The Scientific Romances of
J.-H. Rosny Aîné

THE MYSTERIOUS FORCE
And Other Anomalous Phenomena

Vol. 3

The Scientific Romances of
J.-H. Rosny Aîné

THE MYSTERIOUS FORCE
And Other Anomalous Phenomena

translated, annotated and introduced by
Brian Stableford

A Black Coat Press Book

Acknowledgements: I should like to thank John J. Pierce for providing valuable research materials and offering advice and support. Many of the copies of Rosny's works and critical articles related to his work were borrowed from the London Library. Also thanks to Paul Wessels for his generous and extensive help in the final preparation of this text.

Visit our website at www.blackcoatpress.com

Table of Contents

Introduction

This is the third volume of a six-volume collection of stories by J.-H. Rosny *Aîné* ("the Elder"), which includes all of his scientific romances, plus a number of other stories that have some relevance to his work in that genre.[1]

The contents of the six volumes are:

Volume 1. THE NAVIGATORS OF SPACE AND OTHER ALIEN ENCOUNTERS: The Xipehuz, The Skeptical Legend, Another World, The Death of the Earth, The Navigators of Space, The Astronauts.

Volume 2. THE WORLD OF THE VARIANTS AND OTHER STRANGE LANDS: Nymphaeum, The Depths of Kyamo, The Wonderful Cave Country, The Voyage, The Great Enigma, The Treasure in the Snow, The Boar Men, In the World of the Variants.

Volume 3. THE MYSTERIOUS FORCE AND OTHER ANOMALOUS PHENOMENA: The Cataclysm, The Mysterious Force, Hareton Ironcastle's Amazing Adventure.

Volume 4. VAMIREH AND OTHER PREHISTORIC FANTASIES: Vamireh, Eyrimah, Nomaï.

Volume 5. THE GIVREUSE ENIGMA AND OTHER STORIES: Mary's Garden, The Givreuse Enigma, Adventure in the Wild.

Volume 6. THE YOUNG VAMPIRE AND OTHER CAUTIONARY TALES: The Witch, The Young Vampire, The Supernatural Assassin, Companions of the Universe.

The first volume of the series includes a long general introduction to Rosny's life and works, which there is no need to

---

[1] *Le Félin géant* (*The Giant Cat* a.k.a. *Quest of the Dawn Man*) and *Helgvor du fleuve bleu* (*Helgvor of the Blue River*) will be reprinted in their original English translations in a seventh volume.

7

repeat here; the following introduction will therefore be limited to a brief account of the stories included in this volume, which will be supplemented by a more detailed commentary contained in an afterword.

"Le Cataclysme" was initially published in 1888 as "Tornadres" and reprinted until the more familiar title in a volume with "Les Xipéhuz" (1887; tr. in vol. 1 as "The Xipehuz") by the press associated with the *Mercure de France* in 1896. The latter volume might well have been produced as a direct response to the success in England of H.G. Wells's early scientific romances—Henry Davray, Wells's French translator, was on the editorial staff of the *Mercure*—and certainly had the effect of initiating Rosny's reputation as a French anticipator of Wells, although it was issued at a time when Rosny had abandoned such work, and was not to resume his experiments in speculative fiction for more than a decade.

Like its companion-piece, "Le Cataclysme" can now be seen as spinoff from the speculations that Rosny dramatized in a less conventional fashion in "La Légende sceptique" (1889; tr. in vol. 1 as "The Skeptical Legend"), featuring a temporary interaction between different kinds of matter, initiated by virtue of a cosmic incident. When Rosny returned to the writing of scientific romance, under the influence of Maurice Renard's propagandizing in favor of "scientific marvel fiction," he picked up the theme of "Le Cataclysme" for much more elaborate development in *La Force mystérieuse*, which was serialized in *Je Sais Tout* in 1913 before being reprinted in book form by Plon in the following year. Rosny subsequently produced an abridged version of the latter story for publication alongside "Les Xipéhuz" and "La Mort de la Terre" (1912; tr. in vol. 1 as "The Death of the Earth") in the collection *Les Autres vies et les autres mondes* (Cres, 1924) but I have reproduced the fuller version here.

The third item translated here, *L'Etonnant voyage de Hareton Ironcastle*, was issued by Ernest Flammarion in 1922 in a series of *Romans aventures*, for which it might have been specifically commissioned. Flammarion had become Rosny's primary publisher during the war, after a substantial gap in the author's production, following the propagandistic *Perdus?* [Doomed?] (1917) and *Confidences sur l'amitié des tranchées* [Secrets of Friendship in the Trenches] with three sentimental novels and reprints of several of his earlier works in the latter vein. In addition to Rosny's full-length books, Flammarion issued two novelettes by Rosny as booklets in a series entitled *Une heure d'oubli*, both of which were imaginative fiction, presumably written to order: *La Jeune Vampire* (1920; tr. in vol. 6 as "The Young Vampire") and *Le Trésor dans le neige* (1920; tr. in vol. 2 as "The Treasure in the Snow"). The structure of the narrative of *L'Etonnant voyage de Hareton Ironcastle* suggests that part three of the extant text might well have started out as another exercise in the same vein, but that it grew too long, with the result that Rosny decided—or was advised—to add the preliminary material to convert the novelette into a novel. On the other hand, the fact that *L'Etonnant voyage de Hareton Ironcastle* features an American hero might reflect an ambition to have the story translated; Rosny may well have been aware in 1921 that translation rights to his novel *Le Félin géant* (1918 as a serial; 1920 in book form; tr. as *The Giant Cat*, 1924) had been sold in the USA.

Although *L'Etonnant voyage de Hareton Ironcastle* did not sell translation rights at the time of writing, it was eventually translated into English for publication by DAW books in 1976 as *Ironcastle*, but that translation was handed over by DAW's proprietor, Donald A. Wollheim, for extensive modification by Philip José Farmer. Although Farmer's revisions fill in some lacunae in Rosny's rather hurried text, thus smoothing it out, and definitely qualify as improvements from the viewpoint of the casual reader, the fact remains that the DAW text is not a true reflection of what Rosny actually wrote, and I think that the present, more accurate, translation is therefore justifiable.

Oddly enough, Don Wollheim's primary reason for commissioning the revision—as he explained to me on the one occasion when I met him, while *Ironcastle* was in press—was that he felt it unacceptable, in the context of an adventure story, that Hareton Ironcastle should spend so much time praying. The only reason the character does that, however—it is not something that Rosny or any of his other male heroes would ever have thought of doing, although weak women (like Luce in "Le Cataclysme") often fall back upon prayer in times of crisis—was that Rosny was trying to make him into a plausible American, and had evidently formed the impression that Americans tend to be pious Bible-addicts. As to how he had formed that impression, we can only guess. I, of course, have left the praying in, along with the frequent references to the Bible made by Ironcastle and his sister.

Ironically, from the viewpoint of the present exercise, one of the effects of Farmer's modifications was to convert *Ironcastle* into a story of the same kind as "Le Cataclysme" and *La Force mystérieuse*, explaining the anomalous life-forms encountered in the final phase of the story as the result of an intrusion of extraterrestrial life on the Earth's surface. Although Rosny does not specifically exclude that hypothesis, there is no evidence to support that interpretation in the original text; even so, the exoticism of the "alternative evolution" featured in the story is considerably greater than the hypothetical constructions featured in the lost land stories collected in volume two of the series, so the novel is as fittingly located here as it would have been there.

The version of "Le Cataclysme" from which I derived my translation is the one in the 1896 Mercure de France volume. The version of *La Force mystérieuse* I used is a reprint of the Plon book. I used the 1922 Flammarion edition of *L'Etonnant voyage de Hareton Ironcastle*.

Brian Stableford

THE CATACLYSM

I. Symptoms

On the Tornadre plateau, for several weeks, nature palpitated and equivocated in anguish, the whole of its delicate vegetable organism shot through by intermittent electricity, symbolic signs of a great material event. The free beasts on the farms and in the chestnut plantations were not as quick to flee quotidian perils; they seemed to want to get closer to human beings, wandering around the tenancies. Then they came to an extraordinary decision, sounding an alarm: they emigrated, going deep into the valley of the Iaraze.

As the nights fell, in the gloom of forests and thickets, there was a drama of nervous animals furtively quitting their lairs with hesitant steps, often pausing and stopping, melancholy to be fleeing their native land. The somber and languid howling of wolves alternated with the muffled grunts of wild boars and the sobbing of ruminants. Ashy silhouettes were gliding everywhere, generally toward the south-west, over cultivated ground beneath the open sky: great antlered skulls, heavy tapir-like bodies with short legs, and slimmer beasts, carnivores and herbivores alike—hares, moles, rabbits, foxes and squirrels. The batrachians followed, the reptiles and the wingless insects, and a week ensued in which the south-western direction was flooded with inferior organisms, a frightful vermicular population, from the hopping silhouettes of frogs to slugs and snails, through the marvelous wing-cases of carabid beetles and horrible crustaceans that live under stones in eternal darkness, to worms, leeches and larvae.

Soon, nothing remained but winged creatures. Then the birds, filled with unease, increasingly clinging on to branches, fearful of flying, saluted the twilights with more subdued songs, often leaving the locality for a large part of the day. The crows and the owls held great assemblies; the swifts gathered together as if for their autumnal migration; the magpies became agitated, cawing all day long.

The mysterious terror spread to the slaves: the sheep, the cattle, the horses, even the dogs. Resigned, in the confidence of their humble serfdom, all expecting salvation from humankind, they stayed on the Tornadre plateau—except for the cats, which had fled in the early days, returning to savage liberty.

As the evenings went by, a confused sadness, an asphyxia of the soul, took possession of the inhabitants of the tenancies and the proprietors of the estate known as the Corne: the confused anticipation of a cataclysm—which, however, the topography of Tornadre belied. Being distant from volcanic regions and the ocean, insubmersible—having only a few streams—and compact in texture, what form could the threat possibly take?

It was felt nevertheless, electrically, in the rigidity of small branches and blades of grass at certain morning hours, in the singular attitudes of foliage, in subtle and suffocating effluvia, unusual phosphorescences and the prickling of flesh by night, which caused the eyelids to rise, condemning the individual to insomnia, in the extraordinary behavior of livestock, often stiffening, their nostrils open and tremulous, and *turning their heads toward the north.*

II. The Astral Downpour

One evening, at the Corne, Sévère and his wife were finishing dinner next to the half-closed window. A crescent moon was wandering near the zenith, pale and full of grace, above the vast perspectives, and rising mists decorated the western frontier. A troubling spell—an ardor of the nervous system, a suddenly awakened obscure commotion—kept them silent, impregnating them with a particular aesthetic sensibility, a profound wonderment relative to the nocturnal splendors.

A harmonious tremor welled up from the trees in the garden; at the rear, visible through the gate to the avenue, there was an enchantment of confused objects, the crop-fields of the Tornadre, the blanched farmhouses, the friendly mystery of human lights and the vague slate-covered steeple of the rustic church. The masters of the Corne were moved by that, troubled by the vibration of their nerves. The commotion being keener along the spinal column, however, the wife dropped the bunch of grapes that she was plucking, her lip trembling.

"My God! Is it going to go on forever?"

Sévère looked at her, with a strong desire to give her courage—but his own soul was in a stupor, obscured by an imponderable force.

Sévère Lestang was one of those grave intellectuals slowly seeking the secret of things, studying nature without impatience, disinterested in glory—but he was a man as well as an intellectual; his eyes were gentle and courageous, and he had a desire to *live his life* as well as developing his faculties. His wife, Luce, was a nervous mountain Celt, delicately graceful, amorous and captivating, but a trifle somber. Under the calm and attentive protection of her husband, she was like certain infinitely frail flowers that live in the inlets of great rivers, between large shady leaves.

"If you want," said Sévère, "we can leave tomorrow."

"Yes, please!"

She came closer to him, seeking refuge, murmuring: "They say that one can't keep a foothold any longer, you know, especially in the evening…that something takes hold of you and carries you away! Well, I don't dare walk quickly any longer, my steps draw me on so…and one climbs stairs effortlessly, but with a constant fear of falling…"

"You're mistaken, Luce. It's a nervous illusion." He smiled, pressing her to him—but he too, with a terrible malaise, had perceived that incomprehensible lightness. Sometimes, before dusk, had he not wanted to walk more rapidly, to get back to the Corne, and found his stride lengthening, transformed into bounds, launching him forward with frightening speed? With his equilibrium lost, having difficulty in remaining vertical, experiencing a sensation of ataxia at each footfall, he had reverted to a slow pace, clinging to the ground, solidly, seeking large patches of sticky ground.

"You think it's an illusion?" she said.

"I'm sure of it, Luce!"

She looked at him, while he stroked the fringe of her hair, and she suddenly realized that he was as nervous as she was, electrified by a profound anguish: no longer a refuge for her, but a poor frail creature confronted by enigmatic powers.

Then she went paler, her teeth chattering.

"The coffee will settle you," he said.

"Perhaps."

But they sensed the deceit in their words, the poverty of any tonic, or any human remedy against the approaching Unknowable—against that vast metamorphosis of phenomena, in which terrestrial life no longer participated, which had been troubling the flora and fauna, the animals and the plants, for weeks already.

They sensed the deceit. They did not dare look at one another, instinctively afraid of communicating their presentiments, of doubling their distress by nervous induction. And for long minutes, they listened inwardly, in their flesh, to the dull and confused echo of Mystery.

A fearful housemaid brought the coffee; they watched her leave, unsteadily, not daring to question that anxiety, similar to their own.

"Did you see how Marthe was walking?" asked Luce.

He did not reply, looking in surprise at the little silver spoon that he had just picked up. Perceiving his fixed stare, she looked at it in her turn, and exclaimed: "It's green!"

The little spoon was, indeed, green, with a pale emerald gleam—and they suddenly noticed the same tint on the other spoons, and all of the silverware.

"Oh, my God!" cried the young woman. Raising her finger, she began to recite, in a low voice, whispering painfully:

"When the Silver goes green,

"The *Roge Aigue* will come

"Devouring the Moon and stars…"[2]

These words, an ancient and vague prophecy that the peasants of the Tornadre plateau had handed down through the ages, made Sévère shudder. They both had an impression of darkness and fatality, colorless and soundless, beyond all anthropomorphism. Where had the poor rustics obtained that oracle, now so serious? What science, what observations of remote eras, what cataclysmic memories, did it symbolize?

Sévère had an immense desire to be far away from Tornadre, remorseful at not having obeyed the sure instincts of the animals, at having dared to follow poor cerebral logic rather than the warning of Nature. "Do you want to leave this evening?" he asked Luce, ardently.

"I'd never dare leave the house before morning returns!"

He thought that it might be as perilous to venture out by night as to stay at the Corne; he resigned himself to it, thoughtfully. A great lamentation interrupted his thoughts: feverish whinnying, the dull banging of horses struggling against the stable-door. The dog howled, and the clamor spread along the length of the Tornadre plateau, echoed by other animals, terrified ruminants and braying donkeys. At the same time, there

---

[2] I have left the key words unaltered, because they are deliberately misrendered in such way as to conserve a certain ambiguity. *Roge* is only one letter away from *rouge* [red] or *rogue* [arrogant], while *aigue* is subtly distinct from both the masculine and feminine forms of *aigu/aiguë*, whose usual meaning is "pointed" or "sharp," although the term is also used as a noun to signify a diamond, referring to its "water" rather than its facets, by analogy with *aigu-marine* [aquamarine]. The readiest inference to be drawn, therefore, might be reckoned as "red gem"—but the other possible implications should not be left out of account.

was a greenish glow in the sky, and a shooting star passed over, huge, with a resplendent tail.

"Look!" said Luce.

Other meteors welled up, isolated at first, then in small groups, all with bright nuclei and leaving long trails, miraculously beautiful.

"It's the night of August 10," said Sévère, "and the star-showers will increase…there's nothing abnormal about it."[3]

"Why, then, are our lamps growing dimmer?"

The Lamps were, in fact, lowering their flames; a superior electrical density enveloped everything, a terror, not of death, but of exasperated life, of supernatural dilatation—so that Sévère and Luce clung on to the furniture in order to *weigh more*, in order to *perceive contact with solid material*. A strange pressure lifted them up, robbing them of their sense of balance. They felt that they were in a new atmosphere, in which the ether acted with a *living* power, in which something organic—extra-terrestrially organic—was disturbing every drop of blood, orientating every molecule, intruding into the very marrow of their bones, and gradually stiffening every hair on their bodies.

In addition, as Sévère had predicted, the stellar downpour accelerated, the entire concavity of the firmament filling with bolides. By degrees, it was mingled with an unknown phenomenon, persistent and increasing: voices. Faint, distant, musical voices, a symphony of tiny strings in the celestial depths, a sometimes almost human whisper, reminiscent of the ancient Pythagorean harmony of the spheres.

"They're souls!" she murmured.

"No," he said. "No, they're Forces!"

---

[3] August 10 is the usual peak of the Perseid meteor shower, consisting of particles left behind by Comet Swift-Tuttle; the shower has been observed for the last 2000 years, and is sometimes known as "St. Lawrence's tears" because August 10 was the day of his martyrdom.

Souls or forces, however, it was the same Unknown, the same hermetic threat, the pressure of a prodigious event, the blackest of human fears: the Shapeless and the Unforeseeable. And the voices went on, above the murmur of things, frightfully gentle, essential and subtle, taking Luce back to the Humility of childhood, to Worship, to Prayer:

"Our Father, who art in Heaven…"

He did not dare smile, the beating of his heart increasing as if to burst his arteries, while his masculine mind—more curious about causation than his wife's—tried to imagine what magnetism, what extraterrestrial polarities, were working upon this corner of the globe, and whether it was the same in the valley of the Iaraze.

Outside the plateau, however, since the commencement of the phenomenon—and Sévère had gone down to the river again that very day—no one had perceived the unfamiliar symptoms. The animals and people there were living tranquilly. Life preserved its normal form there. Why, though? What correlation was there between the sky and the plateau, what cycle of phenomena—for the prophecy of the peasants of Tornadre implied a cycle—regulated this great Drama?

A misfortune occurred: a triumphant assault by the animals against the old stable door. The Corne's three horses appeared, bucking and foaming at the mouth beneath the pale rays of the sinking Moon,

"Here, Clairon!" called Sévère.

One of the horses approached, the others following. Never had there been a scene as phantasmagoric as the three long heads hollowed out in the light and shadow, in front of the window, their large eyes bulging, sniffing Luce and Sévère, visibly questioning, with a return of vague confidence in the master, a troubled idea of the power of the person who fed them. Then, for no obvious reason—perhaps an increase in the meteor shower—with absolute terror in the depths of their large eyes, their nostrils more cavernous, the mad panic of their race took hold, and they tore themselves away from the window whinnying, and fled.

"Oh, how they're leaping!" said Luce.

They were, in truth, running with an amazing gait, in enormous bounds. Suddenly, at the far end of the garden, confronted by the iron gate, the most impetuous rose up like a winged creature, and cleared the obstacle.

"You see! You see!" cried Luce. "He too has no more weight!"

"Nor the two others," he added, involuntarily.

Indeed the other two black shadows, rising up, without even brushing the bars, leapt more than four meters high. Their agile silhouettes, carried vertiginously across the fields, diminished, evaporated and disappeared. At the same time, a manservant appeared outside, alone and timid, hardly daring to come forward with the fearful step of a little child.

Sévère felt an infinite pity for the poor devil, realizing that everyone else at the Corne must have shut themselves up in their rooms, prey to the same increase in terror as the Masters.

"Let them go, Victor!" he called. "We'll find them later."

Victor came closer, holding on to trees, then the wall, and the shutter. "Is it true, Master," he asked, "that the *roge aigue* has come back?"

Sévère hesitated, preserving the modesty of his intelligence and his doubt in the midst of the sinister events, but Luce could not be silent.

"Yes, Victor."

A bleak silence fell, the three individuals equalized by the sensation of the supernatural—but Sévère was still examining, questioning himself about the connection between the phenomenon and the meteorites. He studied the increasing rain of stars, the stream of supreme beauty from the depths of the Imponderable. A new observation alarmed him: that the sad fragment of the Moon sinking toward the horizon could not be providing the light that persisted over the landscape. Looking westwards, he watched the satellite disappearing, its convexity ready to collapse, adjacent to the western horizon.

A few minutes more, and then it was gone—but the light over the Tornadre plateau persisted, as if emanating from the zenith: only a few degrees to the north, according to the indication of its shadow. Was it from the zenith, then, that the phenomenon was coming? He turned his face to it, slowly. There, an amethyst glow, a lenticular glimmer, was thinly displayed like a slender cloud, with a maximum radiance toward the north.

Sévère thought that these things would have been a delight to behold, without the creeping of the flesh, the sepulchral threat and the presentiment of death falling from the Heavens upon the Earth.

III. The Appearance of the Aigue

"Look!" said Luce. She had perceived the light in her turn; more affected than Lestang, she was pointing at it.

Victor, clinging to the window on the outside, was shivering with fever, as if he were drunk, occasionally coming round with a sigh, and ever-increasing horror.

Up above, the light was increasing. As it did so, the whispering voices of the firmament faded away, and an enormous silence weighed upon the Tornadre plateau. Then, faint at first, a light from below appeared to reply to the other, light fringes floating over the treetops and over all the plants. It was delicately and wildly heart-rending. On the three people, so dissimilar, it made an almost identical impression, of funerary lamps or a pyre, an immense conflagration that was about to engulf Tornadre and all its inhabitants.

Luce moaned, almost unconsciously, and uttered a desperate plaint: "Oh, I'm thirsty!"

Sévère turned toward her; the tenderness of his heart, his love for the Celtic mountain woman, gave him strength. He fought against his desire not to move, to end his existence there, at the window, with the bottom frame in his clenched hands. Swaying, he went to fetch a glass of water—but he continued questioning himself, astonished that the atmosphere was cool, almost cold, in spite of all the subtle fire in the heavens and on Earth.

He had great difficulty bringing back the water; the glass in his hand was so light that he had no sensation of holding anything, and had to grip its base with all his might. He lost half the liquid en route.

Luce took a gulp, and spat it out, nauseated. "It tastes like iron filings…like rust!"

Sévère sipped the water, and had to spit it out in his turn; it was metallic and powdery. They both looked at one another for a long time, desperately. The veils of memory lifted, across so many charming years, on the moment when they had glimpsed one another for the first time in the Real World, the appeal of their nervous systems, amorous thereafter. Delicate and indefatigable periods of adoration. (Oh, what long, elevated, immense hours, woven of divinity, revive beneath the nebulous portico of the past!) And their gazes embraced, in an infinite pity for one another. Was this truly the death-agony? Would they have to leave their young lives behind like this, dying of asphyxia, thirst and that hideous impression of anti-gravity, that *non-contact* with matter. Oh Lord!

Personally, Sévère, so full of vital force, did not want to admit it, in spite of everything. Curiosity subsisted in his skull through the knell, making it attentive to the exterior again. The marvelous and lamentable drama continued to evolve; an opera of subtle fires, colossal corposants, lit up the distant landscape; at the summits of the tall trees, slender and flickering at first, and displaying the infinite scale of the spectrum, flames multiplied, trembling on every twig and the tip of every leaf, and then spread to the lower vegetation, the bushes, the grass, the stubble.

Every protrusion of vegetation thus had its glow, directed upwards at the sky.

Above the dream-like glimmers of that fiery landscape, birds were flying in flocks. They had finally decided to flee.

Super-electric creatures, they had initially resisted these phenomena, which were doubtless less antipathetic to their organisms than those of terrestrial animals. Crows, with somber cries; sparse but infinite flocks of sparrows, goldfinches, chaffinches and warblers; intelligent groups of magpies, swifts, swallows, in traveling formation; and raptors in ones or twos, all headed southwards with an excited chirping and twittering that was almost speech.

Again, Sévère concentrated on the innumerable flames, which were neither fusing with one another nor giving out any appreciable heat; they were also, as he looked at them so directly, elongating into fine strips, building towers and Gothic monuments with billions of dazzling spires.

He was interrupted by a raucous cry, emitted by Luce.

"Hold me down! Hold me down...I'm being carried away!"

He saw his companion delirious, livid and cramped, her breast rising in a pitiful attempt to breathe. His own heart became weak; he was overcome by an absolute and infinite desperation, while he held on to Luce with a mechanical gesture. Shivering, she gazed at the shining plateau, and spoke confusedly:

"It's the other world, Sévère—it's the immaterial world...the Earth is about to die..."

"No, no," he whispered, aware of the vanity of his words, "it's a Force...a magnetism...a transformation of movement."

A lower voice made him start: that of the hypnotized Victor, who had woken up: "the *Roge Aigue!*"

Sévère leaned out. Less than 20 degrees from the north he saw a large rectangle the color of rust, with an irregular border, as if excavated from abysms of sulfur. Gradually, it became brighter, as transparent as a wave, a veritable lake extended over the north, over which ran wrinkles of a paler red, similar to waves. And around the red lake, over the entire sky, a green darkness appeared, which turned blue and darkened, casting a profound jade shadow over the southern extremity.

The stars had died away. Nothing remained by that sky of red water and green water, of green gem and jade darkness.

What was it? Where had it come from? And why this enormous influence on the Tornadre? What power of special induction, and what affinities, were prowling around the firmament? These questions racked Sévère's brain, but did not spare him at all from the stupor that had taken hold of Luce and Victor on seeing the peasant prophecy fulfilled. He no longer doubted that death would come swiftly, that the heart which was galloping so terribly in his breast was about to burst and shut down forever...

Meanwhile, her dying face raised toward the heavens, Luce began to recite, with a poignant solemnity:

"When the Silver goes green,

"The *Roge Aigue* will come

"Devouring the Moon and stars..."

Releasing a heavy sigh, she collapsed against the window-sill, rigid, with her eyes closed.

IV. Toward the Iaraze

Motionless at first, devoid of strength, Sévère drew his wife toward him. Was she dead? Had she vanished forever? Black laughter—the laughter of unavoidable destiny—rose to his lips, and the word "forever" circulated in his skull in an ironic manner—that "forever" which, so far as his own existence was concerned, might not extend beyond the next hour.

His grip on Luce grew tighter then, becoming unhealthy. He lifted the poor woman up, holding her across his chest...

Then, suddenly, bizarrely and delightfully, a kind of relief overwhelmed his entire body: *firmness on the ground, weight, had returned!*

What! Chance must have told him to do it; he had not arrived theoretically at the idea of combining someone else's weight with his in order to recover a sense of material security.

Reanimated and solidified, in spite of the oppression in his breast, a flood of courage and hope ran through him now, which further augmented the consequences of the event, including the singular ease with which he was holding Luce in his arms like a little child. Then, his heart skipping a beat, his memory reverted to the catastrophe, forgotten in the shock of glad emotion. Was Luce dead?

He listened carefully, with his ear upon the young woman's breast; the inconvenient sound of his own arteries prevented him from hearing anything. She was not stiff, though—but she was so pale! Her eyelids opened upon unmoving eyes.

"Luce! My darling Luce!"

A sigh; a slight movement of the head. He discerned a very faint breath—of life! His will-power was reinforced; he resolved to make every effort to save her.

He stood there for a few minutes, thinking, then shrugged his shoulders. What good was calculation? It was necessary to act like a brute, the least of organized beings, and flee straight ahead until he reached the banks of the Iazare. And with no further hesitation, taking the shortest route, he climbed on to the window and leapt through it nimbly, shouting to Victor:

"Get hold of something heavy. Release the dog and go to warn your comrades. See how I'm carrying my burden. That's how anyone might save himself. Do you understand?"

"Yes, Monsieur."

And Sévère ran off at a trot, his tread steady but oppressed, his breath whistling, troubled by the electricity, which was livelier and more debilitating outside. He went out of the garden gate, and found himself in open country. In its prodigious majesty, the red lake seemed to magnify the stellar abysses even further. Its glory, at its palpitating edges, with the softness of stained glass, delicate and resplendent, terminating in lace, orange cinders and dendrites, almost overwhelmed the zenith. No other stars could be seen any longer. Here and there, a fine serpentine line—a streak of fire—ran from the extreme north to the extreme south. On the ground, on the flat surface of the Tornadre plateau, the fires persevered every-where, a taciturn inferno: an inferno without heat, or even consumption.

The colossal candles of large trees and the torches—infinite in number—of the short grass, the steep ascensions, the great never-ending polychromatic bows devoured by the neutralization of forces and indefatigably recomposed, filled Space with a terrible and beautiful life. Sévère marched on, going through it, closing his eyes periodically when he had to cross excessively flamboyant zones. Luce's hair emitted a torrent of sparks which dazzled and blinded Sévère. Instinct guided him south-westwards.

Every few minutes, a farm appeared, which served him as a landmark, but one in which he had no great confidence, so uncertain were appearances rendered by the infernal transfigu-ration.

A moment came when he thought he had gone astray; in front of him there was a pool, with reeds rising up like aveng-ing blades, and willows with pale emerald leaves. Fireflies were moving continually over the surface. There was a suffo-cating odor of phosphorus and ozone. He felt the soft ground beneath his feet, the confused attraction of hidden water. He tried to get his bearings, but in vain. He knew, however, that it was Cilleuses pond, less than 500 meters from the edge of the plateau. He went around it and marched for ten minutes—and found himself back at his point of departure.

If he remained there miserably, his great effort would be wasted.

"Come on, Sévère!"

He gets under way again, striving to recognize some landmark, some familiar sight, but weakening in that research, convinced that he will fall unconscious within an hour, to die in the open countryside.

Suddenly, he makes a discovery: a sharp little promontory, the only one on the pond, from which he can deduce which direction to take. From then on, it seems that he has wings, progressing in a straight line, and ending up finding a little path that he knows well, which he never leaves thereafter. He cannot estimate the duration of the journey—perhaps half an hour, perhaps ten minutes, or even five—but he has come to a halt, overwhelmed amazement, before a black gulf parallel with the blazing Tornadre: an abyss of darkness beneath his feet, which something separates from the phosphorescent outpouring flooding the plateau.

"The slope! The slope!" He repeats the word; full of strength, he begins to go down a sinuous path at a run.

Already, he feels a physical well-being; the induction is decreasing, the lights are becoming steadily sparser, as gentle as will-o'-the-wisps, and the moist and tepid air is more breathable. On the other hand, Luce's weight is becoming harder to bear. It is breaking his arms and slowing him down.

He falls down, collapsing on the slope without the interposition of any root or branch. Then, as he resumes his course, out of breath, indomitable instinct masters his nerves.

Eventually, to his immense joy, he hears the running of the Iazare, and perceives imminent salvation through his every pore. Only a few more steps! Already, the peril can scarcely reach him in this environment, where, the mysterious influence having been reduced to a minimum, there is already the healthy, vital terrestrial nature of old, hospitable to humankind.

He does not stop, sweating and haggard but full of strength. Finally, the vale arrives, with the river sobbing in the darkness. With a loud cry, a violent and dolorous delight, he lets himself go.

Luce is lying across his knees. Momentarily, he turns his head to look back and upwards, irresistibly. A vague glimmer is wandering over the slope, brighter toward the edge of the plateau; that is all he can see of the vast conflagration, which is little enough compared with the glare of the nocturnal sea in

the era of its fecundation. The firmament is especially astonishing, the *Aigue* having vanished, leaving only the red-
ness—a kind of aurora borealis. The shower of bolides continues to fall.

"What's going on?" he wonders. "Why that enormous
dissimilarity between the Tornadre and the Iazare?"

Eventually, he leans over Luce. She is still pale and motionless, but her breath is perceptible—the breath of sleep rather than unconsciousness. He calls out to her, raising his
voice: "Luce! Luce!"

She shivers, and moves her head gently. That is an infinite joy amid the gloom, and, with sobs of happiness, he em-
braces her, and continues calling out to her. He murmurs a few
tender words.

Finally, the eyelids open and the young woman's gaze,
full of dreams and darkness, falls upon Sévère.

"Ah!" he cries. "We're finally victorious. The Tornadre
has not devoured you."

Standing up, with his arms folded, he conceives a desire—the promise of climbing up again, alone, toward the
south-west, to follow the story of the cataclysm. Voices are
raised on the slope however, and the sound of barking.

Understanding that it is the Corne's servants, Luce and
Sévère wait for them, embracing one another, in a bliss so
great that tears are streaming down their cheeks.

Note

Monsieur Sévère Lestang has, in fact, published the story
of the Tornadre cataclysm (*chez* Germer-Ballière). For seven
days the *Aigue* was visible over the plateau, and the conflagration with *neither heat nor consumption* persisted for those
seven days—as attested, in addition to Monsieur Lestang and
the inhabitants of the plateau, by a scientific commission that
arrived on the final day of the phenomenon. There were some

dead to mourn, but relatively few, the majority of individuals having fled after the beginning of the night of August 10.

As for the conclusions of the scientific investigation, it must be confessed that they were entirely negative; no plausible theory was offered. The one interesting fact, which might prove, at a later date, to lead to some discovery, is this: the Tornadre plateau rests on a rocky mass of about 150 billion cubic meters, which is evidently of stellar origin; it is *a colossal bolide*, fallen near the Iaraze valley in prehistoric times.

THE MYSTERIOUS FORCE

To Jean Perrin and Emile Borel [4]
Their admirer and friend,
J.-H. Rosny Aîné

Part One

I. The Disease of Light

Georges Meyral's reflection in the looking-glass seemed
to be subject to misty zones, which sometimes retracted and
sometimes broadened out slightly; it seemed to be less luminous than it should have been.

"That's not right!" the young man complained.

The two electric lamps, on examination, seemed normal,
and the looking-glass was wiped clean. The phenomenon persisted. It still persisted when Meyral had replaced the lamps,
one after the other.

"Something's happened to the mirror, to the electricity,
or to me."

---

[4] Jean Perrin (1870-1942) was a noted physicist, whose ac-
complishments included a demonstration that "cathode rays"
were streams of negatively-charged particles and an explanation of solar energy in terms of hydrogen fusion. Emile Borel
(1871-1956) was a mathematician who helped to elaborate
Einstein's theory of relativity; Rosny might have met him via
his wife, who wrote novels under the name Camille Marbo.

A hand-mirror revealed identical peculiarities; in consequence, the looking-glass was above reproach. To eliminate his own vision from consideration, Georges summoned his chambermaid. That haggard creature, with a tanned face and the eyes of a pirate, examined her own image. At first, she did not notice anything, for she had almost lost any sense of coquetry; then, without having been subject to any suggestion, she declared: "There seem to be stripes, and also some mist."

"My eyes are innocent!" Meyral remarked. "Bring me a candle, Marianne."

Two minutes later, by the light of the candle, the phenomenon was confirmed, aggravated by a thickening of the zones. It was reproduced in various rooms of the house and then on the gas-lit stairway. Thus, neither the electricity, nor the mirror, nor Meyral's eyes could be suspected of any anomaly peculiar to them. It was necessary to revert to more general hypotheses. They flowed. It was logical first to consider a singularity of the light. But what evidence was there that the perturbation did not extend to the whole environment? Where did that environment stop? It might be the house, the street, the neighborhood, the entire city, France, Europe…

Meyral lapsed into an impassioned reverie. He was a man of 35, of the kind that is thin but muscular. At first glance, the eyes distracted attention from the rest of his face: those eyes, the color of beryl, speckled with amber, were vigilant but distracted, and had passed from excessive confidence to anxiety or suspicion. His scarlet mouth advertised a childlike mind; his forehead was drowned by fleecy and curly hair that would not obey the metallic brush.

Meyral was one of those scientists for whom the laboratory is a battlefield. Intoxicated by the world of cells, by the depths of its "substrata," he sought the origins of life in hazardous mixtures, in the bosom of the primitive and the murky evolution of colloids. The anomaly that had just taken him by surprise plunged him into one of those crises of exaltation in which he thought he glimpsed "other planes of existence."

Time was pressing, though. He was due to visit Gérard Langre, his master, whom he admired more than any other man. He finished dressing, and did not forget to take a pocket mirror with him.

Three times he stopped in front of mirrors to contemplate his reflection therein. While he was examining it outside Revelle the tailor's, a cracked-crystal voice called out to him: "Do you think you're handsome, darling?"

He perceived a young woman whose eyes were both mocking and pathetic.

"It's not me that I'm looking at!" he said, distractedly.

"Oh, right!" she said, laughing. "It's your father?"

"The phenomenon's persistent."

"I believe you! Is it worth the price of a little drink, this phenomenon?"

Meyral started laughing. "I'll buy you a little drink, if you care to look attentively into this mirror and tell me what you see."

She looked at him in alarm. *He's crazy!* Knowing that one has to humor the whims of madmen, she obeyed meekly. "All right—I'm thirsty!"

"Pay careful attention."

She did so, willingly.

"What do you see?"

"My face, of course!"

"Nothing odd?"

The girl opened and closed her eyes several times. "There are little lines of some sort, which aren't usual."

"Well," said Meyral, with a smile, "that's the phenomenon—and here's the drink." He handed her an effigy of Leopold II.

There was some excitement on the terraces—the squawking of many people. At the corner of the Rue Soufflot, policemen were breaking up a fight.

Mankind's in a bad mood!

The young man arrived at Gérard Langre's home just as 9 p.m. was chiming at Saint-Jacques-de-Haut-Pas. The physic-

31

ist came to open his door himself. He was an excitable and careworn old man whose head was inclined to the right; he had so much exceedingly white hair that he was nicknamed the Lighthouse. "My maid's in bed," he said. She's suffering from a crisis of faith and horrible presentiments."

"Why do you have such a gloomy servant?"

"Gaiety gets on my nerves."

Langre led a disconnected life. His difficulties with the universities had led to a needy youth. Full of genius, endowed with the stubbornness and skill of great experimenters, he was embittered by the sight of been overtaken by the men that his discoveries and publications had inspired. He worked with such rudimentary apparatus and such restricted materials that he only obtained any results by virtue of the miracle of his obstinacy, his vigilance and his professional acumen. A lofty vision made up for the wretchedness of his laboratories.

His worst setback, which ate away at his soul, was the matter of rotary diamagnetism. He had been carrying out the experiments that were to elevate diamagnetism to the rank of guiding principles when he had taken Antonin Laurys into his laboratory. Laurys, an admirable assimilator, was known for three or four minor discoveries of a parasitic order. In collaborative work the young scientist could render immense services, but he lacked the vision that pierced the clouds. Left to himself, he would have carried out tasks of completion or clarification, especially "variations." He charmed Langre by means of his eloquent understanding and eulogies, of which the poor man, worn out by fatigue and overwhelmed by injustice, was in dire need. One morning, gripped by a fervor of confidence, Langre told the story of his miseries and showed him the wretched apparatus with which he was investigating rotatory diamagnetism. He had obtained two results that were both characteristic and abominable.

Contrary to his habit, Laurys did not seem to understand very well. His eulogies missed the point; his admiration was lavished on tangential issues. Three months later, he informed the Académie des Science of an important discovery, which was none other than Langre's discovery, but incontestable, surrounded by the guarantees conferred by experiments carried out with excellent apparatus and choice materials.

Thunderstruck, then feverish, and mad with indignation, Langre had protested vehemently. The other, having made a modest and deferential reply, had distributed anonymous notes that referred to claims anterior to Langre's, and the latter's disagreements with the university. As it diverged, the quarrel became obscured. Gérard came to be seen as a chagrined individual prone to illusion and accustomed to make reckless accusations. By way of defenders he had two or three obscure young men to whom the major journals were closed, but he lost the greatest discovery of his life as one loses an inheritance. He never got over it.

Having grown old, deprived of honors, possessed of the kind of shaky renown that attracts a few acrimonious rivals and a few solitary enthusiasts, poor, harassed and ill, he roared at seeing Laurys glutted with appointments, plastered with decorations and saturated with a glory that promised to be immortal. The defeated man did, however, have Georges Meyral, and to have such a disciple filled him with pride. "I'm glad you came," he said, after a pause. "My day had been full of sinister obsessions and awful hypochondria." He shook Meyral's hand with both of his own; his eyes were blinking, staring, hollow and lamentable. "I'm so tired and so alone!" he stammered, with a kind of shame. "At times, at dusk, I feel that wind of imbecility of which Baudelaire spoke passing over my brow."[5]

Meyral looked at him with concern. "I too haven't been my normal self," he replied. "It's as if I'd drunk too much

---

[5] Actually, what Baudelaire referred to having sensed, in his diary (on January 23, 1862, while slowly dying), was "le vent de l'aile de l'imbecillité" [the wind of the wing of imbecility], but later quoters of the phrase, including Emile Goudeau and Catulle Mendès, often shortened it in the same fashion as Langre.

coffee. My maid seems particularly excitable—she's talking to herself. To cap it all the crowds seemed rather ill-tempered this evening." He saw *Le Temps* lying on a table and picked it up. "Excuse me, old friend!"

Unfolding the ample newspaper, he searched through the columns. "Here you are—human agitation is increasing: suicides, madness, murder. It was already detectable yesterday."

Interested, Gérard leaned over the newspaper. There was a brief pregnant silence. "You're not speaking lightly," the old man said. "What do you think?"

"I think something unusual is happening in this part of the planet! Have you looked at yourself in a mirror?"

"In a mirror!" said Langre, surprised. "This morning, perhaps, to comb my hair."

"You didn't notice anything?"

"Nothing. I don't pay much attention to myself, though."

Meyral picked up one of the two oil-lamps that was lighting the room and carried it to a mirror. "Look."

Langre studied his reflection with the precise attention of an experimenter. "Damn it!" he muttered. "There are zones…"

"Aren't there? *There's something wrong with light.* Since when, I don't know. It was only just now, when I was dressing to go out, that I noticed it…"

"Have you made any useful observations?"

"I've limited myself to verifying the phenomenon—I even checked it out on the way, in front of Revelle's clothing store."

The two men meditated, with the vague and almost dazed air of scientists absorbed in conjecture.

"If light is *ill*," Langre finally said, "we need to know what it's caught!" He went to a table where a variety of optical equipment was visible: prisms, lenses, plates of glass, quartz, tourmaline and Icelandic spar, Nicol prisms,[6] spectroscopes, mirrors and polariscopes.

---

[6] The Nicol prism, invented by William Nicol (1770-1851)—which consists of two precise fractions of a crystal of Icelan-

Langre and Meyral each took a plate of glass, in order to verify whether refracted light confirmed the anomaly presented by reflected light. Nothing was evident at first; it took a few moments for Gérard, and then Georges, to notice a certain nebulosity about the edges of images. They made up piles of plates; the nebulosity became more obvious, the contours of the image becoming delicately iridescent.

"A small anomaly," Langre uttered. "One has to be looking for it, since the refractory milieu of the eyes don't alert us to it."

Meyral stuck a black thread to one of the plates. Having orientated the edges in various ways, he remarked: "A double refraction is perceptible, but the extraordinary index scarcely differs from the ordinary one—and as there's no trace of an axis, I presume that each ray conforms to Descartes' law."[7]

"No axis!" Langre muttered. "That's absurd, my boy!" He lowered his eyebrows in irritation.

"There's nothing to permit the assumption of an axis. Whatever orientation I try, the images remain immutable."

"Then it's necessary to presume a double refraction in an isotropic milieu? That's insane."

"Yes, provisionally, it's insane," Meyral agreed.

Gérard put down the pile of glass sheets, bad-temperedly. His eyes, still keen, were reminiscent of a raptor's. Eventually, having verified the distance of the images

---

dic spar, glued together with Canada balsam—was the first device commonly used to polarize light.

[7] The law known in France as Descartes' law, popularized by the great philosopher's *Discourse on Method* (1637) was first discovered in 984 by Ibn Sahl and had been rediscovered at least twice before Descartes' publication; outside France it is generally known as Snell's law, after Willebrord Snellius, who had published it in 1621. It states that the ratio of the sines of the angle of refraction and the angle of refraction is equal to the ratio of the velocities of light in the two media through which a refracted ray is passing.

several times over with the aid of micrometric projections, he moaned: "That's crazy! Both rays follow Descartes' law."

He reached angrily for a plate of Icelandic spar and placed it on a pamphlet. An immense consternation contracted his features; he raised his hands toward the ceiling. "There are *four* images."

"Four images!"

They stood there open-mouthed, in a silence that mingled curiosity, bewilderment and anguish.

Gérard was the first to speak. "Our astonishment is stupid! The second experiment is the demonstration of a logical extrapolation. Since the glass yields two images, the spar must necessarily yield four."

"All the present images must appear in duplicate to us," Georges noted. "Undoubtedly, the difference in the refractive indexes is too small to register on the retina."

"There's also our annoying power of accommodation!" the other complained. So saying, he directed a cluster of parallel rays of light at a flint-glass prism, while Georges intercepted the spectrum on a screen.

"The encroachment is visible. The red overlaps the orange, the yellow intrudes on the green. Everything's happening as if one were imperfectly superimposing two near-identical spectra."

Meanwhile, Meyral had moved over to a polarization apparatus; he directed a beam of red light into it.

"There's no need to ask you the result!" the old man exclaimed. "You haven't obtained its extinction."

"That's correct."

"Ergo, the light is definitely duplicated over the whole extent of the spectrum—*and it's not a phenomenon of refraction!*"

"No," Georges agreed, pensively, "it's not a phenomenon of refraction. Each ray seems to have an independent existence, refracting and polarizing in almost exactly the same manner as its twin ray. There's a very slight inequality at the point of departure—which is to say, in the normal indices of refraction—but, thus far, we haven't observed any other dissimilarity. It's a disconcerting mystery."

"It's a terrifying mystery—an intolerable negation of all our experience, and I can't even glimpse the shadow of an explanation. All things considered, the problem is this: given a ray of light, let's suppose that it can duplicate itself without any intervening refraction or reflection, and without undergoing any polarization. We have a complete aberration."

"Let's take note of the fact, though," Meyral suggested, timidly, "that the overall intensity of the light seems to have decreased. Thus, the light is duplicated, but weakened. The duplication, in consequence, could have taken place at the expense of a part of the available luminous energy."

"And how can that be explained?" exclaimed Gérard, aggressively.

"It can't," the young man conceded. "At least it tends to save the principle of conservation."

"In this instance, I don't care about the principle of conservation! It's more of a hindrance. I prefer the idea of an external energetic intervention, responsible for the malady of light. At least I'd have some hope of capturing the perturbatory energy in the semicircle, whereas, if it's a diminution…"

"Why should a diminution be undetectable? We might find some residue! And a diminution isn't simply an inversion of an exterior intervention."

"Bah! Any hypothesis seems puerile. Experimentally, we've scarcely brushed the surface of the problem. What's happening is so significant that I'm ashamed of having quibbled. Let's get to work!"

"Let's get to work!" Georges agreed, with an excitement equal to the old man's.

They were going to the large table in order to resume their experiments when a shrill ringing sound was heard in the corridor.

"The telephone! At this hour! What primate can have anything to say to me?" Langre headed for the apparatus, with a resentful expression. "Hello? Who's there?"

37

The receiver emitted a distressed voice that made the physicist blanch. "It's me…Sabine. Come quickly. It's a dangerous attack of neurasthenia. He's almost insane!"

He did not waste any time demanding explanations. "You have to get out, get a cab and have yourself brought here."

"That's impossible. He's locked me in with the children. You're the only one who can do anything. He won't listen to anyone but you…"

"All right—I'm on my way!" Langre dropped the telephone receiver and raced into his laboratory. "My daughter needs my help," he announced. "That wretch Pierre has gone mad! Wait here for me."

"I'd rather go with you. You might need help."

Langre did not accept immediately. As his emotion increased, his anxiety abruptly became intolerable; he was almost dizzy—but it did not last. "Yes, come," he said. "He regards you as something of a friend. Between the two of us, we'll calm him down." Pensively, he added: "He's not insane, though?"

"He might be—*tonight*."

While the automobile carried them away, Langre thought about the disastrous marriage that aggravated his melancholia. He had always disapproved of his daughter's choice, and judged it incomprehensible. Why had she preferred that taciturn hypochondriac to so many others? Pierre Vérannes was graceless, with a headstrong character and a brutal temper, and his intelligence was scarcely above average.

"There's no accounting for taste!" sighed the father.

It was not a matter of unaccountable taste. Nothing about the straightforward Sabine fitted in with the qualities or the faults of Vérannes. She did not like his looks. In fact, *she had not chosen him*. He was the one who had wanted her, with a savage forcefulness and intolerable stubbornness. In order to win her, he had been able to suppress his rude impatience, tame his frenzies and hide his brutality. He had only displayed his melancholy. Humble and somber, he appeared to be a great human drama, bearing an infinite amount of anxiety, sacrifice, and the appearance of wanting to die that bowls women over.

The brevity of his conversations, and their fearful and furtive appearance, far from working to his disadvantage, had been helpful to him; they permitted an extreme density of emotion, hid the awkwardness, the gaps and the linkage of souls, excused incomplete sentences and gave a subtle or mysterious meaning to the play of his expression. Sabine's youth and the vicissitudes of her existence also worked in his favor. By virtue of her father's ravaged life, she knew the story of unjust suffering and the legend of misunderstood greatness only too well. The man's features, his tone of voice, his gestures, his breathless manner and his ardent pallor of jealousy corresponded strangely to that legend. Sabine had shivered at the thought that she might treat Pierre as society had treated Langre. Her compassionate soul had yielded to the drama.

The illusion was total, for she loved Vérannes. She did not love him as she might have loved a more well-balanced man, better suited to her nature, but she did love him. Social destiny is as restricted as it is complex. Those who are made for one another brush past one another in the street, at the theatre and on social occasions, but, close as they may be, are separated by incommensurable distances—or, rather, separated by subtle isolating factors. In consequence, choices are falsified. An obscure fortune determines them, in which our own will is negligible. Sabine had yielded to Vérannes because the momentary combination of encounters and coincidences had decided it.

Afterwards, she paid the price. Trapped, jealously ill-treated, asphyxiated by anxiety, she lived the corrosive existence of women surrounded by suspicion. Because her husband loved her, she became a little tremulous creature, who was safe neither by day nor by night, neither among others, nor in the petty desert of the hearth, neither during caresses, nor at work. In the vast and intimate worlds alike, there was nothing that was not dangerous. A word or silence, a gesture or something read, a star or the light of a lamp—anything might excite the wild beast. Some days, every minute suggested peace, serenity and trust: she had not left the house; she had not seen anyone; no footstep had sounded in the garden; the red sunset was decaying delightfully into black night...but all the same, the suspicion was born, like a little flame at the tip of a blade of grass; it increased, it took possession of Pierre's soul, filled him with odious and sinister impacts...

Two children had come along; that had not been able to cure the somber man. Although he was not very perspicacious, outside the things he knew—his microscopes and his electrical coils—Langre eventually realized that his daughter was unhappy. When she saw that he knew, she hid it with less courage. Intermittently, he intervened. Vérannes was afraid of the old man, of whose worth he had a vague idea and whose bitter eloquence fascinated him.

II. The Red Night

The car moved at great speed. People hurled insults as it passed by; the crossroads vomited forth furious creatures; the driver made superfluous gestures, moving his head in a maniac fashion or replying to the vituperations with hoarse shouts and blasts of his horn.

"The wretch is excited!" Meyral murmured, when they reached the Pont d'Alma. He was subject to a certain intoxication himself. Langre's eyes were glistening wildly beneath his huge white eyebrows. That hyperesthesia made the young man more anxious as it seemed to increase.

He was not surprised to see four well-dressed pedestrians in the Avenue Marceau fall upon one another with mighty blows of their walking-sticks. A woman ran in front of the car shouting ominously, and the driver, who only avoided her by a miracle, laughed like a hyena. Near the Arc they ran into a huge brawl; several hundred individuals, howling and brandishing weapons, had surrounded a few policemen with the attitude of guard-dogs. Suddenly, the shouting became terrible: an automobile, having crushed several people, projected its driver into the crowd.

It was only a glimpse. The Avenue du Bois-de-Boulogne opened its wide expanse; the vehicle leapt forward like a racing-car. Other bolides were vibrating in the semi-darkness, and light was streaming from almost every window.

"The fever's spreading," Meyral muttered, with exasperated melancholy. "Dementia is scything through humankind like a cavalry charge."

The car stopped in the Rue Marteau, in front of a small town house built of lumps of millstone punctuated with red brick. A meager garden preceded it, which contained a poplar, a few yew-trees and hollyhocks.

"We'll keep you on!" said Gérard to the driver.

The driver pulled a face. "As you wish!" he croaked. "Provided that it's not for long—I need my rest. I've been on the go for 15 hours."

He had, to be frank, a face like a dog, with bloodshot and candid eyes, but he was very excited. Meyral looked at him with anxious attention. *He's quite normal!* He thought. Aloud, he said, gently: "We'll try not to keep you waiting for too long."

The man struck an expression that was almost cordial.

As Langre extended his hand toward the bell, the door of the little house opened suddenly; bare-headed with untidy hair, a man leapt into the garden and rushed toward the gate. "Father-in-law!" he exclaimed, with wild amazement. In a thunderous voice, he added: "Where's Sabine? Where are the children?"

"How should I know?" Gérard replied, impetuously.

They looked at one another through the bars, like wild beasts. Their eyes were glittering in the same way; the same mistrust clenched their jaws. In that first moment, inflamed by the mysterious influence, they seemed ready to leap upon one another—but the anger gave way to anxiety.

"Yes, how should I know?" Langre went on, plaintively. "Twenty-five minutes ago I was at home, and Sabine…"

"…Was still here," Pierre agreed, feverishly.

"She can't have gone far, then," Meyral interjected, standing some distance away from the gate.

Vérannes turned to him with a peevish expression, but the observation had struck home.

"Have you searched the house and the back garden thoroughly?" demanded the old man.

"Everywhere! I've searched everywhere!"

"Did she leave alone?"

"She took the two children with her, and a chambermaid."

"Then we have only to divide up the field of research," said Langre. "You search the neighboring streets, Vérannes. Meyral, the cab-driver and I will explore a wider area."

"I don't want strangers getting mixed up in my private life!" cried the husband, wildly.

"You don't want?" said Langre, exasperatedly. "You don't want! It's time to put an end to all this, isn't it? For the moment, you're not Sabine's husband—you're a criminal! You shouldn't even be participating in our search. If I consent to let you involve yourself, it's because, in the circumstances, you're going to conduct yourself like a worthy man. Yes, you've behaved like a maniac—you'll answer for your iniquity."

Vérannes was convulsed by hatred, anguish and resentment. All the same, he was subdued. Silently, he limited himself to making a curt rude gesture, and then he ran back into the house.

"He's gone to look for the manservant," muttered Langre. "There's no point waiting for him. Let's start searching."

"Where?"

"Along the Avenue du Bois."

"That's not my opinion. Your daughter took an opportunity to save herself, while her husband was upstairs for some

reason or other. She can only have had one idea in her mind—
to seek refuge with you."

"She knew that I was coming."

"She knew it, she was counting on it, and surely hesitated before going out—then, fear got the better of her, fear
inspired by the conduct of Vérannes who must have said
something crazy, but also born of the over-excitement she
shares with all of us. So she ran away, and I believe she's hiding, fairly close by. One of us ought to wait—the other ought
to go to the Metro station in the Avenue du Bois, the one in
the Avenue de la Grande-Armée, or to the nearest cab-stands."

"You're right! The chambermaid who went with Sabine
will come back here to tell me. I'm astonished that she isn't
here already."

"*This is a very difficult night!*" Meyral grumbled.
"Who'll wait?"

"It's better if it's me. Take the car."

Georges wasted no time. He gave an order and climbed
into the cab just as Vérannes came out of the house again. The
driver took off at speed. In two minutes, the vehicle reached
the Avenue de la Grande-Armée, where Meyral inspected the
cab-rank. Then he went down into the Metro. He bought a
ticket and went as far as the platform. A few men and women
were waiting there, showing signs of impatience.

As the physicist came out again, the clerk shouted at him
angrily: "What are you doing?"

"That's none of your business!" Meyral replied.

"I need to know why you went in without a reason."

The man did not insist. Georges went back into the avenue. There was a lot of noise there. In a restaurant ablaze with
light, men and women were singing, howling or yapping. Two
prowlers on the threshold of a bar were threatening to stick a
knife in the owner. The passers-by wore unusual expressions.

It's getting worse! Meyral thought.

He was about to give an order to the driver when he spotted the little Gare de Ceinture, which he had never used, and
of whose existence he was almost unaware. It was an excellent

place to wait. After avoiding a group from which incoherent chatter resounded, Georges reached the entrance. It was empty—which disappointed him. He examined the dusty ground feverishly, along with an old man bent over in front of the booking-office, a pneumatic clock that marked 11:30 p.m. The place seemed bleak and sinister.

The young man was gripped by a terrible impatience. "A ticket to Saint-Lazare," he said to the clerk.

The woman shivered, and stamped the ticket with a shaky hand.

Where will all this end? Meyral asked himself, as he went down the staircase. *My excitement's getting worse—other people's must be getting more aggravated too. Are we all going to be raving mad before the night's out?*

He was shaken by a spasm, but did not pause in his march; the platforms and the rails seemed even more sinister than the waiting-room. The lighting was pitiful; two shadows were wandering around miserably, and Georges' heart skipped a beat. He had just perceived a seated woman in the distance, hidden behind a column. There was a child next to her and she was holding another on her knee.

"Sabine!" he whispered.

Memories rose up, so sweet, so fresh and so sad that he was shaken to the core of his being. He suppressed them, and presented himself before Madame Vérannes with a calm expression. She could not have seemed more alarmed if she had seen a wolf. Her small hand was visibly trembling; she clutched her child to her convulsively; the light in her eyes gleamed like starlight. Suddenly, she displayed an exaggerated astonishment and an inexplicable terror. "Is it by chance that…" she stammered. She stopped short.

"It's not by chance," he said. "I was looking for you."

"You were looking for me?"

She smiled vaguely; she seemed calmer and almost joyful. She was a sparkling creature, by virtue of the brightness of her blonde hair, piled up on her head, and her complexion of convolvulus and wild roses, but pathetic by virtue of her large, unsteady and timid eyes.

"When you called your father, I was with him," Meyral went on. "We came together. He's waiting for you near your house, for we expected that you'd send the chambermaid to meet him."

"She should have reached him by now," she whispered.

"You don't want us to go and find him?"

She uttered a faint wail: "Oh, no! No! I don't want to go back to the house tonight—I don't want to risk running into..." She did not finish; fear took hold of her; her lips moved soundlessly.

"We'll wait, then," he said, disturbed by the poor creature's anxiety. "It's not very far."

By means of a surge of sentiment analogous to the previous one, she reassured herself generally: "Oh, how nervous I am!"

"We're all nervous tonight," he replied, mechanically. His tone was marked by gloom and malaise. His memories were still flowing, a cruel, destructive and magical host. "Perhaps it would be better to wait upstairs?" he added, by way of diversion.

She approved the suggestion with a nod of the head. Gently, Meyral picked up the little girl who was sitting beside her mother, while Sabine brought the baby.

They had not long to wait. Scarcely five minutes had elapsed when Langre and the chambermaid came into view. Gérard displayed an excessive joy; his hands were trembling. He had the taut smile of old men, in which even happiness is mingled with something unstable and tragic. His keen eyes never ceased looking fondly at the two children—the uncertain family that was supposed to extend into the far future.

"What do you want to do, my darling?" he murmured, eventually. "Do you want to go back to your husband?"

She uttered the same plaint that she had addressed to Gérard: "Oh no! Not now. Perhaps never again." In a low and intense tone, she added: "I've tried, father; I've fought hard. I

45

think I've been resigned, perhaps courageous—but I can't any longer. I can't do it any more!"

"It's not me who'll force you to see him again," her father replied, somberly.

When the group got back to the Avenue de la Grande-Armée, a baseless quarrel was convulsing two hosts of frenzied individuals. The racket was getting louder; shady individuals were roaming near the barrier. It was impossible to find a supplementary vehicle; it was agreed that the chambermaid would take the Metro.

At first, the driver barked, angrily: "I'm not an omnibus!"

"No, but you're a good fellow," Meyral retorted, sharply, "and you'll help out these good people." He pointed to the young woman and her children. The cabby, gripped by abrupt compassion, tapped himself on the sternum and exclaimed, in a generous tone: "One has a heart! And benevolence!"

The car moved through deserted streets. Agitated silhouettes were perceptible at intervals; almost all the windows were lit up. Nothing got in the travelers' way until the church of Saint-François-Xavier; there erratic bands surged into the road, composed of artisans from Grenelle or Gros-Caillou. They were moving rapidly, in the same direction. Sometimes, a cry echoing from mouth to mouth ended up as a unanimous shout. The automobile was greeted with vituperation and insults.

One plaster-encrusted individual with the arms of a gorilla croaked: "Take it back! Take it back!"

With every rotation of the wheels the crowd became denser; men were emerging from the side-streets unrelentingly, and the driver, after swerving a few times, was obliged to slow down.

"Are you trying to squash the workers?" jeered a black-faced man with a flat nose and circular eyes.

"I'm a more conscientious worker than you!" howled the driver. "And I'm in a union!"

"Then f--- off to the Bois with your bourgeois!"

"They're not bourgeois. They're good fellows—and a woman and two kids!" He was barking like a huge mastiff in the night, terrible and raucous.

The man with the round eyes was already 30 meters behind.

A loud roar emanated from the Gare Montparnasse: "Death! Death!"

Almost immediately, a song rose up, in successive waves, like a tide:

> "*C'est le grand soir, c'est le grand soir,*
> "*C'est le grand soir des exploiteurs!*"[8]

"In God's name!" groaned the driver. "This is it! The red night's arrived!"

The automobile went forward slowly, without exciting any protests, for the driver had started singing along with the rest of them, and the chorus emerged from his throat like a roar:

> "*Les bourreaux mordront la poussière*
> "*Lève-toi, peuple aux mille bras,*
> "*Nous allons tuer la misère;*
> "*La nuit rouge monte là-bas!*"

Innumerable hordes were running toward the station. Six large aircraft were directing the beams of searchlights amid the stars.

In the car, Langre and Meyral, who were very pale, looked at one another. "Is it the revolution?" asked the old man.

---

[8] The words of this stirring revolutionary song—which proclaim that the day of "the exploiters" is done, that "the executioners will bite the dust," exhorting "the people with a thousand arms" to rise up because "we're going to kill poverty," and declaring that "the red night is rising in the distance"— produce no hits on Google, so it is possible that Rosny composed them himself, although he might well have heard them sung in the days when he used to hang around with nihilists and assorted revolutionary socialists.

"It's an episode of it," Meyral murmured. "An order must have reached the suburbs; hundreds of thousands of men are on the march."

Suddenly, the song quavered and broke up. A wave ran through the crowd; the multitude slowed down and gunshots resounded, isolated at first, and then in incoherent salvoes.

"The cops! The cops! Death to the cops! Murderers! Have their hides!"

A detachment of police arrived, which drove back the crowd; with roars and complaints it broke up, bumping into masses emerging from the Rue de Vaugirard, the Rue du Cherche-Midi and the Rue de Sevres: insane faces with frantic eyes, reminiscent of marine froth and phosphorescence.

Behind them, the police formed a black raft, compact and solid, which oscillated without breaking. Everyone fled from them. Further shots crackled, and there was a charge; the hounds fell randomly on the ragged remnants of the crowd, breaking heads, recklessly kicking fallen bodies in the belly with booted feet. A boundless fury was exciting the assailants; the roars and growls of carnivores replied to the screams and blasphemies of the victims.

An immense rumor filled the Avenue du Maine, however; as incoherent as a squall, it exhaled jeers, threats and exhortations—and then a rhythm took possession of it, channeling the enthusiasm, the war-cry giving it a soul:

"Nous allons tuer la misère.
"La nuit rouge monte là-bas!"

A man with a skeletal torso, six feet tall, was brandishing a scarlet rag; a horde of laborers was following him, their arms interlinked and their bearded heads held high. The raft of policemen was fragmented and broken up. The tide of fugitives came back from all directions. The soft thud of falling bodies was audible, the impact of skulls on pavements, and the screams of the wounded and dying.

"Forwards!" howled a colossal voice. "To the Ministries, the Elysée Palace, the telegraph offices!"

The storm of noise broke, and the multitude broke into a frantic run in the direction of Montparnasse. For ten minutes the flow seemed inexhaustible; then it thinned out. There were only scattered groups and bewildered solitary individuals, women with ragged hair, idlers and curiosity-seekers leaning on window-ledges.

Then one could see the corpses lying on the pavements or in the gutter; wounded men dragging themselves toward doorways; others panting, howling or coughing…

The aircraft had disappeared.

"It's disgusting!" cried Langre.

"They don't know what they're doing," Meyral sighed—while Sabine, her eyes wide with fright and her face whiter than the clouds, hugged her children in her quivering arms.

The automobile was drawn up at the pavement; the driver had abandoned it in order to charge the police.

"Perhaps it would be better to go back on foot," Georges remarked.

Just then, the driver reappeared, his beard stained with blood and his eyes full of fury. "Poverty is dead!" he howled, showing his canine face at the window. "The reign of exploiters is over! That of the common man is beginning! Ah! Ah! It's ended in suffering…it's all come apart!"

A distant and ominous detonation interrupted him. "Cannon fire!" He leapt back and whirled around. "There you are!" he moaned. "I'll drive you, all the same, before rejoining our brothers. It'll only take three minutes…and then…and then! Oh, and then…"

The words would not come; the veins in his temples were swollen, his eyes were phosphorescent and his mouth agape. A jovial fury was making his entire body shiver.

"More prolos!" he stammered. "Uh oh! More vampires! We're going to settle their hash!"

Having violently taken hold of his machine he climbed into the seat and moved off. The streets were clear; from time to time, a belated group shouted insults or raised brutal fists—but the driver brayed: "Up with the red night!"

When they reached the Faubourg Saint-Jacques, a church bell had started to ring, tolling funereally; a crimson glow was trembling among the stars; the voice of the cannon, resounding at intervals, was suggestive of the speech of the elements, mingled with the incoherent frenzy of human beings.

III. Humanity's Fever

It was 2 a.m. when Meyral left Langre and Sabine. The Rue du Faubourg-Saint-Jacques seemed almost asleep, but the number of lighted windows was still unusual; occasional excited individuals were going along the pavement or springing forth from corners.

The conflagration continued beneath the clouds, and distant detonations could be heard. After Saint-Jacques-du-Haut-Pas, there were more people about; they were swarming in the Rue Gay-Lussac, and forming a dense crowd at the opening of the Boulevard Saint-Michel. Georges succeeded in slipping through next to the railway station.

The spectacle became sinister there. All the lights were out in the direction of the Odéon; the far end of the boulevard was like a black abyss, in which helmets and breastplates were glinting confusedly. At intervals, the cavalry charged—into empty space. The clinking of iron could be heard, and an equestrian mass was seen to surge forth; the crowd roared terribly.

That heterogeneous crowd, in which revolutionaries seemed to be scarce, was scarcely spoiling for a fight. Continually traversed by surges of rage and panic, it was subject to a mysterious excitement, which the soldiery shared. Occasionally, a long moan went up, and it was evident that wounded men were lying in the darkness—but the drama was further away; the revolutionaries had suffered a defeat in the Latin Quarter and, after the destruction of the street-lights and the looting of a few shops, had gone back to join the hordes submerging the Boulevard Saint-Germain, the quais, the Louvre and the Champs-Elysées.

"Our brothers are victors out there!" growled a clean-shaven individual, whose upper lip continually drew back to reveal chalky teeth. "It's the end that I prophesied: biting the wooden pavements!" He thrust his yellow face into Meyral's. "We're going to take it back! Why shouldn't we do it here and now?" He pointed to the head of the boulevard, toward the Observatoire and, gripped by a sudden excitement, exclaimed: "Let's set fire to that! It'll only need 20 of us. First, we need volunteers! Who's coming with me?"

Pale faces emerged from the shadows, but the clatter of hooves became audible at the same time; two rows of breastplates seemed to float through the air; the howling multitude ran away in panic.

How will all this end? Meyral wondered, retreating along the façades of the buildings. *If the excitement continues, all humankind will be crazy by tomorrow morning—including me.*

After making tiresome detours, he succeeded in getting home. His maid, Césarine, was waiting for him, horribly haggard, drunk on drama and terror. She had spent hours in a dark closet, in the company of old clothes, decrepit boxes and broken crockery.

"Monsieur!" she moaned. "Monsieur!" Dirty tear-strains streaked her face. "Are they going to murder us, roast us alive or smoke us out like rats?"

The creature's effervescence exasperated Meyral. Nervously, he studied her reddened face, the sparkling eyes behind her tears, and the hair that had escaped from her curlers to hang down like the remnants of a threadbare mane. He felt a desire to break a flask over her head or chase her away with blows from a pestle. At the same time, he felt sorry for her; he understood her smoldering terror and the consequent leaps of her imagination.

"Before anything else, go to bed!" he ordered. "Go to bed right away. Do as the cockroaches do—get back into your hole; you'll make yourself ill staying awake. The best refuge is upstairs, in your room. No revolutionaries will take it into their heads to climb up there, and what if they did? They don't want anything from servants."

These words gushed forth like water from a cracked basin. He made expansive gestures; his consciousness was falling apart, without his ceasing to maintain a certain self-control. "Jump to it!" he went on. "It's here that your precious life is in danger. Up there is an oasis—a spring in the desert, a haven of safety. Climb up, I tell you! Get on with it!"

She listened in bewilderment, shaking the gray wisps of her hair, indecisive at first, but then convinced. Suddenly, she grabbed her little copper lamp and ran away up the service stairs, without even bidding her master goodnight.

He took refuge in his laboratory, and at first the overexcitement seemed to increase. Memories were roaring like torrents and becoming intolerably colorful, waves of hope alternating with asphyxiating anxiety. "To work, pitiful atom!" he exclaimed.

For a few minutes, he attempted to carry out experiments. His hands were shaking; his retinas received quivering images; his thoughts, as discontinuous as his movements, fled randomly.

"It's worse than being drunk!" he sighed. "Meanwhile…what about the phenomenon? It persists, the phenomenon, but isn't it decreasing? The indices of refraction… Sabine…Langre… What will become of France?"

The vertigo became unbearable. Georges abandoned the polarizer in which he was analyzing a ray of red light, took a few steps at random and let himself fall into an armchair, struck down by drowsiness.

He woke up at about 8 a.m.; immediately, he had the impression that his excitement had disappeared. Only the anguish persisted, sharp and keen, but normal. The events of the previous evening were strangely unsteady in his memory.

He called Césarine. She came running, yellow with fatigue, her lips like minced veal. "Oh, Monsieur!" she murmured. She was obviously frightened and harassed, but not as haggard as before.

"What about the mob?" he asked.

"The President has been killed, but the quarter is peaceful," she replied. "They're collecting the dead."

"Who's collecting the dead?"

"The Red Cross, along with the cops and other people."

"So the government is victorious?"

"I don't know, Monsieur. So they say. I can't hear anything any more, and even the fires seem to be extinct."

"Bring me the newspapers."

"There aren't any, Monsieur."

"Damn!" Georges growled. He was not surprised—only anxious—an anxiety that was a trifle slow and ponderous, with shivers that made his heart leap like an animal woken up with a start. He drank a hasty cup of chocolate, put on his overcoat and went out.

The weather was warm, the sky covered with nickel-plated clouds in which there were gaps. People were passing by leadenly. A fruit-seller was hawking Burgundy cherries in a tearful voice; the grocer's boy was arranging boxes with a pensive air; the butcher was slicing meat with a dirty and distracted hand. Everyone seemed weary. An old woman told a bread-carrier: "Tomorrow, there'll be no more Republic. It's Victor who's taken the *fauteuil*!"

As he got closer to the Boulevard Saint-Michel, Meyral ran into the vestiges of the mob. Many shops were closed; police platoons and cavalry squadrons were circulating in the roadway. The brutality of men was revealed; leaves had been torn from the trees, street-lights were twisted, shutters gaped open, staved in by iron bars, windows were missing panes.

The dull and pale spectacle was simultaneously reminiscent of demolitions, awakenings the morning after drunken sprees, crystallized fury, frightful lapses into unconsciousness and mortal skirmishes.

A human fever, Meyral thought, *already dissipated in the night of time!*

The police would not let him through. He had to go round by the Rue Monsieur-le-Prince and cross a section of the Luxembourg. When he came in the vicinity of the Rue Gay-Lussac, newspaper-sellers surged forth waving their papers tumultuously.

"*L'Eclair!*"

"*Le Journal!*"

L'Eclair and *Le Journal* had only two pages each. Posters informed readers that, for want of compositors, press-operators and power, it had been necessary to restrict the print runs to whatever could be contrived. The headlines read:

Death of the President of the Republic.

Mob triumphant and vanquished.

Fire and Blood in Paris.

The Battle of the Boulevards and the Champs-Elysées.

The Siege of the Ministries.

It seemed that the revolutionaries had taken the Ministry of the Interior by storm, invaded the Central Telegraph Office, massacred the police and routed the Municipal Guard and the Dragoons. At 3 a.m. they had taken possession of the Elysée Palace and captured the President of the Republic. A vast fire had ravaged the Boulevard des Italiens; another had devoured the stockrooms of Au Printemps;[9] bombs had demolished the fronton of the Palais Législatif; anarchists and apaches had swarmed through the first, second, seventh, eighth and ninth arrondissements, where they had instituted looting; the damage was estimated at 50 or 60 million francs.

That was the moment at which General Laveraud had come on to the scene. He had brought five infantry regiments,

---

[9] Au Printemps is a famous department store in the Boulevard Haussmann. When Rosny wrote *La Force mystérieuse* it was fitted out in an Art Nouveau style, but it really was devastated by fire in the early 1920s and the modern version is quite different.

four cavalry regiments and several batteries of light artillery, and had massed these troops in the sixteenth arrondissement. The men had exhibited an extreme overexcitement, and the general himself had manifested a savage humor—but that bad mood had not detracted from his military qualities; it had rejuvenated them. It seemed that he had decided not to take any notice of any higher authority. He began by sweeping the Avenue du Bois de-Boulogne and the Avenue de la Grande-Armée with cannon-fire; the revolutionaries there had scattered. Then, disposing his batteries, he ordered the bombardment of the Champs-Elysées and the Faubourg Saint-Honoré, where countless fanatics had accumulated. The shells had scythed them down like grass.

The revolutionaries' panic had been as feverish as their audacity. When the avenue was clear, Laveraud's troops had moved forward to the roundabout; then there had been a brief battle. The rioters' elite held Saint-Philippe-du-Roule, the Rue du Faubourg-Saint-Honoré and the Elysée. They withstood a hail of projectiles for a quarter of an hour, and then gave way in their turn. Charges of infantry and cavalry had swept the streets clean as far as Saint-Philippe—and then the butchery began. The troops had fired relentlessly into the massed crowds, held immobile by their own numbers; shells had smashed the presidential palace.

Then by the light of fires and the dawn, a white flag had been raised, and Laveraud consented to listen to negotiators. They were three men drunk with rage, gunpowder and blood.

"We hold the President!" the most frenetic declared. "If your troops don't pull back, we'll kill him like a hyena."

"And I," Laveraud replied, shaking with fury, "will give you five minutes to evacuate the Palais."

"Be careful! We shan't hesitate—especially me!" He turned a purple face toward the general. "I, most of all, will not hesitate!"

"I have but one order to give," growled Laveraud. "Your extermination!"

The revolutionary withdrew, vomiting threats. Five minutes later, the bombardment resumed; at 4 a.m., Laveraud went into the Elysée. The President's cadaver was lying on the steps of the Palais, but the Revolution was defeated.[10]

Is it defeated? Meyral wondered, in amazement.

He studied the people surrounding him, astonished by their gray faces. There was an excessive contrast between this calm and the convulsions of the night. He felt internally dull and worn-out himself.

Oh yes, it's defeated. The rhythm has disappeared—the exasperated rhythm that drove it to murder.

He made haste to get back to Langre.

The old man had only just woken up. He seemed vague and somber.

"*He*'s been here," he murmured. "After grinding his teeth, complaints and curses, he left—but he'll be back!"

"When did he come?" Georges asked.

"At 3 a.m.…exhausted…without a hat, with a gash in his neck. When he left, a boundless fatigue had flattened us both."

"Me too!" Meyral whispered.

"Sabine and the children are still asleep. We must save her, Georges. I don't want her to fall back into the hands of a

---

[10] When Rosny wrote *La Force mystérieuse* the President of the Republic was the aged and inert Armand Fallières, who was widely despised (Maurice Renard's *Le Péril bleu* also singles him out for scathing criticism). It is obviously Fallières that Rosny has maliciously in mind here, but while the novel was being serialized Fallières was replaced by the far more dynamic Raymond Poincaré, and readers of the subsequent book version would inevitably have assumed that it was his corpse that was ignominiously laid out on the steps of the Elysée Palace. Given that Rosny owed Poincaré a considerable personal debt—he was the lawyer who won the long legal battle to establish the Académie Goncourt—this must have caused him some slight embarrassment.

maniac." He roused himself and became animated. His tragic face appeared beneath the weary mask. "I committed a crime in giving her to him; I've committed another in leaving her to suffer."

"You didn't know."

"I hadn't the right not to know. Undoubtedly, I'm a poor social observer—the laboratory had stripped away my sensitivity to human beings—but one doesn't give one's daughter away without obtaining guarantees. I should have consulted my friends...you most of all, who are not entirely the slave of attitudes to matter. You would have warned me."

"I don't know."

"Yes, you know. Don't treat me with a degrading indulgence. You knew!"

"I guessed," said Meyral, softly, "that she could not be happy with that man. And since then, I've seen..."

"You've seen her suffering! You knew she was in danger. You should have told me."

"I didn't think I had the right."

"Why?"

A blush of shame rose to the young man's cheeks. He made an interrupted gesture expressive of embarrassment and doubt. "Scruples," he murmured.

Langre could not decipher the gesture, nor interpret the word. "Unfortunate scruples!" He fell into a grim reverie.

"Did you know that the revolutionaries have been defeated?" Meyral said, suddenly. "And that the President of the Republic is dead?"

"I don't know anything!" Langre exclaimed. He shook his head violently, a red tint spreading over the colorless swarthiness of his cheeks. "I detest my contemporaries," he said, gloomily, "but I'm ashamed nevertheless to be so uninvolved in their drama!"

"We couldn't have done anything about it! Our humble presence would only have aggravated the disorder. It's not that I regret. Our role was elsewhere—and we haven't been able to fulfill it. Who knows what has happened while we've been asleep? Who knows what prodigious observations we've missed—and humankind with us—unless others…?"

"Unless others have taken our place!"

They looked at one another, full of the profound anguish of scientists who have let the moment of discovery pass.

"Why should it be too late?" Langre muttered.

"Yesterday, before I went to bed, it seemed to me that the phenomenon had decreased. I wasn't able to make completely sure; fatigue got the better of me—but this morning, the great calm succeeding the hyperesthesia of the multitude surely indicates a metamorphosis of the environment."

"Well, let's get to work—since you don't have anything urgent to do."

As soon as they had carried out the initial experiments—the simplest and sketchiest—no further doubt was possible; the refraction of light had returned to normal. At the most, they discerned, after a passage through a pile of glass plates, a few confused zones in the spectrum obtained by means of a flint-glass prism: traces of abnormal infringement. Attempts at polarization gave scarcely any result.

"We've lost the game!" groaned Langre, in a chagrined tone. "It's the fault of that abominable Vérannes. While we were embarking on an absurd adventure, *the others* were at work." His despairing eyes searched the invisible for those unknown rivals that iniquitous destiny had sent to haunt them. "For after all," he went on, bitterly, "everyone involved in optics…"

"Who knows?" said Meyral, thoughtfully. "Perhaps they had other things to look at than what we have seen."

"But the basis of the phenomenon was there to be studied! Why wouldn't they have devoted themselves to it more passionately?"

Georges shrugged his shoulders imperceptibly. Confronted with the accomplished fact, he did not know how to answer. "Undoubtedly," he said. "But what can we do about it? I think, moreover, that the evolution of the phenomenon will continue. Exceedingly interesting things are happening…I sense it!"

"Oh, you sense it!" Langre cried, ironically.

Meyral had picked up the flint-glass prism. He looked at the spectrum projected on a plate, with the sort of distracted attention that one frequently encounters in laboratory men. "It seems to me," he said, "that there's an anomaly in the violet."

Langre shivered, in a fashion comparable to that of a war-horse that hears the trumpet sounding. "What anomaly?"

"Firstly, a certain pallor…and then again, one might think that the violet region is less extensive. I might be mistaken, for my *personal equation* is certainly disturbed this morning."

Without saying a word, Gérard began taking measurements. "You're right! The extreme violet is eroded."

An emotion equal to that of the previous day contracted their faces.

"Let's verify it!" said Georges.

They verified it. After experiments exact to the micrometer it became evident that the extreme region of the violet was lacking, and that the neighboring region was reduced in intensity.

"Approximately a 30th of the spectrum has disappeared!" Langre concluded. "In consequence, the ultra-violet…"

There was no need to go on. Already, Meyral was helping him to set up new apparatus. The observations were decisive. The absence of any simple chemical or phosphorogenic effect left no doubt as to the disappearance or extreme enfeeblement of ultra-violet radiation.

"You're right," the old man murmured, nervously. "The disorder persists—and the continuation is as disconcerting as the beginning!"

Successively, they analyzed light produced by electricity, gas, wood and coal; they all manifested the same lacuna.

"Something awesome is happening!" the young man sighed. "If the anomaly is general, the worst hypotheses become plausible. What's going to happen in Europe tonight?"

He picked up the newspapers that he had thrown on a table and searched for news from the provinces and overseas. They were innocuous, apart from three items transmitted before the mob had invaded the Central Telegraph Office: a brief dispatch announcing troubles in Marseilles; another relating to the sabotage of a battleship; and a third recording an unexpected excitement in London.

"We can, at least, conclude that the disturbance extends over a considerable area," Langre said. "Let's see if any other papers have appeared." He rang a bell; the maidservant was not long delayed in showing a yellow-patched face.

"Go and buy some newspapers, Catherine."

"If I can!" she replied, acrimoniously.

"You will be able to," Meyral remarked, cocking an ear. Wild shouts announcing the sensational editions of the newspapers were audible.

Catherine went out, with a tragic expression. She came back with *La Presse, Le Journal, Le Petit Parisien* and *Le Figaro*. The first pages were devoted to the vanquished mob, but in the following pages numerous telegrams testified to the morbid state of the entire human family. In Madrid and Barcelona the revolution was victorious. Homicidal riots had bloodied the Italian peninsula. There had been violent skirmishes in Berlin, Hamburg, Dresden, Vienna, Budapest, Prague, Moscow, St. Petersburg, Warsaw, Brussels, Amsterdam, London, Liverpool, Dublin, Lisbon, New York, Chicago, Buenos Aires, Constantinople, Kyoto and 50 other cities: battles everywhere, after a period of frenzy, ending in a strange torpor. The mob had triumphed in Mexico, the Brazilian state of São Paulo, Athens and Canton—and doubtless in many regions that the disorder had isolated completely from the world.

"That leaves us in no doubt!" said Langre, throwing *Le Figaro* aside. "The entire planet is affected."

"And no news of a scientific nature!"

"Oh well—let's get back to work!"

They worked doggedly for an hour searching for further characteristics. They only found one: the region of red and orange acted with unexpected intensity on fluorescent substances.

"That region," Meyral remarked, "even seems to be more luminous than usual."

"By comparison, undoubtedly. What remains of the violet must be weakened; I imagine that the indigo, and even the blue, are deleteriously affected. Note that the daylight has a yellow tinge."

The tragic maidservant abruptly came into the laboratory. "Madame Sabine wants to see Monsieur."

"Is she afraid to come into the laboratory?" Langre asked.

"It's because Monsieur is working."

"She won't disturb us."

Sabine's blonde plaits appeared. Her expression displayed neither agitation nor fear, but a listless melancholy, which deepened her dark blue eyes. Meyral looked at her covertly, with a gentleness full of resentment. That hyacinth and convolvulus complexion, the allure of an undine in moonlight, such glossiness, harmony and freshness—it was the fairy tale that had led his youth astray. By departing with the other, Sabine had changed all the legends…and he had not forgiven her. At the sight of her, he experienced the weight of defeat, and the corrosion of the defeated; on evenings saturated with aromas, stars and adventures, she depleted the splendor of the world.

"I woke up late!" she said, excusing herself.

"You were worn out by fatigue," her father replied, after embracing her. "We've all fallen victim to a bizarre drowsiness. How are the children?"

"They're asleep."

"They were awake until 3 a.m.!"

Sabine had moved toward Georges. "I'll never forget!" she said.

61

He clenched his fist in order not to reveal the immense shiver that shook his being. The past reappeared, with its springs and verdant hills.

"Yes, you'll do well not to forget!" exclaimed the old man. "Without Georges, time would have been lost—and time, on that ferocious night…"

Anxiety inundated the young woman's face. "What's happened?"

"Frightful things, my poor child! Perhaps less frightful than…" Cutting his own speech short with an abrupt gesture, however, he began again: "The mob has been dispersed; the city and the nation are tranquil; our surroundings remain in the chaos in which we flounder from our first breath to our last sigh!"

Sabine took these words to mean that there were no longer any but individual dangers. Thinking about Vérannes, she became feverish. "I can't live with him any longer!" she whispered.

"You'll live with me," Gérard declared. "I behaved like an unspeakable idiot in allowing that man to take you away. I can't repair the inevitable, but I can cut the mooring-rope!"

She broke into a smile. She was not far-sighted; the future was lost in the fog into which it fades for savages—but a menacing image made her shiver. "What if he becomes violent?"

"Let him come!" growled her father, impetuously. He put his hand on Meyral's shoulder. "He will find me, and he will find this fellow." He continued, with a mixture of anger and bitterness: "Oh, why wasn't it you, my son, who loved Sabine!"

Georges went pale, and a convulsive smile passed over his mouth.

IV. The Twilight of Life

The day was peaceful. Radiotelegrams announced the end of the agitation over the entire planet, save for the southern states of the Argentine Republic, Tasmania and New Zealand, where an appreciable decrease in feverish symptoms was still observable. As time went by, though, new anxieties increased incessantly. They scarcely reached the social underworld, but, swiftly disseminated by men of superior culture, they brushed the intermediate strata.

Scientists kept track of the "malady of light" with an ardent anxiety. Experimenters had discovered the singularity initially observed by Meyral. Without adding anything substantial to the observations made by Langre and Georges, their observations confirmed, to the extent of its disappearance, the phenomenon of abnormal double refraction—or, rather, the duplication of light.

In Paris, Berlin, London, Brussels, Rome, Amsterdam and all of Central Europe, the end of the first phase of the phenomenon had occurred at about 3:30 a.m. It had been manifest slightly later in Eastern Europe and in Asia, and later still in the northern regions. It was delayed in North America, except in high latitudes. In the tropics, and especially the southern hemisphere, the delay was further accentuated. All the times were corrected to Greenwich Mean Time. It appeared that the phases had nothing to do with the Sun.

As for the new phases, they followed their course. After 7 a.m., the hour at which—in Paris as in London, Liverpool, Amsterdam and Jena—the disappearance was ascertained of a narrow band of the extreme violet and all the ultra-violet rays, a progressive paling and disappearance of the remainder of the zone was observed. Nevertheless, at 7 p.m., a part of it remained—but the indigo appeared duller.

Various secondary phenomena followed. Firstly, it was ascertained, as Langre and Meyral had done, that the brightness and fluorescent power of the orange and red were increasing continuously. Soon, it was also observed that these two colors were acquiring singular chemical properties, although not very pronounced. On the other hand, the electrical conductivity of metals was decreasing; iron was the most greatly affected. Communications via submarine cables became capricious. Although transmission by terrestrial wires remained normal for those of medium length, it deviated over long distances. The production of Hertzian waves became more difficult. Work in electrical factories became subject to numerous malfunctions.

The perturbations became more marked during the night. By morning, the violet zone of the spectrum was invisible. Communication by submarine cable was no longer possible. The major telegraph lines were scarcely functioning, and only intermittently. All electrical factories had been shut down. Chemical reactions were becoming capricious in factories as in laboratories, and some had ceased to work. In consequence, wood and coal were burning poorly, giving dismal flames. Terrestrial magnetism was weakening; compass-needles were giving uncertain indications, which rendered navigation perilous. The planet was illuminated by a yellowish light.

That was a funereal day. A breath of the end of the world passed over humankind. Individuals sensed the immensity of the phenomenon and its frightful mystery, and huddled together nervously, gripped by the instinct of the herd. The phantasmagorical creatures that herald cataclysms were seen to surge forth—but no one knew anything! The men of the laboratories and those of books, the scientists who numbered the stars and those who weighed atoms, could not even offer a conjecture to the terrors of the multitude; their power was limited to minute description of the episodes of the drama.

The third night saw the last electrical communications disappear. Batteries gave derisory currents; dynamic induction seemed to have been abolished; no apparatus produced Hertzian waves any longer. In the morning, people found themselves deprived of the nervous system that had united them "innumerably" all over the world. By the evening, they averred that they were inferior to people of the olden days; steam abandoned them in its turn. Alcohols, petroleums and even wood and coal had become inert. To produce a little fire it was necessary to have recourse to rare products—which, they felt certain, would not be long delayed in sinking into chemical death.

In three days, therefore, and without any clue as to the origins of the catastrophe, humankind found itself reduced to impotence. People could still navigate by sail or by oar, and harness horses to their carriages, but they were prohibited from lighting the fires whose red caress their savage ancestors had felt in the fringes of forests, in the profound plain or on the banks of rivers.

One infinitely enigmatic thing was that life went on. The grass continued to grow in the meadows, the wheat in the fields, the leaves at the tips of little branches. Beasts and humans accomplished their subtle functions. In sum; *organic chemistry seemed to be intact.* Not entirely, though: a coppery tint was mixed with verdure; human skin became ashen; everywhere, physiologists perceived a slowing down of pigmentary functions. Emotional sensitivity also seemed to have decreased. Undoubtedly, creatures were agitated by a continual fear, but the "pulsations" of that fear were less violent than at the beginning.

Because the threat extended over the entire world, it seemed less terrifying. People did not experience the individual outrage that is by far the most bitter and intolerable. Among the old, the sick, the disabled, and even more so in those suffering from some mortal disease, a sentiment of "revenge" attenuated the distress. Outside of these psychological elements, however, there was a narcosis. The nerves lost their customary sensitivity; cuts and bruises awakened no more than a muted pain; the imagination was weighed down and impoverished. Only deductive intelligence showed no weakening. As for the spirit of observation, what it lost in promptitude it seemed to regain in precision and constancy.

On the morning of the fourth day, Langre and Meyral, after a meager breakfast, held a consultation in the laboratory.

"The blue has almost disappeared!" the old man murmured. He was pale and distressed; his eyes had lost their fever; a stupor had slackened his fervent expression. "Nothing can save humankind," he affirmed.

"Quite probably," Meyral agreed. "The chances of salvation are small—nevertheless, they're not zero. That depends on what I call the *trajectory* of the cataclysm—for I don't believe for a moment, old friend, that these phenomena are durable. They will pass."

"When?" asked Langre, morosely.

"That's the nub of the problem. If we assume that the phases are regular and comparable, we can extrapolate their limit."

"What limit? I can see several of them! In the end, all light and infra-red radiation will disappear, or the destruction will stop, whether at the green, the yellow, the orange or the red—so many limits!"

"The limit would then be the end of all radiation and the end of all superior life. I assume that mammals cannot survive the disappearance of the yellow and the orange, even admitting that the last phase is brief. There's no point in anticipating that eventuality. Let's imagine, however, that the crisis reaches its maximum when it reaches a part of the yellow radiation, and that a reaction then begins. It seems evident that the briefer the phases are, the better our chances of survival will be. Well, it took three days to consume violet, indigo and blue; it will therefore require about a day to make green disappear. Let's say one day to eat into the yellow. In 48 hours we'll reach the limit, and then the retrogression will begin."

Gérard looked at is companion pityingly. "My poor child! When all human calculations are so utterly ridiculous, how can one still construct hypotheses? There's no reason why all the radiations shouldn't vanish, to the very last."

"I perceive, however, a certain 'compensatory' logic in the progress of the phenomenon. In addition to the fact that the red and orange have definitely become more intense, the temperature is very nearly normal. That last fact permits a hope."

"A very feeble hope!" Langre protested, bitterly. "Certainly, it might signify that the energy lost by one part of the spectrum tends to increase another, but that might only be a residue of the transformation. If we assume that radiations of the visual order are being gradually converted into unknown energies, one has to expect reactions—but those reactions don't prove that the conversion won't proceed to the end. Then again, I can't believe, even for a moment, that humankind can support the disappearance, even temporarily, of the green waves! I've always held that it's a color essential to life." He concluded, with a humorless laugh: "For the time being, it's possible—and in any other circumstances I'd say probable—that the phenomenon will be transitory; its initiation was too abrupt and its evolution too rapid for our logic to see it as anything other than an immense accident—but what is our logic worth?"

He fell silent, and resumed work.

For half an hour, they devoted themselves to melancholy experiments. Then Meyral sighed. "Is the accident due to interstellar space?" he wondered.

"As a mere perturbation of the planet, it seems excessive," Langre retorted, "and as a perturbation of the Sun, implausible; it would be necessary to complicate the solar influence infinitely to imagine that the abolition of superior waves is so exactly similar by night and by day…for the slightest fire lit by humans and for the light of the stars. I'm inclined to admit that the catastrophe is interstellar in origin."

"Then it would influence the Sun, and in that case too we should discover differences between its diurnal and nocturnal action?"

"But differences infinitely smaller than if the Sun alone were involved. No matter—we must search for them. Perhaps an attentive reading of our experimental journal will reveal one of them…in which case…" A little of the bitter enthusiasm that had sustained him against the denials and spoliations of justice swelled up in his face. "Poor old maniac!" he muttered, striking his breast ironically. "Miserable dream-machine! Humankind is about to perish, but you…" A cold shiver made his shoulders quiver. "I can't do any more!" he groaned. "Let's gather together—unite our petty lives before sinking into the formless fog."

Meyral listened to him with an immense compassion, which also poured out over himself. "Yes," he replied, "we must be together; it's necessary not to separate yourself from your family any longer—even for an hour. It's ungodly!"

"Catherine!" shouted the old man.

The gloomy maidservant appeared. In the coppery light, she displayed a face in which terror had hollowed out holes and wrinkles. Her pupils were dilated, like those of a cat in twilight.

"Tell Madame Vérannes that we're waiting here for her and the children—and Berthe and Césarine too," said the old scientist, in an amicable tone. "You can stay with us too, if you prefer."

"Oh, yes, Monsieur!" she exclaimed. "I'd certainly prefer that!" The herd instinct was manifest in the gesture of her arms, extended toward her master; she had confidence not only in the old man, of whom she was deeply and faithfully fond, but also in the enigmatic instruments on the tables and against the walls.

"There are no letters?" he asked. "Or newspapers?"

"Neither letters nor newspapers; Monsieur knows that I would have brought them."

"Alas!"

"Perhaps there'll be a midday paper—like yesterday."

A few minutes later, Sabine appeared with the children and her chambermaid. Césarine followed them furtively. The reddish light hardly concealed the pallor of their faces, but the children were not manifesting any sadness, although a certain languor was affecting their gestures.

Mental turmoil had made the young woman thinner. She had little hope left. Her long ordeal with Vérannes and Langre's dramatic existence had dragged her down into black depression. Having so often envisaged the worst, she was scarcely astonished by the immense and subtle disaster that threatened humankind. A mystical correspondence had been established between that total misfortune and the afflictions accumulated within her. Although she envisaged the fatal denouement without rebellion, however, she suffered bitterly on behalf of others; she also endured an immeasurable remorse for having made such a ridiculous mess of her youth.

Her gaze interrogated Langre's face fearfully. The old man looked away, but she deciphered the nuances of his impatient features, inept at concealment.

"Is it year 1000?" she said, for she did not want to terrify Berthe or Césarine.

"We don't know."

She heard the bell tolling at Saint-Jacques; then there was a piercing cry in the street.

"The newspaper!" said Catherine.

Three minutes later, she brought a sheet of paper entitled *Le Bulletin*—a makeshift paper printed on a hand-press, into which a group of journalists and scientists condensed the news. It contained nothing superfluous; anecdotal style had been abolished therein.

Langre read it avidly. Apart from a few details, the information of a scientific nature told him nothing that he did not already know. The other facts were merely consequences of the general fact, but one of them was alarming; in Paris, mortality had tripled in the last 24 hours, and it was increasing exponentially. Between 8 a.m. and noon, the physicians had certified 39 deaths; between noon and 4 p.m., 44; between four and 8 p.m., 58; between eight and midnight, 82; between midnight and 4 a.m., 118; between 4 a.m. and 8 a.m., 177. In total, 518. Two out of three invalids had been carried off by a mysterious and rapid illness, without any manifest suffering save for a terrifying crisis of anxiety that manifested itself about an hour before death. That anxiety ended in a state of stupor, followed by a coma. No fever was observed, although the movements of the patients were accentuated, at the commencement of the malady, by shivers and contortions. The pupils were constantly dilated, the skin dry and red—a brownish red, that was not a consequence of blood-flow.

Langre handed the paper to Meyral, saying: "It's the turn of living chemistry!"

"Alas!" said Georges, in a low voice, when he had read it in his turn. "If I hope against hope, it's because the morbid crisis was, it seems, bound to have set in sooner or later—in a slower manner than the other!"

Langre was pacing back and forth. Sabine, divining that the news was ominous, preferred not to interrogate the two men. What good would it do, since she expected the worst? As for Berthe, Catherine and Césarine, huddled in the corners, they had given up on understanding anything, and had put their destiny in the hands of their masters.

Meyral continued reading. Brief paragraphs noted that animals were affected to various degrees; the disease was hitting herbivores hard; on the other hand, dogs—and cats especially—were proving more resistant than humans. Domestic birds were becoming sluggish, without their mortality being much higher than usual. It had not been possible to determine statistics relating to wild birds or insects, but their vitality appeared to have been reduced.

The two men looked at one another grimly.

"If the green radiations disappear…" Langre began. He set about examining the solar spectrum attentively. For a quarter of an hour, the men made precise measurements. Then Meyral whispered: "It's eating into the green!"

There was a miserable silence. All comment seemed derisory. The chill of oblivion enveloped that islet of individuals, lost in a boundless catastrophe.

Through the windows, they could see the Val-de-Grâce and the Luxembourg, in a light reminiscent of artificial fireworks. A few people were wandering along the pavements, like phantoms; a black silence had settled over the neighborhood. Meanwhile, noon resounded from the nearby tower, and the chimes took on an inestimable grandeur, as if emerging from the depths of the ages, quivering with millenary memories.

"Lunch time!" said Langre, mechanically.

Catherine stood up in the corner where she had huddled up and said: "I'll serve it."

Ten minutes later, they were reunited in the dining-room. There was fruit, biscuits, conserves and wine. Langre and Meyral eyed the foodstuffs suspiciously, fearing that they might have become inedible. The first mouthfuls, however, revealed that they were unaffected—and in spite of everything, the meager meal had its satisfaction. They all felt hungry—a "lazy" but continuous hunger—and the wine revived them; its confused gaiety, extending through their bodily fibers, awoke an unexpected confidence.

"In a way, the cataclysm is merciful to living organisms!" said Meyral.

Langre drank a large glassful to combat the pessimistic fog that was thickening his mind, and smiled. "We'll get out of it!" he lied.

He had picked up little Marthe and placed her on his knee. He was like a man condemned to death, in whom opium or morphine had both excited the sensation of nothingness and soothed distress. An extraordinary tenderness filled his old heart—the love of a father and a grandfather amalgamated with the love of the human race, and the love of all terrestrial life, which was enveloped by a force incomparably more cruel than all the forces that had assailed creatures through the myriad ages of the past.

"Let's go see our fellows!" he said, moved by a sudden and violent desire.

Scarcely had he spoken than the same desire overwhelmed Georges, Sabine and the servants. All of them, to the extent of their instinct and intelligence, felt the overarching linkage of the species.

The Rue des Feuillantines was deserted. Passers-by were circulating in the Rue Saint-Jacques and the Rue Gay-Lussac, walking furtively in the reddish light. Those who were moving in couples or groups scarcely addressed a word to one another. It was reminiscent of those twilights described by northern poets, which are not the twilights of a day but of an era. The absence of vehicles would have been sufficient to render the city silent; noises dissolved in the soft atmosphere; the pedestrians' boots seemed fur-lined. All the faces displayed melancholy, bitterness and a dread that attenuated their lassitude.

In the Boulevard Saint-Michel the crowd became dense. Young men, abandoned to the herd instinct, formed gangs; poor pale girls with purple lips slid mournfully along the pavements as if they had just been to mass. Here and there, the white head of a scientist or philosopher protruded. They met artisans, domestics, shopkeepers, rentiers, factory-owners, street-walkers, beggars, and even a flower-seller, offering faded lilacs with a bewildered expression.

The subtle boundaries that divided up instincts, tastes and mentalities continued to separate these individuals, maintaining a vague hierarchy. Besides, the crowd was mild-mannered and slow-moving. The nature of the catastrophe, the sinister subtlety of its vicissitudes, restrained brutal impulses. Even fear was contained, as if dilated by amazement. There was a great unity of emotion: simple minds felt as keenly as the most intellectual how contradictory this adventure was to human destiny. That the Earth might swallow its inhabitants, that the seas might drown the continents, that a deadly epidemic might carry off all living things, that the Sun might go out, that a fiery star might burn them or a displaced planet crash into ours—they were conceivable events, in the image of things that had happened since the beginning of the world...but this fantastic death of light, this dying of the colors, which affected the humblest of flames as well as the rays of the Sun and those of the stars, derisively gave the lie to the entire history of animals and men!

"They're accepting it more easily than I would have imagined," Langre observed. "After all, why not? The destruction that threatens all of them would otherwise threaten them

72

each in turn. How many are avoiding cancer, kidney failure, nights of choking, facial neuralgias—everything that threatens infimal creatures!"

His speech was not at all consoling. The human race, which he had thought that he scorned and hated, had become strangely dear to him. Although the expectation of his own death and that of his family was sufficient to fill his heart, he experienced a sacred horror and a fraternal pain that far surpassed his own drama.

That horror was even more profound in Meyral. He watched the multitude with tender compassion. In the depths of his inner being a religious sentiment emerged, for he was one of those people for whom the future of humankind is a passion and a promise. The energy and the persistence of the species had always excited his own energy and the sense of his persistence.

As they passed Cluny, Sabine started and drew her children closer to her. A few seconds later, Meyral shivered in his turn; he had just seen Vérannes.

What does it matter? he said to himself. *He's only one more wretch.*

In the orange light, Vérannes had a sulfurous and debilitated appearance. He was on the other side of the street, half-hidden in the crowd; he had obviously seen the young woman.

"What are you looking at?" asked Langre. Turning his head, he perceived the man in his turn. The sight reanimated him to the point of wrath. He made a threatening gesture. A rearrangement of the crowd hid Sabine's husband, and they saw that an adolescent had just fainted; two men were holding him up. A rumor spread—the rumor of a languid crowd, slow in its emotions.

Then, in quick succession, a student collapsed against a façade, and a child rolled on the pavement. They were picked up and taken away; there was a sort of collective breathlessness.

"The disease is getting worse!" murmured a tall, thin man who was coming along the boulevard. Langre and Meyral recognized Dr. Desvallières.

"What disease?" asked the physicist, mechanically.

Desvallières, who was preparing to cross the road, extended his hand to Langre. "I don't know," he confessed. "The planetary disease? These last three hours have been terrible. Furthermore, the deaths are increasingly sudden."

While he was speaking they heard a faint cry for help. A woman had just collapsed on the pavement. A policeman and two workers lifted her up. Her eyes were wide open; her gaze was visibly becoming extinct by the second. Desvallières, leaning over her, felt her neck at the location of one of the carotid arteries.

Confused words strayed from the edges of her livid lips: "Cécile...I want...ah!"

"She's dead!" the physician declared.

Horror paralyzed Sabine; her eyes were full of tears.

Meyral whispered in Langre's ear: "We need to go home as quickly as possible. I'm afraid of mental contagion."

Before the little group had turned the corner of the Rue du Sommerard, they saw another old man who had fainted in front of the Café Vachette and a little girl inanimate in an artisan's arms. Langre had taken hold of Sabine's hand; Meyral was carrying one of the children and the servants were lengthening their stride. In the Rue Saint-Jacques, which was almost deserted, the pedestrians were no longer idling; all of them were hurrying home. In straw-colored sky the Sun was visibly reddening ominously.

The route seemed interminable; an increasing fatigue slowed down their progress, and the anguish would have been terrible if their ability to feel pain had not been strangely reduced.

"Finally!" sighed Langre, when he found himself at the door. He gave Sabine a swift push, for he could see men in the distance carrying an inert body.

Three minutes later, they were reunited again in the tiny fatherland of rooms. The relief of refuge! The immense peril ceased to be perceptible. They drew closer together, like children seeking the security that comes from being together in the same nest, in the midst of mysterious elements.

It did not last. A terrible sick feeling turned their weakness tremulous; they frightened one another with their faces, whose pallor took on a coppery tint, in which the secret of the moment inscribed its threat.

Furtively, Meyral had moved toward one of the large laboratory tables; Langre followed him.

"The green's decreasing!" said the young man, in a low voice.

"What's perhaps equally serious," replied Langre, in the same tone, "is that the temperature's falling—it seems that the brightness of the red has stopped increasing. *There's no longer any compensation…*"

"One degree—that's not much, and could be due to normal causes. As for the brightness of the red, if it has stabilized in the elevated region, it's increased in the vicinity of the infra-red. It even seems…yes, it seems that the region has enlarged slightly…"

They measured the width of the red band with a micrometer gauge.

"It's enlarged."

"It's just another kind of compensation," said the old man, bitterly.

V. The Grim Reaper

Langre shivered. The tragic maidservant was shivering too; a sudden chill penetrated the depths of their flesh. That chill was followed by a period of excitation and fear. An intolerable distress weighted up the napes of their necks.

The chambermaid, Berthe, was prowling along the walls, like an animal searching for a way out. "Death! Death! Death!" she croaked. She turned round, as if she had been shot in the head, raised her arms in a gesture of supreme anguish and suddenly collapsed on the floor.

Langre and Meyral lifted her up. She was shivering, in brief fits, her cheeks hollowing out between her jaws. Her eyes remained wide open, losing their gaze fantastically.

"Berthe! Poor Berthe!" moaned Sabine. She loved the young woman, for her gentleness and her patience.

"Berthe's dead!" murmured the dying woman. Her hands were groping in empty space; then a tragic smile contorted her lips, and her gaze continued its extinction.

"Fetch a doctor!" Langre ordered.

The tragic maidservant headed unsteadily for the door, but Meyral got there ahead of her. A few more words spilled confusedly from the dying woman's lips, like pebbles in a stream. She released a groan, then a croak, and slipped away into eternal darkness.

The doctor that Meyral brought was a thickset and bandy-legged man whose beard was going gray on the left, while remaining black on the right. He studied the corpse indifferently, and stammered: "We don't know any longer! This disease has no name. If it continues, no one...no one...!" He made a gesture of renunciation, and looked into Berthe's open eyes silently. "Their gaze!" he sighed. "That gaze has never existed before!" He shook his head and mechanically buttoned up his overcoat. "Nothing to be done! The afflicted are dying. Our presence is futile...futile!" Passing his hand over his forehead, with a gesture of immense lassitude, he added: "They're waiting for me elsewhere...they're waiting for me everywhere!" He slipped out of the laboratory like a specter.

An hour went by, crushing and monotonous. They waited there, in unspeakable expectation, lost in the bosom of mystery to a greater extent than shipwreck-victims in the depths of the ocean. Their only relief was their weakness. It gave them long intervals of numbness, during which thoughts and sensations became physiologically distant, so slow and indecisive that they diluted the suffering. There were atrocious, glacial awakenings, in which their souls filled with terror and anguish squeezed their throats like a noose. The awakenings and torpors corresponded to a rhythm; they were manifest simultaneously in the adults and the children.

At about 5 p.m., Langre and Meyral observed that the temperature was dropping more rapidly.

"This time, the intensity of the red rays is stable!" murmured the old man, in an ominous voice. "The end is approaching…" He was interrupted by a knock on the entrance door. "A visitor?" he groaned, with faint irony.

The tragic maidservant dragged herself to the antechamber; they heard an exclamation and whispering, and then a tall silhouette appeared on the threshold of the laboratory.

"Vérannes!" growled the old man.

"Yes, Vérannes," the visitor replied. He displayed a humble expression, hollow and pitiful. His tall stature seemed compressed; a continuous shiver was agitating his muscular hands. "I've come," he continued, in a supplicatory manner, "because everything's about to end—and I wanted to die with my children and the woman I love."

"You don't deserve it!" Langre cried.

If Vérannes had arrived while the crisis of numbness was still in force, perhaps he would have been greeted without resistance—but the phase of excitement was nearing its peak; the sight of "the enemy" exasperated the old man and drove Sabine to despair.

"No!" Gérard continued, his excitement mingling with a sort of delirium. "You don't deserve to die with your victim, and we don't deserve to have our last moments disturbed by an odious presence."

"I'm a wretch!" sighed Vérannes. "My sins are irreparable, but remember that they drew their source from a boundless love! Remember, too, that these poor creatures are my children. I'm not asking for any compassion. Give me a corner in a room where I can tell myself that I'm close to the woman I love…Sabine, won't you have pity on me?"

"Yes, yes…let him stay!" sighed the young woman, hiding her face.

There was a long silence. The chill seemed to increase; the red light surrounded people like a pyre about to consume them; death was hovering in the terror, and they were all shivering lamentably.

"What should I do?" asked the old man, turning to Meyral.

"Forgive!" replied the young man.

"Forgive—never!" Langre protested. "But I'll endure his presence."

"Thank you!" Pierre sighed, faintly. He was shivering more than anyone else; one might have thought that his face was growing thinner by the minute. "Where shall I go?" he asked, after a further silence.

"Stay with us!" said Sabine.

He grasped his wife's hand, sobbing, and kissed it like a slave.

Another hour went by; dusk was approaching. Through the western window they could see an immense crimson Sun; the clouds seemed to be steeped in coagulated blood.

Vérannes seemed to have been drowsy for some time. His head was slumped on his right shoulder, one of his eyes was closed, the other half-open. He was breathing harshly, like a hunted animal. Suddenly, he raised his head, examined the laboratory and his companions with a distant gaze, and whispered; "Hideous things…are happening."

Then he got up. Shaken by long tremors, he began to move toward the crepuscular window. One might have thought that he was about to hurl himself through the window—but he turned back, retraced his steps, and knelt down beside Sabine.

"Oh," he groaned, "Forgive me…have mercy on me. I loved you so much. You cannot know what you were to me…all life, all springtime, all the beauty of the Earth! Every beat of my heart wanted you to be happy! For your love, I was ready for any crucifixion! But I was so afraid of losing you! And that fear tortured me like an implacable beast; it made an executioner of the man who cherished you more than himself." He had grasped Sabine's little hands, and was lavishing kisses upon them. "Can't you…forgive me?"

"My heart holds no rancor," she murmured.

"Thank you!" he said, in a raucous sob. He stayed there, as if in prayer; then, as the tremor in his limbs increased, he turned his convulsive face to the sunset and began prowling along the wall. "Death!" he gasped. "Death!"

Meyral caught him just as he was about to collapse and sat him in an armchair. His teeth were chattering; his gaze was glassy; his hands were groping feebly. He shook his head two or three times, in a lugubrious manner, and after an abrupt exhalation of breath, disappeared into eternal darkness.

Then Sabine, with a loud scream, threw herself on his body and gave him a kiss. They all stood around the pale statue. The profundity of death dissolved their rancor. In the distance, beyond the branches, the immense Sun was vanishing. It was possible that no human eye would ever see it again.

"We exchange a unique spark," Meyral quoted, "like a long sigh charged with farewells."[11]

Humbly, he studied Sabine. In the declining light, he went back in time to his youth, when all his dreams hovered around the maiden, like a flock of wild doves: luminous Sabine, perfumed Sabine…her long hair with the magic of Eden! She was free now; boundless hopes might have flourished around her…but it was the end of the world!

The sunlight had abandoned the window; a dusk of bloody ash wandered amid the clouds. Night came, thick and mur-

---

[11] Meyral is quoting Baudelaire again, this time from "La Mort des Amants;" he is obviously fond of the poem, because he will soon quote the last three lines of the sonnet, which follow on directly from these two.

derous. In a few minutes, the temperature dropped several degrees.

"It's going to get very cold," said Langre, "and very dark. The Moon won't rise until after midnight. We must wrap up!"

"Should the children be put to bed?" asked Catherine.

"Not in their room," the old man replied. "We shouldn't be separated. Let's go fetch cloaks, blankets and mattresses before it gets dark."

A crude bed was made up in the laboratory. Everyone had put on warm clothing. They made a hasty meal, while the last light lingered in the distance. A few red stars appeared in the desert of the sky: the Evening Star, Altair, Vega, the Diamond of Cygnus,[12] Aldebaran, Jupiter, Capella. The smaller stars would remain invisible.

The crisis of torpor began. Somnolence evaporated the sadness. With a large surge of effort, Langre, Meyral and Sabine took measures against the increasing cold.

"It's winter…eternal winter!" the old man sniggered, dully.

Forms faded away, becoming no more than patches of darkness.

"Ah! Ah!" Gérard's raucous voice resumed. "We shan't see the green rays disappear!"

In the semi-sleep that was numbing her, Catherine moved as stiffly as a somnambulist. She was holding a box of matches, and sought instinctively to strike a light. As if in a dream, she said: "Will there never again be fire?"

They could no longer see; they were drowned in darkness; the faint light of the red stars could not even impart a glow to the windows, magnifying-glasses, mirrors and prisms.

When the children had been put to bed, Catherine and Césarine went unsteadily to lie down in their turn.

"My poor little Sabine! My dear Georges!" stammered the old man. He drew them toward him; already in the grip of

---

[12] Deneb.

torpor, he whispered; "This is the last night of the human race! Oh, we would have been able…I've loved you so dearly! Nevermore…"

They listened, chilled to the bone. The cold was becoming intolerable.

"Goodbye!" sobbed the old man. "The Ocean of the Ages…" The words died away in a surge of pain and tenderness.

Langre still had the strength to help Sabine lie down beside her children; then he let himself fall on to a mattress.

Meyral remained standing, alone.

A dream filled him: the immense dream of humankind, a dream of centuries and millennia. In the infinite darkness, on the surface of a black star, he saw once again the dawns of his childhood, as young as the first dawns of the upright animal as he lit a fire on the bank of a river or on a hill.

In spite of the cloak in which he was swathed, he felt the cold sinking into his limbs.

Millions of my peers are living their final hour! he thought.

Then he heard the jerky breath of his companions. His shivering intensified; a great weakness made his muscles contract. Instinct carried him to his mattress. He wrapped himself up in the blankets, and collapsed like a dead weight.

VI. Dawn

When he woke up, faint copper-colored light was filtering through the eastern window. He remained utterly tremulous for a minute, still filled by the weight of his dream. Gradually, his mind cleared and organized itself. The horror of the dream appeared. The cold had become unbearable; it had frozen Meyral's face…

He looked around, blurrily perceiving the mattresses on which his companions were lying. No breathing was audible in the great silence.

"They're dead!" Meyral stammered, terror-stricken.

He stood up, his head reeling; he moved to the nearest mattress and confusedly made out a shock of white hair. Mortal anguish immobilized him; he almost went back to his own bed to await the decree of the invisible. The strength that was within him, and did not want him to despair before the last sigh, reanimated him. He felt Langre's face.

The face was cold. No breath seemed to be exhaled from the lips.

Georges dragged himself to the other beds, one by one. All the faces were as cold as the old man's, and no respiration raised their breasts.

"Nothing!" sighed the young man.

He leaned over Sabine for a longer time; a whimper escaped him. His pain had something too vast and too religious within it, however, to burst out in tears. Kneeling in the dark, ready to die, since all those he loved had now disappeared, and since all his human kin were condemned to death, but filled with wild rebellion, he could not yet admit that the long effort of ages was sinking into that abominable oblivion.

For some minutes, that rebellion shook him to the very core of his being; then he discovered a grim grandeur in the catastrophe. It appeared to him to be almost beautiful. Why should it not symbolize the infinite resources of the world?

The sacrifice of one humankind counted for little more, in the inexhaustible cycle of forces, than the sacrifice of a beehive or and anthill. The millennia during which the generations emerged from the sea had followed one another were as fleeting in the life of the Milky Way as a second in the life of a man. Perhaps it was admirable that the long tragedy of Beasts and Plants should end in a disdainful destruction...

What had terrestrial life been but a war without mercy, and what had humankind been, if not the species that had massacred, enslaved or degraded its inferior kin? Why should its end have been harmonious?

"No! No!" Meyral protested. "It's not admirable—it's hideous!"

His thoughts were beginning to slacken and slow down. The numbness was gripping both his limbs and his intelligence again. He was no longer anything but a tiny shivering and dolorous entity. He folded up beneath enormous forces like an insect in the autumn cold.

Soon, his thoughts became disconnected; even images became rare; instinct dominated him. Painfully, he went back to his bed and buried himself in its blankets.

The dawn had come, then the daylight: a daylight that resembled polar nights when the aurora borealis rises amid the clouds. In the large laboratory, nothing moved.

Again, it was Meyral who woke up. At first, he stayed in the limbo of dreams, his eyes half-closed and his thoughts captive. Then reality took him by the throat, fear increasing like a horde of wild beasts. Sitting up on his elbow, he looked for a long time at the vague and motionless forms of his friends.

"I'm alone! All alone!"

Horror filled him. Then he experienced a kind of delirium. No idea or impression seemed graspable; they swirled around like blades of grass in a stream. That vertigo gave him a sort of strength; he succeeded in standing up, and there was no longer any but a single sensation, ardent and intolerable: hunger.

It drew him out of the laboratory and took him to the kitchen, where he ate greedily and haphazardly: a few biscuits, some sugar, a little chocolate. The meal was efficacious; his thoughts became lucid again, and a vague optimism inflated the young man's chest.

"Until the end! It's necessary to keep going until the end!"

The pain came back, however, as soon as he was back in the laboratory He dared not lean over his companions; he wanted to conserve a glimmer of hope—and to grant himself a delay, he headed for one of the large tables.

The thermometer registered seven degrees below zero.

"Twenty-three degrees below average!" the scientist murmured, mechanically.

Then he analyzed the solar spectrum. All of a sudden he quivered. The green zone was stable! Or, at least—which came to the same thing—it had hardly decreased at all.

"Given the rhythm of the phenomenon," he soliloquized, "the green should have disappeared. It's probable…" He interrupted himself, examined the zone again, and continued—for it soothed him to formulate his thoughts: "It's probable that the green was eaten away more profoundly. Therefore, the reaction must have begun." He repeated, in a mystical tone: "The reaction must have begun!"

That gave him the courage to go back to his friends. First, he leaned over little Robert. The child's face was still cold; no breath was perceptible. Meyral felt his chest, and tried in vain to find a heartbeat; his limbs were stiff, but their rigidity seemed incomplete.

Successively, the young man examined Langre, little Marthe and the servants. He scarcely dared to touch Sabine's cheek. Their state appeared identical to Robert's.

It's not rigor mortis! Georges thought.

Besides, their temperature, taken in Langre's and Robert's armpits, was nearly 20 degrees. Meyral assured himself that that temperature was not getting any lower.

"They're alive! A precarious life, to be sure…a minimal life…but they're alive! Oh, if the reaction were to continue…"

His emotion, ardent at first, decreased. He thought that the torpid phase was about to overtake him again; if he went back to sleep, they would be alone in confrontation with the deadly forces!

After an expectant quarter of an hour, he determined that his present state was different from the previous day's states.

His sensitivity was deadened, his movements a trifle slow, but he was not experiencing either torpor or stupor. On the contrary, he was quite lucid.

While continuing to observe his friends, he resumed measuring the zones of the spectrum. Soon, he was certain that the green rays were not decreasing. He took extraordinary precautions for the next experiment, which he postponed until later in order to reduce "the contingency of the personal equation," and made a few observations with the polariscope.

At 10 a.m., the thermometer indicated nine degrees below zero; in that respect, the situation was getting worse. Nevertheless, a change was observable in the condition of the invalids, Meyral was no longer in doubt; neither Langre nor Sabine, nor either of the servants or the children, was dead. Their state seemed to be intermediate between that of creatures in hibernation and pathological lethargy. The peril was profound, though. They would probably be unable to resist the cold, even though the young man had heaped more blankets upon them and wrapped up their heads carefully.

At 10:30 a.m., Meyral decided to resume checking the solar spectrum. He released a loud yelp; in spite of his apathy, his face was convulsed by an overpowering hope. The green zone had increased—the reaction had begun!

"Ah!" he stammered, his eyes full of tears. "This hideous drama won't go all the way to the end, after all!"

In that first minute he forgot himself; his frail form disappeared into the ocean of creatures; he thought only of the salvation of Life. Then his apathy reappeared. He scarcely shivered as he wondered: *What if it's just a simple stutter in the phenomenon?*

By noon, it was impossible for him to repress the certainty: the green zone continued to increase. Unfortunately, the thermometer fell to ten degrees below zero. In spite of his cloak and blankets, Georges felt bitterly cold.

A hunger similar to that of the morning having gripped him again, he devoured more chocolate, biscuits and sugar. The meal did him good, but made him sleepy. Curled up in an armchair, with his feet wrapped in an eiderdown and his head well-covered, he sank into unconsciousness.

When he woke up again, he felt over-excited, and feverishly assured himself of his companions' condition; their illness was stable. Then he launched himself toward the apparatus.

The green had reached its limit again, and the blue rays were beginning to reappear!

Meyral's doubts dissipated then. His soul expanded like an April primrose. It was a great hope—the hope of resurrection, as vast as the dawn of a universe. All the poetry of Genesis swelled the young scientist's heart. Fervently, he recited:

"And afterwards an angel, opening the doors,

"Faithful and joyful, will come to reanimate

"The tarnished mirrors and the dead flames."

It was a festival of the infinite, a star's springtime, a beatitude from which the gleams of the Milky Way oozed forth. And in that great minute, he did not doubt the salvation of his companions of the Ark.

When the excitement had passed, he understood that the circumstances remained obscure and redoubtable. The cold was still punishing; the lethargy, although it was no longer imperious, had not shown any sign of amelioration. In truth, those immobile beings, whose breath was inaudible and whose pale faces remained strangely stiff, bore more resemblance to the dead than the living.

"*If I could only light a fire!*" Meyral thought.

Taking a chance, he made the attempt. Matches would not strike; no chemical combination could be started; the electrical apparatus remained inert. With extreme slowness, however, light continued to climb back toward the superior waves. The blue band became increasingly clear.

At about 3 p.m., there was a second phenomenon of "return;" the compass needle, insensitive until then, began to point north-west, 15 degrees away from its normal position. That seemingly-trivial fact gave Georges considerable pleasure; terrestrial magnetism was the constant whose disappearance had made the deepest impression on him.

"Electricity will reappear in its turn."

It did not reappear for another hour, in the Holtz apparatus—but no matter how vigorously the young man made the machine turn, he could not obtain a spark.[13]

Returning depression crushed him. It was not the same sadness as before—the sadness of the planetary drama—it was a purely human distress. He continued making sure that his companions were alive, but it seemed more improbable with every passing minute that he could reanimate them. And as despair assumes a form appropriate to the circumstances, what distressed him now was wondering whether, even if life were reborn everywhere, the divine light would resume its creative work, and whether his former master or Sabine would witness the resurrection.

Only warmth could save them, he thought—but the night would undoubtedly pass before he could obtain fire. Several times he tried, by means of changes in position and massage, to produce some effect on the children, whose vitality inspired him with more confidence than that of the adults.

The time went by rapidly, in spite of all his anxieties. The Sun was already descending over the leafy crowns of the Luxembourg, and its orb was growing by the minute. Within half an hour it would disappear, and less than an hour later, there would be complete darkness. The Moon would not rise until 2 a.m.

Meyral, simultaneously drawn by his emotion and his scientific curiosity—which even the near approach of death had formerly been unable to extinguish—multiplied his expe-

---

[13] Wilhelm Holtz (1836-1913) developed an electrostatic induction generator in 1865, which—as the text makes clear—converted physical energy into static electricity. A similar device had been invented independently by August Toepler, so such devices are usually known nowadays as Toepler-Holtz machines.

riments. They were all in agreement in the evolutionary sense; the compass-needle gradually drew closer to its normal position; the Holtz machine, without yet yielding sparks, revealed stronger tensions; the blue region of the spectrum, in spite of the approaching sunset, never ceased to increase.

"Fire! Fire!" moaned Meyral. "The cold will get worse during the night. Their weakness is excessive, their reactions are insignificant. Oh, for a fire!"

Dusk arrived, less somber than the previous day's; scarlet fires wandered over the summits of the Luxembourg…and all of a sudden, the Holtz machine began to produce sparks. They were brief and coppery sparks, but they filled the physicist's heart with hope. He contemplated them drunkenly; he listened to their slight crepitation, which reminded him of the flight of certain insects—and an idea occurred to him.

He connected little Marthe's head to the positive pole and one of her feet to the negative pole. Then he turned the machine carefully, keeping watch on the tension. Nothing. The body remained inert. Georges accelerated the motion. Soon, a palpitation was discernible, which agitated her lips and raised her breast: Marthe was breathing!

For some time, Georges maintained the rotation. The result remained the same. No matter! The experiment demonstrated, conclusively, the persistence of life in the little girl.

Darkness fell again. The cold shadow thickened in the long room—but it was not the fearful shadow of the day before. The great constellations were almost complete; the seven stars of the Great Bear were visible. Furthermore, the thermometer stood three degrees higher than the preceding night.

An immense lassitude overcame Meyral, but that lassitude too was normal. He did not resist sleep—what good would it do? Without light, was he not reduced to impotence? There was still the feeble light of the Holtz machine, but to obtain it he would have to harness himself to the machine. It was better to sleep. While he rested, the forces of normality would continue to resume their empire…

VII. The Resurrection.

When he woke up, broad daylight was streaming into the laboratory. Immediately, in spite of a residue of fatigue, the young man felt a considerable well-being. The light that inundated the room was almost similar to the light of a fine spring morning. Undoubtedly, it remained confusedly crepuscular, but how different it was from the sinister light of the preceding days!

As soon as he was on his feet, Georges threw himself toward the apparatus. He uttered a cry like those he had uttered in his adolescence when the morning seemed promising. The greater part of the blue zone had reappeared.

"The reaction is more rapid than the action," he said, rubbing the palms of his hands together. "We'll reach the indigo before noon."

That first movement, which lasted less than a minute, was so impetuous that he had forgotten the plight of his friends. The sight of extended bodies suggested nothing to him but the idea of sleep. Then his heart lurched. Gripped by dread again, he ran to Langre. The old man was in the same position he had been in the previous evening, but Georges observed important changes, one after another: he was breathing again; his heart was beating feebly and his pulse was perceptible, although slow. It was the same for the children, Sabine and the servants. Even so, their sleep was still profound.

"Saved! They're saved!" Meyral affirmed, with a quiver of joy.

In those delightful minutes, doubt seemed impossible. Georges gazed out over the Luxembourg, saturated with light, and savored the young morning like a child. He decided that he would wait two more hours before waking them up, feeling strongly that, in the circumstances, it was necessary to let nature take its course.

As on the previous day, a terrible appetite hollowed out his stomach. He devoured biscuits, stale bread and chocolate sensuously. The taste of foodstuffs seemed to have been renewed, altogether finer and more intense.

"That's the best meal of my life!" he murmured, slightly intoxicated. "That stale bread is incomparable, and the aroma of the chocolate sweeter than the perfume of may-blossom, lilac and newly-mown meadows."

He worked enthusiastically, varying and refining his experiments and accumulating notes. When Saint-Jacques-du-Haut-Pas chimed 11 a.m., he started. Should he intervene or wait a while longer? Incontestably, the condition of the dreamers was continuing to improve. Sabine's pulse and those of the children were almost normal; Langre's was accelerating, along with those of the servants. They were all breathing fully.

In addition, the temperature was climbing; an hour before it had passed zero and was approaching four degrees. The Holtz machine was giving off eight centimeter sparks. The blue rays had regained their integrity; the indigo zone was beginning to emerge.

"Fire?" muttered Meyral.

He struck a match, and went pale. The flame ignited: the sacred fire, the savior fire! What a thrill to see it creep along that paltry morsel of wood! Meyral forgot his science and became the naïve creature who sees a divinity in flame. He went to get a bundle of firewood and some coal from the kitchen.

A few minutes later, there was a roaring fire in the stove. Then the heat began to spread its waves around. Before noon, the thermometer stood at 16 degrees.

On reflection, Georges had judged that no intervention could do as much for his friends as the gradual rise in temperature. He waited, going from one to another, scrutinizing their faces or feeling their wrists. Gradually, the pale faces of Sabine and the children took on color. It was little Marthe who made the first movement; her right arm tried to push back the blankets that had become too heavy. Then she sighed and, after blinking a few times, her eyes opened.

"Marthe!" cried Meyral, joyfully.

"I'm hot!" the child replied. Her blue eyes looked at Georges, vaguely at first. "Mama!" she called.

Sabine shivered. A vague smile passed over her silvery face.

"Sabine!" said the young man.

The large eyes opened like marvelous flowers. Sabine, half-plunged in a dream, continued smiling.

That was the delightful episode of the resurrection; the immense joy of rejuvenated families filled Georges' breast.

"Have I been asleep?" Sabine asked, studying the cabalistic furniture of the laboratory in surprise.

"You've all been asleep!" Meyral replied.

Suddenly, she shivered; fear made her face tremble; she remembered. "Are we going to die?"

"We're going to live!"

She raised her head. She saw little Marthe, who turned her joyful and innocent face toward her.

"Are we saved, then?"

"We've come back to life! The creative light has triumphed over eternal darkness. Look at the Sun, Sabine. In a few hours, it will have become the great Sun of our childhood again."

Sabine turned to the window, and saw the air repossessed by brightness, the sky beginning to resume the shade with which generations had colored their most beautiful dreams.

"Life!" she sighed, while tears of ecstasy gleamed on her eyelashes. Then she blushed; she dared not look at Meyral any longer.

He turned away, and Sabine, remembering that she was not undressed, lifted up the blankets and appeared in the dark costume that she had put on the day before last, as a sign of mourning.

When she stood up, a certain anxiety came back into her being. She called to Langre and her little son. The blonde head and the white head stirred.

91

"Let them wake up by themselves," Meyral advised. "That's the best way!"

She acquiesced, and carried Marthe to one of the windows.

The Luxembourg was the garden of her youth; as full of life as in the time when the past and the future had melted into the same dream...

When she turned round, she saw Georges looking at her with humility—and they were like the Man and the Woman in the land of Seven Rivers, when Agni devoured the dry flesh of trees and the bright herds passed over the hills.[14]

"Where am I?" asked a grave voice. Gérard had just woken up. A stupor was confusing his brain. His old soul had difficulty emerging from oblivion; distractedly, he sought to pull himself together. "The laboratory? Sabine...Georges..." He released a long groan; his ideas were beginning to take form. "Is this the last day?"

"It's the new life!" Meyral replied.

With a violent gesture, Langre threw back his blankets; his aggressive and combative humor emerged from the mist. "What new life?" he demanded. "Light..."

"Light is victorious!"

Gérard's eyes gleamed beneath his bushy eyebrows. "Don't give me false hope, Georges," he said. "Have the green rays reappeared?"

"The green rays, the blue rays and even the majority of the indigo rays."

"The sunlight!" said the clear voice of Sabine.

One by one, the servants and little Robert had woken up. Delightedly, Langre contemplated the daylight that was streaming through the windows. "When did it begin to climb?" he stammered.

"Thirty-six hours ago."

---

[14] Agni is the god of fire—incarnate in sacrificial fire—in Vedic religion, India being the "land of the seven [sacred] rivers."

"Then we've been asleep for…"

"For nearly two days."

"What about you?" murmured the aged physicist, with muted anger. "Did you witness the resurrection, then? You've seen the world reborn! Why didn't you wake me?"

"It was impossible."

Langre remained pensive and melancholy. He was experiencing a bitter disappointment; he was jealous. Then, delight got the upper hand. His old veins transported hope; on the renewed Earth he was about to live glorious days, and finally know justice. "Stand up!" he cried. "We mustn't lose a single one of these magnificent minutes…" And, pouncing on his apparatus like a wolf on its prey, he threw himself into hasty research. He read Meyral's notes avidly. "Ah!" he sighed, periodically. "It's too wonderful…it's too beautiful."

Meanwhile, Catherine made chocolate. In accordance with Langre's wishes, they had that first breakfast in the laboratory. When the fuming liquid appeared, there was a moment of enthusiasm. Even the old scientist paused in his work to participate in the communion, and the humble meal became an incomparable fête.

"Hi ho!" cried Langre, laughing. "We'll have to ration our provisions!"

"We'll probably be short of meat," Georges replied, "but not of flour, sugar, coffee or chocolate. The poor human race must have been decimated…and its stores are intact."

As shadow passed over the bliss, Sabine thought about Vérannes' body, laid out in a neighboring room.

"Hundreds of millions of our peers must have died!" said the old man, in a nervous voice.

For some time, a rumor had been growing in the streets. They could hear the surf-like noise that the clamors of a multitude make. Suddenly, church bells started ringing. Hesitant at first, the sound multiplied and swelled. Saint-Jacques-du-Haut-Pas sounded the Easter of the human race in great volleys.

Part Two

I. The Great Renewal

The next day, the violet rays were reconquered and the human race resumed its routines. Fire reappeared in the hearths, in the blast-furnaces, in the brush and the grasslands. Electric boats resumed their journeys over the resounding sea; cars cluttered the cities; aircraft ploughed through the sky; the telephone, the telegraph and radio waves reassured the multitudes.

People began to calculate the extent of the disaster. A third of humans, a quarter of domestic animals and a few million carnivorous and herbivorous animals in the last virgin forests had fallen victim to it.

Among the westerners, Germany, the United States and Great Britain had suffered the heaviest losses. Germany's population of 66 million had been reduced to 46; there were no longer any more than 65 million people in the United States and 39 million in England. Less deeply afflicted, Italy saw its population reduced to 30 million people, Russia to 90 million, Spain to 15 million and France to 34 million. In Paris, however, and along the Mediterranean shore, the hecatomb turned out to be exceptional. Of its four million inhabitants, Paris lost 500,000; Marseilles was diminished by half, Nice by two-thirds.

For a few days, these losses seemed irreparable, but when the survivors began to be reassured as to their own fate, there was more talk of well-being than grief. Only mothers, and many fathers—such faithful creatures—were subject to profound regrets. Others experienced indifference, or the sly pleasure that follows the death of a relative; the innumerable inheritances created by the disaster became a vast celebration for millions of legatees. The cities having suffered more than rural areas, the social question was temporarily resolved; there was work for everyone, and richly rewarded; there was an abundance of disposable goods; the treasury was enriched to the point that taxes could be reduced, enormous public works undertaken and generous help given to the poor.

The cause of the cataclysm remained mysterious, although conjectures were rife. The majority of scientists favored the hypothesis of an immense flux of energy originated in the interstellar abyss, which had swept over our planet, and perhaps Mars, Venus, Mercury, and even the Sun as well. As the nature of that energy escaped all conception, the hypothesis did not explain anything. No one could imagine why its effect had been to reduce or nullify known forces. A few thinkers also put forward the contrary hypothesis; it was not, according to them, an energetic flux that had passed over, but a torrent of ether particularly avid for energy, and which, in consequence, had absorbed light, heat and electricity in massive doses. In sum, according to some, it was a matter of antagonistic forces, and according to others, of a capture of force.

The latter theory was contradicted by the rapid reconstitution of terrestrial energies: a summery temperature succeeded the cold of the deadly days; magnetism seemed to be increased; chemical actions were manifest with a surfeit of alacrity—which, in many cases, caused accidents, and demanded a surfeit of precautions in factories and laboratories; all in all, it was as if vital force had been saved up.

The overwhelming majority of the survivors disdained these scientific discussions. A marvelous renewal intoxicated souls. The simplest joys acquired a miraculous intensity; the sweetness of existence suppressed almost all of the hatreds, jealousies and frictions that darken the days of human beings.

Langre, Sabine and Meyral savored this happiness in its plenitude. They took refuge in the country, in a location replete with water, trees and greenery. The squat and sullen house was surrounded by gardens. A retired colonel in the colonial forces had had it built, according to his own plans, after returning from Africa. It was somewhat reminiscent of a fortress, but, as might be expected, it was spacious and comfortable. Three gardens produced a surprising variety of fruits and vegetables, as well as tall trees, superabundant flowers and lush grass. It belonged to the colonel's daughter, a stupid creature who, having taken a dislike to it, could not bring herself to sell it, and let it out in order to obtain an income.

The colonel had stuffed the bookshelves with volumes bought from the neighboring châteaux and multiplied its heterogeneous furniture. Light penetrated through a multitude of windows, and one could see, beyond the enclosures, a landscape of Old France, of elegant undulations, in which the crop-fields and meadows alternated with woodlands. Charming hills surrounded the villages and indented a western horizon rich in crepuscular fêtes. Among the beeches and linden-trees, two springs formed a rill that mingled its voice and youth with the gardens.

It was there that they stayed during the world's renewal. Gérard had lugged all his chemical and physical instruments out there, even though, for the moment, he and Meyral were going over their notes, searching desperately therein for some explanation of the scourge that had ravaged the Earth.

This work did not weary them at all. They drew delight from the same well as Sabine, the children, the servants, all the people in the village, and even the animals—for the living seemed to receive something of that surfeit of energy that was observed in phenomena; even the sick savored a certain honey of happiness, which soothed their suffering and enchanted their respites.

The family often went sailing on the Yonne, in a heavy rowing-boat manned by a taciturn villager. Beauty deployed its magic at every bend in the river. An islet planted with reeds, willows and poplars reminded them of castaways. Inlets sheltered armies of green blades; among long strands of waterweed, fish liked their cold and agile lives; the grass grew monstrously; large flocks of crows, nourished by the disaster, passed overhead screeching war-cries.

Meyral ceased to struggle against his affection then. He let it grow, to fill his days like an inexhaustible river and form the substance of his dreams. What did the future matter? If necessary, Georges would pay for the days of his enchantment in pain; at least he would have passed through the gate of ivory and wandered in the enchanted garden.

For a long time, the bright Sabine, sheltered from the enemy male population, paid no heed to any voice. Her charm was at its height; the brilliant silken quality of her hair seemed to increase further; her neck, formerly frail, acquired a thrust, roundness and harmony. The form of her cheeks was perfect; her fresh eyes emitted a gleam of renewal that caused all the passionate creatures of fable to rise up before Meyral.

When the family disembarked on the bank, and the tragic maidservant set out a picnic, it seemed to Georges that they formed a strangely united group, by virtue of the memory of trials undergone in common, and by some indefinable link that grew tighter every day. A large dog, which Langre had acquired in Sens, shared this intimacy; it suffered strangely when they had to leave it alone in the house; its absence was slightly painful for the adults as for the children. Even the old gardener who lodged in an annex at the back of the vegetable-garden, and his grandson—a little boy with silvery hair, scarcely tinged with a hint of straw-color—displayed an extreme pleasure in drawing close to the family. One might have thought that the goat and the donkey experienced an analogous inclination.

Three weeks went by. The solstice had passed. It was the season of long twilights: on some evenings, sitting on the terrace, from which they could see the Yonne, full of beautiful lies that the clouds told after sunset, they had a presentiment of the pearl-tinted dawn, when the fairies of the sunset still dispersed their enchantments. The warmth was extraordinary; it exceeded that of the hottest years, but it was not at all oppressive. There was a fever of gaiety in their veins, which delighted in high temperatures. People and animals alike enjoyed a surprising sensuality in walking over the warm meadows or along the baking roads. Oddly enough, the grass, the foliage and the flowers were not suffering. Every day, to be sure, storms thundered for an hour or more, releasing deluges of rain.

"It's the burning heat of the dog days—of the star Sirius that frightened Virgil," Langre said, one morning, while walking in the garden with Georges and Sabine.

"The Dog Star is lucky for us!" Meyral replied, with a smile.

"It is, strangely…we ought to feel harassed, sometimes by the heat, sometimes by the storms. By contrast, a surprising joy animates everything that crawls, walks or flies. There you go! We're not yet out of the mystery…"

The old man furrowed his bushy brows, with the expression of impatience that came naturally to him—but he was joyful in spite of himself. "I'm a captive of the moment!" he complained. "Never, even when tumultuous youth was burning in my veins, have I known such happiness!" As anxiety returned, he added: "We'll pay for it!"

"We have paid," Georges retorted. He continued: "Have you noticed the need to gather together that the people of the village feel, and which we share? Look!"

The children and Césarine had joined them; Catherine had emerged from the house and was approaching the group; the dog was capering around them, and the donkey, in its stable, uttered appealing cries. In all directions, chickens were pecking, songbirds, pigeons and doves were fluttering; toads were displaying their topaz eyes and three frogs were hopping along the bank of the stream.

"Am I mistaken?" the young man asked.

"Oh, no!" Sabine exclaimed.

"Notice that, instinctively, we've drawn closer to the house—which is to say, the favorable center. What astonishes me more than anything else, all things considered, is that it's not a matter of a social instinct, strictly speaking. We have no desire to join *other groups*, and the groups in the village don't want that either. Yesterday, when I went for a walk on my own along the Yonne, I felt a veritable sense of distress as I distanced myself from all of you."

"We were all anxious during your absence," Gérard said, "as if you had departed on a long voyage."

"We have to let that poor donkey out!" said Sabine.

As if he had only been waiting for these words, the old gardener went to open the stable door. The donkey, a young animal with lively eyes and supple limbs, arrived prancing.

"Bizarre, indeed!" said Gérard, who was very pensive. "I firmly believe that the interstellar adventure has not concluded."

"You don't think that it might happen again!" said Sabine, horrified.

"It's a million to one that the wave that broke over the planet won't come back—but there's a residue. Until that residue is completely expelled or absorbed, we have to expect unusual phenomena…like those we're witnessing."

"That might be pleasant."

"If they remain analogous, no doubt—but I'm afraid things might change!"

"Don't say that!" Georges exclaimed. "Let's enjoy these delightful hours in peace."

Langre did not reply. His anxiety had scarcely any force; his pessimistic faculties surrendered to the universal intoxication.

In the gardens and the fields, the harvest was extraordinary. The fruits attained unprecedented dimensions; there were peaches as large as Jerusalem oranges. The wheat-fields resembled reed-beds. The foliage, as thick and green as the land of Erin, was reminiscent of a tropical jungle. Everything grew in abundance; the granaries and cellars were overflowing. A magnificent improvidence invaded human hearts.

One morning, Langre and Meyral made two exciting discoveries in quick succession. The old man observed that the violet band of the solar spectrum was visibly enlarged, while Meyral observed that a radio-wave detector he had invented was showing an unexpected sensitivity.

"That fits in well with our hyperesthesia and the exaggeration of vegetal growth," Georges said.

"But why haven't we observed it before?"

Minute measurements revealed a few other anomalies, but very tiny. For instance, the electrical conductivity of metals was diminished, but the phenomenon was masked in practice because various items of apparatus—batteries, dynamos, electrostatic machines—had above-normal yields.

"All this," Gérard remarked, "leaves us in complete ignorance. Through all the observations we've made, during and after the disaster, I can only see one *specific* characteristic."

"Obviously!" Georges concluded. "It's that only the yellow, orange and red rays have resisted; they've been subject to an increase in brightness. The infra-red rays too."

"Those closest to the visible spectrum, at least! The others have been subject to the common fate—just like radio waves."

"I find, however, something quite characteristic in the present release of energy. Indeed, the 'disease of light' created the impression that the enemy forces were *devouring* terrestrial and solar forces. The result clearly shows that the antagonism has formed potential energies."

"Exactly!" cried the old man, resentfully. "It's the release of these virtual forces that ought to furnish us with the key to the mystery—but it only provides us with curious but banal anomalies. We also have to account for the singular refraction that marked the commencement of the attack. It's exasperating! And it's ridiculous."

"We can't climb up on our own shoulders!" Meyral concluded, philosophically.

The following days were undoubtedly the most beautiful the human species had ever known. Life—the simplest life—was filled with indescribable grace. An immense florescence covered the Earth all the way to the poles; everywhere, plants revived a new spring. The air was heavy with perfumes; an inexhaustible tenderness floated in the twilight and seemed to color the stars. Nature became virginal again; every meadow evoked the savannah; woods became forests; the crazy increase revived all the mysteries of reproduction.

There was one evening more beautiful than all the rest. It was toward the middle of the heat-wave. After dinner, the family had gathered on the terrace. Immeasurable angles were hollowed out in the depths of the Occident. The unsteady countries of the Clouds simulated the splendors of land, water, forests, mountains, and even the works of humankind. There were not only lakes and marshes, caverns and peaks, amethyst rivers and quicksilver gulfs, savannahs and brush; there were also cathedrals, pyramids, blast-furnaces and a colossal ship, a tabernacle shaded with sulfur, pearl and hyacinth, a pile of chasubles...

The donkey and the goat were wandering over the little lawn; the gardener had taken shelter in the shade of a laburnum, an old Gothic profile with hollow cheeks and a curly beard; his grandson was crawling toward the spring; the dog got up periodically, sniffing the air, its eyes ardent, as if it perceived things invisible to humans; the intoxicated sparrows inflated their little syrinxes and sang recklessly.

Georges was sitting next to Sabine. Clad in white, with her hair gathered into a bun, she condensed the brilliant symbols that make a woman's figure delightful. Every gleam in her eye, every tremor of her silvery neck, the pearliness of her teeth visible between her scarlet lips, and the caress of the light on her slender cheeks, added vivid hues to the beauty of the evening.

At the same time, that bizarre linkage binding the whole group together was tangible.

"I've never been so happy!" murmured Langre.

"Who has been," Georges whispered, "save for those moments that pass like fleeting wings before a window, and vanish into darkness? Who has known the mysterious host for which humans have been waiting since they acquired an imagination?"

Large evening moths passed by with their cotton-wool wings; bats multiplied their sinuous flights in front of the western windows, and Meyral never ceased to contemplate Sabine. It seemed that he was, in some way, part of her; whenever she moved, rapid and delightful currents passed through every fiber of the young man's being.

II. The Living Patches

One morning, while she was dressing, Sabine noticed stains on her arms and chest. They were very pale patches, scarcely tinted with brown. Although their form was somewhat irregular, their contours were made up of curved lines. Sabine studied them with more astonishment than dread, and tried to define them. She could not do it. At the most, they reminded her, vaguely, of slight bruises.

While she was thinking about it, the chambermaid, Césarine, appeared with Marthe and Robert.

"Look, Madame," she said. "It's strange."

Sabine examined the children; the same patches were manifest on their young bodies, but more visible and extending as far as the abdomen. Then, a slight anxiety entered the mother's heart.

"What about you, Césarine?"

The chambermaid unbuttoned her bodice. Her skin was darker than Sabine's or the children's, and also harder; it only took a moment to discover the characteristic patches there.

"The children don't feel ill?"

"No, Madame."

"What about you?"

"Me neither."

"That's what's surprising!" said the young woman.

The anxiety came and went, but the great joy, which seemed to be spread out like an elixir, prevented Sabine from being positively emotional. "I need to consult my father," she said. Putting on a dressing-gown, she went to find the old man, with Marthe and Robert.

An early riser, like most old men, Langre was in his laboratory. In normal times he would have been disturbed by seeing Sabine appear at that hour with the two children, but he showed hardly any surprise.

"*Hannibal ad portas?*"[15] he said, with a smile—but when he had examined Marthe and Robert he became serious. "Unusual, to say the least!" he muttered. "And you're affected too, you say?"

Sabine pushed back the loose sleeve of her dressing-gown. The patches, scarce on the forearm, were more frequent beyond the elbow. They yielded no impression to touch; the skin was still smooth and level. At first glance, they seemed to be uniform, but a brief examination revealed striations, dots and confused shapes.

Langre picked up a magnifying-glass, and the contours revealed a certain regularity; they formed triangles, rectangles, pentagons and "spherical" hexagons. The exterior details were more precise. The dots became ellipses; the stripes were approximately parallel; the shapes were analogous to the general form of the patches. A certain number of delicate pale surfaces were also perceptible.

"I once studied medicine," Gérard declared, "and I never saw anything like this—no, nothing!"

For a few more minutes he inspected little Robert's chest, where the phenomenon was manifest most intensely.

"What about me?"

Having rolled up his shirt-sleeve—the weather was too warm to work in a jacket—he saw nothing. Sabine, however, thought she could see patches; the magnifying glass made them stand out clearly. They exhibited, albeit more indecisively, the particularities already observed. Evidently, the impre-

---

[15] "Hannibal is at the gate!"—a cry of lamentation uttered by the Romans after the loss of a battle near Cannes, according to Cicero.

ciseness of the whole and the details was correlated with the brown color and the horny texture of the skin.

"I was right," said Langre, in a somber tone. "The planetary drama is continuing." For the first time in many weeks, he felt the renaissance of the pessimistic inclination that doubled the bitterness of his vicissitudes. His heart weighed him down like a cannonball. "However," he exclaimed, "we haven't, so far as I know, felt any malaise."

"None!" Sabine replied. "The children have never been in better health."

Meyral came into the laboratory. "Are you talking about the stains?" he asked. "I noticed them yesterday evening, when I went to bed, without attaching any great importance to them. There were only six or seven then—they've multiplied during the night."

"But you aren't worried?"

Georges raised his arms in a gesture of perplexity. "Apparently not," he said. "I've tried to be, but I've discovered nothing deep down inside me but curiosity—and seeing you all full of vigor…truly, I can't see any reason for anxiety."

Perhaps he was bluffing, for the sake of the others, but only to a degree. His words caused the anxiety that Langre's attitude had awoken in Sabine to vanish.

"I couldn't put it better," the old man agreed. "In fact, if I were sure that this would remain inoffensive, I'd be glad. Who can tell whether we might finally learn something?" He smiled. His scientific mania eclipsed the fear of the unknown. "For safety's sake, let's call the doctor," he concluded.

The doctor presented himself shortly afterwards. In his fifties, with a surly face, coarse hair and toothbrush-like eyebrows bristling above his sardonic eyes, he only smiled with one side of his mouth.

"I've just seen the same oddity at the Ferrand house," he said, after looking at Robert's arms and chest. He spoke leadenly, and indifferently.

"What is it?" Langre asked, impatiently.

"I don't know, Monsieur. I've never seen anything like it. If it's not a new disease, it's a malady unknown in France—and, I suspect, in all Europe. Is it even a disease? Nothing proves that. This little boy is as normal as one could imagine. It's the same with the young Ferrands." So saying, he listened to the little girl's chest. "This child too. So, I don't know. I'm at a loss. In this regard, I'm as competent as my dog—perhaps less so."

In the silence that followed, they heard the hour chime in the tower of Saint-Magloire.

"Obviously, it's not usual," the doctor finally muttered. "But for two months, what has been ordinary? Personally, I confess that I no longer have the least space in my brain for astonishment. Nowadays, I find everything natural." He yawned. "Excuse me!" he said. "I'm upset. I get upset every time I leave home; if the journey is a long one, it becomes torture. Happiness is in my bachelor quarters, with my old maidservant, my old manservant, my old horse, my dog, my cat and my livestock. All the inhabitants of the village are the same…"

"The pigeons no longer go far from the loft," Gérard remarked. "Even some wild birds are keeping ever closer to the house."

"Try to go away!" said the doctor. "Tell me how you get on!"

He took his leave, and was visibly in a hurry to get back to his car.

"Well?" said Langre, his eyes fixed on his grandchildren.

"Let's wait and see," Meyral replied, almost insouciantly. "The mystery dominates us to such an extent that we can only repeat the old formula: *Pater, in manus…*[16] The hour is charming, and hope is pampering us."

---

[16] "Father, into thy hands…" Meyral/Rosny takes it for granted that his auditor/reader will recognize Jesus' final words, as reported in *Luke* 23:46, and will know that the sentence concludes "…I commend my spirit."

105

They had breakfast on the terrace, in luminous intimacy.

"I'm going as far as the Yonne," Georges said, then, having had an idea. For three weeks, he had not taken a walk of any real extent on his own.

As he went out of the garden, he felt a need to return to the house that he knew by experience. He did not yield to it; he went along the street that led to the river. As he progressed, a malaise took possession of his entire being. It was as if elastic threads were pulling him backwards. The further he went, the stronger that traction became. At the same time, he had a sensation of the presence and the actions of the people he had just left. He witnessed, with some imprecision, the movements of Langre, Sabine, the children, the servants, and even the animals. Having reached the Yonne, he stopped, in order to carry out a fuller analysis of the state of his nerves.

The pause rendered the traction less painful; it was effective upon his entire skin, his muscles, and also within his skull and his breast—except that, while the part of his body turned toward the dwelling was subject to a sort of chill, the part turned toward the river was contracted by a sensation of warmth.

Georges sought to define the movements of his friends. Each of those movements gave rise either to a traction or to a release. Delicate as they were, these perceptions seemed gross by comparison with others that had no relationship to the usual sensory data, but which, however, were not purely psychic…

He divined that Langre had resumed his experiments; he knew that the children were playing on the front steps with the dog, Chivat, and that the gardener was picking fruit. The manner in which he knew all this was neither tactile, nor auditory, nor visual…he simply knew it. And if, for example, he was excited by the idea that Césarine was combing Sabine's long hair, it was because a visual image superimposed itself on the unknown sensation, almost as if it were being superimposed on something he was reading or a daydream.

"In sum," he concluded, "a part of their life is linked directly to mine. Nevertheless, *I'm not reading their thoughts…*"

He scribbled a few notes in his notebook and resumed his walk. It was difficult, and then painful. The difficulty increased by the minute. When Meyral, having passed the islet, saw the aqueduct come into view, his step became heavy; it was as if he were pulling a cart. Large drops of sweat ran down the back of his neck. At the same time, a sharp pain invaded his entire body; it seemed that his temples were being squeezed between two blocks of wood; his heart faltered; burning sensations shot through his lungs.

He knew that his pains were echoing in the distance, albeit less intensely, *shared out* and diluted.

He kept going as far as the aqueduct. Finally, the fatigue became intolerable and, feeling that he was at the end of his tether, he stopped. "No point in taking the experiment any further!"

The muscular relief was instantaneous. There was no more than a tension, annoying but bearable. The pain also decreased; it took on a sort of static expression: no longer stabbing, but a continuous headache, a sort of intercostal neuralgia and a burning sensation in his limbs

When he returned toward the village, the sensation was almost one of well-being. He walked with extraordinary ease; his weight had diminished. Level with the islet, he broke into a run, and reached a speed greater than he had attained in the days when he had trained for races. In parallel, the pain faded away. As soon as he reached the turning, it disappeared.

He finally reached the spot where he had paused the first time. His stride became normal and, when he started running again, he only achieved a normal speed.

"Your absence has been quite unpleasant for us!" Langre exclaimed, when Georges went into the laboratory.

"Much less so than for me!" the young man retorted. "You were all missing me at the same time. I was subject to an impression of the whole; you only had to tolerate an impression of a detail. Then again, I was making an enormous effort, while you remained relatively passive."

They lapsed into a profound reverie; then Gérard said, excitedly: "I know exactly where you went, and where you paused."

"I know everything that you've done in my absence."

"If I were not prey to the most absurd optimism, I'd be gripped by horror—for everything is happening as if we had become a kind of single entity."

"Is that so frightening?" Meyral whispered.

"It's terrible. It has only to continue for us to share the same personality as our gardener, our dog, our donkey, and the birds in the farmyard…"

"The same personality, yes!" Meyral agreed. "It's certain that we're linked to one another in a strangely organic manner. Is some kind of energy gradually tightening the slack bond that attaches individuals in normal times? If so, it's a simple phenomenon of interaction. Or are there *living* connections forming between us…or, rather, have we been caught in…?"

He interrupted himself and looked at Langre, whose optimism was being pierced in the same way that he had been affected while the doctor had been examining the children.

"Yes," Langre concluded, "We've been caught in an immense trap. *We've been captured by another form of life!*"

III. The Carnivorous Crisis

The patches increased in number and became more precise; the link uniting the group tightened—and the disease, if it was one, proved to be universal; all human beings and all animals were affected.

Everywhere, individuals were forming little agglomerations, united by a strange force. Every day, it became more difficult for individuals to draw away from their nucleus, beyond a certain distance. That distance varied according to the size of the agglomeration and local conditions. In France, it attained its minimum on the Côte d'Azur, in Paris and the vicinity of Lyon; individuals felt ill as soon as they were more than three or four meters way from their family members. Beyond that the suffering commenced, aggravated by increasing fatigue. In other regions, the limit extended as far as 700 meters—in rare cases, to 800 or 900. Germany, the western United States, southern England and northern Italy were characterized by the narrowness of the "area of circulation," to use Professor MacCarthy's expression.

As the phenomenon progressed, the social and individual perturbations multiplied. Individual journeys became impossible. All displacements of any significance required the displacement of the entire group, or exposed it to catastrophes. Until the beginning of August, separations only caused distress; afterwards, they began to be fatal. Energetic, headstrong or imprudent individuals perished in large numbers. The "mortal zone" began at a distance of between 7 and 20 kilometers, according to the region.

The group shared, in part, in the distress of the absentee, but none of its members perished. Any dispersal of the group was, of course, a source of malaise and pain, in proportion to the distances involved; so long as the whole remained within the area of circulation, sensations were produced that were more of less keen, but not painful.

Gradually, social life underwent a metamorphosis. The units of a group were no longer able to work at any distance from one another; the staff of workshops, factories and banks was reduced; production slowed down and often stopped. Fortunately, the abundance of harvests and the somber ravages of the catastrophe largely compensated for these failures. Excursions by automobile became virtually impracticable; they required the driver and each passenger to bring the human and animal members of their agglomeration with them. People made ingenious attempts to form groups of vehicles, and imagined problematic combinations. The railway still offered some recourse, but it became increasingly difficult to obtain "convergent series" of mechanics, drivers, stokers, inspectors, crewmen and passengers.

All civilized people became vegetarians, or almost, the death of domestic animals and some wild animals compromising the health and security of groups. Touching, bizarre and absurd relationships were seen to be established between creatures. Nothing was more singular than the processions of rich people and poor people, dogs, cats, birds and horses circulating in the cities, or gangs of peasants escorted by their livestock, followed by crows, magpies, jays, chaffinches, bullfinches, goldfinches, robins, swallows, hares, field-mice and hedgehogs, and sometimes roe deer or wild boar.

In sum, circulation became almost as restricted as at the beginning of the planetary catastrophe, and the difficulties that were encountered on *terra firma* were reproduced at sea. Nevertheless, the contingencies of navigation had created original liaisons. On some ships, especially long haul vessels, associations were formed between sailors that attached them to their ships as land-dwellers were to their houses. On the other hand, the excessive mobility of their life permitted such mariners to escape the bonds that bound most men tightly together. These privileges, shared by some continental nomads, permitted water transport greater activity, by comparison with other modes of transport. Even so, ships that were immobilized in port were ten times as numerous as the others.

In compensation, other means of communication—ordinary telegraphy, wireless telegraphy and telephones—remained, if not normal, at least sufficient. The lack of personnel was balanced by more restricted needs: tradesmen, bankers and manufacturers inevitably sent few messages.

Until the end of August, the disorder was tolerable. The only people who suffered were those who persisted in leaving the areas of circulation; the only ones who died were those who exceeded the extreme limits assigned to their group. To the others, existence seemed pleasant and singularly intimate. Unknown joys balanced out the inconveniences. Egoism was partially replaced by a restricted but real altruism; everyone participated directly in the life of the group; there was an agreeable exchange of impressions and energies, if not thoughts.

No one savored these new sensations more than Georges Meyral. He spent entire hours observing himself, researching by introspection the sensation of the lives of others. He experienced the strange aerial emotions that came from birds linked to the community; the enigmatic dreams through which something of the obscure souls of the dog and the donkey passed; subtle meditations in which he discovered within himself the reflections of Langre's intellect, Sabine's candor and the youthful impetuosity of the children.

The charm of these emotions was that they embodied simultaneously a sense of collective life and that of intimate life. The latter was not at all compromised. Quite the contrary; it seemed more intense—with the result that there was no diminution, but a net gain.

Even so, hypocritical individuals underwent certain trials, for, if thoughts remained totally indecipherable, actions had their reverberations through the whole group, and powerful sentiments could not be concealed. That inconvenience was compensated by an increasing solidarity, which expelled hatred, anger and jealousy.

There was also a certain "proportionality" in the communication. A perception exclusive to two individuals remained rather obscure to the others. Meyral's love for Sabine was only clearly evident to the young woman; although Langre was not unaware of it, and approved of it, he received no very precise or continuous revelation of it. Sabine, however, perceived it with a troubling acuity; often, when she was daydreaming in the garden or meditating in her room, a blush rose to her temples. There were moments when Georges experienced those rushes that are the storms of the soul.

Sabine defended herself. After so much dolor and humiliation, she retained a terrible mistrust. Love had scarcely ever appeared to her in its charming forms. She saw it as a raw power, a tragic servitude, the intimate cruelty of nature. Without telling Meyral about the odious memory she retained of her marriage, she set love aside from individual good and evil, discerning therein, quite differently from Phaedra, an all-consuming and toxic force. The very candor of her sentiments, combined with a richness of imagination that she inherited from Langre, maintained her in her horror. Less fearful, she might have had a clearer sight of the various combinations of passion.

Georges received the echoing impact of these mental debates. He could not grasp the detail, but what he could grasp filled him with dread. In addition, he drew therefrom a kind of melancholy security; at least he had no need to fear any rival. While Sabine's pessimism lasted, she would not leave her father, and he, Meyral, would be her best friend. He was at the stage in which one believes in negative happiness—in *the happiness of presence*, in the words of one orator.

At length, he began to feel some pain, which increased and troubled his waking hours. He hated being feared, when he knew that he was tenderly enslaved; anguish interrupted his dream, while he felt the urgency of the young woman's apprehension.

One evening, they were walking in the garden in the coppery light of dusk. Gérard was following a path under the linden-trees; the children were playing by the fountain; Sabine and Meyral found themselves alone, in a bed of hollyhocks, sunflowers, irises and gladioli. Because her companion had a heart overflowing with tenderness, she was anxious. The pulsations of that anxiety penetrated into Meyral and gave him an intermittent petty fever. He ended up saying: "Be happy, I beg you! These hours are perhaps the most beautiful that your youth will experience, and you're the one who should enjoy them most. You're free, Sabine."

She blushed slightly, and replied: "Am I, really?"

He turned to her and fell under the spell of her eyes, bathed in the light of the setting Sun, the sparkling curls of her hair and the fearful smile on her scarlet lips.

"You are," he affirmed, forcefully. "You must believe me. No constraint will be imposed upon you, save from outside. Don't you feel that, Sabine?"

"I sense your honesty and your gentleness," she said, in a low voice. "No one is as truthful, no one inspires more confidence in me. It's the circumstances and my own soul that frighten me!" She lowered her charming head. "I'm weak!" she continued, in a sort of lament. "And I've been so unhappy."

"I will never speak to you about my love. You shall know that it exists, and that's all. I shan't break the silence until the day when you give me tacit permission."

"How will you know?"

"I'll know, Sabine. I've come to know you, in certain respects, better than you know yourself."

She offered him her little trembling hand, just as Gérard came back toward the house. "Have you read the papers?" the scientist asked. He was holding *Excelsior*, which he was brandishing nervously.

"Not yet," Meyral replied.

"Well, read this." He showed him the headline of an article on the first page. It read: *STRANGE NEWS FROM WESTPHALIA—THE CARNIVOROUS CRISIS.*

Singular and alarming news has reached us from Westphalia, where—as our readers know—groupism is more pronounced than in any other part of Europe.

For several days, a carnivorous crisis has been rife in the region, particularly to the east of Dortmund. The inhabitants are prey to a hunger for meat that is becoming more violent by the hour, and manifests itself in some individuals with murderous fury. The affected groups steal livestock or hunt game—which has been virtually annihilated—savagely. In some districts there is veritable war; people are killing one another. It is estimated that several hundred people have perished as a result of fratricidal conflicts. The news is confused, for it is dangerous and almost impossible to send groups of reporters, but there can be no doubt about the gravity of the events…

"The sinister era is resuming," said the old man. "We shall pay for these two months of quietude. Oh, I knew full well that the planetary adventure was not over!" He was pawing the ground like an impatient horse; pessimism was entering his soul again, and contracting his features. "Haven't you observed," he went on, "that our happiness is fraying? Undoubtedly, there's a strange sensuality in the air that we breathe, and in the effluvia of plants, but that sensuality is attenuating as the days go by."

It was undeniable. Although, thanks to the fatality of his nature and his age, he perceived it more clearly than the others, Sabine and Meyral nevertheless had a clear impression of it.

"The disease is approaching swiftly," Langre continued. "The disease that has gripped the inhabitants of Westphalia will spread throughout Europe and all over the world. A monstrous war is imminent—which might perhaps spare no one! Take note that the disease is particularly intense in Paris and the vicinity of Lyon; we're caught between two fires. Wouldn't it be better to flee to the south or the north?"

"How can we foresee the future?" said Sabine. "Here, at least, we have our refuge."

"You're right," her father went on, plaintively. "Immense hazard surrounds us. The consequences of our actions evade all calculation. Nevertheless, it's necessary to think about defending ourselves."

"Who can tell whether the events in Westphalia will have a sequel?" Georges put in.

"How can you pronounce such words?" replied Langre, angrily. "Have we ever seen, since the advent of the catastrophe, a single phenomenon that has not followed its course?"

Meyral made no reply. He would have liked to reassure Sabine, but, even more than the old man, he could only hope that the event would be without consequence.

"We must think about defending ourselves!" Langre repeated—and he headed for the laboratory.

IV. The Experiments

They had been making disturbing observations for a week. The patches, after a period of incubation, became clearer. The details of their structure became more easily perceptible; their zones stood out clearly under the magnifying-glass. Motionless at first, they had begun to move, and their displacements made their extraterrestrial constitution obvious. In fact, when they left one region of the skin, the latter retained no trace of their sojourn or their passage, and seemed perfectly healthy; in consequence, the existence of the patches was unconnected with any known phenomenon.

Given that fact, Langre and Meyral tried to determine whether the patches were constituted by material substance. The most subtle measurements revealed no resistance. At the place occupied by a patch, the skin could be pricked or sectioned exactly as if it were in its normal state. Experiments that Langre and Georges carried out on themselves, as well as the tragic maidservant and the dog, were conclusive. Nevertheless, the patches had three dimensions. The microscope revealed that they were elevated above the skin to a height that varied between 8 and 66 microns. Appropriated sections showed that they penetrated the epidermis to a mean depth of 12 microns. They were not transparent, but translucent. The inferior rays of the spectrum gave them bizarre colorations, which defied analysis at first. Electricity caused them to execute movements whose rhythm seemed disordered; chemical reactions only produced indirect effects; they seemed totally immune to the influence of weight and revealed no mass. On the other hand, they conserved their configuration and their zones rigorously.

115

"So they're assimilable to solid bodies," Langre concluded.

"Solids without mass or resistance?"

They stood there meditatively.

"Is it necessary to see them as a kind of matter, though?" asked the old man.

"Yes, if matter, in its turn, is only a form of energy—or, rather, energies."

"Substance, then?"

"*Quien sabe?* Energies, after all, are only manifestations of differences. They're probably substantial, but they have no connection with what we call matter."

"What about the ether?"

"The scientist's ether is childish. I believe in *ethers*, indefinite in number, analogous to one another but not similar."

"Let's not get out of our depth!" Gérard protested, swiftly. "I think it's necessary to consider these patches as a material form of energy."

One morning, they made an important discovery. In order to undertake a series of experiments they had assembled the whole group, human and animal, in the laboratory. Langre, after several attempts, observed the same unusual refraction, albeit much weaker, that had been observed at the beginning of the planetary catastrophe.

"I conclude that there's an essential identity between the patches and the phenomenon that almost annihilated life," he declared. "The patches must, therefore, have originated from the residuum that I've suspected for a long time."

"Must we admit, then, that this residuum is the cause of the extraordinary intoxication that has held sway over the Earth? That's contradictory."

"At least imagine an effect of evolution…"

"Or a reaction of long-neutralized terrestrial and solar energies."

"Perhaps both. In any case, old friend, your work is fundamental."

The next day, Meyral made a discovery in his turn. For some time he had noticed that the orange and red rays had more effect than others on the coloration of patches. He produced an intense red light and directed it at his bare arm. The patches began rhythmic oscillatory movement, so regular that it would have been possible to use it, *grosso modo*,[17] to measure time. While he was observing this relatively expectable phenomenon, however, he experienced a sharp surprise: on the one hand, the patches became colored in the intervals of the zones; on the other, garnet-colored filaments appeared, linking the patches to one another. That was not all; paler filaments appeared in the atmosphere; some extended from Meyral to Langre, while the majority extended to the walls, the windows, the door and even the ceiling.

As soon as he had made the first observations, Georges had called his friend. The old man manifested an anxiety that caused him to tremble. "We're moving into the gulfs!" he exclaimed. "These filaments undoubtedly link *all* the patches—which is to say, the entire group.

"There's no doubt about it. Notice that there are variations in color, surely produced by the various movements of our group."

"And which are probably the result of variations in diameter!"

He fell silent, overwhelmed by a flood of suggestions and images. Although the presence of these "filaments" was no more extraordinary than communication at a distance would have been, they painted a clearer picture of the imperious energy that connected individuals. Countless dreams made their heads spin.

"These links are obviously very elastic," murmured Meyral. "And that's what explains the relative freedom of our movements."

---

[17] Roughly.

117

"Just as the limit of their elasticity explains the *area of circulation*!" said Langre. "But why does anyone who goes out of the area die?"

"Would he die if he drew away very slowly?"

"It seems so, since there has been no report to that effect. The deaths are more or less instantaneous, that's all."

After a further pause, Langre muttered: "Why is the revelatory effect produced by the red rays? Is it certain that it can't be produced by others?"

"Let's try."

In succession, they produced intense beams of violet, blue, green, yellow and orange light. Until the yellow, nothing was revealed. The yellow occasioned the rhythmic movements, but did not display any filaments. Only orange had the same effect as red, but less powerfully—the aerial filaments were scarcely visible.

"Evidently, the effect of the red rays extends—considerably—even to the orange," Meyral concluded. "That's doubtless connected to what we observed during the catastrophe: as the superior rays were extinguished, the red became more intense."

"A further demonstration that the patches are similar in nature to the energy that ravaged the Earth. I'm sure now that it was an energetic flux."

"You don't think that the entire flux was *alive*?"

"No."

"But you think the patches are?"

"I'm sure of it. The phenomenon to which we are victims is organic in kind. Each group, in my opinion, is annexed within a single being."

"With the result that terrestrial life is presently a *double* life."

"A double life, yes. That's the right expression—for the phenomenon isn't purely parasitic; it has increased our power of extension."

"How exciting that would be, if the future weren't uncertain!"

"It's worse than uncertain. Frightful perils are threatening us."

After another pause, Meyral remarked: "I think the visibility of the filaments signifies that they're enveloped by a luminous sheath, for they're evidently invisible in themselves."

V. The Paroxysm

Communications were becoming increasingly slow and difficult. Trains were only running on the major lines, and scarcely served any other purpose than transporting food, merchandise, letters and printed matter. The postal service functioned erratically; correspondence and newspapers were subject to considerable delays, or went astray. The era of sensuality was over. After an indifferent period, people began to feel a lassitude that rendered them almost incapable of work and prolonged the time they spent sleeping.

This torpor only let up in districts where carnivorism developed. There, a fever reigned: a murderous excitement; a demented intoxication that increased to the point of paroxysm.

Carnivorism began with a period of exhaustion. The affected person or animal shivered, remained lying down, in the position of those afflicted by meningitis, and uttered moans that it was impossible for them to suppress. Their temperature fell to 36 degrees, sometimes 35.5. It rose again abruptly to reach 38 degrees, often 38.5. That was a period of excitement and delirium. In animals, it was characterized by frenetic movements; in humans, it gave rise primarily to manias, phobias, delusions of grandeur and delusions of persecution. Soon, the "specific hunger" manifest since the outset of the crisis, became intolerable.

In the regions where there were reserves of meat, carnivorism scarcely existed; a copious meal cut the crisis short. Unfortunately, if vegetable provisions were superabundant, others were run down. There were no more conserves; game became almost impossible to find, either because it was annihilated or because it took refuge in places inaccessible to groups—for individual hunting had become impossible. As for domestic animals, apart from herds sacrificed long before, they all belonged to one group or another; their death caused frightful suffering. In any case, no one would touch an animal of his community; the carnivorous crises, far from destroying the links of solidarity, seemed to render them more invincible. Only the flesh of other groups was coveted.

One Thursday, the inhabitants of the Villa des Asphodèles were waiting impatiently for the newspaper. They had finished their frugal breakfast of peas, fried potato chips, grapes and pears; the chambermaid had begun to serve the coffee.

"Hasn't the paper arrived yet?" Langre asked.

"Monsieur knows that it hasn't!" the domestic replied. "The postman's group makes enough noise!"

That was true; the postman circulated in a numerous company. His retinue, which included numerous young boys and dogs, advertised itself with shouting, laughter and barking. For a fortnight, he had only brought bad news. The Westphalian sickness had spread throughout Prussia, Hungary, Poland and south-western Russia; it had spread to the United States, along the Pacific shore, and the advance symptoms were manifest all over the planet. In Paris, the infection of Montmartre, Belleville and Ternes had been observed; several villages in the Lyonnais region seemed to be afflicted. The Mediterranean coast gave considerable cause for concern.

In Westphalia, carnivorous warfare had decimated the population. In Prussia, the conflict was getting worse by the hour. It had begun in Russia, Poland and Hungary. It was raging in Chicago. Thus far, no "carnivorous homicide" had occurred in France.

The villa's inhabitants remained unaffected. If they aspired to a meal of meat, it did not seem to be in an unusual manner; they merely suffered, slightly, in the manner of people constrained to renounce an old habit. Outside of the sensations of solidarity, which were mostly pleasant, they enjoyed normal physical and mental health—but they feared that terrible events might be imminent.

When Sabine had poured the coffee, Langre and Meyral drank it in silence, slightly feverishly. Suddenly, a rumor became audible in the direction of the village.

"The postman!"

The rumor drew closer; they could make out children's cries, dogs barking, and sometimes the bleating of a goat and the cawing of crows—the postman's house had a derelict tower in which those black beasts had taken up residence.

Five minutes later, Catherine brought in *Le Radiographe* and *Le Journal*. The former only had two pages, the latter four. Langre unfolded the latter feverishly. The news was bad. Carnivorism continued to spread; riots and homicides were multiplying. In some areas, groups were forming alliances against other groups, which gave massacres the semblance of battles.

"Listen to this!" said Langre, abruptly. He read aloud: "Crises of carnivorism have been reported in several garrisons in Russian Poland and Latvia. This is the first time that the disease has run rife among European troops; the reason for that immunity is that soldiers—whose numbers have been considerably reduced by the planetary catastrophe, have stores of meat at their disposal almost everywhere. In Germany, France, England and the other countries of Central and Western Europe, these stockpiles are so large in quantity that governments might be able to surrender a part to the public. It is true that the military personnel are strongly opposed to this, and that the senior and junior officers have sided with the men." He stopped reading. "It's fortunate that these supplies are in the possession of the army," he remarked. "Distributed to the pubic, they would scarcely delay the crises, whereas, if the soldiers did not have them, the carnivorous war would become much more terrible."

Meyral, who was holding *Le Radiographe*, released an exclamation. "Carnivorism is getting worse in Paris and the Lyon region!" He handed the paper to Langre.

The latter read, from the *Stop Press*: "Murders due to carnivorism have been reported in the Butte aux Cailles and the Boulevard Rochechouart. More than 100 people might have died; details are lacking. Circulation is difficult and the reportage groups are not sure. On the other hand, several villages in the vicinity of Roanne are in bloody chaos. The Council of Ministers is in permanent session, but the presence of groups associated with each member of the Cabinet is confusing the deliberations. The Prefecture of Police is almost powerless, for analogous reasons; the Paris garrison is refusing to march against 'the sick'."

"Why is the garrison refusing to march?" asked Sabine.

"It doesn't say," Gérard replied, "but I have a suspicion—the soldiers are in a privileged position; they're afraid it might be compromised."

"What about the officers?"

"You know full well that the officers are in accord with their men, when anyone suggests touching the reserves. It's only to be expected that the officers have become attached to groups of soldiers. The army probably fears that, if it intervenes in the disorder—which will increase from one day to the next—it won't be ready to defend itself when the carnivorous war reaches its climax. You can be sure that the officers know that even better than the men."

Sabine looked at the children fearfully. "What will become of us?" she sighed.

"It's time to think about our own defense!" Langre growled, nervously. He had been thinking about it since the advent of carnivorism; Meyral had given it as much thought as him.

"We're caught between two fires," the old man continued. "If the disease spreads through Paris, the city will precipitate itself upon the countryside; we must expect to see carnivorous hordes arriving. The Lyonnais are no less of a threat.

Anyway, who can guarantee that the peril won't arise from the region itself!"

"At any rate," Georges interjected, "our zone is strangely peaceful. Although its provisions of meat are exhausted, there's no evidence that anyone has yet sustained any harm from a vegetable diet."

"I'm suffering from it!" Langre declared.

"Not in terms of your health, or your humor."

"I agree. Thus far, it hasn't exceeded the annoyance that the deprivation of a habit causes. Nevertheless, far from attenuating, that annoyance seems to be intensifying. Sooner or later, we'll contract the disease—and we need to be able to defend ourselves against that, too."

"How?" demanded Sabine, feverishly, having drawn her children closer to her. "Given that there's no more meat!"

"Perhaps meat isn't indispensable!" Meyral murmured.

Everyone turned astonished faces toward him.

"I have an idea!" he said. "Permit me to keep it secret for a few days."

VI. In the Forest

Two days later, Gérard felt exhausted. He had spent a night replete with hectic dreams and feverish awakenings. In the morning, he complained of an intense cold; he was shivering. At the same time, he was tormented by a fervent desire to eat meat. As the hours went by, that desire became unbearable.

"This is it!" he declared, with revulsion. "I've been infected with carnivorism."

At noon, Césarine was gripped by weakness and shivering in her turn. After lunch, it was the turn of little Marthe; she was shivering, and clung to Sabine or Meyral. Her illness got worse more rapidly than that of the two adults. Her eyes turned back, and she was subject to sudden fits of terror; her shivering was exaggerated into convulsions.

At 2:30 p.m., Meyral instructed the gardener to hitch up the donkey.

"Why?" asked Langre.

"We're going into the forest," the young man replied.

"You must have an idea!" the old man persisted.

"I don't know…I'm not sure. We'll see, out there." His features expressed uncertainty and a sort of apprehension.

Langre shrugged his shoulders, and resigned himself to await developments.

Georges was giving instructions to Catherine when the gardener came to announce that the rig was ready. The rig consisted of the donkey and a cart that was light, but fairly spacious; it served various purposes, especially transporting provisions. Seats had been installed therein for Langre, Césarine and little Marthe.

At any other time, the caravan would have seemed strange, and in some ways absurd. In addition to the family, the servants, the gardener and his grandson, the cart was accompanied by the hens and the cockerel, the guard-dog, three cats, rabbits, a sow and six piglets, a flock of pigeons, sparrows, bullfinches, starlings, titmice, warblers, two magpies, a fat toad, a dozen frogs, two dormice, a hedgehog and a few field-mice—but no insects or crustaceans, invertebrate animals having escaped the mysterious empery, or being submissive to it in a different manner.

The journey through La Roche-sur-Yonne did not excite any curiosity. Such incongruous groups were seen every day, and it was not the first time the residents of the villa had gone out.

The horde—for it was definitely a horde—went through the deserted fields and reached the edge of the forest. The forest was also abandoned. Its rare human inhabitants—those who were permanently resident there—had either fled during the planetary catastrophe or died. The immense wealth "liberated" by the disaster had then retained the fugitives in towns or villages; the forest only offered its eternal fortune—the fortune of primitive times, which humans did not hesitate to abandon for social benefits. Even animals were rare; they had been ruthlessly hunted down to replace the livestock annexed by the groups; in the universal relaxation, no authority had intervened. Furthermore, all the gamekeepers having emigrated, there would have been no one to provide the law with definite sanctions.

"It's virgin forest!" said Sabine, dreamily.

"Without guests!" growled Langre.

Here and there, however, flocks of wild birds escaped into the branches. They were usually disparate mixtures of starlings, robins, greenfinches, wood-pigeons, jays, magpies, blackbirds, pheasants and bullfinches. They were only glimpsed from afar; their various vigilant capacities had been combined. Only crows and starlings appeared in homogenous flocks; even they were more often accompanied by birds of other species. It seemed that these coalitions had given the birds new abilities; their flight from the human beast had a more concerted and sagacious—one might almost say intelligent—appearance.

"They're not easy to reach!" Meyral remarked.

"Inasmuch as we can't track them without immediately revealing our presence—there are too many of us!"

The rolling of the cart was muffled on a roadway invaded by wild grass. The vegetation was prodigious. No one had seen anything comparable to that immense profusion of foliage, those seemingly arborescent ferns, those dark thickets, those millions of plants which, having strewn their seeds, started flowering again.

In spite of the anguish of the occasion, Sabine and Georges were subject to the magic of the spectacle.

"It's the magnificent vitality of primitive times!" whispered the young man.

The sow and the dog often disappeared into a thicket for several minutes; Meyral watched them carefully.

A clearing appeared, where the grasses were engaged in a fierce battle. It widened out; they saw a house appear, invaded by wild plants, with strange outbuildings and covered areas behind it, some of them veritable caverns.

"Where are we?" Langre asked. He was shivering more forcefully and his face was livid.

"In Vernouze's mushroom-farm," Georges replied.

They were all familiar with it. It had been created five years before by Mathieu Vernouze and his two sons, who had planned a large-scale and original cultivation of mushrooms. It had swallowed up the greater part of their fortune, but its success had begun to pay them back when the planetary catastrophe had burst forth. All three had perished, along with most of their assistants. Since then, the immense mushroom-farm had led its own life in the deserted forest. After the cataclysm, it had not tempted anyone; it belonged to distant heirs who had not hesitated to put it up for sale. Throughout the Period of Exaltation, it had not attracted any interest; people were preoccupied with more comfortable properties. When groupism had modified existence and social relationships, it seemed more negligible than ever; it had shared the fate of many other lands abandoned by anxious humankind, diminished and eroded by degrees. Finally, now that a new cataclysm threatened the nations, it was incapable of attracting any interest at all.

"Why have you brought us here?" asked Langre, in a weary voice, adding, in a whisper: "If I could only eat a cutlet, it seems to me that I might be saved…"

The little girl was also experiencing a paroxysm; she was shivering in every limb.

"We're stopping here!" said Meyral. Then, addressing himself to Gérard, he said: "Excuse me, old friend. I have to leave you for a few minutes."

He armed himself with a basket and set off into the labyrinthine mushroom-farm. Like the entire forest, it exhibited an excessive fecundity. In the cavernous or arborescent shade, the mushroom population was growing mightily. Monstrous caps were visible everywhere, fairy rings of pink, scarlet, coppery, russet, bluish and silver flesh. Equivocal, like viscous beasts or bloody lumps of meat, or bursting forth like flower-heads or seashells, the mushrooms seemed endowed with an inexhaustible life. There were 100 species; the spring varieties had grown for a second time in that astonishing early autumn; others had made an early appearance. Georges, who knew them, made out orange agarics, porcinis, white and black morels, milk-whites, red, spotted and hairy agarics, chanterelles, button mushrooms, red amanitas, columellas, field mushrooms and fallow-ground mushrooms—enough to feed a little town for several months.[18]

The young man selected morels, porcinis and domestic mushrooms, which he piled into the basket methodically. When the harvest was complete, he became thoughtful. Primitive sensations, strangely seductive, filled his thoughts. He thought about the many forests, plains and hills, throughout the planet, that had been liberated, and the many others that would be, in their turn…

---

[18] I have translated this list of mushroom varieties as precisely as I can, given that the common names given to such fungi in France and Britain are not exactly equivalent and that Meyral occasionally seems to be offering more than one term for the same referent species. Rosny's list is obviously based on the color plate in contemporary editions of Larousse which accompanies the entry on "Champignons" [Mushrooms] and some of its eccentricities might be the result of casual copying from that list. The strangest of those eccentricities is the manifest presence in the list of more than one variety of *Amanita muscaria*, the fly-agaric, which is highly toxic, and not a species one would normally expect to be found on a farm, but this does seem to be deliberate, as one variety of the species in question (named by Rosny as the *fausse oronge*, although the Larousse plate only supplies that label as an alternative name for the *Amanite tue-mouches* [literally, fly-killing amanita]) is singled out for a specific role later in the text—a singularity that I shall discuss further in the afterword.

"If we survive," he murmured, "we'll see the world of our ancestors again!"

The links that attached him to his group became imperious; he made his way back. The condition of Langre, Césarine and the little girl had worsened; they had plunged into a sort of tremulous torpor. In addition, the gardener had begun to shiver and Sabine was pale.

At a signal from Georges, the gloomy maidservant had taken a small oil-stove from the cart, along with a saucepan and a packet containing butter, salt and pepper.

Ten minutes later, the butter was sizzling in the pan.

"What's cooking?" Langre asked, in a dull voice.

"Porcinis!" Catherine replied.

He shrugged his trembling shoulders and fell back into his torpor. Time passed; the cook supervised the preparation of the dish. Sabina and Meyral maintained a pensive silence. The little girl whimpered occasionally, and the forest rustled like an immense dress.

"It's ready!" said the maidservant, finally.

The porcinis gave off an appetizing odor. Georges placed his hand gently on his former master's shoulder. "Would you care for some porcinis?" he said.

"Why?" the other retorted, looking at the young man in surprise.

"I hope that they'll give you some relief."

Langre shook his head bitterly. "All right!" he growled. "It might as well be porcinis as anything else!"

Except in the periods of coma, carnivorism stimulated the digestive system.

Langre was given a large plateful of porcinis, which he ate with a hearty appetite; the little girl and Césarine ate some too. All three of them chewed and swallowed the nourishment without emerging from their dazed state. When their plates were empty, it seemed at first that the torpor increased. The child, especially, seemed ready to sink into a coma, and Meyral, gripped by anxiety, dared not look at Sabine.

Suddenly, Langre murmured: "I'd like some more."

Immediately, Catherine filled his plate.

This time he ate almost greedily, sitting up, with his eyes wide open. "That definitely seems to be doing me good!" he muttered.

At the same moment, the little girl, raising her head, said: "I'm hungry! Porcinis!"

"I'm hungry too!" murmured Césarine.

Sabine hastened to defer to their desire.

"That's odd," said the old man. "At first, I didn't like the porcinis...I would have preferred bread or eggs—but now it's almost as if I were eating meat." He finished his second portion with an avid and astonished expression. "If I'm not mistaken," he declared, "I could eat more."

"Perhaps it's better to wait," Sabine put in.

"I think," said Georges, "that we might risk another half-portion."

"That's delicious!" Gérard declared, this time. His shivering was becoming imperceptible; a slow feeling of well-being seeped into his heart and brain. His eyes, formerly dull, resumed their aggressive vivacity. Césarine and Marthe also revived, even more rapidly than Langre. Joy returned to the little body full of creative force; Marthe laughed at the branches, the flowers and the profound woods.

"It's paradoxical that mushrooms should have that virtue!" Langre remarked. "How can they replace meat, when milk, cheese and eggs can't? A mushroom, after all, is merely a sponge full of water, with so little nourishing substance! It's almost equivalent to a turnip or a beet!"

"Do you think," Georges asked, "that carnivorism is provoked by insufficient nutrition, in the banal sense? Isn't it rather the lack of some substance characteristic of flesh, which is found there in minute quantities—perhaps even the lack of a certain form of energy that the others are extracting from our organism? If that substance or energy exists in mushrooms in appreciable quantities, what does it matter that they're sponges?"

"Why should it exist in mushrooms?"

"A mystery, alas—like everything that has enveloped us since the origin of the catastrophe. Note, however, that a mushroom is a plant parasite. It lives in a manner similar to that of animals, not at the expense of the mineral but at the expense of life. Given that, one sees more than one analogy between the flesh of mushrooms and that of animals. A similar substance or a similar form of energy might be common to both!"

"All right!" said Langre, who was still too tired to pursue the discussion ardently. "I'm also wondering why you thought of mushrooms."

"I didn't think of them spontaneously. It was the recent avidity of the dog for the rare mushrooms in our gardens that first attracted my attention. I then observed the same avidity among the chickens, the pigeons and, of course, the sow. That gave me pause for reflection."

"I understand!" Langre replied. "I even understand why you hesitated to make us party to your hopes..." He turned his agile gaze in every direction. When he saw little Marthe smiling at him, he had a fit of tenderness, and planted a large kiss on her silvery cheek. Then, observing that the gardener was shivering, he muttered: "There's an opportunity to confirm the experiment—are there any more porcinis?"

Catherine plunged a large ladle into the saucepan and replied: "There are still three or four platefuls."

"In that case, give some to Guillaume."

Guillaume wanted nothing more—not because he particularly appreciated mushrooms, but because what he had just seen had made him want to eat some. He swallowed the portion without enthusiasm, but, like Langre and the little girl, felt no effect at first. After a few minutes, however, he asked for more porcinis, and this time devoured them. His shivering, less intense than the old man's had been, had already disappeared. "That does you good when it hits the spot!" he said, laughing loudly and naively.

"It's evidently a specific remedy for carnivorism!" said Langre. "What surprises me is that no one else has discovered it."

"Is it really the case that no one else has discovered it?" asked Sabine, thoughtfully. "The observation must surely have been made on occasion, but those who have made it didn't think it appropriate to spread it around! They preferred to hoard stocks of mushrooms."

"One can't blame then," said Meyral. "It wouldn't be in the general interest to divide up the cryptogams; everyone would have too small a share. Moreover, as we know very well, the solidarity of groups invariably outweighs general solidarity!"

"But what are we going to do?" Sabine asked.

"That's another matter. This mushroom-farm, I think, can't compare with any natural or artificial reserve—it's sufficient for the needs of a sizable town. Chance permits us to be altruistic, and our interests command us to be, in this respect. Thanks to this mine, we can form a coalition with the inhabitants of La Roche-sur-Yonne, and organize ourselves for the carnivorous war."

"Be careful!" cried Langre. "We'll need to employ cunning and prudence. Human covetousness is full of traps and immeasurable stupidity!"

"We'll operate stealthily," Meyral agreed.

There was no need to demand secrecy from the gardener, the servants or even the little boy; their sentiments reflected those of the group They agreed to load up the cart with a large cargo of cryptogams, which would be converted into conserves in order to guard against the unexpected, for throughout the autumn—which is, strictly speaking, the mushroom season—they would grow abundantly.

"Superabundantly!" said Langre. "That's not what worries me. It's just that, in La Roche-sur-Yonne, we're too far away from the mushroom-farm—and besides, mushrooms need to be eaten fresh. It isn't practicable—in fact, it's almost impossible—for us to make the journey continually. People would notice eventually."

"We can do something quite simple," the gardener put in.

"What's that? Take up residence here?"

"There's no lack of buildings!" the other retorted, with a snigger. "But that wouldn't be very clever." The gardener had a bovine face and sleepy eyes, but his thin-lipped mouth was indicative of a certain guile. "There's the hunting-lodge," he continued. "Monsieur knows that it's well-built, in a clearing, with a big garden around it. It has seven rooms, plus a thatched cottage and a stable, all with cellars attached. It can certainly lodge us all, and a few more besides."

"But it's not ours, Père Castelin!"

A sly smile, sardonic and knowing, creased the man's right cheek. "True! But no one's living in it. The owner's gone to the devil, with the group he belongs to, you can be sure! Although, if you have scruples, there's a middle way. It's for rent. That idiot of a steward will give us permission to spend a few months there, for a small fee. Come on—I can arrange it, I tell you!"

"Where is the steward?"

"Over in Maufre, with his group. They don't go anywhere any more!"

"Won't he suspect something?"

"Well, Monsieur, you know how it is. I'll explain that it's one of your scientist's whims. Perhaps Monsieur doesn't know…"

"That these people take me for a crackpot?"

"Exactly!" replied the gardener, jovially—for, although he could not read his master's thoughts, he participated, like all the other members of the group, in his sensations, and he perceived that Gérard was amused. "Good, for the time being, that's okay. I'll tell him that Monsieur wants to do experiments. I'll wager that neither he nor anyone else will have any suspicion."

"That's what comes of having a good reputation!" said Langre, laughing.

Catherine prepared another dish; this time, she cooked the morels.

VII. The Attack of the Carnivores

Père Castelin had not exaggerated. He rented the hunting-lodge for a minimal price, and the Langre-Meyral group installed itself therein diligently. In addition to furniture, they transported all the laboratory instruments and products.

This installation in the forest was doubly advantageous. It put the group within range of the mushroom-farm, and assured them of a partial security against the invasions of carnivores. It was scarcely probable that such groups would waste their time searching the sylvan wilderness; their prey was to be found in the villages.

For a few days, the servants, Sabine and even the men manufactured mushroom conserves feverishly. Those that were destined for the family were prepared straightforwardly, but Langre, mistrustfully, had vegetables added to those that were to serve the needs of the villagers.

"They have to believe there's a *recipe*," he claimed. "If not, they'll come to pillage our stores—and I'm also fearful of indiscretions that would expose us to other dangers."

"I don't think there's much danger of indiscretions," Sabine replied. "The solidarity of groups is too strong."

"And each group contains naturally-discreet individuals, who dominate the others," Meyral added.

In the village, carnivorism manifested its symptoms everywhere. After accumulating provisions at the villa, Langre and Meyral resolved to help the sick. They presented themselves at the postman's house first, where the disease was becoming perilous. After a period of coma, the postman was exhibiting an ominous excitement. He received his visitors with a sly air, and it required Sabine's intervention to persuade him to take the "medicine." The effects were both more rapid and slower than in the forest—more rapid because, after the first mouthfuls, the postman felt a sort of intoxication and developed a passionate fondness for mushrooms; and slower because it required considerable doses to make the irritation disappear. After he had devoured several jars of conserves, the man was seized by an enthusiasm that expressed itself in joyous whoops. Applied to the other members of the group, the remedy revealed itself to be infallible.

All the inhabitants of the village were treated, in succession, without a single failure. Then confidence overflowed; the "sorcerers"—as Langre and Meyral were familiarly termed—acquired an influence that, in the formidable mystery of the moment, took on a religious aspect. That influence extended to the hamlets of Vanesse, Collimarre and Rougues, which were like the village's advance forts. It spread no further; as Sabine had foreseen, the groups kept the secret.

In any case, communications were increasingly rare and difficult. The mail, the telegraph and the telephone were no longer functioning at all. Sinister rumors spread obscurely from one parish to the next. There was talk of grim invasions; formidable events were anticipated.

Heedful of the advice of Langre and Meyral, the village was fortified; ditches were dug, makeshift barricades erected. Rifles were polished, along with pitchforks, axes and knives. In the forest, the gardener, aided by a group from La Roche-sur-Yonne, had blocked the exits and made a careful study of the mushroom-farm and its caves. Langre and Meyral manufactured explosives and, having dug holes, set up mysterious traps.

A month went by; their fears eased; people enjoyed a health more stable than usual.

One night, Sabine, Langre and Meyral were snatched from their sleep by gunfire, which the directions of the wind rendered more persistent.

"One would think," said Meyral, leaning out of a window, "that it was coming from Rougues." Rougues was the hamlet most distant from the village, adjacent to the forest three kilometers from the hunting-lodge.

The night was stormy. Immense clouds were racing over the treetops; a wan Moon shone amid the chaos; the shadows, sometimes ashen and sometimes silvery, made the woodland palpitate strangely, their moving soul seemingly fleeing through the sky.

The watchers' anxiety was growing by the minute; it was communicated to the group; the gardener went out on to the granite step; the dog was barking frantically; the goat was bleating and the donkey's hoarse braying was audible, while the birds fluttered around in the darkness.

"The horror's approaching!" whispered Sabine.

"What shall we do?" asked Meyral.

There was no possible doubt: the hamlet of Rougues had been attacked by the carnivores. The intensity of the fusillade testified to the large number of the assailants.

"We can't let them be massacred like this!" the young man continued. "We must try to do something."

Langre looked at Sabine. "Yes, we must!" she said.

The whole house was awake, even the children.

"It would be futile," said Gérard. "It's certainly too late."

As if to confirm these words, the fusillade, after a few fits and starts, died away. The forest fell back into its dream.

"The drama's ended!" murmured Langre.

"But how?"

"In the defeat of the hamlet."

"Is that certain?" Meyral demanded. "Even if it is, should we remain inactive? Our own safety requires a reconnaissance."

"I don't have any complaint about that," Gérard said, "except that a reconnaissance would require the complete abandonment of the lodge. None of us can cover three kilometers alone—nor even two of us."

"Let's try. I'll be the scout. The gardener and his dog can form a relay to facilitate my movements. I certainly won't be able to reach Rougues, and I won't attempt it—that would be putting the whole group at risk—but I imagine that some of the unfortunates will have been able to run away, and their first impulse must have been to come to us."

Two minutes later, Meyral was heading towards the hamlet, with the gardener and his mastiff. Their progress was relatively easy at first; it became difficult 500 meters from the lodge, and then painful. The gardener stopped a kilometer away, bathed with sweat. Meyral continued on his way with palpitations and choking sensations; a thousand attachments held him back, with so much force that he could barely travel two meters a minute. At 500 meters, he stopped, exhausted. His head was buzzing, rent by a migraine; he felt stabbing pains all over his body.

At least I'll have done my duty!

In spite of the forces pushing him back toward the house, he waited for ten minutes, his ears pricked. Finally, he heard footsteps. Soon, he was sure of it. Two men and a woman were running through the ashy glimmer.

They're running! How can they be running? Georges asked himself, bewildered—for he imagined that they were linked to a group.

Soon they were nearby. In the moonlight, which streamed through a gap in the clouds, Meyral made out two middle-aged individuals with bristly hair, one of whom was vaguely reminiscent of King Louis XI. The woman, who was younger, had a crazed and funereal face.

They recognized Meyral and began to utter hoarse laments.

"They've all been killed…all killed!" the woman cried. "And we're going to die!"

The men, in their turn, shouted even louder; their pupils were dilated like a cat's; their lips were drawn out in a mad rictus; it was evident that their physiology had been disrupted by the fracture of the group.

"Try to follow me!" he said.

All four of them started running toward the lodge. The run seemed to have a calming effect on the fugitives from Rougues; it was a delight for Meyral. They found the gardener, who—without asking any unnecessary questions—joined the party.

The lodge appeared; Meyral had got back to it in a quarter of an hour, and would have taken even less time without his companions.

The fugitives were taken into the room that served as a drawing-room. Their faces seemed more haggard, their rictus smiles were accentuated. It was impossible for them to stand still; one of the men paced up and down near the wall; the other marched around a table; the woman stamped her feet with sudden jumps, and their eyes revealed an intolerable terror.

From their story, stammered chaotically in fits and starts, it emerged that a numerous company had mounted a surprise attack on Rougues. Before the inhabitants had been able to take stock of the situation, the stables and pig-sties had been demolished and the animals killed or wounded with axe-blows. Attracted by the noise and even more so by the links that attached them to the animals, the people of Rougues had raced outside. They had been greeted by sustained gunfire. The attackers, massed at first around the houses, had rapidly dispersed—they were no longer visible; only their continuous and murderous fire indicated their positions. The men of Rougues had tried to respond; surprise and an unusual bravery—a collective, vertiginous bravery—had precipitated them simultaneously in an assault on their enemies. Their losses, far from intimidating them, enraged them; all of them, even the women and the children, had continued their hazardous course, in the hope of reaching and massacring the murderers. The latter had retreated, retrenched, and continued their salvos. In this fashion, they killed three-quarters of those under siege. Then excitement was succeeded in the survivors by a feverish terror; they fled pell-mell, at random, making the same circuits several times over. The assailants exterminated them like hinds in a clearing.

"Had they no animals with them?" asked Langre.

137

"They had!" replied the oldest of the fugitives, whose name was Pierre Roussard. "We saw them, but they kept them at a distance."

"A necessary strategy," Meyral observed. "The animals would be easier to kill than the humans…and the humans' fate is linked to theirs."

The woman screamed, raised her arms as if to grab hold of something, and collapsed in a heap. She was no longer moving; she was stiff, her limbs extended. Her fall somehow caused her companions to fall too, but while Pierre Roussard collapsed into an armchair, the other sank down gradually in a corner, where he remained huddled.

For a minute, Meyral and Langre remained paralyzed. A thrill of fear passed through them. It was Sabine who leaned over the woman and tried to bring her round. The body remained inert and breathless.

"She's dead!" Georges whispered.

Her heart was no longer beating; a mirror, placed against her mouth, revealed no vapor. As for the men, they were unconscious, Pierre Roussard less profoundly than the other.

"It's the rupture of the group that has killed her," said Gérard, sadly. "And them…"

He did not finish; a funereal stupor dilated his pupils. The rustling of the forest evoked perils more hideous that those of the centuries when bears and wolves devoured solitary travelers…

For several seconds, the dog had been showing signs of anxiety. Outside, the hens were clucking; pigeons and songbirds had taken flight in the cloudy moonlight. The nervousness of the animals was communicated to the humans; they perceived fluidly that something was approaching.

The impression intensified. Soon, it was evident that living beings were moving toward the lodge. The dog sometimes growled, sometimes sniffed the shadows feverishly. Finally, they began to hear a dull rumor. Meyral, Gérard and the gardener hastened to lock the doors all around the lodge and arm themselves.

In the woods, human forms appeared.

"Who goes there?" shouted Georges.

"Friends!" replied a clarion voice. "We're from Collimarre."

"It's Jacques Franières," said the gardener. "What's happened to them?"

"Nothing good," said Gérard.

"This way!" shouted Meyral.

They could now make out a horde of men, women, children, livestock, dogs, birds and rodents. At the head marched Jacques Franières, an athletic individual whose barrel-shaped torso rested on the legs of a rhinoceros.

"What news?" asked the gardener.

"The region's been invaded," Franières replied. "Roche and Vanesse are surrounded. We had time to take refuge in the forest."

"There are more than 1000 of them!" moaned a pale individual, lamentably.

"Have they attacked?"

"Not yet—the brigands are keeping their distance."

Distant gunfire interrupted the peasant. Weak and intermittent at first, it became furious.

"That's the village!" said Franières, his ear cocked.

A long shudder passed through the groups; even the beasts held their breath, subtly penetrated by the human's terror. An immense despair hovered in the air.

"Let's organize our defenses!" said Langre. His voice was imperious; it lent the circumstances a tragic force. The rustics submitted to his authority with superstitious docility. After a pause, he went on: "We must hide the women and children. It's also necessary to hide the animals; they're too easy to kill—their death would weaken us dangerously and threaten our lives!"

"There's no shortage of cellars, fortunately," said Père Castelin.

"The men can conceal themselves behind the barriers, the walls and the retrenchments," Langre went on. "Who are the best shots?"

Jacques Franières and three other men came forward. In addition, the gardener was a marksman and Meyral had practiced shooting passionately since his adolescence.

"We need a detachment in the mushroom-farm," Georges said.

The rustics looked at one another, indecisively. They all wanted to stay with the "sorcerers."

"It's necessary!" the young man said.

Jacques made the decision. "That will be us," he said. "What do we have to do?"

"First, hide carefully—and don't budge. You know the place; it will be easy for you to remain invisible…until you get the signal."

"What signal?"

"When the lodge bell begins to ring, you'll mount an attack with rifle-fire—without breaking cover. If the bell is no longer working, I'll substitute a trumpet-blast."

Franières' group listened fearfully.

"You won't be in any more danger than us," Langre interjected, almost rudely. "On the contrary! It's in everyone's interest to expose you as little as possible."

These words from the "old sorcerer"—the more redoubtable of the two in the peasants' eyes—were decisive; the party headed for the mushroom-farm.

A bleak silence followed their departure; the very forest seemed more immobile. The breeze had died down; a vast nimbus covered the Moon, only letting a paltry light filter through; pale vapors floated among the branches. A few stars were visible in the gaps in the clouds; there was no other sound but that of the distant fusillade.

Meanwhile, the animals, women and children were sheltered. Guided by Langre, Meyral and the gardener, the riflemen had chosen their spots. There was no shortage of ammunition, or of weapons. In addition to the rifles brought by the peasants, the lodge contained an entire armory of revolvers, carbines, pistols and cartridges. The weapons of inferior quality and the dubious ammunition were distributed to the poorer marksmen. Langre and Meyral distributed the petards that would reinforce the fusillade; they also made ready grenades that they had manufactured themselves, and which could be thrown by hand in case the enemy attempted an assault.

Would the enemies come at all, though? The forest, in which so many ambushes could be hidden, and which offered such scant resources, would scarcely tempt carnivorous gangs. They would almost surely disdain it, if they had not perceived the flight of the people of Collimarre.

An hour went by. There was no suggestion of any approaching danger, although the dogs, the birds and the livestock displayed some agitation. That agitation might well have been attributable to the anxiety of the humans, which was inevitably propagated to their inferior kin.

The attack on the village proceeded through phases marked by the periodicity of the fusillade.

"The defense is energetic," Langre remarked, as he and Georges were examining an array of switches disposed at the back of the lodge.

"That's lucky for us."

"Yes, if the bands are intensely concentrated—but there's undoubtedly some incoherence, and the difficulties of the siege might convince some of the besiegers to seek their fortune elsewhere."

Within the last few moments, the agitation of the animals had become tumultuous. The dogs were growling or barking abruptly. The horses were manifesting the overexcitement peculiar to them. The birds were flying around hectically. Two owls were uttering fantastic plaints. The cocks were crowing.

Then the dogs all started howling together, and the horses neighed. A breath of panic passed through them.

"They're here!" cried a haggard adolescent, brandishing an old revolver.

Fear suddenly spread from soul to soul—but Langre said, with an imposing gravity: "Courage will save us!"

Within the crowd, which the mysterious force had rendered a hundred times more hypnotizable than normal crowds, an imperious confidence succeeded the terror.

"Everyone to his post," continued the old man. "Don't open fire until I give the order."

The lights went out one by one; the lodge and its gardens no longer received any but the changing light of the sky; the men took up the positions that had been assigned to them. Armed with long-range rifles, Meyral and Langre remained inside the lodge, close to their apparatus. Distress was relegated to the depths of the unconscious; the two men understood, better than by means of intelligence—with all their instinct and all their sentiment—that emotion had to be abolished. While they waited, they checked their equipment and made the final preparations.

They began to hear muffled voices, the growling of animals and footfalls. They were coming from the west, but the rumor gradually extended to the north and south. Meyral made out the first of the vertical silhouettes. They were advancing slowly, uncertain and careful. They increased in number. Soon, he could count 50, quickly reinforced by others that were arriving obliquely. In the rear, one could perceive— vaguely with the naked eye, distinctly through binoculars—the profiles of animals.

Suddenly, the scouts stopped, and their halt successively determined the halt of all those following them.

"They've seen the lodge," said Meyral.

The pause lasted several minutes. Then a slow encirclement commenced. Individuals coming from the west continually veered to the right or the left. That movement, clear to Langre and Meyral, remained rather vague for the lodge's other guests, who were less well-positioned and reliant on the naked eye. They all deduced, however, that the enemy was getting ready to surround them.

"Wouldn't it be better to open fire now?" Langre muttered. "The surprise might cause a panic."

"Undoubtedly," Meyral replied. "But apart from the fact that it would be regrettable to kill without definite provocation, a panic might be followed by a reaction."

"As you wish, my son!" the old man replied. "I share your scruples...but they'll become culpable if they compromise the safety of our own people, and those who've accepted our command…"

He broke off, and directed his binoculars southwards, where a compact assembly had formed. Suddenly, that assembly moved toward the lodge; then a column emerged from the north, supported by two groups to the west. Meyral and Langre watched them approach, very pale.

"For Life or Death!" whispered Gérard.

Meyral picked up his rifle, while the old man flicked the switches rapidly. The electric beams of searchlights darted forth. Surprised by the sudden glare, the enemy masses stopped or became turbulent. Gunshots crackled; they were unable to hit anyone.

"Fire!" Meyral ordered.

A salvo echoed in the depths of the woods. Four or five attackers fell. The others took shelter behind trees and bushes.

"Cease fire!"

The searchlights went out. A black silence, undisturbed even by the animals, descended upon the area. The noise of an expiring fusillade, coming from the direction of Roche, was hardly perceptible.

The silence lasted several minutes. Then, as mysterious orders circulated, the forest lit up with flashes of gunpowder, and a storm of bullets rained upon the lodge.

"Lie down! Lie down!" shouted Georges, taking cover himself behind a thick wall.

The searchlights came on again. Their sharp light revealed the ambushes, and the lodge's defenders only fired intermittently, all the more invisible because the glare of the searchlights, distant from the retrenchments, blinded and deceived the aggressors. Sometimes, a savage yelp or a resounding scream announced a wound or death-throes; sometimes, too, a unanimous clamor emphasized the fury of the besiegers.

Thus far, none of the men from Collimarre had been hit, while the enemy horde had sustained several deaths.

At first, Meyral had hesitated to commit homicide, but the vicissitudes of combat, the hypnosis of peril and the sentiments of solidarity dispersed his scruples. Favored by his position, by the maneuvering of the searchlights and his natural skill, he had shot down several adversaries. The old gardener had clocked up three victims; four other marksmen were demonstrating their redoubtable qualities. Deaths and injuries echoed physically through the carnivore groups, causing sharp pains and a sort of dark intoxication, which were emitted in howls.

There was a pause. The carnivores kept still behind the trees or in the bushes; their plaints and threats continued to be heard.

"They're preparing something!" Meyral murmured. He switched off the searchlights. Beneath the thick clouds, darkness fell like a block of stone; the breeze drew a sound like a stream from the treetops.

Soon, the sentiment of a new danger sent a collective thrill running through the groups, which gradually became intolerable.

One of the searchlights lit up again and began a slow rotation. Its violet light cut through the darkness like a sheaf of swords—and they could see, to the north, an unhitched cart loaded with brushwood and foliage, which was advancing. It was rolling along ponderously, moved by an invisible force. Immediately, Langre and Meyral guessed its purpose: the carnivores were going to try to blow the lodge up.

The maneuver should have been familiar to them, since they had set up its equivalents in the forest; it was, in any case, appropriate to solitary habitations. Gradually, the attention of the besieged forces became fixed on the enigmatic machine. It caused little anxiety at first; then, as memories surfaced, a few sharpshooters began to comprehend. A frisson spread from neighbor to neighbor, and the dogs barked frenziedly.

"Castelin and Bouveroy, fire at the side and the wheels!" Meyral commanded.

To the left of the lodge, a steady fusillade erupted; the besiegers replied with a hail of bullets—and the cart continued its slow progress. Hampered by the fire of Castelin, Bouveroy and Meyral, its course had deviated, into the shelter of a clump of young beech-trees. It soon reappeared to the right, where, protected by the carnivores' violent fire, it could move more easily. The men pushing it remained invisible.

"At the wheels!" Georges repeated.

The wheels must have been hit, but their functioning was undisturbed. At length, the cart arrived 100 meters from the retrenchments.

"The grenades...on command!" shouted Langre, as the vehicle emerged into an open space.

It advanced more rapidly. Meyral darted the beams of several searchlights to the left, which guided the fusillade and caused the vehicle to swerve.

"They're nearly there!" the young man whispered, in Langre's ear.

The clamor of the carnivores became triumphant. Shocked by the approach of disaster, the defenders of the lodge held their breath. Once more, the lights went out. Meyral found a switch and flicked it with a nervous hand. Then livid flames sprang forth from the ground; an explosion shook the forest; the earth shook and split; fumaroles erupted; and the cart collapsed in the darkness.

"Long live the sorcerers!" howled strident voices, while three crippled shadows limped away. Only one got away; Castelin and Bouveroy laid the other two low.

The cart was burning. The flames, creeping at first, in the bosom of a vortex of smoke, jetted forth in scarlet blades, copper lacework, and heavy waves of purple; they projected their formidable life, drawn from the mysterious depths of force, the abysms of the creative world and the unsoundable

145

inferno of the atom, into the woods and over the lodge. Thunder split the air; beech-trees splintered; the cart was blasted into sparkling smithereens, to the tops of the trees—and the windows of the lodge imploded.

"Those bombs were destined for us!" said Gérard.

The event stirred the souls of the peasants to the utmost depths; faith entered into them, which filled them with bravery and made them loyal servants of the will of Langre and Meyral. By virtue of its repercussion within the groups, that faith attained a power of supernatural unanimity.

In the firelight, the carnivores gazed at the pale lodge and the reddened gardens; obscure legends sprang to mind, and terrorized them. Then, in a fit of rage—a rage born of the *physical* sensation of losses suffered, they uttered a fantastic groan, in which pain and exaltation were confused: the voice of the human and the voice of the animal.

It was like the unleashing of the sea. A hundred frenzied men rushed to assault the lodge.

"Fire!" yelled Langre.

Meyral fired without pause; within the mass, every one of his shots struck home. Castelin, Bouveroy and all the other able-bodied men accelerated the fusillade—but the carnivores' thrust seemed invincible. In the glare of the searchlights they saw twisted faces, fluorescent eyes and howling mouths. An obscure fatality was guiding those men and rendering them similar to elements.

"Grenades at the ready!" warned the old man. He flicked a switch. Thick smoke belched from the ground; 12 or 15 men were thrown up into the air with soil, roots and plants; the others bounded like wolves, wild boars or leopards. One of them roared: "Attack!"

That was the life-or-death moment. The defenders' fire was still increasing; the lodge bell began to ring, slowly at first, like a knell, and then with insistent strokes. The quickest of the aggressors were already within ten meters of the retrenchments.

"Throw the grenades!" Langre commanded.

146

The young men from Collimarre were standing up. One of them grunted, rotated his arm and threw the first grenade; several others followed, tracing luminous parabolas; all of them, exploding sharply, split chests, opened bellies, smashed bones, or carried away fragments of flesh and limbs.

Frightful laments rose up; terror slowed down the carnivores' charge—but the rear-guard, less surprised and not quite understanding what had happened, continued bounding forward. As soon as they were within range, grenades flew through the air; they carried away ranks of men; skulls were seen rolling on the ground like cannonballs; the strokes of the bell and the dazzling searchlight-beams rendered the scene more sinister still.

"Attack! Attack!" repeated demented voices.

The woods crackled; a fusillade emerged from the sylvan shadows, while the booming voice of Franières resounded like the roar of a bull.

There was panic. There was a superhuman clamor of screams of terror and long laments uttered by the women, children and animals left in rear—and the carnivores scattered into the trees.

"Should we pursue them?" Meyral asked.

Langre only reflected momentarily. The collective soul was within him, which masked the danger.

"We must!" he said.

Soon, the groups from Collimarre and the inhabitants of the Lodge surged forth *en masse*. To render the pursuit more effective, men blew trumpets and horns they had taken down from the walls: a crazy and discordant music spread through the forest.

Progress was slow, however, although they had hoisted the wounded and the children on to horses or oxen. Nevertheless, a few limping laggards were overhauled, whom the peasants shot down mercilessly. Then they discovered men, women, children and animals rolling on the ground, prey to the sickness that had killed the peasant woman from Rougues. Meyral and Langre forbade their companions to finish them off. In any case, a considerable event hypnotized them: the village was nearby. They perceived scattered fires and a swarming multitude, and heard rifle-fire.

"Halt!" cried Meyral. "And silence."

He climbed up on to a sort of mound and, with the aid of his marine telescope, scrutinized the landscape. From the outset, he saw that the defense of the village was stubborn. Although the aggressors had been able to take possession of two solitary farms to the extreme south, the retrenchments were holding up well, and the assaults had been energetically repelled. The present attack lacked vigor and consistency; a propitious diversion would doubtless sow disorder and discouragement among the carnivores…

They would be able to approach under cover, from the east, and attack the enemy from the height of a ridge, where the marksmen would be able to remain under cover.

When he had examined the enemy positions in detail, Meyral came down from the mound and, drawing Langre aside, explained his plan to him.

Gérard adopted it resolutely. He was living in a lucid dream, which was further enlarging the sense of personality. Fear had been abolished; peril became a kind of abstraction. That state of mind, which did not exclude prudence, was established in all the groups. Even the women and children were subject to a collective hypnosis, which suppressed their customary sensitivity.

When Langre gave his orders, he encountered no hesitation; the men marched off with a fatalistic serenity. They reached the crest of the ridge without encountering any obstacles; the carnivores' entire attention was focused on the village. Even their animals, weary of so many alerts and maddened by the incoherence of the battle, only manifested an uncertain anxiety. The forces defeated in the forest had veered northwards. Disorder was predominant. The savage hordes retained a kind of organization, however, carrying out certain tactics and tricks—but their experience was limited and they were guided by instinct rather than intelligence.

VIII. The End of the Battle

Langre and Meyral arranged the sharpshooters behind the crest. The position proved to be excellent and difficult to outflank: pools of water defended it to the right and a quarry to the left; it overlooked a terrace on which the majority of the besiegers were massed, and herds of animals were perceptible, hidden in an enclave inaccessible to the men of Roche, but easy to reach from above.

"Don't fire before the command!" Langre had said.

Some of them had brought grenades; the women had picked up weapons before leaving the lodge. Meyral had brought a large reflecting lantern, whose light was almost as powerful as that of the electric searchlights; he was carrying it veiled.

An expectant pause. The clouds were thickening further. A grayish darkness hung over the location, pierced by a milky gleam in the east. There was a sort of truce between the combatants, but from the height of the crest several files of carnivores could be seen heading for the terrace. Pale fires, splashes of light, accompanied intermittent fusillades.

"The rogues are preparing an assault," Langre muttered. "Are we ready?"

Meyral distributed trumpets and horns to a few women and young boys; they would only make use of them at the moment when the men of Collimarre opened fire.

Suddenly, shouts went up; a thunderous fusillade was launched from the terrace; a command resounded and a savage horde precipitated itself toward the retrenchments of the village.

"Fire!" yelled Langre.

Georges unveiled his lantern and projected its dazzling radiance upon the carnivores. Castelin, Franières, Bouveroy, and even the poorer marksmen, ravaged the swarming masses. The trumpets and horns sounded. An immense cheer went up from the village, followed by desperate rifle-fire. Bewildered, the assailants collided with one another in disarray, carried by their momentum, gripped by eddies and refluxes, or stopped by the fall of their companions.

The attack was not broken, however. An energetic advance guard ran toward the village retrenchments, followed by hypnotized files. The center whirled around bizarrely. In the rear-guard, a tall man shouted out as he climbed the slope. A bullet had almost torn away one of his ears, and he howled, exasperatedly: "Take the hill!"

Gradually, his fever infected the others; raucous voices roared; the hypnosis increased and became invincible; enslaved bands climbed up toward the men of Collimarre…

The fusillade redoubled. Every shot fired by Meyral or Castelin hit the target; Franières and Bouveroy worked tirelessly and effectively; the cacophony of trumpets and horns seemed to be the discordant voice of the Earth…but the assailants were still climbing. If they succeeded in precipitating themselves on their adversaries before the depressive phase kicked in, the latter would inevitably be crushed.

The steep slope, bristling with obstacles, slowed down their march; sometimes, the carnivores seemed harassed, but then the ascent resumed and the huge lantern illuminated haggard faces, wolfish eyes and gaping mouths…

Soon, the leading group drew close. It advanced with hoarse cries, tightening up in a kind of gully, between two ribbons of stone.

The movement had been anticipated. Langre waited attentively until the defile was filled with men, and then he commanded: "To you, Gannal, Barraux and Samart!"

Those three men were holding grenades at the ready. They stood up slowly and took aim. The projectiles were seen to describe parabolas, to fall upon the crowd accumulated in the gully, and rebound in flamboyant shreds. There was a grim clamor, howls of terror, panting bodies, scattered limbs and floods of red liquid: the advance-guard's attack was broken…

At the rear, though, other men were running, going around the blocks of stone and appearing in two hordes on the flanks of the men from Collimarre. A brutal fusillade greeted them; then, in response to an order, Barraux, Gannal and Samart threw more grenades. The effect was horrible; it broke the charge on the left. To the right, 30 stubborn individuals continued the climb. The last grenades sprang forth from the ridge…but six or seven assailants reached the crest. One of them spun round and collapsed; the others launched themselves forward, croaking. The colossal Franières slashed at them with an axe; Barraux, Gannal, Samart and ten others stabbed them with pitchforks, beat them with heavy cudgels or whirled swords. Meyral laid about him with his rifle-butt…

That secured the victory. All along the slopes, the survivors were fleeing vertiginously, while the last aggressors died on the crest.

Although several were wounded, the men of Collimarre gave voice to a long howl of triumph, to which a clamor from the village responded. Meyral, Franières, Bouveroy and Castelin were already firing on the carnivorous masses, and their intervention was salutary. The attack against the retrenchments of Roche, violent until then, weakened. The right wing retreated under an ardent fusillade; the left wing ceased advancing. Langre directed the piercing rays of a searchlight at the latter wing and ordered the fire to be concentrated there, while he grabbed hold of a horn himself and blew it lustily.

This maneuver coincided with the carnivores' loss of heart; they saw a stampede propagate magnetically from the east to the north, and from the south to the west. To accelerate it, Gérard selected 20 men and told them go down as far as the gully. The effect was decisive. When those men appeared on the crest, the besiegers who were still hesitating thought they were seeing a crowd, and beat the retreat. Scattered at first, the mass of carnivores reassembled in the north; it faded away gradually into the pearl-tinted darkness. Here and there, a human or a quadruped spun round and collapsed, struck down by the mysterious malady that Meyral called "rupture sickness," or a bird, after a jerky flight, fell to the ground.

"We're saved!" roared Franières.

His cry rang out like a fanfare of hope. The unanimous joy spread from individual to individual, making the women and the children laugh, the quadrupeds quiver, and a flock of pigeons, sparrows and bats to whirl around the crest of the hill.

Standing up on their retrenchments, the defenders of La Roche-sur-Yonne cheered Langre, Meyral and the men of Collimarre.

Epilogue

I. La Roche-sur-Yonne

That night saved the inhabitants of La Roche-sur-Yonne, Collimarre and Vanesse. The defeated carnivores did not attempt any offensive return; they spread out toward the north, where they met Parisian hordes that annihilated and devoured them. Having returned to the village, Langre and Meyral organized its defenses to the point of rendering the retrenchments inaccessible to the bands roaming the region, none of which was very large. Two or three of these bands attempted nocturnal raids, but retreated before the glare of searchlights, the number and glare of which gave warning of a significant garrison and redoubtable means of defense.

As their losses had been minimal, save for the hamlet of Rougues, the groups affected only experienced tolerable suffering, which did not cause any deaths. The harvests of the mushroom-farm sufficed to strangle carnivorism. The general state of health was better than in normal times. The supernatural links uniting the groups acquired a charm that seemed to increase with familiarity.

The collaboration between Langre and Meyral attained an extraordinary unity. Although there was no telepathy, save for certain sensations, identical thoughts eventually arose from the nervous connection. It happened so often that the physicists had the same idea or the same intention that it became impossible for them to distinguish whether a discovery belonged to one or the other. They no longer tried to do so; they gladly abandoned themselves to a solidarity that multiplied their inventive faculties tenfold. Their discoveries increased in number and in depths. Those discoveries sometimes excited them, and sometimes plunged them into a sort of ecstasy.

After numerous attempts, they created a colloidal solution whose active substance extracted spores from fly-agaric mushrooms. Prepared in particular conditions, the solution seemed perfectly isotropic, but when traversed by the lines that bound the members of the group together, it had a weak duplicatory effect on light-rays, especially the violet rays. If the test-tube or flask containing the solution was between Langre and Meyral, the duplication was hardly discernible; it became more apparent when several individuals were gathered in the laboratory, particularly when they were arranged in such a manner that the lines traversed the liquid in parallel.

As soon as they had carried out the first experiments, the scientists became convinced that it was not, strictly speaking, a matter of double refraction, but of facts entirely comparable with those that had preceded the Planetary Catastrophe.

For a week, no further discovery was made. Langre and Meyral sought to increase the intensity of the phenomenon. They succeeded by arranging two rows of humans and animals. It did not take them long to make a new observation concerning the violet rays: those rays weakened perceptibly when the lines of communication were more forceful, and the relevant rays tended to form a right angle with the relevant lines. By prolonging the experiment, the disappearance was determined of a limited zone of violet radiation.

"We're entering the gulf of unknown energies!" Langre exclaimed, trembling with joy.

Meyral was as excited as the old master. They persisted, and, enlarging the scope of their experiments, had recourse to three other groups from the village, chosen from those which included the highest proportion of humans. The zone of transformation was enlarged; they contrived the disappearance of a considerable range of violet rays, a weakening of indigo radiation, and a slight discoloration of the blue rays. In sum, the physicists reproduced almost all the phases of the Planetary Catastrophe.

In spite of stubborn efforts and the most ingenious equipment, they were unable to make the blue rays or the

154

green rays disappear altogether, but they made other discoveries. The first showed that, if subjected to the directed action of groups for a long time, the colloidal solution retained durable traces of the experiment. By prolonging the poses, it was observed, with the aid of red light, that lines parallel to the filaments persisted in the liquid. These lines were a weak reproduction of the lines that linked individuals in the same group together. By means of patience and ingenuity, they succeeded in increasing their visibility—and, undoubtedly, their diameter. They could then render them perceptible with the aid of orange, and even the less refrangible yellow radiation—but the other rays did not seem to have any effect on them.

"There's no doubt, however, that the effect exists," said Georges.

It did, indeed, exist. A series of particularly subtle experiments showed that the filaments weakened violet radiation.

"Weakening them and making them disappear is the same thing," Meyral remarked. "We have, therefore obtained *fixed* lines of force that have the properties of the mysterious phenomenon."

An ultimate experiment, made with the aid of an exceedingly narrow beam of violet light, taken from the edge of the ultra-violet zone, ended in the vanishing of the beam.

"One more step," Langre sighed, always more excited than his companion.

The step was taken. After being isolated for a fortnight, one of the solutions, which had caused a relatively considerable range of violet rays to disappear, began to emit an unusual quantity of electrical and calorific energy.

"Indirect reversibility," murmured Langre, in an awed tone.

"Which explains the period of exaltation," Georges added. "We're probably reaching the limits, old friend. We've far exceeded our fondest hopes! Not only have we reproduced the phenomenon in its broad features, but we've succeeded in retaining a form of it as stable as our material forms. Perhaps we'll be able to reach a conclusion."

"We shall—and boldly!" cried Gérard, spiritedly. He interrupted himself; a rumor was growing in the street.

"The postman!" said Georges, who had gone to the window. "One might think that he were bringing correspondence."

"Is social life resuming?" said Langre, incredulously.

"A newspaper!"

Césarine brought in *Le Temps*, printed on four small pages. The two men considered this social message with a strange affection. Was this the end of the accursed era, the return of human harmony, or merely a lull in the storm? For a fortnight, the region had been tranquil; roaming bands were no longer seen, but no group dared to chance itself in the fields and villages, which the carnivore war had made into wilderness or places to be feared.

Le Temps announced that the scourge was losing all its impetus. Carnivorism was dying out; in France, it was thought that it only subsisted in a few remote districts. Its decline had been rapid, even abrupt, and coincided with a perceptible relaxation of bonds of solidarity. A few groups in Auvergne and Touraine were showing symptoms of dissolution. Normal existence was beginning to resume in the big cities. Trains were running intermittently. The principal telegraph lines were functioning for several hours a day. Newspapers were being printed in Paris, Lyon, Marseilles, Bordeaux and Lille. The losses due to carnivorism, however, were seemingly immense. In Paris, a fifth of the population had been immolated or had perished in the wake of the massacres. Equally grave losses had been sustained in the Lyonnais region, and even graver ones in a few large cities and some foreign territories. *Le Temps* estimated the average losses to be a tenth of the European population.

"We've been extremely fortunate!" said Meyral.

"Thanks to our dietary regime and our victory over the carnivores! On the other hand, we haven't yet observed any decrease in the cohesion of our group, nor the other groups in the village."

"I fear that that might also be a consequence of the diet. Our return to normal will undoubtedly be slower than everywhere else."

"Damn it!" said Langre, who seemed worried.

Every day, the news got better. The supernatural link that had shackled societies was fading away rapidly. Individual action was resuming. Automobiles were reappearing on the roads; numerous trains were circulating on the railways; the postal service, the telegraph and the telephone were functioning with a degree of regularity; a few aircraft were flying over the devastated region. Newspapers increased in number. The cultivation of the land was resumed. Factories and workshops reopened, one by one.

By the spring, only sparse traces of "groupism" remained, and only in places where the malady had been benign. Among these places, some manifested a noticeable relaxation of the collective bond; others, much rarer, revealed no significant amelioration. It was soon discovered that such persistence corresponded with a particular dietary regime—the regime that Meyral had introduced in La Roche-sur-Yonne. Remarkably, the belated groups did not experience any distress, and even enjoyed some singular privileges; humans and animals seemed invulnerable to parasitic diseases, with the result that mortality was very limited. In Roche and Collimarre, only one old man had died during the winter.

Nevertheless, Meyral—and Langre especially—felt a certain anxiety, although it was only manifest periodically. As for the people of the village, after an interval of mistrust, they were reassured; there was nothing unpleasant about their situation. They accomplished their tasks as well as ever; the domestic animals worked as well as they had in the past, perhaps better. For the time being, the rustics remained steadfastly loyal to the "sorcerers"; their faith, by virtue of collective repercussions, was almost religious.

In one sense, this situation pleased the physicists; it permitted them to push their experiments to the end, to check their tiniest details and to multiply the proofs. The La Roche-sur-Yonne memoirs revolutionized the scientific world. Although they clashed on a few points with English, German, American, Italian and Russian scientists, Meyral and Langre left their rivals' most subtle investigations far behind—and when they announced an official verification of their discoveries, all the academies in the world sent delegates. The date of the session was fixed for April 20.

From the 15th on, people became anxious to ensure themselves a place. Between the 17th and the 19th, La Roche-sur-Yonne filled up with a population whose origins rendered it incongruous. Small Japanese, bronze-skinned Hindus, black Africans and people of mixed origin rubbed shoulders with tall Scandinavians, sturdy Germans, haughty Anglo-Saxons, quick Italians and placid Slavs.

It was necessary to arrange the apparatus in the gardens, in garages that sheltered them from the solar rays. For those experiments that required near-darkness the spectators were reduced to filing through in little groups.

At first, some spectators—especially those who claimed to have made significant discoveries themselves—manifested a certain skepticism, but the astonishment and admiration gradually grew to the point of enthusiasm. The two principal facts—the destruction of violet rays and the conservation of lines of force—positively excited the scientific audience.

When Langre gave a synthetic summation of the investigations carried out at La Roche-sur-Yonne, he was interrupted by ovations, but the speech concluded in silence.

"There can scarcely be any doubt as to the nature of the catastrophe that almost destroyed animal life on our planet. A storm of energies swept through the space that surrounds us, but these energies have only distant analogies with ours. Even so, the analogies exist, since our energies were subjected, during the passage of the interstellar cyclone, to modifications which, in some instances, ended in veritable destructions.

"From experiments that a favorable combination of circumstances allowed us to pursue a little further than our glo-

158

rious colleagues, it can be deduced that these destructions were, in fact, metamorphoses. A general proof of that was provided, after the cataclysm, by the great afflux of energies that gave vegetation an extraordinary luxuriance, and which determined the strangest vital excitement in humans. The particular proof, Gentlemen, we were fortunate enough to produce in this very place; it is, we believe, more decisive than the other.

"From the sum total of our verifications, we dare to conclude that the incident energies comprise, in addition to unimaginable forms, a considerable number of longitudinal, or rather helical, oscillations, with the peculiarity that the transverse component of the waves is excessively reduced. When these waves encounter luminous waves, there is a conflict which, if sufficiently prolonged, ends with the disappearance of ultra-violet, violet, indigo, blue and even green waves.

"These various waves are literally vanquished by the unknown waves. Nothing any longer remains but yellow, orange, red and infra-red waves. The yellow waves resist the attack. The orange, red and infra-red waves go further; they win the battle, succeeding in transforming a part of the unknown rays. We have also observed, along with our illustrious colleagues, that during the planetary catastrophe, the red and orange zones exhibited a slight increase in brightness. Fluorescent phenomena demonstrated that it was the same for the infra-red; even so, beyond a certain wavelength, it seems that the phenomenon changes qualitatively or becomes more complex.

"The conflict between the red rays and the unknown waves is particularly fascinating, because it reveals itself more clearly to the eyes of observers. In fact, we observe that the lines of force uniting our group become perceptible when one illuminates the routes of their passage with red light. This perceptibility is indirect; it results from the conflict of waves—the red rays form a sort of sheath around the connecting lines, which are beams of helical waves.

"Many processes will remain permanently obscure—including, no doubt, the effect of the mysterious energies on chemical phenomena. We may, however, hope—and we are carrying out further research in this regard—to furnish a few suggestions regarding the perturbations to which various other forms of energy are subject. In the present state of affairs, it is best to leave such delicate problems until later.

"We must now, Gentlemen, engage with the most troubling of enigmas—by which I mean the astonishing series of organic phenomena which, by turns, charmed and terrified our species. The facts that emerge from observation and scientific experiment are of two kinds, some physiological and others physico-chemical. We shall say little here about the former, which are outside our competence. Nevertheless, let us recall the singular properties of mushrooms with respect to carnivorism, and the remarkable effects of our colloidal solution, prepared with the aid of the spores of the fly-agaric mushroom. These are indications appropriate to interest not only physiologists, but also—and even more so—those involved in physical chemistry.

"As for groupism itself, on the one hand, it seems likely to remain a mystery, but on the other hand, there is no doubt that it depends on a double organic environment: the terrestrial organic environment and an external organic environment. In other words, people and animals have been a terrain of cultivation, doubtless unfavorable but possible, for seeds that have come from interstellar space. It is permissible to conjecture that each animal and human group was the prey of one of these seeds, *ergo*, of a living being. The individuals that developed thus at our expense, inevitably emerged from the energetic environment that was so harmful to light.

"We know, with an approximate precision, about two of the elements comprising our prodigious parasites: firstly, the patches that are the first symptoms of the disease; and secondly, the networks of linkage.

"The physical properties of the patches are familiar to you. They exhibit no resemblance to our matter, and yet they behave like solid bodies—like ultra-solid bodies, I might say, since they resist all means of destruction or even deformation.

They seem so perfectly permeable to all our substances that one might conclude that impermeability does not exist for them. We have not been able to discover any appearance of mass in them, but they extend in all directions. They must contain waves analogous to those which destroy violet radiation and augment red radiation, since, in sum, they cause the former to pale slightly and slightly increase the brightness of the latter. On the whole everything occurs as if we were dealing with stabilized energies.[19]

"The same observations apply to the threads that connect the individual members of a group together, in a more precise and more striking manner. Here, in fact, we obtain not only a weakening of violet radiation, but their destruction, provided that we consider a thin pencil of rays, and the effect on red rays is manifest. Finally, we succeed, in our colloidal solutions, in immobilizing threads exactly as we can immobilize fluid currents, by solidifying them in some manner. Given that, it is difficult to deny that the energy-storms that swept the terrestrial surface are capable of a permanence of form comparable to the permanence of our solid bodies.

"Does that mean that we can take the analogy to its limit? We do not think so. There are enough differences between the unknown energies and our matter-energy system for the same terms to be unable to serve the two modes of existence—and yet, the analogies are real, since we see a part of our energies absorbed and transformed by the invading energies, and, on the other hand, the latter—more weakly, admitted—absorbed and transformed by our energies. The exaltatory phase that followed the catastrophe's depreciatory phase was a partial restitution of the lost forms of energy.

---

[19] Rosny inserts a footnote here: "The reader is not unaware that our matter is considered by illustrious modern scientists to be a straightforward complex of energies." The idea of the interchangeability of mass and energy was not as familiar in 1913 as it is nowadays; although Einstein had published his famous equation quantifying their equivalence in 1905.

"Permit me, Gentlemen, to conclude with a hypothesis—which, in our opinion, we consider as the imperious sugges-tion of observation and experiment. Considering that the inter-planetary storm gave rise to a cycle of phenomena which is, on the one hand, analogous—albeit distantly—to our physico-chemical phenomena, and which is, on the other hand, more distantly but certainly analogous to our organic phenomena, we may conjecture that it is a *world*, or a fragment of a world, that has encountered our Earth. To all evidence, this world belongs to a system very different from our solar system. It does not follow that it is associated with systems beyond the space occupied by the Milky Way and the other nebulas.[20]

"It might be that our space includes different kinds of un-iverse, some of which are capable of partial interaction with one another, and others almost complete in their mutual indif-ference and even their mutual permeability. In the latter case, the coexistence of universes, whatever their proximity, would not give rise to any perceptible disturbance, while, in the for-mer case, cataclysms proportionate to the analogies are possi-ble. The world that has just passed through our system did not have enough analogy with ours to destroy our Earth—the pla-netary mass does not seem to have suffered any serious mod-ification—but there was sufficient to attack our superficial energies and to threaten life. Had there been a slightly higher

---

[20] Rosny inserts another footnote: "Langre is here using the term 'nebulas' in its double meaning." The term was, of course, employed by astronomers to refer to any light-source that remained telescopically vague, although it had been known for more than a century when *La Force mystérieuse* was written that some were actually distant star clusters—other "island universes" or galaxies—while others were lu-minous clouds of gas within the Milky Way. In stating that Langre is conserving both meanings, Rosny is emphasizing the physicist's contention—which he is about to elaborate—that the nebula within the Milky Way might be inherently mysterious, involving one or more kinds of "alien energy."

degree of analogy, or a less rapid transit of the catastrophe, terrestrial animal life would have disappeared.

"In any case, we posit the hypothesis that we have been subject to the collision of a world, incapable of compromising the existence of our world or even of troubling its progress through space, and that that world includes, as ours does, an organic regime.

"Let is conclude with a word of consolation. It is highly improbable that such an accident will be repeated, at least for thousands of billions of years—and the residues of energies and unknown entities that still persist in our midst have ceased to be dangerous. The recent experiments carried out on the groups of La Roche-sur-Yonne, to which we were party, seem conclusive in that regard: the parasitic organisms are doomed. Thanks to our equipment, we can calculate approximately the curves of their decline. Our special alimentation has sheltered us from crises, and the crises themselves have become less redoubtable: the living webs that envelop us will only pose a serious threat if we attempt premature separations; it is necessary to wait for the webs to break of their own accord.

"Is it necessary to confess, Gentlemen, that we await that denouement without impatience, and even that we would like to see it delayed for some months yet? At La Roche-sur-Yonne, we have only suffered—and not very much—for a very short time; exceptional circumstances preserved us from the ordeals to which the vast majority of our peers were subjected. Our solidarity has ended up being so pleasant that we shall sometimes regret it when we have finally recovered our individual independence—and my scientific egoism will cause me to regret it more than anyone else, for it is all too evident that it has been extraordinarily favorable to my collaboration with Georges Meyral.

"Nevertheless, Gentlemen, you do not know how profoundly happy we are to see the human family delivered from the most frightful nightmare to which it has ever been subject since the time when our ancestors lit the first fires and stammered the first words."

An immense storm of applause resounded through the gardens; a sea of faces surged forward, and old Whitehead, laden with years and honors, gave the accolade to the two physicists, declaring: "Posterity will class your discoveries among the most astonishing that the genius of our species has made."

The acclamation resounded thunderously, the hands tumultuously raised and an ardent enthusiasm lighting up every eye. Langre, his eyelids bathed in tears, felt that the glory of which he had despaired during so many trying days had finally been conferred upon him, and would never be rescinded.

II. Sabine

Sabine advanced beneath the copper beeches at a dreamy pace, and when she emerged from the shade, she seemed to be very close to the beautiful clouds that were gathering in the west. The light was peculiar and variable; the branches were quivering, and Sabine considering the stream and its noble poplars, savored the living warmth of the breeze. The fervor of young races swelled her bosom; she no longer saw life as a wood full of pitfalls, and there was a certain recklessness in the way she shook her tresses.

While she abandoned herself to the strange population of dreams, she heard someone approaching and turned round. Meyral emerged from the shade. He came forward rather fearfully; his large bright eyes dared not settle on the young woman. She watched him come toward her; when he was close, he murmured: "In a few weeks, we'll be free."

A melancholy expression passed over their faces. The bonds that had united them for long months had become so weak that they only sensed them in moments of excitement. At that moment, in the dully stormy air, confronted by the landscape of Old France, they shared the same regret.

"I can't rejoice on that account," she replied. "It seems to me that I shall be alone." She bowed her head and added, in a whisper: "I love the mysterious creature that unites us!"

"Do you?" he said, in his mystical voice. "You can't imagine how sad I was, just now, while considering the frail lines that still join us. I thought I could feel the pulsations of the death-agony of the Being in which we're living; my blood ran cold."

"I knew that! I shared your suffering."

"We have ended up, if not knowing it, at least living partly in accordance with its nature. The strange space in which it exists, that space devoid of surface and depth, how clearly I sense it! And that alternative duration in which each pulsation extends in part into the past! I have its rhythm *fully* within me—a rhythm that renews all our ideas regarding the essential nature of things…"

"Ah!" she said. "Most of all, I'm struck by its sadness. It knows that it is in exile, exiled forever, separated from its world by an inexpressible infinity. Its dolor is reflected in me; I was unaware of it at first, for I was unaware of the creature itself; then communication was established. I think and live in association with it!"

"It was also unaware of us! Isn't it one of our most thrilling sensations to perceive its gradually increasing consciousness of our existence, and its attachment to us?"

"Oh, yes!" she sighed. "How sensitive we are to its lamentation! And what poetry is mingled therein…"

"Only the music of the masters can give us a very distant impression of it, if that music becomes absolutely internal, invading every nerve with its profound mystery…"

There was a long silence. Then she fixed Meyral with her gaze. Their hearts beat faster.

In a slightly hoarse and curt tone, she said: "I also know why you have followed me."

"Sabine!" he said, tremulously. "I was resigned, and I can be again—but take care not to give me any false hope; the awakening would be abominable!"

She only hesitated momentarily before saying: "Suppose I wanted to take you into my confidence?"

"Oh!" he cried, with a joy that was ready to change into distress. "Don't let me glimpse anything if you don't love me!"

She smiled at him, with a woman's tender malice; an immense sliver ran through him; all the beauty of the world passed by in a hurricane of love. Kneeling down in front of her, fearful and fretful, he said, in a broken voice: "Is it true? You're not mistaken…it's not compassion? I don't want compassion, Sabine."

She took his hand and leaned toward the imploring face. "I believe that I shall be happy!"

"Ah!" he sighed.

The past was no more—or, rather, the present moment contained all life, all time and all space. He remained kneeling on the sacred ground on which Sabine stood; the religion of family filled his breast, and when the long blonde hair touched his lips, he knew that his destiny was complete.

HARETON IRONCASTLE'S AMAZING ADVENTURE

Prologue
The Fantastic Land

Rebecca Storm was waiting for the Spirits. She was holding a gold pencil-holder lightly, with its point on a pad of gray paper. The Spirits did not arrive. "I'm a poor medium," she sighed.

Rebecca Storm had the Biblical face of a dromedary, and almost the same sandy hair. Her eyes were visionary, but her mouth, fitted with the teeth of a hyena, which could have crushed marrow-bones, provided a realistic counterweight.

"Am I even worthy? Do I deserve the Beyond?" That anxiety ravaged her. Then, hearing the clock chime, she headed for the dining-room.

A tall man, a perfect symbol of the type invented by Gobineau,[21] was standing by the fireplace. Hareton Ironcastle,

---

[21] Arthur, Comte de Gobineau (1816-1882) was one of the pioneers of the race theory that became fundamental to paleo-anthropology in the latter half of the 19th century; he was also a statesman and a prolific writer of fiction. The reference here is to his theory of the superiority of the "master race," whose ideal type Rosny had adopted for the heroes of almost all his prehistoric fantasies and adventure stories. Whereas Gobineau identified that stereotype as "Aryan," however, Rosny had attributed it to original inhabitants of Europe who were displaced by successive waves of invaders from the east, including the "Ariès" (see "Eyrimah" in vol. 4). In the story that followed Rosny takes care on several occasions to express

with his rounded face, hair the color of oat-straw and the gray eyes of a Scandinavian pirate, still retained at the age of 43 the skin of a blond virgin.

"What does 'epiphenomenon' mean, Hareton?" Rebecca asked, hoarsely. "It ought to be blasphemous."

"It is, at least, a philosophical blasphemy, Aunt Becky."

"And what does that mean?" asked a young woman who was finishing eating a grapefruit, while the butler served bacon and eggs with Virginia ham. The tall fair-haired young women that once inspired the sculptors of goddesses must have been made in her image. Hareton focused his gaze on tresses shaded with amber, honey and wheat-straw.

"It means, Muriel, that if your consciousness didn't exist, you would continue to eat that ham and ask me questions exactly as you are doing—except that you wouldn't know that you were eating and asking me questions. To put it another way, the epiphenomenal consciousness exists, but everything happens just as if it didn't…"

"The people who invented such absurdities can't have been philosophers!" exclaimed Aunt Rebecca.

"Yes, Aunt…they were philosophers."

"They ought to be locked up in a sanitarium."

The butler brought eggs and smoked bacon for the aunt, and toast and two small sausages for Hareton, who did not like eggs. The teapot, the hot bread-rolls, the fresh butter and the pots of jam formed islets on the sparkling table-cloth. The three diners ate religiously.

Hareton was finishing the last piece of toast, with black-currant jam, when the butler brought in the mail. There were letters, a telegram and newspapers. The aunt captured two letters and a magazine called *The Church*. Hareton grabbed the *New York Times*, the *Baltimore Mail*, the *Washington Post* and the *New York Herald*. He opened the telegram first, and,

---

dissent from the profound horror of miscegenation that infected Gobineau's thesis.

with a half-smile whose significance remained unintelligible, said: "We're going to see my nephew and niece from France."

"I ought to be horrified by them," the aunt remarked.

"Monique is fascinating" Muriel declared.

"Like a necromancer who had taken on the appearance of a young woman," said Rebecca. "I can't look at her without a perverse pleasure…it's a temptation…"

"There's something in what you say, Aunt," Ironcastle agreed. "Think of it as if Monique's mind had a kind of bark…a good shot of honesty and honor would put her right…"

From an envelope that bore a Gondokoro stamp he extracted a second envelope, filthy and covered with stains, to which the wings and legs of crushed insects were still attached. "This is from our friend Samuel," he said, with a sort of reverence. "I can smell deserts, jungles and marshes!"

He opened the envelope carefully. His features clouded over. It took a long time to read. Occasionally, he exhaled forcefully, almost whistling. "Here's an adventure," he said, "that surpasses anything I thought possible on this ignominious planet!"

"Ignominious!" his aunt retorted. "The work of God!"

"Is it not written: 'And it repented the Lord that he had made man on the Earth, and it grieved him in his heart'?"[22]

Raising an uncertain eyebrow, Rebecca drank her black tea.

Muriel, seized by curiosity, said: "What adventure, Father?"

"Thou shalt be as the gods, knowing good and evil!" Ironcastle muttered, shrewdly. "I know that you can keep a secret, Muriel, if I ask for your word in advance. Will you give it to me?"

"Before Our Lord," said Muriel.

"And you, Aunt?"

---

[22] *Genesis* 6:6.

"I will not invoke His name in vain; I shall simply say: yes."

"Your word is worth all the pearls in the ocean."

Hareton, who was apt to repress emotion, was more agitated than his expression showed. "You know that Samuel Darnley set off in search of new plants, in the hope of confirming his theory of cyclic transformations. Having passed through terrible places, he's reached a land unexplored not merely by Europeans but by any living men. It's from there that he's sent me this letter."

"Who carried it?" asked Rebecca severely.

"A native, who probably reached a British outpost. By means of which I'm ignorant, the letter got to Gondokoro, where it was thought appropriate, in view of its decrepitude, to insert it in a fresh envelope…"

Hareton lost himself in thought, his eyes seeming empty and hollow.

"But what has Mr. Darnley seen?" Muriel persisted.

"Oh!" Ironcastle started. "Yes—the land where he is differs fantastically, in its plants and animals, from any other land on Earth."

"More than Australia?"

"Much more. Australia is, after all, nothing but a vestige of ancient ages. Samuel's country seems to be as advanced as Europe or Asia, perhaps more so, in its general evolution…but it has taken another path. One must suppose that, many centuries—perhaps millennia—ago, a series of cataclysms reduced its fertile regions considerably. Presently, they're not much larger than a third of Ireland. They're populated by mammals and reptiles of a fantastic sort. The reptiles are *warm-blooded*. There is also a superior animal, comparable in intelligence, but not in its physical structure or by the nature of its language, to humans. The vegetables are even stranger, being improbably complex, and actually holding humankind in check."

"This reeks of witchcraft!" muttered the aunt.

"How can plants hold humans in check?" asked Muriel. "Is Mr. Darnley claiming that they're *intelligent*?"

"He doesn't say so. He limits himself to writing that they have mysterious faculties, which don't resemble any of our cerebral faculties. What he's sure of is that, one way or another, they're able to defend themselves and conquer."

"Are they mobile?"

"No. They can't change location, but they're capable of sudden and temporary subterranean growth, which is one of their modes of attack or defense."

The aunt was annoyed, Muriel was astounded, and Hareton was gripped by the internal overexcitement typical of Americans.

"Either Samuel has gone mad," proclaimed the aunt, "or he has fallen into the domain of Behemoth."[23]

"I'll have to see for myself," Ironcastle replied, mechanically.

"Christ!" protested the aunt. "You don't mean that you're going to go join the lunatic!"

"I shall, Aunt Becky—or, at least, I shall try. He's expecting me—he's not in any doubt as to my determination."

"You're not abandoning your daughter!"

"I shall go with my father," Muriel affirmed, placidly.

There was anxiety in Ironcastle's eyes. "Not into the wilderness?"

"If I were your son, you wouldn't raise any objection. Am I not as well-trained as any man? Haven't I followed you to Arizona, the Rocky Mountains and Alaska? I'm as resistant to fatigue, privations and climate as you are."

"Even so, Muriel, you're a girl."

"That's an obsolete argument. I know that you're going to undertake this journey, and that nothing can stop you. I also know that I don't want to suffer for two years waiting for you to come back. I'm going with you."

"Muriel!" he sighed, emotional and rebellious.

---

[23] Rosny inserts a footnote: "The aunt is evidently adopting the opinion of those Church Fathers who consider Behemoth to be an emblem of Satan."

The domestic reappeared, with a shiny tray. Hareton picked up a visiting card, which read: PHILIPPE DE MA-RANGES. In pencil, someone had added: *And Monique.*

"Here we go!" said Hareton, almost joyfully.

A young man and a young woman were in the drawing-room.

Men like Philippe de Maranges are found in the Ce-vennes, with faces in which every feature is marked with a secret ardor, in which the eyes are the color of rocks. The visi-tor was almost as tall as Ironcastle, but it was Monique who captured the gaze. Reminiscent of some young witches illumi-nated by torchlight or a pyre, she made Rebecca's unease un-derstandable. Her black hair, devoid of any shine, seemed to the aunt to be even more infernal than her eyes, garnished with long bristling stamens, which were all the darker for being framed by child-like sclerotics.

Delilah must have looked like that! Rebecca said to her-self, with fearful admiration.

An invincible attraction made her sit down next to the young woman, who emitted a faint odor of amber and lilies-of-the-valley.

By means of indirect questions, Hareton progressed quite rapidly to the point of Maranges' visit.

"I need," the latter confessed, "to go into business."

"Why?" asked Hareton, nonchalantly.

"For Monique's sake, especially. Our father has left us an inheritance debilitated by debts that are all too definite and credits that are altogether doubtful."

"I fear, dear boy, that you're not cut out for business. You'll have to abandon yourself blindly to a manager, to whom you'll have to give a percentage of the capital. I don't know anyone in Baltimore, but my nephew, Sydney Guthrie, might. Personally, I'm ridiculously incapable."

"It's quite true," Philippe sighed, "that I scarcely have a vocation—but needs must."

Hareton considered the young witch fondly. She con-trasted so perfectly with the fascinating Muriel that he paused to admire the contrast. "There," he muttered, "is an irrefutable objection to theories that extol one superior race: the Pelasgians were the equal of the Hellenes."

Maranges avidly savored Muriel's proximity.

"I seem to remember that you're a good shot?" Hareton said. "And the war has accustomed you to ordeals. I can, therefore, make you a proposition. Would you subject yourself to the ordeals of a Livingstone, a Stanley, or your Marchand?"[24]

"Don't you know that I've always dreamed of such a life?"

"We'd recoil in disgust from the majority of our dreams, if they became practicable. People love to imagine themselves in situations for which they're not naturally cut out. Imagine uncomfortable and dangerous countries, hostile—sometimes cannibalistic—tribes and peoples, privations, fatigue, fevers. Would your dream consent to become a reality?"

"Do you think it's comfortable for three people to freeze at an altitude of 5000 meters in an imperfect and capricious flying machine? I'm ready, on one condition—that the adventure will provide Monique with a dowry."

"The land where I'm going—for I'm the one organizing the expedition—contains living treasures that won't interest you; it also contains precious minerals in abundance: gold, platinum, silver, emeralds, diamonds and topazes. If you're lucky, you might capture a fortune. If you're unlucky, your bones will dry out in a desert. Think about it."

"Hesitation would be stupid. But do I *deserve* a fortune?"

"In the wilderness, a good marksman inevitably renders immense services. I need dependable men—of my own class, and, in consequence, associates. I'm counting on recruiting Sydney Guthrie, who's in Baltimore and planning to undertake a voyage of this sort."

"You mentioned living treasures?" said Philippe.

---

[24] Jean-Baptiste Marchand crossed Africa from west to east in 1898.

"Forget them! That doesn't concern or interest you."

Hareton became inward-looking again, as indicated by his hollow eyes.

Aunt Rebecca smiled maliciously.

The young women exuded the alarming and sweet charm that brought human love out of animal selection, and Philippe mingled Muriel's tresses with the mysterious lands where he was going to rediscover the primitive life.

Part One

I. The Inexorable Night

Evening was about to embrace the ancient forest, and fear, made up of fears accumulated by countless generations, agitated the herbivorous animals. After so many millennia, the forest was almost unaware of humankind. In its obscure and inexhaustible perseverance, it remade the forms engendered before the days in which the Cromlechs and Pyramids were built. The trees remained masters of the region. From dawn to dusk, by day and by night, under red and silvery rays, unvanquished by time and vanquishers of space, they maintained their taciturn realm.

In a formidable region of the forest, branches cracked. A hairy creature detached itself from a baobab and lay down on the ground; its four black hands remained half-closed. It bore a rough resemblance to the deadly animal that had lit the first fire in the ancient darkness, but its jaws and torso were more like those of lions.

Long numbed by an opaque dream in which the past was misted over and the future did not feature at all, it finally voiced a hoarse and soft call. Four creatures emerged: females with the same black faces, the same muscular hands and strange yellow eyes that gleamed in the gloom. Six little ones followed, full of the joyful grace that is the gift of young creatures.

Then the male led his harem toward the Occident, where a vast red Sun, less harsh than the midday Sun, was sinking into the branches.

The gorillas reached the edge of a clearing, hollowed out by fire from the clouds, where the stumps of burned trees persisted, with islets of grasses and ferns. On the far side of the

175

clearing, four monstrous heads rose up among the lianas. They were contemplating an extraordinary spectacle.

A fire! A few upright creatures were throwing branches and twigs on to it. The flames, still pale, were growing with the dying of the sunlight. In the brief twilight they became pink, then scarlet, and their life seemed ever more redoubtable.

The male lions having roared, with elemental force; the large gorilla growled dully. The lions had no knowledge of fire. They had never seen it running through the dry grass or devouring branches; they were only familiar with the importunate light of storms. In the depths of their instinct, however, they feared the heat and palpitation of the flames. The male gorilla knew. Three times he had encountered fire roaring in the forest and spreading immeasurably. Images passed through his opaque memory, of an immense flight, thousands of terrified feet and myriads of terrified wings. He bore scars on his arms and breast, which had been intolerable wounds.

While he paused, prey to sparse memories, his females had drawn closer; the lions, moved by curiosity and uncertainty, marched towards the unusual spectacle with light and heavy steps.

The upright creatures watched the large wild beasts approach.

Within the ring of fires, there were 15 men as black as the gorillas, resembling them in their heavy faces, enormous jaws and long arms. Seven white men and a woman of their race had no analogy to the anthropoid apes save for their hands. There were camels, donkeys and goats. An ancient terror was manifest in waves.

"Don't shoot!" shouted a tall blond man.

The roar of a lion sounded, like the voice of primitive times; the brutal mass of the two males, with their manes and vast shoulders, testified to a terrifying strength.

"Don't shoot!" the blond man repeated. "It's improbable that lions will attack us—and the gorillas even less…"

176

"Improbable, no doubt," replied one of those holding a rifle. "I don't think they'll come past the fires…and yet…" He was almost equal to the blond man in height, but was different in his build, his amber eyes, his black hair and ten indefinable nuances that implied another race or another civilization."

"Twenty rifles and the Maxim!" put in a colossus with granite jaws, whose malachite green eyes were flecked with amber and copper in the firelight. His hair was the same color as the lions'. His name was Sydney Guthrie; he was from Baltimore.

The two male lions roared in unison; the fires lit their compact faces from the front. The anthropoids watched the upright creatures, perhaps thinking that they were captives of the fire.

A servant had unpacked the Maxim machine-gun. Sydney Guthrie loaded his rifle—an elephant-gun—with explosive bullets. Sure of his aim, Philippe de Maranges watched the nearest lion. None of the men was positively afraid, but they experienced a thrill of anxiety.

"In Europe," said Maranges pensively, "when there were still bears in the Alps and wolves in France and Germany, they were only a vague reflection of the times of the mammoth, the rhinoceros and the gray bear. Here there are lions and great apes identical to those one might have encountered 50 or a 100,000 years ago…in the vicinity of a paltry human family armed with clubs, behind a pitiful fire!"

The lions' advance caused the gorillas to beat a slow retreat.

"Pitiful!" Ironcastle replied. "They were more skillful than us in making fires. I can imagine sturdy males, dexterous and muscular, behind enormous fires, who made lions tremble. They might have had miserable evenings, but they must have had magnificent ones. My instinct prefers their time to ours."

"Why?" demanded a fourth interlocutor—an Englishman, whose face was reminiscent of the great Shelley.

"Because they already had the joy of being human without the infernal foresight that spoils all of our days."

"My foresight doesn't make me suffer!" Sydney replied. "It's a staff on which I lean, not a sword suspended above my head."

He was interrupted by an exclamation. Hareton pointed his finger at a little anthropoid that had slyly advanced toward the lions. It was chewing grass near to a clump of ferns. One of the male lions executed a six-meter bound, while the large gorilla and two females ran forward, grunting. Having reached its prey, however, the lion knocked it down with a thrust of its paw.

"Oh! Save it! Save it!" cried a fearful voice. A young woman had stood up—one of those tall blondes who are the glory of the Anglo-Saxon race, Philippe de Maranges raised his weapon, but he was too late; the male gorilla attacked. It was quick, wild and formidable; the black hands clenched around the yellow throat, while the large predator, thrust its muzzle forward, dug its fangs into the ape's breast.

The monstrous beasts swayed from side to side; their panting breath was audible, and the creaking of their enormous muscles. A claw ripped shreds of flesh from the gorilla's abdomen; the gorilla, without letting go, planted its teeth in the carnivore's neck, near the jugular…

"Splendid!" exclaimed Guthrie.

"Terrible!" sighed the young woman.

All of them, hypnotized, contemplated the large red wounds and the reactions of the colossal organisms. The passion of the Romans in the circus carried away Hareton, Philippe, Sydney and Sir George Farnham. Beasts too remained spectators: the three lions and the four female gorillas, one of which was clutching the injured infant gorilla to her breast.

The lion choked. Its vast mouth ceased to bite and opened wide; its claws struck out at random. The gorilla's teeth having sheared through the carotid artery, a scarlet jet streamed over the grasses.

The claw dug into the belly for the last time; then the masses collapsed, and the black hands released the bloody throat. The colossi remained motionless.

178

Carried away by a panic fury, Sydney Guthrie grabbed a flaming branch and threw it at the lions. The men howled. An obscure fear gripped the souls of the carnivores, frightened by the death of the large male; they quit the clearing and disappeared into the depths of the forest.

Surprised by his own action, Guthrie started to laugh. The others remained serious. It was as if they had just witnessed, not a battle between two beasts, but the combat of a lion and a human—and Hareton's voice awoke echoes in the depths of their consciousness when he remarked: "Why shouldn't our ancestors have had the strength of that anthropoid?"

"One might think," the young woman exclaimed, "that the gorilla had moved…"

"Let's go see," proposed Sir George Farnham.

Guthrie examined his elephant-gun. "Let's go!"

"Let's not forget to take torches," Ironcastle added, placidly.

They took torches and went out through a gap between the fires.

The female apes recoiled from the creatures armed with fire, and only paused on the edge of the clearing, from which they contemplated the recumbent male with an obscure anguish. He was no longer moving; his head rested on the belly of the lion, whose mane was crimson, and whose large yellow eyes were vitrified by death.

"Nothing to be done!" Sydney remarked. "Besides, what would be the use?"

"None," Maranges replied, "but seeing it survive would have given me pleasure."

"It seemed so very like a human being," Muriel whispered.

Hareton took a little mirror from his pocket and put it close to the gorilla's mouth. "He's not dead, though," he concluded, displaying a fine mist on the glass. "Even so, how can he recover? He's lost several pints of blood."

"Can't we try?" the young woman asked, timidly.

"We shall, Muriel. The vitality of these brutes is incredible."

Three men carried the gorilla into the ring of fires, where Ironcastle began to disinfect and dress his wounds.

The females had come back. They were moaning strangely in the starlight.

"Poor creatures," said Muriel.

"Their obscure memories forget quickly," said Maranges. "The past hardly exists for them."

Ironcastle continued to examine the wounds. "It's not impossible that he'll live," he concluded, admiring the anthropoid's enormous torso.

"This brute is at least a distant relative of our earliest ancestors…"

"A distant relative! I don't believe that our ancestor was a monkey or an ape!"

Ironcastle continued dressing the wounds. The gorilla's chest was palpitating slightly; it remained plunged in unconsciousness. "If there were a chance for him to recover in the trees…he needs care…by abandoning him…"

"We shan't abandon him!" cried Muriel.

"No, darling, we'll only abandon him if our safety requires it. All the same, he's a burden."

There was a brief muffled exclamation. The oldest of the natives, a man the color of mud, pointed to the north side of the clearing. His hand was trembling.

"What is it, Kouram?"

"Squat Men!" the man moaned.

The clearing seemed deserted; the howls of the wild beasts were sparse and distant.

"I can't see anything," said Maranges, raising his binoculars.

"The Squat Men are there," the old African affirmed.

"Are they redoubtable?"

"They're men born of the Pitiless Forest, cunning and ungraspable."

"Over there!" cried Sir George. He had just glimpsed an upright silhouette among the ferns. It had already vanished; beyond the luminous ring of flames, all they could see was the black forest beneath a sky white with stars.

"The poor devils must have few weapons," said Guthrie, shrugging his shoulders.

"They have poisoned assegais, stone axes and pikes" said Kouram. "Always in large numbers, they're skillful at setting traps, and they eat…" The old man hesitated.

"What do they eat?" said Guthrie, impatiently.

"Their victims, Master."

The fires roared and flickered like living creatures; at intervals, a crackling reminiscent of a plaint was heard; sparks rose up like a swarm of fireflies, and the forest sent forth a light breath, full of sly gentleness and ferocious mystery.

II. The Squat Men

Kouram recounted the legend of the Squat Men, born of the Forest, the Marsh and a Beast from the Clouds.

No one is sure that they are human. Their eyes emit a green glow by night and can see in the dark; their torsos are broad, their limbs short; their hair resembles the fur of hyenas; they have no noses, only two black holes above the mouth; they live in tribes, the least of which includes 100 warriors; they are unskilled in lighting fires, scarcely cook their food, and are ignorant of metals; their weapons are made of wood and stone.

The Squat Men do not know how to cultivate land, nor weave cloth, nor bake pottery; they nourish themselves on meat, nuts, tender shoots, young leaves, roots and mushrooms. They wage war implacably, devouring the wounded and prisoners, even women—and especially children. An inextinguishable hatred animates the Squat Men of the North, who have red hair, against those of the South, who have black hair, and those of the West, who are proud of their blue breasts.

They are not increasing in number; they are diminishing with every passing generation. Their courage scorns death, and does not weaken under torture. In their faces, they resemble buffaloes as much as men; they give off an odor that resembles the odor of roasted flesh.

When Kouram had finished, Maranges asked: "Have you seen these Squat Men?"

"Yes, Master. I had scarcely come of age when they took me prisoner. I was to be eaten. The fire was ready to cook me. The ones who held me had red hair. They were laughing because they had other prisoners and dead men whose wounds were still bleeding. They had tied us up with lianas. The sorcerers were chanting slowly, in an unknown language. They were waving axes and flowery branches…

"Then howls came through the branches, then sharp assegais. The Squat Men with blue breasts had come. There was a battle. I freed myself from the lianas and fled toward the plain…"

Kouram fell silent, becoming contemplative. The times of his youth were crowding within his arid brain. There was consternation in Hareton's gaze, which was fixed on Muriel's sparkling hair. Maranges looked at the young woman and sighed deeply. Sydney Guthrie, however, considered the darkness without fear or anxiety. His youth, his vigor and a joy that came naturally to him hid the future from his thoughts. By virtue of his travels in the Orient, Sir George Farnham had contracted a little of the fatalism of Arabs and Mongols.

"What can these wretches do?" said the colossus. "The machine-gun alone would suffice to wipe out a tribe, the elephant-gun to reduce them to shreds. Maranges and Farnham, as skillful as Leatherstocking,[25] have rifles that fire 20 bullets

---

[25] Bas-de-Cuir [Leatherstocking] is the appellation usually used in France to refer to James Fenimore Cooper's archetypal

a minute. Even Muriel is a fairly good shot. All our men are well-armed. We can exterminate them at a range 20 times greater than that of their assegais."

"They know how to render themselves invisible," Kouram replied. "When an assegai strikes a man or an animal, we do not know where it has come from."

"The ground is bare around our fires…there's nothing growing there but a few ferns and grasses..."

Something whistled in the darkness; a long slender streak passed over the flames, and they saw a little black goat shiver. The assegai was embedded in its flank.

Then the vast starry night became hostile. Hareton, Guthrie, Farnham and Maranges peered into the darkness. They saw nothing but the female anthropoids, whose gleaming eyes were searching the darkness.

Old Kouram had uttered a feeble plaint.

"Can't you see anything?" asked Maranges.

"Master, I can only see that clump of ferns."

Philippe raised his rifle and fired three times, at three different heights. They heard two raucous cries. A dark body leapt up, fell back, and began crawling through the short grass. Maranges hesitated over finishing the fugitive off. The latter disappeared, as if he had been swallowed up by the ground. Long sinister cries—sounds reminiscent of the howling of wolves and the mocking laughter of hyenas—echoed over the clearing and in the forest.

"We're surrounded," Hareton observed.

Silence was restored uniformly. The Southern Cross marked 8 p.m.—and the little black goat, uttering a desperate bleat, collapsed and died.

Kouram, having retrieved the assegai, held it out to Ironcastle. The American examined it attentively and said: "The point is granite. Set up the tents, Kouram."

---

character Natty Bumppo, more often known in England and America by his other nickname, Hawk-Eye.

The tents were erected. One of them was large enough to serve the entire expedition as a dining-room or conference-room. All of them were made of thick canvas, solid and impermeable.

"They wouldn't protect us against bullets," Hareton remarked, "but these assegais won't get through the surface."

When the white men were gathered in the big tent, the men served millet and roasted Cercopithecus.[26] The meal was melancholy; only Guthrie seemed to retain a considerable optimism. He savored the roast, and the millet spiced with red pepper, and remarked: "We'll have to carry out a beat!"

"A beat?" Maranges exclaimed.

"The area around the camp needs to be free, for a distance that exceeds the range of their damned machines. The important thing is to sleep without being disturbed."

They listened with a sport of bewilderment.

"But a sortie would expose us to the assegais," said Iron-castle.

"Why?" asked Guthrie. "That's not necessary."

"Come on, Sydney! It's no joking matter."

"It's you who doesn't remember, Uncle Hareton. I anticipated poisoned arrows. I sent to New York for the necessary vestments…"

"That's true—you mentioned it to me…and I didn't give it another thought.

Guthrie burst out laughing as he finished a slice of Cercopithecus. "Hello!" he said. "Kouram—send someone to fetch the yellow trunk."

Ten minutes later, two natives brought a rather flat trunk upholstered in fawn-colored leather, at which everyone looked with ardent curiosity. Sydney opened the case carefully, displaying a thick pile of garments resembling mackintoshes.

---

[26] *Cercopithecus* is a genus of long-tailed monkeys; the adventurers' sense of biological kinship with other primates obviously extends no further than the great apes.

"A new cloth," he said. Metallic—as supple as rubber. Here are gloves, masks, leggings, hoods…"

"Are you sure that they're proof against arrows?"

"Hold on…" He unfolded one of the mackintoshes, fixed it to the side of the tent and said to Ironcastle: "Would you like to throw the assegai?"

Hareton picked up the weapon and took aim. The spear rebounded from the garment.

"The cloth's still intact!" Maranges observed. "The granite point only caused a dent."

"There can't be any doubt about that," the American went on. "Padding and Mortlock furnished the merchandise— the world's leading company in its area. The Squat Men will waste their venom. Unfortunately, there are the camels, the donkeys and the goats—if they were to perish the loss would be irreparable. That's why I want to flatten everything around the circle where men might hide."

"A tree-trunk and three or four clumps of ferns!" remarked Sir George.

Sydney put on the most voluminous of the garments, fixed a flexible mask over his face, unrolled the leggings from the ankles to the knees, and said: "Let's set things to rights!"

Farnham, Ironcastle, Maranges, Muriel, Kouram and the two white servants, whose names were Patrick Jefferson and Dick Nightingale, imitated him.

"Let's start on the side opposite the one where the animals are located," said Ironcastle.

The scarlet horned Moon was climbing above the depths of the clearing and its rays were soaking the millennial forest like an imponderable wave.

"It's astonishing that these brutes haven't launched any more assegais," said Maranges.

"The Squat Men are patient," Kouram replied. "They've understood that we have redoubtable weapons, and they'll only attack us directly if they have to. Good as they are at hiding, there's not much cover around the fires…"

"You don't think they'll give up their project, then?"

"They're as stubborn as a rhinoceros! They'll follow us as far as the edge of the forest. Nothing can discourage them—and if we kill any of their warriors, the more we kill, the more their hatred will increase."

Farnham, Hareton and Muriel, armed with binoculars, were examining the remoter parts of the site.

"Nothing!" said Hareton.

"No, nothing at all," Farnham agreed. "We can get going." He had picked up a long-handle axe, which was very sharp, to do the work of a sickle.

Muriel leaned over the gorilla. It had not come out of its coma, and resembled a corpse.

"He'll pull through," said Maranges, softly.

The blonde head was raised again, and the young people looked at one another. A notion as imprecise as the nocturnal branches swelled Philippe's bosom. Muriel was calm, and slightly suspicious.

"Do you think so?" she said. "He's lost almost all his blood…"

"Half, at most…"

A whimpering voice made them turn their heads. The female anthropoids were still there. The little ones and one of the mothers were asleep; the others were on watch.

"They're anxious," said Kouram. "They know that the Squat Men have us surrounded…and they also know that the male is among us."

"They won't attack us, will they?" Ironcastle asked.

"I don't think so, Master; you haven't finished off the gorilla…they can smell him!"

"Let's go!" said Guthrie.

The little troop went through a gap and found themselves outside the circle. First, Guthrie headed for the nearest clump of ferns and cut it down with a few sweeps of the axe. Then he mowed down the long grass, felled the stump of a palm-tree and moved toward the bush at which Maranges had fired. When he had got rid of it, there was no more cover within assegai range in which the Squat Men could render themselves invisible.

"But how was the wounded man able to disappear?"

"Into a ditch," Kouram replied. He overtook Maranges and Guthrie. "Here it is."

Guthrie, Maranges and Farnham caught up with him in two strides.

They perceived a man lying in a crevice, completely motionless. Hair as red as a fox's fur covered his skull and was gathered in tufts on his cheeks. He had a cubic skull, truncated at the jaws, which seemed to be set directly on the shoulders, skin the color of peat, and flattened arms that terminated in extraordinarily short hands, the general form of which was reminiscent of the carapace of a crab. His feet were shorter still, with vague, scarcely-existent toes seemingly covered in a horny substance. Ample shoulders and a broad, thickset torso justified the race's name.

The man was almost naked; blood had coagulated on his chest and abdomen; a belt of raw animal-skin maintained a green axe and a stone knife. Two assegais lay in the crevice.

"The three bullets hit him," Kouram remarked, "but he's not dead. Shall we finish him off?"

"Don't do that!" exclaimed Maranges, horrified.

"He's a hostage," said Guthrie, phlegmatically. He bent down and lifted up the Squat Man as he might have lifted up a child. A sort of groan resounded; half a dozen assegais whistled through the air, two of which struck Kouram and Guthrie. The colossus burst out laughing, while Kouram informed the invisible enemies, by means of gestures, that their attack had been in vain.

Farnham's keen eyes scanned the cover. There was little enough of it. About 50 meters away, however, there was a bush that might have concealed two or three men.

"What should we do?" Sir George asked.

"It's essential that they're scared of us! No attack can be permitted without response. Fire!"

Shouldering his elephant-gun, Guthrie fired toward a patch that stuck out in the center of the bush. The shot was followed by an explosion and a furious clamor. A body reared up and fell back, inanimate.

"Poor brute!" sighed Philippe.

"Don't waste your pity," Sydney replied. "The poor brutes are murderers by design and cannibals on principle. There's no other way of informing them of our strength." He put the body of the unconscious man under his arm and headed back to the camp. The white servants got rid of all the hiding-places that Maranges and Guthrie had not attacked. No man could hide within a radius of 100 meters, however cunning he might be.

Sydney deposited the Squat Man next to the gorilla. Hareton took responsibility for dressing his wounds; the injured man uttered two or three groans without coming out of his swoon.

"He's not as badly wounded as the anthropoid."

Kouram studied the Squat Man with hateful apprehension. "Better to kill him," he said. "It'll be necessary to watch him continuously."

"We have ropes!" said Guthrie, lighting his pipe. "The night will be calm...and tomorrow, it'll be light."

Having taken off her mask and metal hood, Muriel contemplated great Orion, a constellation of her native land, and the Southern Cross, which symbolized the unknown land. Philippe was enchanted in the presence of the girl, who was reminiscent of the oreads, the nymphs who haunt the forest at dawn, and the undines who spring forth from crepuscular lakes. In the sinister wilderness, she brought the man's thoughts into focus. The moment was all the more redoubtable for it. Philippe paled at the thought that the peril that threatened the males threatened her even more...

"Can't we do anything for those poor creatures?" she said, pointing to the female anthropoids.

188

"They have no need of us," he said, smiling. "The entire forest is their realm, where everything in which gorillas delight grows in abundance."

"But you can see that they aren't going away. Their anxiety is visible...they must be afraid of the red Squat Men. The Squat Men haven't attacked them though."

Muriel was speaking almost mysteriously, all the more seductive for being lost in the primal forest, in the bosom of the same traps that menaced, at the dawn of humankind, the ancestors from whom her precious form distanced her even more than the millennia.

"They haven't attacked them," he said, "because they're saving their weapons..."

"For us!" she said, with a sigh, turning her head toward Ironcastle, who had finished bandaging the Squat Man,

His heart full of a tragic softness, Philippe savored the stellar space, the luminous grayness that was soaking the confused regions of the undergrowth and the flexible daughter of America, similar to the daughters of the pale isle where the pagan Angels who had charmed Saint Gregory had once lived.

III. The Water-Hole

The lot had fallen to Hareton to take the first watch. Three natives watched with him, scanning the perimeter of the clearing.

It was a night similar to all the nights of that forest, a night of ambush and murder, of triumphs and miseries, a storm of yelping, roaring, howling, belling, croaking and cries of agony, flesh devoured alive, bellies swollen and bellies consumed, anguish, terror, ferocity and greed, the feasting of some and the horror of others, suffering nourishing sensuality, death restoring life...

Every night for the last 100,000 years, Hareton thought, *every night without respite and without mercy...every night*

189

*the charming or ingenious beasts, which have so much diffi-
culty in growing, have perished thus in accordance with inconceivable necessity...and are perishing still! Lord, how
mysterious your will is!*

The pale light of the firmament weighed lightly on the
black night of the forest; odors drifted, as fresh as springs, as
sweet as music, as intoxicating as young women, as savage as
lions, as equivocal as reptiles...

A heavy melancholy gripped the American. Full of remorse for having brought Muriel, he could not understand his
weakness. *It is necessary to believe*, he said to himself, *that
every man not only has his hour but also his season of madness.*

Because he was energetic in action and followed his
projects through, he could not understand his irresolution in
respect of Muriel. She had never left him. She was the last
member of his immediate family, Hareton having lost his two
sons when the *Thunder* was torpedoed off the Spanish coast.
Since then, he had been unable to resist the desires and determination of his daughter.

As dawn approached, a mist settled on the clearing and
rendered the view less clear; the veiled moonlight deformed
the shapes of the trees; the stars were enveloped by a pale tulle
in which they vacillated like feeble night-lights.

Then, for no reason, Ironcastle imagined Muriel carried
off by Squat Men, and frightful images tormented him.

Three jackals paused, turning towards the fire. Hareton
considered their dog-like muzzles, pointed ears and vigilant
eyes with a kind of sympathy. They fled into the undergrowth;
everything fell back into a vast silence.

The enemy is there, though! the voyager said to himself.

Nothing revealed his presence; the forest seemed to be
alone with its predators, thousands of herbivores having ex-
pired by tooth and claw.

In spite of everything, Hareton submitted to the vast
charm of that silence punctuated by slight sounds: the crackle

190

of the flames, the rustling passage of animals, the sighing of the leaves...

A whiter vapor rose up to the stars: the imponderable vapor of first light. The dew hissed in the fires; the three attentive men scrutinized the primordial light that seemed to be born as much of the trees as the firmament. The moving deception of the dawn passed in a moment; daylight had arrived in the unsoundable depths; millions of fearful insects rose up, no longer fearful of life.

Hareton took a little Bible from his pocket and read, with the awe of his race:

"He turneth rivers into a wilderness, and the watersprings into dry ground;

"A fruitful land into barrenness, for the wickedness of them that dwell therein.

"He turneth the wilderness into a standing water, and dry ground into watersprings.

"And there he maketh the hungry to dwell, that they may prepare a city for habitation."[27]

Putting his hands together, he prayed—for his life was divided into two watertight compartments; in one was his faith in Science, in the other his faith in Revelation.

There! he said to himself. *It's a matter of rendering the animals invulnerable. I would have been able to save the goat by cauterizing its wound...*

A shadow fell beside him; before turning around he knew that it was Muriel. "Darling!" he murmured. "I was wrong to obey your will."

"Are you so sure," she said, "that we would not have run greater dangers without leaving our own country?"

She took the little Bible from her father's hands and, turning the pages at random, she read: "Surely he shall deliver thee from the snare of the fowler, and from the noisome pesti-

---

[27] *Psalm* 107:33-36.

lence."[28] She sighed, and added: "Who knows what's happening in America?"

A jovial laugh interrupted her; the giant figure of Guthrie loomed up in front of the dying flames. "What could be happening that is not the repetition of what was happening before our departure? I assume that thousands of ships are filling the ports of the United States, that the railways are transporting city-dwellers who are leaving the beaches to return to the cities, that the factories are humming, that the crop-growers are thinking about the autumn sowing, that honest people are taking their evening meals—for night is falling there—and that buses, trams and automobiles are filling the streets of Baltimore."

"Undoubtedly," said Philippe's grave voice, "but there might also be great cataclysms."

"An earthquake?" asked Farnham.

"Why not? Is there a conclusive reason why England and France should be eternally protected from earthquakes? In any case, the United States is familiar with them. But I was thinking about something else…"

Bright daylight—a creative and murderous light—took possession of the forest. The last fires were put out. The dazzle of wings appeared in the realm of the braches.

"What are we going to do?" asked Hareton.

"Eat breakfast," Sydney replied. "Then we'll hold a council of war."

Kouram gave the necessary orders; two natives brought tea, coffee, pickles, jams, biscuits, smoked buffalo and sausages.

Guthrie ate with the joyous zest that he brought to all meals. "How is the gorilla?" he asked Kouram.

"He's still unconscious, Master—but the Squat Man is beginning to wake up."

Philippe served Muriel's breakfast; while crunching biscuits and drinking tea, the young woman studied the surround-

---

[28] *Psalm* 91:3

192

ings. "They're still there," she murmured. She pointed to the group of anthropoids, which had slept close to the fires.

"That's strange," Philippe replied. "Kouram's right, I think; they're afraid of the Squat Men—who can scarcely spare a thought for gorillas, though, when they're watching enemies like us!"

Muriel's large turquoise eyes became thoughtful. In a whisper, Philippe said to himself: "*And, like her, dread to see the days end, of those who die with her!*"[29]

Having finished his smoked buffalo and coffee, Guthrie said: "Now let's make a plan. As long as we stay in the clearing, we'll be protected from the Squat Men. To attack us, they'd have to come out in the open. Except that we can't stay in the clearing without water and wood. There's water a mile away…wood is indispensable."

"What will we gain by making camp?" asked Maranges.

"We'll be able to work to render as invulnerable as possible those of our men who can't be equipped with the metallic mackintoshes," said Ironcastle. "We can also search for the best means of safeguarding our animals, the loss of which would be a disaster."

"What if the damned cannibals receive reinforcements?"

Hareton turned an anxious face to Kouram. "Is that possible?"

"It's possible, Master—but the red Squat Men rarely make alliances, except against the blue-breasted Squat Men. Their tribes live far apart."

"It would be more likely, then," Philippe observed, "that our besiegers would encounter others of their kind during a march."

---

[29] These are the concluding words of "La jeune captive," written by the poet André Chenier on the night before his execution, during the Terror, in 1794; the poem's immediate reference is to Aimée de Coigny, who was guillotined on the same day. The version in the Flammarion text omits a significant comma, which I have restored to the translation.

"We'll make camp, then?" asked Sydney, insouciantly.

"That's my opinion," Ironcastle replied.

"And mine," Sir George agreed, placidly.

"How's the water-supply, Kouram?"

"We don't have enough for the camels, the donkeys and the goats to drink. We were counting on the water-hole."

"Then a sortie is unavoidable."

Beyond the circle of embers and the bare zone there was nothing but islets of ferns, grass and brushwood—and then the mysterious realm of the trees. The water-hole was invisible.

"The camp needs to be well-guarded," said Guthrie. "You, Uncle Hareton, are the best machine-gunner; you ought to stay, with Muriel, Patrick Jefferson and most of the natives. Farnham, Maranges, Kouram, Dick Nightingale, two men and I will make a sortie as far as the water-hole. It's a pity that we can't take a camel…"

Ironcastle shook his head. A vast anxiety was weighing upon him. He did not like the idea of the sortie at all. "We can wait a while longer!"

"No!" Guthrie retorted. "If we wait, we'll be running even greater risks. We need to decide now."

"Sydney's right," said Philippe.

The party making the sortie was fitted out with mackintoshes and metallic masks. Guthrie had his elephant-gun, an axe and two revolvers. Maranges' and Farnham's armaments were identical, except for their rifles. Dick Nightingale carried a solid broad-bladed dirk.

"Let's go!"

The words fell like the vibration of a tocsin. A slight shiver shook the young woman's shoulders. The forest seemed more ferocious, more immense and more deceptive. Philippe took a last look at the girl from Baltimore.

It was the natives who took the lead. Kouram had a subtle experience, purchased by ten brushes with death; the others opened their keen senses to the surroundings. The three of them formed a triangle with a broad base. Philippe, whose hearing was extraordinary, followed Kouram. Sydney took long slow strides, his great strength reassuring the natives even more than the elephant-gun or Farnham's and Maranges' infallible carbines. The others brought up the rear.

They headed eastwards. A warthog went by under the palm-trees; antelopes ran away; the Squat Men remained invisible. At the edge of the clearing, Kouram, craning his neck, spotted green shadows.

"Watch out!" said Philippe. Among the slight cracking sounds and furtive sliding—the almost-imperceptible noises that seemed to be the breath of the forest—he thought he could hear some kind of organized movement, which drew away and reformed to the rear.

Trails seem to have been marked out—ancient pathways along which animals, and sometimes humans, had passed for centuries to go to the water-hole. The little troop tightened its ranks, with Kouram still in the lead, followed closely by the other two natives.

"Perhaps they've decamped?" Guthrie whispered.

"I've heard too many bodies slipping through the plants," Maranges replied.

"You have the ears of a wolf!"

Kouram paused; one of the men put his ear to the ground. Philippe had already heard. "Someone's moving over there," he said, pointing at a thicket to the right of a baobab.

"It's them," said Kouram. "But they're also in front of us…and to the left. They're surrounding us. They know we're going to the water-hole."

The invisible presence became nerve-racking. They were caught in a supple, moving and solid trap—a living trap that only moved away to close in more effectively.

In the green light, a silvery reflection revealed water, mother of all creatures. As they drew closer, they made out a small lake. Giant water-lilies displayed their petals; a flock of birds took off with the long clatter of wings; and anxious gnu stopped drinking.

Extended between shores more capricious than the fjords of Norway, thick with feverish and avid vegetation, the lake was almost shapeless.

The expedition stopped near a sort of promontory where the plants had been ripped up by elephants, rhinoceroses, lions, buffaloes, warthogs and antelopes. Clear and almost fresh, the water-hole was presumably fed by a subterranean spring; three small streams carried the water away.

The men drank avidly. Less inured to the paludal bacteria, the white men, having filled their water-bottles, poured a few droplets of a yellowish liquid into them.

"Now the canisters!"

A clamor fantastic and terrible went up, which had a sort of rhythm to it—two howls followed by a groan. Human forms emerged and disappeared. Then silence fell again, as penetrating as a lull in a storm.

"That's the voice of 100 men!" Kouram murmured.

The faces of the natives had become leaden and ashen. Farnham and Guthrie scanned the undergrowth. Guthrie, standing tall like Ajax, son of Telamon, raised his powerful elephant-gun...

Assegais flew, which struck the metallic garments fruitlessly or fell into the lake.

"We *would have* been killed!" observed Sydney, placidly.

"These assegais might be useful," Sir George remarked, picking up the one that had rebounded from his breast. "They're as dangerous to them as to us."

"Yes, these degraded worms are supplying us with weapons..."

The canisters having been deposited on the promontory, the little troop waited, arranged in a semicircle with the lake behind them. All the animals had fled; the banks were deserted. A single funereal bird skimmed the surface of the water.

"What are they waiting for?" Guthrie exclaimed, with a hint of impatience.

"They want to see if the assegais have been fatal," Kouram replied. "The poison only acts after a time of 1000 paces."

Nothing was audible but the distant voices of parrots and a monkey ululating on the far side of the lake. The silence seemed interminable. Then the clamor resumed, more raucous than before, and two bands of Squat Men charged. There were at least 60, red-bearded, armed with pikes, clubs or jade axes.

"Fire!" cried Farnham.

He and Maranges, taking aim with infallible precision, had put four men down by the time the elephant-gun raised its resounding voice. The latter's effect was monstrous; arms, legs, feet and red bones were scattered. A head could be seen suspended by its hair from the branches of a baobab; entrails were writhing like blue serpents.

Howling with terror, the Squat Men beat a retreat and dissipated, save for one group that had surged out of the reeds, which fell upon the travelers wildly. A blow from a club knocked Kouram down; assailed by two Squat Men, a native collapsed, and two adversaries appeared in front of Philippe. Red lead made their faces bloody; as their eyes shone, their stout arms raised green axes.

Parrying the blows, Maranges laid out one of his antagonists on the ground, while the second, attacking obliquely, brought down his weapon—but Philippe had stepped aside. Carried forward by his momentum, the Squat Man came too close to the bank; then, lashing out with his boot, Maranges kicked him into the lake.

Guthrie confronted three Squat Men. They hesitated, alarmed by the giant's stature. Sydney knocked one aggressor's pike out of his hands, grabbed him by the neck, whirled him like a club and hurled him at his companions. Sir George, coming to the rescue, felled the stoutest of the aggressors with the butt of his gun.

There was a rout. The Squat Men who were uninjured fled into the shelter of the reeds; the wounded crawled toward the forest, and—as had been agreed—Guthrie sounded the whistle-blasts, one long and two short, to signal to Ironcastle that the danger had passed.

"We need prisoners," Farnham remarked, taking hold of a fugitive.

Guthrie and Dick having done likewise, four wounded men remained in the victors' hands.

"How's Kouram?" said Maranges, anxiously.

Kouram replied with a sigh, followed by a groan. The thickness of his hair and the solid bones of his skull had saved him. The second native was already on his feet, with no other damage than a broken collar-bone.

Twenty minutes later, the expedition returned to the camp. They formed up into a square, in the center of which the captives were dragged. Twice, the war-cry of the Squat Men echoed in the woody arcades, but there was no attack.

When he heard the fusillade, Ironcastle, ready for combat, brought the machine-gun forward; Guthrie's signals calmed him down. During the interval that followed, his anxiety began to increase again. He was about to make a sortie of his own, in spite of everything, when the expedition emerged from the eastern edge of the clearing.

The caravan advanced slowly, delayed by the captives.

"No losses?" Hareton shouted, when Philippe and Guthrie were close enough.

"None...only one man with an injured shoulder."

Involuntarily, Muriel turned to Maranges, whom she liked for his character and sensitivity. "Were there many of them?" she asked.

It was Guthrie who replied. "Sixty attacked head on; ten came from the reeds. If that's the whole tribe, our victory is almost certain."

"It's not the whole tribe," Kouram declared.

"He's right," said Philippe. "There were voices behind them. When the attack failed, the reserves didn't put in an appearance."

"How many warriors do you think there are?" Ironcastle asked the old man.

"At least ten times the fingers of the hands, and another five times," Kouram replied.

"A hundred and fifty. They can't take the camp by storm…"

"They won't try," said Kouram, "and they won't attack again in large numbers until they've drawn us into a trap. They know our weapons now. They know that the assegais are useless against the yellow cloaks."

"You don't believe they'll give up trailing us?"

"They'll be all around us as surely as the light is over the forest."

Ironcastle bowed his head pensively.

"We can't prepare our departure in one day," Maranges put in, fearful for Muriel.

"That's certain," agreed Hareton, whose anxiety had the same object. "But we need water and food, for ourselves and our animals."

"I don't think they'll attack us again on the path to the water-hole," said Sydney.

"No, Master," Kouram agreed. "They won't attack today, or tomorrow. They'll wait for us to leave. The livestock will be able to graze, under the protection of the rifles."

The speakers felt the unknowns of men and circumstances weighing upon them. Between them and their fatherlands were forests, deserts and oceans; close at hand, a strange enemy, human and bestial, which had scarcely changed in a hundred centuries. That enemy was poorly armed, in a derisory manner, but terrifying in the force of their numbers, their cunning and their stubbornness. In spite of their rifles, their machine-gun and their armor, the travelers were prey…

"How are the wounded?" asked Maranges.

Hareton pointed to a small tent. "They're in there. The man has regained consciousness, but he's extremely weak. The gorilla is still torpid."

They turned their attention to the captives. None was dangerously wounded. With their compact faces, smeared with red lead, their ferocious eyes and barrel chests, they gave rise to grim and equivocal impressions.

"I think they're uglier than gorillas!" said Guthrie. "There's something of the hyena and the rhinoceros about them."

"It's not their ugliness that strikes me," said Hareton, "but their expression. That expression is human, but it's humanity at its worst. It reveals, to an extreme degree, a viciousness that one doesn't find in monkeys or other men."

"What about panthers…or tigers?" queried Muriel.

"They're *naïvely* ferocious," Hareton replied. "They're not malevolent. Malevolence involves a kind of strange transcendence of the worst of carnivores. That transcendence only attains its full development in our peers. To judge by their physiognomy, these Squat Men are among the most malevolent of human beings."

"That's still a kind of superiority!" muttered Farnham.

Kouram, who had listened without understanding, said forcefully: "Don't keep the captives! They're more dangerous than serpents! They'll make signals to the other Squat Men. Why not cut off their heads?"

IV. The Python and the Warthog

For three days, the travelers worked to prepare their departure. An antelope having been captured by the natives, Ironcastle carried out experiments with the poisoned assegais; immediate cauterization neutralized the effects of the poison.

"Good!" said Guthrie, who had watched the experiments. "Now we need to try it on one of the captives."

"I don't have the right!" his uncle replied.

"As far as I'm concerned, it's a duty," the nephew replied. "To hesitate between the lives of brave men and that of one of these bandits is mere folly."

Armed with an assegai, he went to fetch one of the captives, who were under guard in a large tent. It was the most thickset of the group; he was fully half as broad as he was tall. His round eyes fixed upon the giant with superstitious ferocity. After a brief hesitation, Sydney pricked the Squat Man on the shoulder. The man stiffened; his face expressed hatred and disdain.

"There you are, Uncle Hareton—I take the sin upon myself alone. Be the good healer!"

Ironcastle swiftly cauterized the wound. After half an hour, no symptoms of poisoning had appeared.

"You can see that I did the right thing!" the colossus concluded, taking hold of the Squat Man again. "We're sure now that cauterization can save men as well as animals."

As Kouram had predicted, there was no further attack.

Every morning, an expedition set out for the lake. Two camels were taken, covered in strong canvas—the canvas that was used to repair the tents. The natives brought back forge, which added to the grass and young shoots that the camels, donkeys and goats grazed in the clearing.

The Squat Men remained invisible; there was no indication of their presence.

"One could easily believe that they'd decamped," Maranges said, at the end of the fourth day. He had been listening to the rumors and slight noises of the surroundings for some time, with ears keener than a jackal's.

"They won't decamp until they're forced to," said Kouram. "They're all around us…but far enough away for us to be unable to hear or smell them!"

The captives were scarcely feeling the pain of their wounds, except for the one that had been taken on the first evening. Retaining an impassive attitude and constantly on the alert, none of them responded to the signs by means of which Ironcastle and his companions attempted to make themselves understood. Their faces, as immutable as stone masks, seemed no less stupid than the faces of hippopotamuses or rhinoceroses. Nevertheless, two influences gradually generated light in their obscure souls. At the sight of Guthrie, their eyes dilated ferociously; at the sight of Muriel, those same eyes reflected a vague mysticism.

"It's through the two of you that we must try to tame them," said Hareton.

Those words did not satisfy Maranges; something in the bestial pupils irritated his affection.

Another event engaged the travelers' interest. The gorilla had recovered consciousness. His debility was extreme; he shivered with fever. When he realized that he was in the presence of humans, he manifested a weak, genuinely fearful emotion; his eyelids quivered, and he tried to raise his head, but, sensing his impotence, became resigned. Because no one did him any harm, and repetition has more effect on animals than humans, he became accustomed to his entourage. Save for a few recurrences of aversion or fear, he received the explorers' visits placidly; those of Ironcastle, who fed and cared for him, became agreeable to him.

"He's certainly less untamable than these Squat brutes!" said the naturalist. "We'll domesticate him…"

The expedition was under way again.

The immense forest seemed far from inextricable. The trees, often monstrous—especially the baobabs and the fig-trees—rarely formed clumps. Lianas were not abundant, nor were thorny trees and bushes.

"This forest is comfortable," remarked Sydney, who marched at the head with Sir George and Kouram. "I'm astonished to have encountered so few humans here."

"Not so few!" Farnham retorted. "In the outskirts, we counted at least three sorts of natives, which implies numerous tribes—and we're being pursued by the Squat Men, who are not negligible."

"They're the ones who prevent other men from extending further," Kouram remarked.

There were a great many contrasts between Farnham and Guthrie, although both of them were typical Anglo-Saxons—with a hint of Celt in the American. Sir George had an internal life as powerful as Ironcastle's, while Sydney's consciousness was scattered in gusts. In times of peril, Farnham retreated into himself, to the point of seeming indifferent or plunged into reverie. At such times, it was as if all his emotions had been banished, chased into the mists of the unconscious; in the forefront of his mind, there was only the vigilance of his senses and the calculations of purely objective thought. By contrast, peril excited Guthrie violently, and during combat he was seized by a sort of light vertigo, which he enjoyed tremendously, and which did not prevent him from maintaining control over his decisions and his movements.

In sum, Farnham had an earnest bravery, Guthrie a joyful bravery.

Their opinions differed as much as their character. Sydney, like Aunt Rebecca, mingled spiritualism and occultism with his faith, while Sir George conformed to the rites of the Church of England, which he accepted integrally. Each of them admitted the diversity of sects, provided that the fundamental prescriptions of the gospels were followed.

Two days went by without incident. In the silent and hermetic forest, only a few furtive animals fled before the caravan. Even the birds were silent, except for the parrots, which raised their strident voices intermittently. There was no trace of humans. Farnham and Guthrie thought that the Squat Men were staying behind them; even Kouram doubted their presence.

In the afternoon of the third day, the trees became more widely spaced, and they found themselves in a sort of forested savannah, in which wooded islands alternated with expanses of grass and desert sands. The region was divided into two quite distinct zones; to the east, the savannah was increasingly predominant; to the west, the forest continued, interrupted by clearings. The explorers kept to the borderland of the two regions, in order to ensure themselves of the advantages of both.

A marsh overlapping the edge of the forest, encroached on the savannah, edged by tall papyrus, whose umbels trembled in the gentle breeze that was incessantly rising and fading away. All around was a haunt of reptiles, moist, chaotic and uneven. Giant water-lilies spread out their bowl-like foliage, enveloped by algae hospitable to tenebrous animals, while birds of beryl, plush and sulfur fled as the human approached.

"We'll stop for lunch and a siesta," Hareton proposed.

While the men installed the caravan beneath the baobabs, Muriel, Sir George, Sydney and Philippe explored the shore of the marsh.

Muriel paused near a creek. Around sacred flowers, immense butterflies of fire and jonquil, and scarlet, gray-green or turquoise flies danced their light sarabands; a frog as big as a rat jumped into the torpid water; the occasional appearance of flaccid forms, or the emergence of a gaping mouth, and the hectic flight of black fish testified to the presence of monstrous life.

A fabulous apparition drew Muriel out of her contemplation. More than any of the creatures encountered in the age-old forest, it evoked obscure forces, the frightful chaos of the world. A larva as thick and long as a tree-trunk, covered in a damascene bark, it crawled with a repulsive agility, guided by a tiny head with eyes like glass beads. Everything that was hideous about an earthworm, a leech or a slug was manifested therein on a colossal scale. It stopped; it was impossible to tell whether it had seen the young woman—its mineral eyes had no gaze.

A savage disgust and a sinister vertigo congealed Muriel's flesh, and the scream that rose to her larynx could not be completed. Before the power of this creature issued from inferior regions, which seemed a vile prodigy, her terror was more profound and her revulsion more frightful than before the ferocity of a tiger or a lion.

The threat was still latent. In the tenebrous instinct of the python, the upright creature had no familiar form—but Muriel's trembling legs collided with a tree-trunk; she stumbled, fell to her knees, and seemed smaller. Excited by her fall, the python crawled rapidly, coiled its vast body around the young woman—and the charming individual was no longer anything but the reptile's prey.

Again she tried to scream; horror stifled her voice; the head of the python reared up before her pale face and her beautiful dying eyes; the giant worm's muscles choked off her breath and caused her vertebrae to creak. She felt her consciousness vacillate; death floated above her; her mind sank into darkness…

Sir George and Philippe were marching in single file along the shore of the marsh. The water, the grass, the reeds and the bushes displayed the immeasurable frissons of life.

"This place exhibits a terrifying fecundity," Sir George remarked. "The insects especially…"

"The insects are the abomination of the world!" Philippe interjected. "Look at these flies...there isn't a single corner of this place of which they haven't taken possession. There they are, ready to annihilate everything and devour everything. We shall perish by the insects, Sir George…"

As he was speaking, Sir George, having rounded a clump of papyrus, uttered a horse cry and his eyes grew wide.

"That's frightful!" he exclaimed.

Immediately, the same fear passed through Philippe.

On the promontory, the python had finished wrapping itself around Muriel and was squeezing her in its formidable vortex. Her scintillating head had slumped on to her shoulder, and a horrible charm emanated from that grace, captive of the monster.

Instinctively, Philippe had raised his rifle, but Sir George shouted: "Revolvers and knives!"

They bounded forward; reaching the promontory in a flash. There was no way of knowing whether the creature perceived their presence. It undulated, quivering, entirely devoted to its voracious task.

Simultaneously, Sir George and Philippe peppered the head with revolver shots, and then began slicing through the enormous body. The coils loosened and came undone. Philippe had grabbed hold of the young woman and he laid her down on the grass. She was coming round already, a haggard smile on her oread's face.

"You mustn't say anything to my father!"

"We shan't say a word," Sir George promised.

When she was on her feet again she laughed lightly, the joy of being alive still mingled with fear and disgust. "That death was too vile! You've saved my life twice over!" She looked away, because she wanted to see the strange corpse of the python.

Guthrie was also following the shore of the marsh. In his own way, he admired that frightful creation, which converted mineral substances into living matter inexhaustibly. As far as the eye could see, the water nourished the paludal vegetation and offered glimpses of the fabulous animality that swarmed in its depths.

"If there were land and water everywhere," Guthrie muttered, "the entire planet would be alive…and yet, water can sustain it almost by itself. What a damned prodigy the Sargasso Sea is! I thought our steamer would never get out of it! That incomprehensible world, from sperm whales to zoophytes, and from sharks to the Argonauts that inhabit its gulfs! And within the gulfs, at depths of 5000, 10,000 meters, the abyssal creatures…in truth, as the Bible says, we have superior waters and inferior waters filling the Expanse…and the whole Expanse is alive. It's magnificent and disgusting!"

A grunt cut his soliloquy short. It had come from a phantasmagorical bay full of muddy redoubts of vegetation and firm ground where 20 herds might have found refuge. A hundred paces away stood a fantastic animal, a sort of long-legged wild pig with a colossal head, a swollen face full of warts, an opaque muzzle armed with sharp and trenchant curved tusks, and bare skin, its hair being concentrated along the spine in a long mane.

By Old Nick, the young man thought, *that's a warthog, and a damned fine example of the species...*

The animal grunted. Brutal and bad-tempered, incoherent, ferocious and courageous in its mentality, it only recoiled in confrontation with a rhinoceros, an elephant or a lion. Even then, if cornered, it accepted the battle; how many times in the millennial darkness had a lion succumbed to thrusts of curved tusks? Ever ready for combat, though, the warthog does seek it out. That requires a moment of madness, the savage and ferocious enchantment of lust, fear transformed into fury, or the necessity of clearing a passage.

This one was grunting because it suspected an attack. Between velvet tufts, the little eyes gleamed, and the verrucose cheeks were visibly quivering.

"We're short of provisions," Guthrie muttered.

Even so, he hesitated, indulgent toward well-constructed beasts. This one, a male in the prime of life, had what was required to father a thousand redoubtable warthogs—and Guthrie, like Theodore Roosevelt, held that there would be animals of noble heritage for a long time yet, handsome or monstrous, exceedingly fast, strong and cunning.

As he was meditating, a second warthog emerged from the marsh, and immediately afterwards, ten more frightful and superb snouts. They were all grunting, anxious and surly—and suddenly, starting to gallop, they seemed to hurl themselves upon Guthrie. He threw himself to the left, while the herd held its course—but the large male that had emerged first came on blindly.

Guthrie did not have the time to unsheathe his weapon or take aim; the long tusks were seeking to disembowel him when, with a mighty blow of his fist, formidably swung, he struck the beast behind the ear. That blow, squarely delivered, caused the warthog to stumble; it drew back, coughing. Its eyes flashed fire.

Sydney laughed—a barbaric and joyful laughter—proud of having shaken the powerful beast, and he shouted: "Halloo! Time! Come on!"

The warthog resumed the attack, which the American avoided with a sidestep to the left; then his fists fell like hammers, on the neck, the flanks and the snout. The beast whirled, moved sideways, and charged, panting.

The antagonists found themselves on the edge of a ditch, and suddenly, grabbing hold of the warthog's foot and shoving its shoulder, Sydney launched it into the mud.

The animal struggled there, got up and made for the other side, while Sydney, more glorious than Hercules, the conqueror of the Erymanthian Boar, shouted: "I grant you mercy, monster of the marshes!"

V. The Beasts' Cave

The plants of the forest region increased in number; the trees, more abundant, with larger crowns and thicker undergrowth, rendered the march difficult. It was necessary to retreat to the savannah. Inhospitable, it consisted of red earth and lamentable grass, alternating with rocky surfaces; purple snakes slid into the crevices, blue lizards warmed themselves on rocks; here and there, an ostrich raced away into the wilderness…

Then there was nothing more than rocks and lichens, pale corroders of the stone, in the course of the centuries…

Finally, the ridges and indentations of a chain of hills loomed up.

Having climbed up to a summit, Guthrie called out enthusiastically. Lost between three millennial solitudes—the forest, the savannah and the desert—a lake extended its inexhaustible waves.

The forest, filling the Orient with its arboreal nations, was separated from the savannah by red rocks and dead sands, where even lichens perished. After a scrubland, the savannah took possession of the Occident.

By virtue of that conjunction of territories, the lake entertained on its shores all the strange beasts of the desert, the sly predators of the grassland, and the countless guests of the branches: the ostrich and the giraffe, the baroque warthog and the monstrous rhinoceros, the hippopotamus and the wild pig, the lion, the leopard and the panther, the jackal, the hyena and the wolf, the antelope, the zebra, the dromedary and the quagga, the gorilla, the hamadryas baboon, the hooded guenon, the elephant and the buffalo, the python and the crocodile, eagles and vultures, storks, ibises, cranes, flamingos, egrets and kingfishers…

"An admirable wilderness, created for all the animals in the Ark," said Guthrie. "For how many thousands of years has this lake bore witness to its immense life, which humans will have destroyed or domesticated before the end of the 20th century?"

"Do you think they'll destroy it?" Farnham queried. "If God wills it—but my own opinion is that He won't. Why? For 300 years, has He not visibly protected civilization? Especially Anglo-Saxon civilization. Is it not written: 'Replenish the Earth, and subdue it; and have dominion over the fish of the sea, and over the fowl of the air, and over every living thing that moveth upon the Earth'?[30]

"But what is not written is 'Destroy!' Now, we have destroyed terribly, Sydney, without mercy and without discernment. The work of God seems to be in the fragile hands of humankind. We have, it seems, merely to make a gesture. We are making that gesture. It will lead us to our ruin…while free creation will flourish again. I can't believe, you see, that everything has been preserved for such a long time, to the marsupials and Ornithorhychus of Australia, to perish under human hands. I can distinctly see the abyss that is about to open; I can see the nations dissolving once again into peoples, peoples

---

[30] *Genesis* 1:28.

209

into tribes, tribes into clans…in truth, Sydney, civilization will die, and the savage life will be reborn!"

Guthrie burst into loud laughter. "I predict," he said, "that the factories of Europe and America will belch smoke over all the savannahs and consume all the forests! Nevertheless, if things turn out differently, I won't be one of those bursting into tears. I'll accept the revenge of the Beasts!"

"I shall accept it," Farnham replied, mystically, "because it will be the will of the Lord."

A herd of savagely graceful quaggas and baroque gnus raced over a promontory, while three ostriches advanced on to a sterile beach, by virtue of the need for open space that is the intelligence of their instinct. Buffaloes also emerged, along with baboons hidden in the bushes, and an old rhinoceros covered with its elaborately folded armor, heavy, indolent and formidable in the total security of a strength that intimidates lions and braves elephants. Then, fearful and swift, their long necks and delicately-horned heads looming over all the other animals, several giraffes came running.

"An enigma!" muttered Sir George. "Why these strange forms? Why the hideousness of that rhinoceros, and the absurd heads of those ostriches?"

"They're all handsome by comparison with that one!" said Guthrie, pointing to a shapeless hippopotamus. "What can the significance be of those monstrous jaws, those hideous eyes, that body of a giant pig?"

"Be sure that all this makes marvelous sense, Sydney…"

"I'd like it to," said the colossus, insouciantly. "Where are we going to set up camp?"

As they examined the locale, they were hypnotized by a spectacle. Colossi had just emerged from the edge of the forest. They were marching, grave, redoubtable and peaceful. Their legs were like tree-trunks, their bodies like rocks and their hides like mobile bark. Their trunks extended like pythons and their tusks formed vast curved pikes. The Earth trembled. The buffaloes, warthogs, antelopes and quaggas moved out of the way of the monstrous herd. Two black lions retreated into the trees; the giraffes raised their heads anxiously.

"Don't you think that elephants are reminiscent of giant insects?" Guthrie said.

"That's certainly true," Sir George retorted. "I liken them to dung-beetles, galofas, and even more so to Cyclommata.[31] There must be females weighing 10,000 pounds there, Sydney! It's a glorious spectacle."

The immense herd went into the lake. Water spurted; vibrant trumpeting shook the expanse, while mothers watched over elephant calves as big as onagers and as playful as puppies.

"If it weren't for humans," said Farnham, meditatively, "there would be no other creature as powerful in the world...and that power wouldn't be malevolent..."

"Not everyone concedes that! Look over there, at the solitary rhinoceros on his promontory. He won't retreat before the most formidable nobleman with a trunk. But let's not forget about the camp."

"Over there, near the forest but in the savannah, I can see a bare region between three rocks, neither too close to nor too far away from the lake," said Sir George, extending his right arm, while his left maintained his binoculars level with his eyes. "It will be easy to build and maintain a fire there."

---

[31] This reference is gnomic in French as well as English. The first of the three terms Sir George uses is *bousiers*, a common name that translates easily as "dung-beetles," but the others seem to be derived, not necessarily correctly, from Latin terms. Rosny's "*cyclomattes*" is presumably intended to refer to *Cyclommatus elephus*, a giant variety of stag-beetle, but the only marginally-relevant uses of *galofas* I can find—in English—are to a blood-sucking fly (whose proboscis might, I suppose, be thought vaguely reminiscent of an elephant's trunk).

Guthrie examined the location and found it satisfactory. "Nevertheless," he replied, after a pause, "I'd like that other place, hollowed out in the brushwood in the form of a semicircle, just as much. If you like, one of us can explore that while the other goes to the three rocks."

"Wouldn't it be better to go together?"

"I think we can each ascertain enough details to let us decide. From here, the places seem equally good. If we find, in the final analysis, that all is well, we can play heads or tails. Let's save time…"

"I'm not sure that we'll save any, but we probably won't lose any," Farnham concluded. "All right—although I don't like splitting up."

"For less than an hour!"

"All right! Which one do you want?"

"I'll take the three rocks."

Although he marched rapidly, Guthrie, accompanied by Kouram and another man, took nearly half an hour to reach the edge of the forest. The place was more spacious than he had anticipated; he judged it comfortable. Two of the rocks were bare, with red walls; the third, which was much larger, had projections and crevices. Banyans were growing in a cleft, and there was a black hole that had to be the opening of a cave.

"Kouram," said the colossus, "you examine the terrain from here to the pointed rock, and your comrade from here to the rounded rock. We'll meet back here."

"Be wary of the cave, Master!" Kouram remarked.

Guthrie replied with a whistle, and headed toward the indented rock.

It formed a surprising architectural assembly: a cracked tower, a pyramidal trunk, the sketches of obelisks, pointed and rounded arches, vague frontons, gothic spires—and everywhere, the indefatigable labor of lichens, pellitories and the weather…

212

The wild place might be made hospitable. The cave and the large crevices sketched out dwellings that a little handiwork might render invulnerable to predators, or make a fortress against humans.

This is where we ought to camp, Guthrie thought.

He recalled Kouram's words: "Be wary of the cave." Guthrie mixed variable doses of temerity and foresight. As reflective as Ironcastle himself, but with more impetuosity, he suddenly yielded to the traps, risks, hazards and excitements of an adventure—and then the release of his enormous energy prevented him from struggling against himself, and his sporting experience gave him an excessive confidence. At boxing, no amateur could resist him; he would have taken on Dempsey. He could carry a horse with its rider. He pounced like a jaguar...

The cave was even larger than he had imagined. Membranous wings stirred; a nocturnal bird opened its phosphorescent eyes in the gloom; crawling beasts were moving sinuously. He had to switch on his electric torch.

The American saw a swarm of subterranean creatures, which the light caused to flee into fissures. An irregular vault was carpeted by fruit-bats, several of which dropped away, frightened, with little squeaks, and started whirling around jerkily on their silent wings.

Tunnels appeared, ominously, and, at the back of the cave, two fissures let in an indecisive light.

The traveler went into one of these fissures, which rapidly became too narrow. Then, directed by the beam of his torch, Guthrie had a disturbing vision. At the end of the fissure, in the lateral wall, there were two holes with broken edges, one inclined to the right and the other to the left, allowing the sight of further caves. They had to open on the western side of the rock, which Guthrie had not yet seen; a confused light penetrated into them, through which the electric beam traced a violet cone.

In the cave to the right, three male lions and two females were standing up, frightened by that unusual light. Lion cubs were moving in the shadows. These families of wild beasts, strangely associated, had a grim poetry. The males were the equals of the extinct lions of the Atlas Mountains and the females made him think of blonde tigresses.

"Life is beautiful!" the colossus thought.

He started to laugh, excitedly. These redoubtable beasts were at his mercy. Two or three shots of the elephant-gun, and the savage kings would enter the eternal night. The ancient soul of the hunter asserted itself. Guthrie shouldered the butt of his weapon. Then a scruple, and also prudence, caused him to look away, and he shivered from head to toe.

A second cave had just appeared, with even more formidable inhabitants. In none of the vast American menageries had Sydney ever seen lions comparable to those that were getting to their feet in the gloom. They seemed to emerge from the depths of prehistory, giants similar to the lion-tiger and the *Felis spelaea* of the Chellean caves.

Living thunder echoed from the red granite. All the lions roared in unison. Guthrie listened to them, breathless with enthusiasm. Once again he raised his weapon—but he beat a retreat, shaking his head and yielding to inexpressible sentiments.

We shan't camp here, he thought.

When he got back into the open air, he headed swiftly toward Kouram and the other man, who were walking toward the rocks, and signaled to them not to go any further. They waited for the giant, who hastened his pace, thinking that the lions might emerge from their lairs at any moment. Their roars died away. Animals with a mediocre sense of smell and a slothful intelligence, they were undoubtedly still hypnotized before the fissure from which the mysterious light had sprung forth.

A growl split the air. A lion had just surged forth, with a lioness.

They were not the immense predators of the second cave; even so, their size took Kouram by surprise. There was a nonchalance in their attitude. The moment had not come when these sovereigns of the fauna would deploy their terrible energy. More so than the tiger, the lion falls from grace outside the shadows. For love or war, it requires the pale stellar light, the crystalline blackness of night.

Even so, flanked by the lioness, the lion came forward slyly, almost creeping. Sydney checked his rifle and made sure that his Bowie knife was loose in its sheath. He had six bullets in his revolver…

A further roar pierced the air; a colossal lion emerged in its turn from the shadow of the rocks.

"Damn it!" Guthrie cursed. "We're playing heads or tails with death."

The first lion started running. In six bounds it crossed half the distance that separated it from the American—but the lion-colossus remained motionless, in a wild dream, still full of the shadows of the cave.

There was no further possibility of flight. Sydney faced the lion head-on, while Kouram and his companion raised their rifles. Three shots rang out. The bullet from the elephant-gun grazed the lion's skull and exploded 200 feet away. The men's bullets passed by harmlessly.

With three enormous bounds, the beast attacked. The blond head came down like a rock. It came down exactly where the man was, but the man had moved. Against the teeth and claws, there was the trenchant blade of the Bowie knife. The elephant-gun had spoken a second time, in vain, because the beast's leap and his own movement had not permitted Guthrie to take aim. One of two lives was about to enter the eternal darkness.

The natives took aim again, but it was an impotent gesture, because Guthrie was between them and the beast and they did not trust their skill.

In order to scare the lion, Guthrie uttered a savage yell; the lion retorted with a growl. Then their momentum brought them together. The lion lunged, its claws splayed, its mouth wide open, from which granite fangs emerged—but the man had his own weapon. He braced himself and thrust with the

Bowie knife, which buried itself entire in the animal's breast and dug into its depths.

The beast did not fall. It lashed out with its claw, which cut into the American's side; its enormous maw tried to seize his skull. Sydney realized that the Bowie knife had not reached the heart; he struck the lion on the nose with his left fist, and the muzzle recoiled. Then, withdrawing his weapon, the man struck again, by default, at the shoulder.

Panting hard, the upright colossus and the carnivorous colossus persisted. It was the beast that collapsed...

A shadow veiled Guthrie's vision. With a supreme effort, his head having struck the rock, he fought to stay conscious. The lioness was no more than three bounds away, followed close behind by a black lion. Sydney was conscious of the danger and stiffened himself for a mortal struggle; before his muscles were able to react, the two beasts would tear him apart...

Meanwhile, Sir George had just appeared in the distance, and Philippe materialized simultaneously on the crest of the ridge. They both raised their rifles, both taking aim at the lioness. Scarcely had the shots rung out when the beast whirled around and collapsed, hit in the head. As she fell, she bumped into the black lion, interrupting its run; it stopped and sniffed the dying lioness. Further shots were already ringing out, and the black lion, in its turn, bade farewell to the forest, the savannah and the intoxicating nights.

The entire caravan had come running, the men howling with joy, and Guthrie forced himself to his feet. There was no more danger. In the distance the colossal lion had disappeared behind the rocks. A formless dread made the other wild beasts recoil.

"I wasn't far from knowing what's on the other side," muttered Guthrie, slightly pale, but full of a joy that he did not try to hide, as he shook the hands of Sir George and Philippe. "There can't be many riflemen of your caliber, even in the Cape!"

"No," said Hareton, who had arrived with Muriel, "but it's definitely necessary not to get separated."

"The Master is right," Kouram added. "And we must not forget the Squat Men. Kouram has seen their tracks; Kouram would not be surprised if they were setting a trap."

VI. The Latent Pursuit

Life ingeniously repaired the obscure fibers of the gorilla and the caves of flesh where death had labored in the wreckage. Beneath hard vaults, in the depths of blanched orbits, his eyes began to scrutinize the universe again. A bitter suspicion persisted in the animal's soul. He knew that he was the captive of equivocal creatures which resembled him somewhat. Sometimes, his forehead creased strangely; images floated in his mind, which recreated lost locales and his female companions...

When the human approached, his hair prickled; instinct raised his arms against the mortal danger that any creature might pose. There was, however, one whom he welcomed affectionately. When Hareton appeared, the man of the woods raised his heavy head with a gleam in his eyes. He studied that pale face patiently, that fair hair, those hands which had calmed his suffering and nourished him. In spite of recurrences of anxiety and surges of mistrust, sovereign habit and salutary repetition—the origins of all security—gradually enveloped Ironcastle's gestures.

The gorilla trusted him. The man's every gesture became reassuring. The beast knew that there was someone in the vast world from whom he could expect food, the source of life, on a daily basis. Because they were renascent, these impressions were more profound and almost meditated. There was a vague exchange between the dissimilar mentalities.

Soon, Ironcastle's presence was a pleasure. When the man appeared, the beast, reassured, submitted to the presence of others—but when Hareton drew away, a primitive defensiveness seethed in the huge breast.

The Squat Men were not tamed. An indomitable hostility gleamed in the depths of their pupils. Their opaque faces either remained strangely stiff or expressed flashes of homicidal aversion. They accepted care and nourishment without any glimmer of gratitude. Their mistrust was manifest in the long preliminaries that preceded their meals. They sniffed and prodded the foodstuffs interminably. Only Muriel seemed not to awaken their hatred. They watched her untiringly, and occasionally, something indecipherable agitated their heavy lips.

It was evident that they were perpetually on the alert. Their eyes gathered every image; their hearing absorbed the slightest rustle.

After the incident with the lions, their vigilance seemed more intense. One morning, Kouram said: "Their tribe is close by. *It is talking to them.*"

"Have you heard voices?" asked Ironcastle.

"No, Master. They aren't voices…they're signs in the grass, in the earth, the leaves and the water."

"How do you know?"

"I know, Master, because the grass is cut at intervals, or braided, because there are grooves in the earth, because leaves are turned back or torn away in ways that beasts never do…because crossed wisps of straw float in the water. I know, Master!"

"You don't know what all that means?"

"No, Master. I don't know their signs…but they can't be thinking about anything but doing us harm. And those we've captured are becoming a danger to us. We need to kill them or torture them."

"Why torture them?"

"To get them to give up their secrets."

Ironcastle and his companions listened in amazement.

"But what can they do?" Guthrie asked.

"They can help set traps for us."

"We have only to watch them more closely and tie them up."

"I don't know, Master. Even tied up, they can help their tribe."

"If they were tortured, would they talk?"

"Perhaps one of them is less brave than the rest—why not try?" Kouram asked, ingenuously. "We can kill them afterwards."

The westerners made no reply, aware of the incompatibility of their mentality and the African's.

"We need to listen to Kouram," said Ironcastle, pensively, when their guide fell silent and withdrew. "He's a very intelligent man."

"Listen to him, no doubt," Guthrie muttered, "but what more can we do than we're doing? Fundamentally, his advice is the only wisdom. It's necessary to torture them and then kill them."

"You're not going to do that, Guthrie!" Muriel exclaimed, horrified.

"No, I won't do it, but it would be legitimate to do it—if only for your sake, Muriel. These men are infernal vermin, ready to commit any sin—a collection of criminals—and you can be sure that they wouldn't hesitate to cook and eat us."

"Wasted words," Ironcastle interjected. "We shan't kill them, much less torture them. Anyway, they can't tell us anything, since we can't understand them."

"Kouram might be able to understand them."

"No—he can only guess. That's not enough."

"You're right," said Philippe. "We won't debase ourselves. Even so, what are we going to do with them? Their presence is a danger."

"Your question is a reply," Sir George remarked. "Shall we set them free?"

"No! Not yet. Is it impossible, by combining the cunning of Africa and the cunning of the West, to deceive their acuity?"

Ironcastle raised his eyebrows, then looked at Philippe fixedly.

"Since the earth, the grass, the leaves and the water are speaking, can't we deform the signals?"

"I've thought of that," said Ironcastle. "We can certainly try. Moreover, it's an elementary precaution to blindfold the captives' eyes when we're on the march, or, even better, put hoods over their heads. At night, we can keep them in a tent."

"It's also necessary to gag them." Guthrie added. "And stop up their ears…"

"They'll be very unhappy!" Muriel sighed.

"Not for long. Kouram claims that they won't leave the forest. They've never been known to advance more than one day's march into the plain. Well, the forest isn't endless."

"Let's call Kouram back," said Sir George.

Kouram listened silently to what the white men said. "That's good!" he replied. Kouram will be alert; his companions too—but the Squat Men's cunning is inexhaustible. It's always necessary to fear an escape. Look what I've just found."

He showed them some fig-leaves tied together with strands of grass; the tips of several leaves had been removed; other leaves had been pierced symmetrically.

"One of the captives dropped this sign near a bush—and it certainly says more than one thing." He sighed, raising his hands to his face. "Why not kill them?"

The surveillance became more scrupulous and more severe. All day long, the captives' faces were veiled; by night, a sentry was posted in their tent. When they were permitted to take exercise within the camp, their legs were hobbled. In spite of all this, they were an incessant object of anxiety.

Through their impassivity, Ironcastle, Philippe and Muriel thought they were beginning to discern the cunning in their eyes and the slight quivers of their lips or eyelids by which they revealed their hatreds and hopes. When they could no longer see during the day their rage was manifest. A sly menace emanated from their attitude; the least patient uttered words that they divined to be insulting…but then they seemed to become resigned. In the bivouac, by the light of the fires, they dreamed mysteriously, as motionless as cadavers.

"Well, are they still 'talking' to the others?" Philippe asked Kouram one evening.

"Still," Kouram replied, gravely. "They hear and they reply."

"But how?"

"They hear by way of the voices of jackals, crows, hyenas and leopards. They reply by way of the ground."

"You're not erasing their signs, then?"

"We're erasing them, Master—but not always, because we don't find them all. The Squat Men are more cunning than we are!"

That night was rendered more charming by a breeze that blew from the land toward the lake. The scarlet flames of the fires rose up; life could be heard growling in the depths of the woodland. Philippe studied the Southern Cross, and its tremulous reflection in the water.

Abruptly, Muriel sat down next to him. Enveloped by red light, mingled with the blue penumbra, she was an almost fluid apparition in the profound life of the desert. He breathed in her scent, a sweetness that occasionally generated anguish; she awoke everything that was mysterious in the hearts of men. Soon, the moment became so moving that Philippe felt that he would never forget it.

"There's no resemblance at all between this night and a night in Touraine," he said, "and yet, it makes me think about a night in Touraine…a night on the bank of the Loire, near the Château de Chambord…as reassuring as this one is redoubtable."

"Why redoubtable?" Muriel asked.

"Here, all nights are redoubtable. Nature hasn't lost any of its dark charm."

"That's true," the young woman whispered, shivering as she remembered the python's coils. "But I think we'll miss these nights."

"Profoundly. Life has been newly revealed to us…and how powerfully!"

"We have seen the Beginning of which the Book speaks."

He bowed his head, knowing that it was necessary not to say a single word that might contradict Muriel in the beliefs that had been handed down to her by generations of mystical women and men. Like Hareton, she lived two isolated existences; in one was the state of faith, which reason never touched; in the other, a terrestrial destiny unfolded in which she thought freely, and according to the circumstances.

"Then again," he added, with a hint of anguish, "you've irradiated us with the life of your beauty. There could not be a sweetness more profound. With you, Muriel, we have never entirely left the world in which men are dominant; with you our tents are dwellings, our evening fires a hearth; you are the image of the most charming and consoling aspects of what man has wrought—our best hope and our most tender anxiety."

She listened curiously, delicately moved, and knowing that she was loved. Although there was a disturbance in her own heart, she did not know as yet whether she preferred Philippe to all other men, and she reserved her own testimony. "You mustn't exaggerate," she said. "I'm not very important…and I'm often a burden rather than a consolation."

"I'm not exaggerating, Muriel. Even if you were less brilliant, there would be an incomparable grace in seeing you sitting among us, so far from the white fatherland."

"Oh well," she murmured, "that's enough talk about me for one evening. Look how the stars tremble gently in the rippling waters of the lake." She sang, in a near-whisper: "*Twinkle, twinkle, little star. How I wonder what you are!* I can see myself again, as a little girl, beside a lake in my own coun-

222

try—it was evening then, too—while a voice sang that innocent little song."

She started, and turned her head—and they both saw a thickset form, crawling. It passed through the zone of the fires and threw itself into the lake.

"One of the prisoners!" Philippe exclaimed.

Already, Kouram, two men and Sir George were running forward. They stood there, eyes fixed on the surface of the water. Obscure forms were moving about—batrachians and fish—but no human form was visible.

"The canoes!" ordered Hareton.

These were collapsible canoes that were made ready in a trice. Two crews protected by armored clothing set off upon the lake—but their search was utterly in vain; the Squat Man had either succeeded in his escape or drowned. They did not know how he had escaped, for he had taken his bonds with him, and completely deceived the two sentries guarding the captives' tent.

"You see, Master," said Kouram, when the canoes had come back.

"I see that you were right," Ironcastle replied, sadly. "That Squat Man has been more cunning than us."

"Not only him, Master. It's the tribe that set him free."

"The tribe?" Guthrie exclaimed, skeptically.

"The tribe, Master. It gave him a weapon with which to cut the cords…and perhaps the water that burns."

"What is the water that burns?" asked Hareton, anxiously.

"It's a kind of water that emerges from the ground, Master. It burns grass, wood, cloth and skin. If the Squat Men had poured it into the hollow of a stone, the fugitive might have made use of it."

"We'll go see!"

The ground on which the tent was pitched had not retained any trace of a corrosive substance.

"Kouram likes legends!" Guthrie muttered.

"No," said Sir George. "Here's a fragment of rope, evidently burned." He displayed a fragment scarcely half a centimeter long, one end of which was charred.

Ironcastle raised his eyebrows. "Capital! Kouram isn't exaggerating."

"Where's the proof that the rope was burned by a corrosive?" Sydney asked. "Perhaps the captive made use of a stray firebrand."

"No," Sir George affirmed, as he continued to examine the rope fragment. "This isn't the burn of a flame."

"Then why have they waited so long to make use of their damned liquid?"

"Because the water that burns isn't found everywhere, Master," said Kouram, who had heard the exchange. "One may walk for weeks, even months, before finding it."

"We were wrong not to have brought dogs," said Philippe.

"We should have had some brought from the Antilles or Vera Cruz before the departure," Hareton said, "but we didn't have time."

"We could train jackals," said Guthrie, half-earnestly and half-facetiously.

"I'd prefer to trust myself to the gorilla," Ironcastle replied. "He detests these Squat Men intensely."

"You're right, Master," Kouram put in. "The man-who-does-not-talk is the enemy of the Squat Men."

"Do you think he might be trained?"

"You might try, Master—but only you!"

Hareton tried to train the anthropoid. For the first few days, nothing seemed to penetrate the granite skull. When the gorilla was put in the presence of the captive Squat Men, an extraordinary agitation made the ape quiver, and his eyes—becoming rounder, fluorescent and green-tinted—expressed a menacing fury and a mysterious dread.

After a few days, there was a sort of explosion in the brute's mentality, like the abrupt blooming of certain tropical flowers. Intelligence scintillated in fits. Then the beast seemed positively to understand that it was to keep watch on the prisoners; it crouched down before their tent, sniffing the odious emanations and staring into space.

One evening, while Hareton was staring into the fire, Kouram appeared beside him.

"Master, the man-without-speech has sensed the Squat Men approaching. They're close to the camp."

"Is everyone at his post?"

"Yes, Master. Anyway, it's not an attack that we have to fear."

"What, then?"

"I don't know. It's necessary to keep watch on the food-supplies, the captives and the ground."

"The ground? Why?"

"The Squat Men know caves that their ancestors hollowed out."

Hareton understood what the man meant, and went to see the anthropoid. The ape was violently agitated; he was listening and sniffing; the hair on top of his head stood up at intervals.

"Well, Sylvius?" Gently, Hareton placed his hand on the animal's shoulder. Sylvius responded with a vague movement, sketched a caress and voiced a dull groan.

"Go, Sylvius!"

The animal headed toward the western extremity of the encampment. There, his agitation became frantic. Crouching down, he began digging in the earth.

"You see, Master!" said Kouram, who had come after them. "The Squat Men are underground."

"The camp is situated above a cave, then?"

"Yes, Master."

Hareton remained deep in thought for a wile. Kouram lay down and stuck his ear to the ground. "They're there!" he said. Sylvius' groan seemed to agree with this statement.

A frightful cry cut through the darkness: a woman's cry, which made Hareton shiver. "That's Muriel!" he exclaimed.

He bounded toward the young woman's tent. The native set to guard it was lying on the ground, motionless. Hareton lifted the flap of canvas that sealed the tent, and shone the beam of his electric torch inside.

He did not see Muriel.

VII. Muriel in the Night

In the middle of the tent there was an oval hole, through which two men might pass. To one side, there was a block of green porphyry.

Shouting an alarm call, Hareton ran forward. Ill-formed steps descended into the darkness. Without waiting, Ironcastle went down. When he reached the last step he saw a subterranean corridor—but after some 25 meters, the route was blocked by a collapse of earth and stones.

Philippe, Sydney and Sir George arrived. "Damn it!" howled Guthrie, gripped by a savage fury.

"We need to organize ourselves," said Sir George.

Vertigo whirled within Philippe's skull, and his heart sounded a tocsin. They all groped around in the hope of finding an exit.

"Send for spades and pick-axes, Kouram," Sir George commanded.

After a brief interval of exasperation, Guthrie recovered the practical sensibility of his race and his nation. "My rock-drill!" he said.

Before the departure he had anticipated the possibility of encountering some obstacle of stone or earth. Accompanied by Dick and Patrick, he went in search of the apparatus. It was an ingenious machine which could, according to circumstances, be operated by hand or driven by gasoline. Comparatively light, it only needed two ordinary men to transport it.

Ten minutes later, the drill was in place, and Sydney had filled its fuel-tank. It began its work, and opened up a passage five times as quickly as spades and picks could have done.

Ironcastle was the first to launch himself into the opened passage. The light of electric torches showed no trace of the passage of Muriel and the Squat Men. Soon, it was necessary to duck down; then the fissure became so narrow that it was impossible to advance two abreast.

"It's up to me to take the lead," Guthrie declared, in a forceful and almost imperious tone. Pulling Hareton back as the latter tried to remain at the head, he added: "No, Uncle, no! Here, my strength is our best safeguard. I'll break through any obstacles more easily than you, and I'll be better able to reckon with anyone who dares to start a fight!"

"But the corridor might become too narrow for you," Hareton objected.

"I'll lie down and you can crawl over me."

While debating the issue, Guthrie moved forward. It was all the more logical that he should take the lead because he—along with Sir George and Patrick—had put on a costume impermeable to assegais.

Although he had to crouch down further, the tunnel did not become too narrow. The pursuers bent down so far that a little further would have made it necessary to crawl, but then the ceiling rose up, the passage broadened, and Sir George uttered an exclamation. He had just spotted a little handkerchief that belonged to Muriel.

Hareton took possession of it and pressed it to his lips.

"At least that confirms that she passed this way," Guthrie remarked.

A feeble radiation penetrated into the subterranean passage, and—almost abruptly—the lake appeared, beneath the light of a quarter moon.

For a few moments, the companions studied the water, in which Sirius, Orion, Virgo and the Southern Cross were reflected. Jackals were yapping on the plain; colossal frogs raised voices as resounding as those of buffaloes.

"Nothing!" murmured Sir George.

Three islands displayed elongated arborescent masses. They were what attracted the passionate attention of the troop.

"That's where they must have taken her!" Hareton exclaimed, plaintively. Large tears ran down his cheeks; his normally-impassive face was entirely distorted by pain. "I've done something unforgivable," he sobbed. "I deserve torture and death a thousand times over."

Philippe's despair was equal to the father's. A nameless horror darkened his soul, rendered even more intolerable by his impotence.

Guthrie, his eyes phosphorescent, waved his fists at the islands.

"There's nothing we can do," said Sir George, authoritatively. "We'll lose any chance of saving her if we continue to expose ourselves needlessly."

They examined the shore. It was almost a sheer cliff. They could not think of climbing up it. There would surely be Squat Men in hiding who would have annihilated all those who were not wearing impervious clothing in a trice. Where they stood, beneath overhanging rocks, with the lake open all the way to the islands, no surprise attack was possible.

"What shall we do?" asked Hareton sadly. In his pain, he felt a need to entrust command to a calmer mind.

"There's only one thing we can do—return to the camp the way we came, man the canoes and explore the islands."

"Right!" said Guthrie, his excitement beginning to yield to the positive instincts of a hunter. "Let's not leave an opportunity for another abduction. Let's move quickly. I'll guard the rear."

"No!" objected Sir George. "For the retreat, Sydney, it's better that it should be me. I can turn round more easily if it's necessary to face the enemy."

Sydney gave in; the little troop rapidly retraced its underground route. When they reached the drill, the Englishman murmured: "We're lucky. The exit might have been blocked."

It took more than half an hour to get a collapsible canoe into a functional state. Hareton and Philippe worked in the trance of those condemned to death, but a dark determination coordinated their efforts. Like Guthrie, they thought it necessary not to lose any opportunity.

Sir George was to guard the camp, with Patrick, Dick Nightingale and the majority of the Africans. The pursuit expedition thus consisted of Ironcastle, Guthrie, Philippe, four natives—including Kouram—and the anthropoid. The last-named played a role analogous to that dogs would have played.

The men had been given capes of tarred canvas that assegais would have difficulty penetrating, but the gorilla would not tolerate any kind of clothing.

Before embarking, they tried an experiment. Sylvius, allowed to move freely, immediately headed for the tunnel. In consequence, it seemed improbable that the Squat Men had been on the surface, at least in close proximity to the camp. On the other hand, Muriel's transportation up the cliff seemed impracticable. Everything converged on the hypothesis of a flight across the lake.

"All aboard!" concluded Guthrie, since a choice had to be made.

The motor juddered, and the boat ploughed through the torpid waters. It stopped at the first island, where Ironcastle, Guthrie and Philippe landed with the anthropoid, which gave manifest signs of irritation.

"They came this way," Hareton concluded.

A crocodile slid into the lake; furtive animals glided through the mist, and large-winged bats flew through the branches. The man of the woods, however, having sniffed the ground, suddenly launched himself across the island. He had become wild and formidable again. His ancient soul was reborn, and all the instincts that guided him through the mystery of the forest.

"He's free!" muttered Guthrie. He'll only have to get it into his head to climb into the trees, and we'll never see him again."

Having crossed the island diagonally, the gorilla arrived at a little creek. Philippe bent down and picked up an object glinting among the reeds; it was a tortoiseshell hair-pin.

"Muriel!" the father groaned.

The anthropoid grunted, but did not move again—and when Hareton put a hand on his shoulder, he made an almost human gesture.

"No doubt about it," Guthrie affirmed. "The vermin set sail again. Let's visit the other islands."

There were three of them, and a few islets. The explorers found no further trace of the passage of the Squat Men.

"Oh Lord," Hareton prayed, with his joined hands pointing to the stars, "God of Heaven and Earth, have pity on Muriel. Take my life, and let her live!"

Part Two

I. The Aerial Men

Ouammha, the Blue Eagle, climbed up into the baobab. Three huts there contained his wives, daughters and sons. The Blue Eagle had snowy threads in the dark weave of his hair, but there was still strength in his limbs, courage in his heart and cunning in his granite skull.

His amber gaze wandered among the Palmyra-palms, the oil-palms, the doum-palms, the pandanus and dragon-trees, punctuated by fig-trees and Andropogon grasses. The baobab formed large islands within them. For centuries, they had accommodated the huts of the Goura-Zannkas, the Sons of the Star. Conical, reminiscent of large termitaries, the huts were resistant to the sunlight and solid against the rain.

Ouammha commanded the five clans of the tribe. It included 500 warriors, armed with jade hatchets, clubs and assegais. There were other tribes to the east, and others still in the Valley of the Dead. They made war against one another, because humans multiplied superabundantly. Prisoners of both sexes were eaten. Sometimes, the tribes made alliances to repel the Squat Men, who coveted their abundant territory.

That year, a war had just been concluded. Ouammha's men, having defeated the Sons of the Red Rhinoceros and the Black Lion, had captured 50 warriors and 60 women; feasts were being prepared that would continue until the new moon. They had been plunged neck-deep into the lake, and would be marinated there until the hour of their consumption; it would make their flesh tender and more flavorsome.

The fires had been lit in the Great Clearing. Ouammha knew the words he had to say and the gestures he had to make in order to appease the Powerful Entities that were in the Water, the Earth, the Wind and the Sun.

The Goura-Zannkas understood the hierarchy of Forces. In the Invisible, there are those that resemble men and beasts; they are the smallest and least redoubtable. Then there are those that have the shapes of great vegetables; their power is inconceivable. Those which have no form and no limits, which flow and change, shrink and increase, and whose language consists of storms, lightning, conflagration and inundation, are not Beings but Entities; compared with them, Beings are nothing!

Once Ouammha was in the baobab, he shouted loudly, and his sons and sons-in-law came out, assembling in the branches. Then Ouammha made a speech.

"Sons of the Chosen Clans—the foremost aerial clans, of which Ouammha is the master—here are my commands. One warrior in ten will set off for the west, the north, the east and over the lake. Unknown men have come, with camels, donkeys and goats. Several are strangers unlike the Sons of the Stars, the Sons of the Red Rhinoceros, the Black Lion or the Marsh, or even the Squat Men. Their faces have no color, their hair shines like straw and their weapons are incomprehensible. Our warriors will surround their caravan. This evening they will camp close to our borders. We shall annihilate them, or make alliance with them! Ba-Louama will lead the warriors, and Ouammha will follow tomorrow with 300 men. I have spoken!"

Ba-Louama therefore selected one warrior in ten, initially from the Blue Eagle's baobab and then from the entire forest, and set out to encircle the men with the colorless faces.

"That is good," said the Blue Eagle, when the expedition had gone. "May victory be consecrated!"

Hegoum, the Man-with-the-Sonorous-Horn, blew toward the four Heavens; the clans gathered in the Great Clearing, and the Blue Eagle raised his resounding voice.

"The Goura-Zannkas are masters of the forest and the lake. The Sons of the Black Lion and the Red Rhinoceros have risen up against us; we have broken their skulls, opened their bellies and pierced their hearts. Their entrails have been spread over the ground, their blood has run like a red river. We have captured many warriors, women and children. Twenty warriors, who have been soaking in the lake all night and all day, are ready for the Great Sacrifice…"

The clans uttered an immense cry, prolonged like the roaring of lions. They were not at all ferocious. In times when the assegai of war was laid down, they had benevolent souls, and met the men of neighboring tribes without fury—but war being sacred, it was a duty to eat the captives.

"Let the fires be lit!" ordered the Blue Eagle.

The fires were it; they struggled against the feeble light of dusk, and their light dominated that of the crescent moon, half of which was silver and the other half gray.

Then, brandishing torches, the clans went down to the edge of the lake. The captured warriors had been immersed there since the previous day. Only their heads were visible, because their bodies were attached to blocks of granite. At the sight of the torches they knew their fate, and were not astonished.

"Sons of the Red Rhinoceros and the Black Lion," Ouammha proclaimed, "on the day of his birth, a man is already ready for the day of his death. Where are the innumerable ancestors? And what will soon become of those who will lead you to sacrifice? Your death is beautiful, Sons of the Rhinoceros and the Lion. You have fought for your clans and we have fought for ours. Many Sons of the Eagle have fallen beneath your assegais. We have no hatred, but it is necessary to obey the Entities, for the Entities are everything and living beings are nothing!"

Already, the captives had been pulled out of the mud. Their legs could no longer support them; it was necessary to carry them to the fires.

They began to laugh when the women, in accordance with the millennial custom, arrived with the millet cakes—for the meal of the vanquished is as sacred as the meal of the victors. The Sons of the Black Lion and the Red Rhinoceros forgot death and devoured the cakes.

233

Meanwhile, Ouammha gave the signal for the ritual dances. A warrior, his face painted red as if he were steeped in blood, beat the dragon-wood drum, while two others blew into reed-flutes. The beats set up a dull counter-rhythm to the monotonous song of the flutes; the warriors' upper bodies began to sway, very slowly at first. As the voice of the flutes accelerated, and the dull drumbeats multiplied, a more confused exaltation lit up in their eyes, while the oscillations of their bodies followed the rhythm of the music and the women joined in with the men.

Then the drumbeat became frantic, the flutes screeched like jackals, and the Goura-Zannkas joined together in a grim saraband. They became entangled, with shrill cries, an oily mass that flowed over the ground, braying, howling and roaring. An intoxicated ferocity shone in their eyes; men and women bit one another; blood ran down their breasts.

Standing still on a mound, with an impassive expression, Ouammha contemplated the spectacle. When the excitement threatened to become homicidal, he uttered three loud cries—and almost immediately, a profound silence was established. The nacreous and mercurial Moon seemed to descend upon the crowns of the baobabs; the light of the pyres effaced the stars—and the captives, having consumed their food, awaited death.

The Blue Eagle gave the signal. Armed with green sacrificial knives, warriors advanced—and several captives, gripped by sudden terror, uttered muted plaints, trying to get up or extending imploring hands.

Each warrior had joined his victim, his eyes fixed on Ouammha. When the chief raised his hand, the jade knives cut the throats and red springs gushed out over the ferns. Then the eyes of the vanquished ceased to swivel, and the quivering bodies became still. Thighs, arms, heads and torsos spread the odor of roasting flesh into the night, and the Goura-Zannkas knew the delicious joy of devouring the Enemy.

234

Then the Blue Eagle issued his commands; as the stars were extinguished in the four firmaments, the Goura-Zannkas rose up in force to combat the Phantom-Warriors.

II. The Bellicose Dawn

About two-thirds of the way through the night, Kouram was on watch by the fire, getting up occasionally to fight off sleep and sniff the air. He knew that the Squat Men were no longer prowling around the camp, since Muriel's abduction. In his savage soul he was delighted by that, for the young woman was nothing to him and he secretly wished that her trail might be lost—but he divined other dangers, for Houmra, the subtlest of the scouts, thought he had glimpsed men on he caravan's flank.

Having sent Houmra and two other natives to investigate, Kouram wondered whether he ought to wake up the chief. There were no white men awake except Patrick, and Kouram did not bother to warn him; although he judged him powerful in combat, he thought him deficient in his sense of smell and discernment.

Situated on the lake shore, in a gully surrounded by fires, the camp was ready for battle. At the first signal, Africans and Westerners alike would be at their posts. Kouram had a religious confidence in the chief's wisdom, the repeating carbines, the elephant-gun and, most of all, the terrible machinegun—but it was necessary not to be taken by surprise. The lake shore did not permit any direct attack, and there was a grassy surface behind the fires where no human body could hide. The nearest cover was 500 paces away. Thus, whatever maneuver the enemy attempted, he could not approach without coming out into the open.

The stars moved on, the Southern Cross positioned over the pole. Eventually, silhouettes appeared and Houmra became visible in the firelight. He had a body as light as a jackal's and the eyes of a bearded vulture.

"Houmra caught sight of men in the direction of the sunset and the direction of the Seven Stars," he said.

"Are there many of them?"

"They are more numerous than us. Houmra was not able to count them. Houmra does not believe that they will attack before the stars have fled the light."

"Why does Houmra think that?"

"Because most of them are asleep. If they were not waiting for other warriors, they would try to surprise us during the night."

Kouram nodded his head, for the argument was reasonable, and he looked eastwards. The sky was not yet pale. The stars, bright in an exceedingly dark sky, were arranged in the order in which they had been arranged before a single man or beast had appeared on Earth. Kouram knew, however, that the gray daylight would extinguish them one by one within an hour.

The silence was deep and pleasant. The animals designated to perish and remake the flesh of other animals with their own were no longer alive. Even the voices of the jackals had died away.

Having received reports from the other scouts, Kouram checked the fires and the sentinels.

"Anything?" asked Patrick, who was on watch at the southern tip of the camp.

"Men are watching us," the man replied.

"The Squat Men?"

"No, men who have come from the forest."

Patrick laughed silently. A man who gave little thought to the future and was full of bravery, he looked forward to battles. "You don't think they'll attack?" he asked. In the firelight, he displayed a head topped with chestnut-colored hair, ultramarine eyes and a long face with a pointed chin.

"They'll attack if they think they're strong enough."

"So much the worse for them," the Irishman growled.

Kouram withdrew, scornful of this response. It seemed to him now that he ought to warn Ironcastle. Going to the chief's tent, he lifted the flap and called out.

Hareton had slept badly since Muriel's disappearance. He got up, put on a jacket and appeared in front of the man.

"What is it, Kouram?"

There was a confused hope in the question: any event, any statement and any thought immediately made him think about the young woman. Chagrin was eating away at him like a disease. In a matter of days, his flesh had weakened; a frightful remorse was corroding him painfully; because he had brought Muriel, he felt as guilty as if he had murdered her.

"The camp is surrounded, Master," said the man.

"By the Squat Men?" Ironcastle exclaimed, with a convulsion of wrath.

"No, Master, by black men. Houmra thinks they have come from the forest."

"Are there many of them?"

"Houmra was unable to count them. They're hiding…"

Hareton bowed his head and reflected sadly. Then he said: "I'd like to forge an alliance with them!"

"That would be good," said Kouram, "but how are we to talk to them?" He did not mean that it was impossible to understand them or to be understood, because he was an expert in sign language, which he had practiced a great deal. "They will throw assegais at anyone who tries to approach them," he said. "However, Master, I will try when daylight comes."

The stars were still sparkling, but dawn was near. The twilight would be very brief; the Sun would appear soon after the initial emanation of diffuse light.

"I don't want you to risk your life," Ironcastle said.

A vague ironic smile creased the violet lips. "Kouram will not take risks," he said, adding, naïvely: "Kouram does not want to die."

Hareton made a tour of the camp and checked the machine-gun. *I should have brought more than one*, he thought. Then he studied the locale: the lake, where the starlight was elongated; the grassland; the brushwood; the distant forest. It was a peaceful moment. Sly nature promised happiness—but, as he respired the velvety air, Hareton's heart was beating horribly.

He turned to the Southern Cross. "O Lord of my salvation," he prayed, "I have cried out to thee night and day…"

He continued in the same vein, mingling despair with hope and faith with dejection. Fever gleamed in his hollow eyes. An ardent remorse continued to gnaw at his heart.

The tropical dawn arrived and passed in seconds; a rapid twilight divided the light momentarily, and already a Sun the color of copper and blood was climbing over the waters of the lake.

"Should I call on them now?" Kouram asked.

"Yes."

Kouram went to fetch a singular flute, carved from the stem of a young papyrus, similar to those used by some of the peoples of the Great Forest. It rendered a soft, uniform sound that expanded into the distance.

Then, making a sign to Houmra, who followed him, he went out of the camp through a gap between two fires.

They took 200 paces into the plain and stopped. No man could advance to within javelin range without being struck down. Kouram raised the flute to his lips again, and drew monotonous and melancholy sounds from it, and then his voice rang out: "The men of the camp wish to make alliance with their hidden brothers. Which of them will show himself, as we are showing ourselves?"

He was not hoping, in speaking thus, to make himself understood to men who spoke a different language, but, like countless generations of savage and civilized men, he believed in the virtue of words, attributing an evocative, organizing and creative power to them.

"Why do you not reply?" Kouram shouted. "We know full well that your warriors are besieging the camp. Houmra of the eagle eyes has seen you in the direction of the Seven Stars and the direction of the setting sun."

There was still no response—but noises could be heard in the depths of the brushwood. Houmra, whose hearing was as subtle as his sight, said: "I think, O wise chief, that other warriors are arriving."

Kouram, gripped by anxiety and anger at the same time, then adopted a menacing tone.

"Let the hidden men place no trust in their number. The white chiefs have weapons as terrible as an earthquake or a forest fire!" He accompanied his speech with a mime. Realizing his imprudence, however, he continued: "We have not come as enemies. If you want our alliance, your chief will be welcome in our camp."

Suddenly, a man stood up, with a roar like that of a buffalo. He had an assegai in one hand and a club in the other. His torso was powerful, his jaws protruding, like those of a wolf. His yellow eyes were gleaming with ardor, courage and covetousness. He shouted unknown words, but his gestures expressed the desire to be victor and master.

"The men of the camp are invincible!" replied Kouram, in words and signs.

Ouammha the Blue Eagle burst out laughing, in a haughty and derisive fashion. He shouted two orders, and the Goura-Zannkas warriors stood up in the bushes, ferns and long grass. They were powerful men, by virtue of their courage and youth; they had the camp entirely surrounded. Hegoum, the man with the horn, blew it in the direction of the rising sun. The Sons of the Star, all armed with clubs and assegais, roared mightily.

And in words and gestures, Ouammha said: "The Sons of the Star have ten warriors for every one of yours. We shall take the camp, with its animals and treasures, and we shall eat the men!"

Understanding that the chief wanted war, Kouram put out his arms, projecting them in front of him and then pointing at the ground. He bowed. "The men of the forest will die like the insects that rose up in the evening over the waters of the lake."

The resounding voice of the Blue Eagle alternated with that of Hegoum's horn. Meanwhile, the Goura-Zannkas formed up in columns; there were four of them, each of about 50 men.

Kouram made one last attempt. His voice and his gestures, in unison, said: "There is still time to make an alliance."

The Blue Eagle, however, seeing his battle columns, felt his power ardently. He gave the signal for the attack.

The camp was ready to receive it. Ironcastle and a native were maneuvering the machine-gun on to the top of a mound. Sydney checked the elephant-gun. Philippe and Sir George were covering the south and the west. The other inhabitants of the camp, ready to fire at a given signal, formed a long elliptical line.

"Don't kill the chief!" Ironcastle shouted—for he hoped to make an alliance with Ouammha, even after a battle.

The horn roared, and Goura-Zannkas spread out on to the lake. Kouram beat a retreat, and 200 grim men started running.

"Fire!" Ironcastle ordered.

The machine-gun, rotating on its axis, launched its hail of bullets, so close together that they seemed to be a liquid jet. The elephant-gun raised its thunderous voice. Sir George and Philippe aimed methodically, supported by the fire of the other riflemen.

It was terrible. Before the Goura-Zannkas' advance guard had covered half the distance that separated them from the camp, more than 60 warriors were lying on the ground. The machine-gun mowed them down in lines; the elephant-gun scattered them in bloody shards of flesh, bones and entrails. Every shot fired by Philippe or Sir George felled a man.

The elephant-gun caused the first stampede; at the sight of warriors torn to pieces, heads and limbs thrown far and wide, the black column coming along the lake-shore was seized by panic and took refuge in the papyrus. Then the machine-gun stopped the group coming from the south, while Philippe's and Sir George's fire, supported by Dick, Patrick and the riflemen, dispersed the fourth column.

In the west, however, the troop led by the Blue Eagle was still redoubtable. The chief was leading them, brandishing his axe and his assegai, and they were already no more than 200 meters away…

Hareton watched them coming. They were the elite: young, vehement warriors, tall and deep-chested, who, if they got into the camp, would throw the natives into disorder and massacre the whites. They were running speedily. Ironcastle only had two minutes to avert catastrophe.

"Damn!" he grunted. Regretfully, he turned the machine-gun westwards; then, methodically, he showered them with bullets. It was as if blades of fire or thunderbolts had swept through the assailants. The men were whirling around like bees in smoke, oscillating and collapsing with cries of rage or agony, or fleeing at random, afflicted by vertigo. Soon, there were no more than ten warriors to follow Ouammha. Ironcastle dispersed them with a single gesture.

The Blue Eagle remained alone in front of the camp. Death was in his soul. The immense force of his race had become, in an instant, that of jackals before a lion. Everything that had swelled his chest with pride, all legend and all reality, vanished before a mysterious power. His pride collapsed into a boundless humility; his glorious memories lay mutilated within him, formless and pitiful.

He raised his club and his assegai. He shouted: "Kill Ouammha—but let it be the hand of a warrior that pierces his breast. Who wants to fight Ouammha?" It was the last surge of his pride, and his voice sounded lamentably. Kouram, who was standing next to Guthrie, understood the chief's gestures. "He wants a single combat," he said.

Guthrie burst out laughing. He surveyed the scene; there was no longer anything there but fugitives, cadavers and the wounded. "I'll give him that consolation," he said.

The giant strode through a mass of hot ashes and, armed with an axe, ran toward the Blue Eagle.

Astonished, the Goura-Zannkas chief watched him come. Although the clans of the Stars included tall men, none ap-

241

proached this pale man, whose strength seemed comparable to that of a rhinoceros. A superstitious sadness weighed upon the soul of the chief, while Guthrie cried: "You want a fight? Here I am!"

Instinctively, Ouammha hurled his assegai, which brushed Sydney's shoulder without even ripping the cloth. In a few strides, the American was in front of the native. The Blue Eagle uttered a sinister cry and raised his club. Guthrie laughed.

The club came down, and so did Sydney's axe, which buried itself in the hard wood and wrenched the weapon out of the chief's hands.

"You've had your fight!" Guthrie jeered. "Now…" Grabbing hold of Ouammha unexpectedly, he threw him over his shoulder and carried him off like a child.

The men in the camp howled mightily. The fugitive Goura-Zannkas paused, gripped with terror, and among those who were hidden in the reeds or the bushes, many moaned, oppressed by the amazement of a prodigy.

"There you are!" said Guthrie, depositing his prisoner on the ground.

Ouammha trembled. He had risked his life a thousand times; no man would have been better able to resist torments and wait impassively for the moment when he would be devoured by the enemy. The fear that was crushing him was not that of a warrior who fears death but that of a man confronted by the Inconceivable. On Guthrie's shoulder he had felt weaker than an infant—and out there, more than 100 Goura-Zannkas were lying dead, while not a single man from the camp had received a scratch. It was as if the assegais and clubs that, since the beginning of time, had killed innumerable men, buffaloes, warthogs and sometimes struck down lions, had suddenly been transformed into wisps of straw.

Mute, his face ashen, Ouammha remained prostrate.

A voice drew him out of his oblivion.

He raised his head slowly, and saw Kouram, who was speaking and making gestures—and because Kouram was black, he felt less crushed.

In sign language, Kouram said: "Would the men of the forest now like to become the friends of the men from the north-west?"

As the signs were repeated and multiplied, Ouammha understood them. An immense astonishment overwhelmed him. He could not conceive that, having been captured, he was not to be reserved for a war-feast…

He studied Kouram, Ironcastle and—most of all—the colossal adversary who had carried him off like a child. Because he had an imagination, he transcended the limits of his beliefs. Men so different from the Goura-Zannkas, so strangely and so terribly armed, might have infinitely different customs. Besides, cunning suggested that, being nomads, it was doubtless in the strangers' interests to leave few enemies behind them. Curiosity too—a sharp, vehement and impassioned curiosity— was stirring in the Blue Eagle. What would he be risking? Was his life not in the hands of the victors? And Ouammha considered that his life was worth that of 100 warriors.

His hesitation came to an abrupt end. He turned to the giant, for whom a boundless admiration was growing within him, and made a gesture of consent. The alliance was concluded.

III. Squat Men and Goura-Zannkas

For some days, the travelers' suspicion was profound. Africans and Westerners alike were ever-ready for battle. They had camped near the trees where the Men of the Stars lived, in an open space on the bank of a river. The clans were wandering around them; men, women and children avid for a glimpse of the fantastic beings that had won the battle without a single one of them being struck by a club or an assegai. No one had any rancor against them. A religious spirit was mingled with the dread they inspired. The sight of Guthrie, especially, filled the Goura-Zannkas with a dazzling amazement; they said to one another: "He is the strongest of all men…he has the power of the Entities…"

Soon, a part of this admiration was transferred to Hareton. By dint of effort, and because he had a gift for languages, he learned the most useful words of the Goura-Zannkas dialect. Aided by Kouram's gestures, he then succeeded in conversing with the Blue Eagle. He knew that the Men of the Stars and the Squat Men had been implacable enemies for a long time. Tradition and legend eternalized tales of combats, defeats and victories, the cunning of the Squat Men at grips with the cunning of the clans.

For more than a generation, however, no one had seen the Red Squat Men, the Blue Squat Men or the Black Squat Men. When Ouammha understood that one of their tribes was nearby, fury made his muscles quiver and his eyes gleamed like those of a leopard at dusk. Hatred rose up within him, ferocious and tumultuous—a hatred that surpassed his person, linking him to superior forces. Hareton realized that. He saw that the alliance was founded on something primitive and indestructible.

"The Blue Eagle will find the Squat Men!" growled the chief. "He will search for them on the waters, in the earth and among the rocks. The Goura-Zannkas are more cunning than jackals."

The American decided to show him the two captives.[32] At the sight of them he leapt up, raising his club to smash their skulls. Kouram stopped his arm.

"Can you talk to them?" Ironcastle asked.

The hatred agitating the Blue Eagle was reflected in the prisoners' thick faces. They too were subject to the power of a millennial instinct.

---

[32] At one point there were five; one escaped, but the others appear to have been forgotten.

Ouammha insulted them untiringly. Over centuries of warfare, the two races had learned to understand one another, at least in essential matters.

"Can you talk to them?" Ironcastle repeated.

"The Eagle can talk to them."

In a dark voice, Hareton said: "Ask them what their people have done with the young woman they have abducted."

Ironcastle and Kouram repeated the question several times, firstly in truncated speech, secondly by means of gestures.

Ouammha understood, and spoke to the captives. The monstrous mouths released sly and silent laughter. Then, one of the captives spoke.

"The Phantom Men will never see the woman with the hair of light again. She is living with the Squat Men on and within the earth. She is the slave of a chief."

"Where are the Squat Men?" demanded the Blue Eagle.

A cold, ironic and hateful scorn came into the eyes of the Squat Man. "They are everywhere!" he said, making a circular gesture.

Ouammha threatened him with his club. The Squat Man remained impassive.

When the Blue Eagle had translated the reply, there was a tragic silence. The image of Muriel, a prisoner among the brutes, was so clear that the unfortunate father uttered a cry of distress.

"The captives will tell me where the horde is!" the Goura-Zannkas chief signed.

"Never!"

"We need to burn their feet!" cried Kouram. "They'll talk then."

When the Eagle understood he shook his head, and was able to make it understood that no torture would be effective on Squat Men.

"We must kill them, then," Kouram went on, ardently. "But for them, the chief's daughter would not have been abducted. But for them, perhaps the Squat Men would have abandoned their pursuit."

That was plausible—but Aesa[33] had passed. Time could not be turned back.

"Do you want to help us to find the Squat Men?" Hareton asked.

A passionate breath inflated the chief's breast. "Ouammha wants to exterminate them!" he howled, waving his club over the prisoners' heads.

The Squat Men's yellow eyes half-closed—and like Kouram, the Eagle shouted: "We must kill them!"

"If they live," said the guide, "even blindfolded, with their mouths gagged and their limbs tied with ropes—even tied up in a sack—they will talk to the others."

"We cannot kill unarmed men," Hareton replied, sadly.

Kouram and Ouammha looked at one another. A mysterious complicity darkened their eyes.

"What will Ouammha do to find the Squat Men?" asked Hareton.

"The warriors will comb the forest, the land and the waters. The sorcerers will consult the Clouds, the Winds and the Stars—and the Goura-Zannkas know all the caves."

"If the Eagle succeeds, he shall have the weapon that kills at 3000 paces," Ironcastle promised, pointing at a rifle.

The yellow eyes scintillated like the star Aldebaran.

Ten minutes later, the Man with the Sonorous Horn assembled the warriors.

Before nightfall, the Goura-Zannkas knew that Squat Men were prowling around the camp. For preference, they stayed underground. Natural tunnels were hollowed out there, often linked up by the working of the Ancestral Squat Men, in the times when the Sons of the Stars had not yet conquered the Forest of Trees and the western shore of the lake.

---

[33] Aesa is a personification of Fate or Destiny, probably originating in Assyria but also recognized by the Greeks.

This discovery tightened the bonds between the clans and the explorers. With a savage passion, the natives searched for traces of the enemy and prepared for war. When the fires were lit around the camp Ouammha reappeared. He paused to contemplate Guthrie, whose stature never ceased to amaze him. Then he said: "The Goura-Zannkas will do battle tonight! They will be victorious—but more surely if the Phantom Men bring their thunderous weapons…"

A clamor interrupted him, and they saw a troop of Goura-Zannkas dragging the two prisoners. By virtue of their stout torsos and their buffalo faces, the odious race of Squat Men was recognizable even in the semi-darkness. A furious delight dilated the Blue Eagle's face. "The battle is imminent now! These will give us their hearts."

Hareton understood, and shivered. "They're prisoners!" he exclaimed.

"Prisoners must be devoured! That is the will of the Earth, the Waters and the Ancestors."

Ironcastle translated the chief's words.

"It's their business," said Guthrie. "One has to respect the laws of one's allies."

Sir George and Philippe remained silent.

Then, coldly, Ouammha shouted an order; clubs were raised; the Squat Men fell, their skulls fractured. "It would have been better to soak them first in the sacred waters," said Ouammha, regretfully—and, seeing that Hareton did not understand, he went on: "I had them killed in order that you would have no regrets…"

"This savage is full of delicate attentions," Sydney remarked, when Ironcastle had reported the Eagle's reply.

Ouammha laughed in a cordial manner. He fixed his eyes on Guthrie and said: "To make victory over the Squat Men more complete, will the Phantom Chiefs help us with the Thunderous Weapons?"

Ironcastle transmitted the request to his companions.

"We ought to take the risk," said Sir George.

"What risk?" Guthrie interjected. "The risk of combat? We neither can nor ought to avoid it."

"The risk of treason," said Hareton. "But I don't think they'll betray us."

"I'm sure they won't!" Philippe exclaimed.

"No," Kouram added, gravely. "They'll be true to their word. And if we help them to destroy the Squat Men, the alliance will be perfected."

Hareton remained thoughtful for a moment, then said: "We'll leave half our men to guard the camp; the others will accompany the Goura-Zannkas. Is that acceptable?"

"We accept."

"Then there's no more to do but select the men."

"The lot will decide," said Guthrie, laughing loudly, "save for me, who will have to go with them."

"Why?"

"Because they want me to."

"That's true," Hareton agreed.

The Blue Eagle's ardent gaze was fixed on the colossus.

The lot designated Philippe, Dick Nightingale and Patrick Jefferson. Six black companions were added, including Kouram.

When the Eagle learned that Guthrie would take part in the expedition he roared with joy. Turning to the men who had killed the prisoners, he shouted: "The Giant Phantom is with us!"

A long clamor greeted this great news, and the man with the Sonorous Horn blew toward the horizons.

IV. The Battle of the Lake

Philippe, with Dick Nightingale, two natives from the camp and 100 Goura-Zannkas, was to explore the northeastern bank and the islands. One of the men was Houmra, the scout with the jackal's ears. No one was better able than he was to discern sounds and threats. When he lay down on the ground, the expanse yielded its mysteries to him; he could distinguish at a distance the heavy tread of a warthog or the even heavier gait of a rhinoceros; he never confused the prowl of a jackal with that of a panther; he could identify the approach of an ostrich, a giraffe, or even a python well before they came in sight; and every cry and murmur, all kinds of rumors, informed him infallibly as to the nature of creatures and things.

One of the Eagle's sons was in command of the Goura-Zannkas warriors. His name was Warzmao, the Python, because he could creep like a reptile and dive deep into the waters for a long time.

Having departed before moonrise, beneath a sky blanched by stars, the warriors followed the curves of the shore. In the feeble astral luminosity the black bodies seemed to be made of a thicker darkness. At intervals, Houmra lay down on the ground, or Warzmao disappeared silently into a thicket. An hour went by without any indication revealing the presence of Squat Men. They were certainly aware that they were being pursued; perhaps they had retreated into the desert—or perhaps they were setting ambushes.

Philippe attempted to see and hear. He had ears as fine as, or even finer than, Houmra, but he had hardly begun to decipher the enigmas of the African night.

"This is a damnable affair!" muttered Dick Nightingale. "How to they expect to fight in the dark? They never find more than one or two of these vermin at a time, and they'd much prefer to die than talk."

Dick was a good servant, loyal and brave, but he talked too much. Although he was whispering, Philippe said: "It's better to keep quiet!"

"Damn it!" said the other. "I defy a wolf to hear me at six yards—and we're surrounded by these men."

That was true. Around the auxiliaries, the Python maintained a mobile cordon of Goura-Zannkas. He did not want to expose them to a surprise attack, not because of them but because of their weapons, which were capable of winning rapid victories.

"Let's shut up, all the same!" Philippe insisted. "And don't worry, Dick—I don't think the Goura-Zannkas intend to fight in the dark, any more, no doubt, than the Squat Men. Be sure that they're not marching without reason!"

Dick shut up, and the expedition continued its monotonous investigations. The ground was carefully examined everywhere, and Houmra, who had divined their allies' motives, often listened for some slight noise deep within the earth.

The wilderness was not silent. Occasionally, they heard the yapping of a jackal, a roar, the cry of distress of a vanquished herbivore, or the plaint of batrachians among the reeds and water-lilies. It was all mysterious, exciting and terrible. A precarious conqueror, man still only possessed a fraction of this savage land, and in the nocturnal opacity he was lost in the bosom of an unvanquished power.

Philippe's heartbeat was intolerably fast. It was not fear; he was only thinking of Muriel. She appeared to him in the phosphorescence of the lake, and in the luminous dust of the stars.

"The Moon's rising!" muttered Dick Nightingale.

Extravagantly blurred by cloud, as red as a poppy, still quite dark but more luminous with every passing minute, it traced a river of light over the lake, and the frogs greeted it with plaintive melodies.

The Goura-Zannkas advance guard had stopped. The scouts crouched down. Then a hundred violent voices roared a war-cry. For a quarter of an hour, there was nothing to be seen but confused flights of projectiles. Those that sprang from clumps of papyrus and grass were aimed at the Goura-Zannkas, who replied by bombarding the coverts with pointed stones.

"Are the Squat Men there, then?" said Dick, brandishing his fist.

The combat was a mere simulacrum. Because of the distance, the projectiles remained harmless. The Squat Men's ambush had failed. They had counted on surprising the Sons of the Stars by means of an unexpected attack, but the scouts had thwarted their plan. Now the adversaries were hesitating, the assegai-points in either side having been dipped in homicidal poison. Before reaching the enemy, the aggressor would sustain serious losses.

Warzmao, who was well aware of that, kept watch on the papyrus. The Squat Men remained invisible, some lying flat in the vegetation, others sheltering in rocky clefts. Sometimes the chief gave voice to a bellow, which the warriors repeated with such force that alarmed monkeys ceased crying out.

Both sides had equal patience, and also hatred—a boundless hatred whose origins were lost in time immemorial. If the Goura-Zannkas, being more impetuous, had not launched an all-out attack, it was because they were aware of their numerical inferiority and the strength of their antagonists' position. Furthermore, the Squat Men had a flotilla of canoes, spotted by the scouts, which ensured a means of retreat across the lake.

"This could go on for a month!" Dick Nightingale complained. "These savages, sir, are damned cowards."

"I don't think so," Philippe replied, almost severely. "They're two exceedingly courageous races." Deep down, he was as impatient as Dick. He had arranged his little troop in the shelter of a mound. If the Squat Men risked a massive attack, the riflemen were to fire at will. They were poor shots, and even Dick was unreliable.

"Are our monkeys on the march?" Dick exclaimed.

Thirty Goura-Zannkas were advancing toward the shore in tightly-knit ranks. They were making a frightful racket, incessantly insulting the Squat Men. One might have thought that they were launching an assault. A cloud of projectiles rose up from the papyrus—but the troops had already come to a halt, out of range. The maneuver was obvious: Warzmao wanted to tempt the enemy with the lure of an easy victory. To increase the temptation, he was holding back the remainder of his warriors.

"Watch out!" Philippe commanded. "Get ready to fire!"

"They won't come out!" Dick grumbled. "This is a war of rabbits."

Philippe, however, gave precise instructions to his riflemen.

The Goura-Zannkas continued to challenge the enemy. The advance guard was now very exposed; at least 700 paces separated them from the bulk of the expedition, and an indentation in the shore permitted the Squat Men to mount a flank attack in combination with a frontal assault. As they also had a considerable numerical superiority over the Goura-Zannkas, the chances of victory were good.

Philippe's heart was beating wildly. It seemed to him that Muriel's fate might depend on the Squat Men's resolve. In his fever, forgetting the obscure horrors and the vile perils, he saw her alive. Imaginary events are obedient to the hazards of the imagination…

There was no revelatory movement in the papyrus, the grass and the rocks—but the harsh voices of Squat Men replied to the vociferations of the Sons of the Star. Then there was a brief silence. In the distance, a flotilla of canoes moved over the lake. It was approaching. A chain of rocks hid it from view.

"Reinforcements!" Dick remarked. "This could get hotter!"

Warzmao had climbed on to a mound. He was undoubtedly hesitant; the position of the advance guard had become dangerous. He did not have time to order a retreat. Frightful roars announced the attack. It was unleashed, massive, crushing and frenetic. Two troops, each of at least 80 men, came forward in tight formation. The one on the flank was evidently attempting to cut off the Goura-Zannkas' retreat.

"Fire!" Philippe ordered.

A hail of bullets decimated the Squat Men on the flank, at which Philippe directed the first wave; seven or eight men fell within an instant.

By some error of their scouts, the Squat Men had no suspicion of the presence of the white men; the precautions taken by Warzmao had deceived them. As brave as bulldogs before the customary weapons, even when poisoned, they were disturbed by the intervention of the thunderous machines. Many of them remembered the battle in the forest, when the Squat Men had suffered an inconceivable defeat in a matter of moments. Hazard determined that the riflemen were admirably placed, and the Squat Men collapsed in clusters.

The troop on the left wailed lamentably. The Goura-Zannkas' advance guard charged the column on the right, which was much more exposed than the one on the left. Warzmao and his men were arriving at great speed. The Squat Men were in turmoil; the mystic terror had astounded them. Like the Athenians at Chaeronea,[34] they experienced the vertigo of defeat, and allowed themselves to be killed without resistance. The Goura-Zannkas' clubs struck them down by dozens, while the fusillade maintained by Philippe and his men continued to fill their obscure souls with horror.

Soon, the Goura-Zannkas having invaded the entirety of the terrain, it was necessary for the others to cease fire. Philippe continued a methodical fire on his own. A few Squat Men attempted a final resistance; a ferocious attack crushed them—and there was an incoherent and furious massacre, a primitive slaughter in which the vanquished yielded to the mysterious destiny of battles and awaited death, no longer trying to rebel against it.

If 30,000 Romans perished at Lake Thrasymenus,[35] more than 100 Squat Men perished on the shore of Lake Savage. Of those who survived, some lay low in the bushes, others threw

---

[34] A decisive battle fought in 338 B.C., in which Philip of Macedonia defeated the Athenians, ended Greek independence and paved the way for the Alexandrian Empire.
[35] A battle in which Hannibal defeated a Roman army led by Flaminius in 217 B.C.

themselves into a dozen canoes moored in an inlet and made for open water.

Other canoes were found—about a dozen of them—each of which could carry a dozen men. Warzmao decided to "clear" the islands that could be seen offshore, where the runaways would doubtless try to hide.

One of the canoes contained Philippe, Dick Nightingale and the riflemen from the camp.

V. Deep in the Earth

Squat Men had been seen to disembark on the northernmost island. Philippe landed there with his men, and a boatload of Goura-Zannkas. The Squat Men's canoes, sheltered in a cove, showed that their enemies were still on the island. It was not heavily wooded. Grass grew with difficulty on the rocky ground, intermingled with lichens; a few clumps of papyrus were growing at the water's edge.

With Dick and six men clad in overcoats impervious to assegais, Philippe undertook a reconnaissance. It revealed no human presence. When the little troop came back to the cove, the oldest of the Goura-Zannkas made signs to Kouram. Three times he pointed to the center of the island.

"That's where *they* disappeared," said Kouram.

Philippe looked. There was a red granite rock, on which nothing grew but bearded lichens, surrounded by a little short grass. "No one could hide there," he objected. "You can see that as well as I can, Kouram. If that's where they disappeared, they can't be above ground."

"They're *under* the ground, Master." Kouram made a sign to the Goura-Zannkas, who nodded his head gravely.

An obscure wave of sensations swirled in Philippe's skull. The human mind is nourished by analogies. Muriel had vanished underground, and it suddenly seemed, strangely, that it would be underground that she would be recovered.

"How does he know?" asked Philippe.

Kouram tried in vain to translate the question, but the old warrior perceived that the Phantom Man wanted to see. He gave a brief order, for he was in command of the expedition, and the Goura-Zannkas headed toward the rock, keeping a sharp look-out. Philippe followed, with Dick and his riflemen.

When they had arrived, the Goura-Zannkas chief called to one of his men. Both of them leaned hard on a crescent-shaped crevice. A block of stone moved sideways, and Philippe saw a black hole extending downwards into the ground. The old warrior held out his arms and pronounced a few words, with a serious expression. He was obviously announcing the presence of Squat Men.

Philippe, Kouram and Dick looked at one another.

"What are the Goura-Zannkas going to do?" Philippe asked.

It seemed that the chief had understood. He pointed at Philippe, Dick, Kouram and the riflemen dressed in impermeable clothing, then to his warriors. At the same time he made signs indicative of succession.

"Master," said Kouram, "he wants us to take the lead—he seems to think that we're invulnerable."

"We nearly are," said Nightingale, with a snigger.

"He has faith in our weapons."

"We'll go first," said Philippe. "We need to set an example."

Dick shrugged his shoulders carelessly; he was a fatalist of almost unlimited bravery.

"Are our riflemen ready?" Philippe asked Kouram.

"They will follow you," said Kouram, having given an order.

Philippe turned toward them. Their attitude was resolute; they had faith. Having seen the white men continually victorious, they deemed them invincible.

"Let's go!" said Philippe, making sure that his hunting-knife moved easily in its sheath and that the rifles were fully loaded.

The slope was fairly steep but quite practicable. Philippe's electric torch projected a violet cone into the darkness. After three minutes the descent ceased; they found themselves in an almost-horizontal corridor, with a cracked floor. Obscure animals fled. The silence was profound.

Turning round, Philippe saw confused heads and scintillating eyes in the gloom. A few Goura-Zannkas warriors crouched down or put an ear to the wall. Others lay down horizontally.

"Well?" Maranges asked.

"They came this way," replied Kouram, who had participated in the investigations, "but we can't hear anything. Perhaps they've fled, perhaps they're waiting for us…who can tell whether they might be lying in ambush in another cave whose entrance we can't see?"

Philippe peered into the mysterious gloom. Glints revealed pieces of quartz, perhaps gemstones, but there was no indication of the presence of living creatures. "Let's press on!"

Warzmao gave an analogous order at the same moment. Two Sons of the Star, skillful in recognizing the tracks of humans and animals, moved to the head of the expedition. They moved slowly, ears pricked, but there was nothing to be seen but stone walls and nothing to be heard but the warriors' muffled footfalls.

Suddenly, one would have thought that lights were shining in the ceiling. They found themselves in a large natural hall, almost hexagonal, and the lights that sprang from the rock were only reflections of electric rays from large blocks of rock-crystal.

"One might think those blocks were polished," Dick Nightingale remarked.

Soon, they made out a series of fissures, each of which was the opening of a more-or-less narrow corridor. Philippe counted ten such exits and turned to the Goura-Zannkas with an anxious expression.

The chief shook his head, but did not seem astonished. He made it known to Kouram that he had expected something of the sort—doubtless in accordance with his ancestors' stories. Evidently, neither he nor any of his warriors had been this far before; tree-dwelling men of the daylight, they did not like to descend deep into the earth.

"What shall we do?" Philippe murmured, full of uncertainty.

"It's worse than a labyrinth!" Dick complained. "Before we'd visited three of these damned holes, the Squat Men would be far away...not to mention traps and ambushes..."

Philippe was overwhelmed by discouragement. All his hopes became chimerical. Besides, what indication was there that Muriel was in these caves? Why would she still be alive? No matter! The momentum of events was beginning to hypnotize the young man. "If the Goura-Zannkas will guard this hall," he said to Kouram, "we'll explore the exits."

"That will be very dangerous, Master."

"No more dangerous that what we've already done."

"Much more dangerous. We'll be exposed to all the Squat Men's traps. The Squat Men are the lords of the underworld."

An ardent impulse was driving the young man, though. "We must!" he said.

Kouram bowed his head fatalistically. "As you wish, Master."

"We'll take half our riflemen. The others will inspire confidence in the Goura-Zannkas. Dick, you'll command them."

"I'd rather follow you!" said Nightingale.

"We need a chief here. If the Goura-Zannkas only see black men, they won't trust them—they'll withdraw."

"All right," Dick said, "but I don't like it..."

Kouram succeeded in communicating Philippe's intention to the Goura-Zannkas all the more easily because the chief had had a similar idea. He offered two skillful scouts to aid the search.

As there was no reason to prefer one exit to the others, Philippe set off into one of the tunnels at random, followed by

257

Kouram and his little troop. The tunnel narrowed and became lower, soon becoming impracticable.

"Either the Squat Men didn't come this way or the stones hold some secret," said Kouram, when they were stopped by the narrowness of the fissure.

"Let's go back," said Philippe, after feeling the walls.

The second fissure ended in a cul-de-sac; the third terminated in a sealed grotto, to which stalactites and stalagmites lent a confused resemblance to some savage temple. The fourth, however, led to a spacious gallery that gave no sign of ending after ten minutes' march.

"This is the way the Squat Men came," Kouram declared.

One of the Goura-Zannkas scouts touched him on the shoulder, and Kouram turned round. The man showed him his hand; the palm was red and moist.

"Blood—it's blood, Master!" Kouram said.

The Goura-Zannkas indicated that they should follow him. Near the wall, there was a red trail.

VI. The Subterranean Water

The Goura-Zannkas scout marched swiftly, sure now that the enemies of his race had passed this way. In the darkness, the little troop followed the violet-tinted beam of the electric torch.

After a few minutes, there was a bend in the corridor. At the same time, the ceiling lowered and the passage narrowed. Soon, the Goura-Zannkas uttered an exclamation. Kouram, who was close behind him, raised an arm. There was no need for an explanation; the torch-beam was reflecting from a shiny surface.

"Water!" said Philippe, despairingly.

Kouram touched his arm. "A canoe, Master."

The sheet of water seemed considerable. It broadened out beyond the little harbor where the corridor ended. A vault rich in crystals reflected the torchlight and gave the subterranean water flecks of diamond, sapphire, ruby and topaz.

Anxiously, Philippe examined the canoe. Why had the Squat Men abandoned it? Should he not fear a trap? The boat, which was quite long but very narrow, seemed fragile; it contained two paddles. There was room for six men at most. Dare they risk themselves on these mysterious waters, in the subterranean darkness, among enemies adapted to a mole-like existence? It was a crazy move, which would almost certainly end in disaster—but Philippe was in the grip of the fever of adventure and a strange exaltation. "I need five volunteers to go with me," he said.

"It's certain death, Master," Kouram replied.

Philippe hesitated momentarily, and was then seized by vertigo. "We'll take four riflemen, Kouram—the rest can rejoin the Goura-Zannkas.

Kouram made no objection. He had said what he had to say. "All right." He pointed to four riflemen, who did not baulk, being full of a fatalistic confidence in the white man, and perhaps feeling safer with Philippe than with Warzmao's warriors.

Philippe examined the canoe rapidly and could not discover any defect. "Let's get aboard."

A few minutes later, the canoe was gliding over the lake. Kouram was paddling like a Pacific islander; Philippe, who had maneuvered canoes of a sort before, made use of the primitive oar comfortably.

The crossing took nearly an hour; then they perceived a flat gray shore, with a low ceiling. There was something sinister about both the water and the shore.

The expedition seemed wretchedly vain. They disembarked, however, and advanced at hazard. The shore was, in fact, only a sort of promontory; as on the other side, there was nothing to the right and left but a granite wall, and they ended up in yet another tunnel. Before going into it, Philippe paused.

No logic was guiding him, and the entire subterranean incursion was contrary to all reason. They would have needed to catch up with the fugitive Squat Men quickly, with sufficient forces to fight them. Now, the latter had the advantage, and doubtless an overwhelming superiority, which would permit them to pick their moment to wipe out the little troop…but the force of inertia pushed Philippe to go on to the end.

For ten more minutes he went forward warily. At intervals, the corridor became very narrow—so narrow that it would have been impossible to march two abreast.

Suddenly Kouram—who had taken the lead—stopped dead. There was a turning. A light seemed to filter from the granite wall.

"Look, Master!"

Philippe was already running forward. They both reached the place from which the light was coming at the same time.

Through an oval opening with jagged edges—a sort of natural bull's-eye window—they saw a grotto, palely illuminated—and a feminine form sitting in the middle of it. Not a native, or a Squat Woman, but a white woman, ornamented with the golden hair of legendary princesses.

Philippe as gripped by a frantic joy. "Muriel!" he cried. He could not help himself.

The young woman shivered and raised her head. Her great slate-blue eyes fixed their gaze on the oval window. "Who's calling me?" she said, in a low and almost indiscernible voice.

"Me…Philippe…"

She reached the opening in two strides.

"You!" she moaned. "You!" Pale, thin and a trifle haggard, she had evidently endured long suffering. "My father?" she asked. "All of you?"

"Safe and sound—but how are you, Muriel?"

"Oh—be careful! They're watching you…they're following you…they're waiting for the moment when they can catch you in a trap. There are no other creatures as stubborn."

"But how are you?" he repeated.

In the bluish light she wore a melancholy smile. "They haven't done me any harm *yet*. Their actions are incomprehensible to me. I'm in the hands of their sorcerers. At times, one might think that they were worshipping me—at others, they seem menacing. I don't know. I'm expecting something horrible." She passed her hand over her forehead; her pupils were dilated. "Get away!" she murmured. "They're masters of the underworld…they must know that you're here. Get away!"

"I have to save you."

"How can you? This grotto doesn't communicate with any other."

"Where does the light come from?"

"From above—the sky…the grotto opens on to a volcanic islet in the middle of the lake. Oh! Wait a moment…"

She passed her hand over her forehead again, in a desolate and fearful gesture.

"Tell me!" said Philippe, avidly.

"I can't. Go back the way you came. It's your only chance of salvation."

"Muriel, I beg you: talk to me!"

"You mustn't risk your life needlessly!"

"We shan't turn back! I'll save you or die. Tell me, Muriel!"

"I can't!"

"I swear to you that we won't abandon you!"

"My God!" she sighed. "Well, I think your tunnel communicates with the islet—but you can't get to it. *They*'re there!"

A growl interrupted her. Three thickset silhouettes had emerged.

Philippe's first impulse was to seize his rifle, but the Squat Men had already surrounded Muriel and dragged her away. Maranges hesitated; it was impossible to aim accurately at the moving group.

"Don't shoot!" Muriel shouted, plaintively. "It will only irritate them!"

He understood the futility and peril of an intervention…and a moment later, Muriel had disappeared; the cave was empty. Nothing remained but the hope of reaching the rocky island indicated by the young woman.

"Come on!" cried Philippe, launching himself into the tunnel.

Kouram and the riflemen followed him.

After running for ten minutes, a light mingled with that of the electric torch. The track ceased to be horizontal, and a rather steep slope rose up in front of the little troop. They climbed it impetuously and found themselves in the open air, in a circular crater with jagged edges, which reflected the Moon's melancholy light. Through a gap they could see the lake, in which the image of the constellations trembled.

"Look! Look!" shouted Kouram.

A canoe was drawing away from the shore, and in the canoe they could see Muriel held by five Squat Men. This time, Philippe was carried away by instinct. Convinced that the young woman would be lost forever if he did not save her now, he raised his rifle.

A shot rang out; one of the Squat Men spun round and dropped his paddle. The other four uttered frantic howls. Already, the rifle had thundered a second time, the bullet hitting a second Squat Man in the head. The survivors started paddling desperately, but with marvelous precision, Philippe shot two more men. The last one threw himself upon Muriel…

That was the supreme moment. The head of the savage and that of the young woman were so close that the slightest deviation would be fatal. Sometimes, they were both in the same line of sight.

Eyes dilated, his hand trembling, Philippe waited…

The man had grabbed hold of Muriel, and seemed to be trying to throw her into the lake.

Vigorous, accustomed to sports, she struggled. Momentarily, she pushed the brute back; their skulls were two feet apart. Then a wild determination took hold of Maranges; his hand ceased trembling—and the last Squat Man tumbled into the water.

The natives howled enthusiastically.

Muriel had seized one of the paddles and was coming back toward the islet. An immense emotion caused Philippe to tremble from head to foot. When the young woman landed, tears were running down his cheeks.

She saw those tears; and a pink tint invaded her pale face. "Oh!" she murmured. "It's as if the world had just been born."

He bowed, and raised the young woman's small hand to his lips. She looked at him gravely, troubled by a joy so profound that it was painful. Raising her joined hand toward the heavens, she said: "Out of the depths have I cried unto thee, O Lord!"[36] Then she said to Philippe: "After my father, you are the one who has given me life!"

"Oh, Muriel!" he whispered. "It seems to me that I would be dead, if you had been carried off!"

They remained momentarily in marvelous silence. Images rose up in tumult, with the incomparable glare that they assume in young people. Then Muriel went on: "We have to get away from here. They might surge out of the ground at any moment. I don't know what miracle allowed you to come through the tunnels, nor why I was so poorly guarded." She studied the inlet where she had landed. "Yesterday, there were more than 30 canoes here. Where are they? Extraordinary things must have happened…"

"We've attacked them, and defeated them, with the help of the Goura-Zannkas!" said Philippe.

"The Goura-Zannkas?"

"Black men with whom we have made alliance. Many Squat Men were able to flee, though. Perhaps there's fighting elsewhere."

"Where's my father?" Muriel asked, anxiously.

"He's at the camp."

---

[36] The opening words of *Psalm* 130 (*De Profundis*).

"We must hurry, Philippe."

"We've left Dick Nightingale and a company of men in the tunnels. They're waiting for us!"

"We can't go back the way you came!"

"What are we going to do, then?"

"Land on the shore of the lake—then send word to our friends."

"So long as they haven't been surprised by the Squat Men!"

"How did you get into the underworld?"

"From an island to the north. The entrance was sealed by a stone."

"I know the island—that's where it's necessary to send the warning. Did they all descend underground?"

The canoe was spacious enough to accommodate Muriel, Philippe and the natives. For a quarter of an hour they paddled in silence. The lake lived its savage existence; here and there, some animal, displaying a misshapen mouth or a scaly back, advertised the eternal extermination of one creature by another.

After a brief hesitation, Philippe had steered the boat toward the northern island. If they found the Goura-Zannkas and the flotilla of canoes there, that would be immediate aid. Perhaps, after all, the Squat Men had temporarily abandoned the struggle. Their defeat had been crushing. Like most savages, they would take their time before seeking revenge…

One of the men uttered an exclamation. He pointed to the north-west, where a somber swarm of canoes was visible. Yet more Squat Men!

A dark anxiety squeezed Philippe's heart. The northern isle was more than two miles away. Would the survivors, who were closer to the island than Philippe and his companions, have time to block the way?

"Quickly!" the young man exclaimed.

The order was unnecessary. The rowers had understood the danger; they were giving their maximum effort. For two minutes, it was impossible to gauge the antagonist's chances

The Squat Men's canoes were moving forward as rapidly as their imperfect construction and paddling permitted. It was a matter of reaching the southern tip of the island before the Squat Men could cut off the route. Two of their canoes were forging some distance ahead of the rest.

"No one fire!" said Philippe. The ammunition was running low. Sure of his own skill, Philippe wanted to keep it for himself. "Is your rifle fully loaded?" he asked Kouram.

Kouram nodded.

The two canoes were approaching the zone of uncertainty. One of them, especially, was advancing at a dangerous velocity. Then, slowly, Philippe raised his weapon.

"One man, at least!" growled Kouram.

He was not mistaken. The shot rang out; a Squat rower collapsed.

The men started laughing, while Philippe selected a new victim. A second later, another Squat Man dropped his paddle—and almost at the same time, furious cheers resounded on the island.

They saw the tall silhouette of Warzmao appear on top of the red rock.

Disconcerted, the Squat Men abandoned the fight. The two leading canoes rejoined the bulk of the flotilla, which disappeared over the starlit waters.

On the island, they found the warriors, augmented by a contingent led by Warzmao. They sent a messenger to look for the men in the underworld.

"This time, I think we're safe!" said Kouram.

Philippe thought so too. Once they had reached the shore, where a part of the Goura-Zannkas forces was waiting—after the expedition had come back from the caverns—the Squat Men would almost certainly renounce any immediate pursuit.

As long as nothing has happened to Dick! Philippe thought.

That anxiety was soon dissipated. Dick and his companions emerged from the red rock. Then the victory was dazzling. Warzmao and his warriors studied the luminous young woman that the Phantom Chief had recovered from the bowels of the Earth with a mystical admiration. Their faith in the invincibility of the white men took the proportions of a dogma. They knew that the Squat Men's ambushes had multiplied in the underworld for centuries; they could not imagine that a feeble troop of men had succeeded in escaping them, while liberating the strange creature with the golden hair.

On the shore they met up with the bulk of the Goura-Zannkas. No alarm having disturbed them in their task, they had gathered the wounded and the prisoners for a solemn feast. There were more than 50 of them.

"It will be a great feast," Kouram remarked; he was not in the least shocked by cannibalism.

"It's frightful!" said Muriel.

"By Jove!" said Dick. "It's not important."

Warzmao's warriors set off for their native forest. Roughly led away, the captives and the wounded followed in the rear-guard. Others were carried, lying on shields or woven branches. The ancestors of the Goura-Zannkas had done likewise in the times when the kings of Assyria had had vanquished enemies flayed "as bark is stripped from trees" and the times when the Hyksos had invaded Egypt. Nothing had changed since those distant eras, and doubtless eras more ancient still. The Goura-Zannkas had the same weapons, the same tools, the same rituals and the same enemies. Many a time, on bellicose nights, Squat warriors had been led away like this to serve as fodder—and many a time, too, had not defeated Goura-Zannkas been mutilated and tortured by victorious Squat Men?

"Yes," Philippe murmured, thinking about these things. "This is a scene of olden times."

He was walking beside Muriel, pensively, and their gazes sometimes met, with a profound tenderness.

"These things will end one day," she said.

"Undoubtedly—but perhaps by virtue of the disappearance of the Squat Men and Goura-Zannkas, under the bullets,

266

bombs or whips of white men…for our civilization, Muriel, is the most homicidal that has ever appeared on Earth. In the last three centuries, we have caused the disappearance of more peoples and populations than all the conquerors of antiquity and the Middle Ages. Roman destruction was child's play compared with ours. Don't you live, Muriel, in a land as large as Europe, from which you have caused the red race to disappear?"

"Alas!" sighed the young woman. The image of her father appeared to her, so clear and so sweet that she avidly extended her arms, as if for a hug. "Are we far from the camp?" she asked.

"Two hours, perhaps."

"What if it has been attacked during your absence?" she asked, fearfully.

"That's almost impossible—isn't it, Kouram?"

"Yes, Master. The Squat Men who attacked us on the lake shore were as numerous as the men of two clans. That almost never happens. The Blue Eagle is over there, with more warriors than Warzmao had—and what can the Squat Men do against the elephant-gun, the rifles and the machine-gun?"

These words reassured Muriel somewhat, and she told the story of her captivity.

The life of the Squat Men was not much different from that of animals. They slept a great deal, even during the day, but when they were active, they could march without respite and unhindered by darkness. They would never have abandoned their pursuit of the caravan. Their sorcerers had carried out mysterious sacrifices, in which warriors chosen by lot were immolated. They had been put to sleep with the aid of plants, and then the veins in their neck had been opened. Their blood had been collected by the chiefs. If the victims did not die, they were granted the mercy of their lives.

"I still don't know why they spared me," Muriel said. "It seemed that, to them, I was some sort of fetish whose presence would give them victory over their enemies."

267

The blood-colored Moon was swelling in the Occident, where it was about to set. The jackals kept watch on the mass of upright creatures; their slender heads popped up occasionally, with their pointed ears, and then vanished into the semi-darkness. A lion displayed its thickset stature on top of a mound; its roar filled the air—then, astonished, it slipped away.

"We're getting close!" said Philippe.

Muriel was exhausted, but they could now see the forest where men lived in the trees.

Suddenly, the column stopped. The advance guard fell back slowly toward the center. Scouts went running off, one by one.

"Are there more of these vermin?" Nightingale exclaimed.

Kouram exchanged signs with Warzmao. The young chief had climbed up on to a mound; his yellow eyes gleamed in the half-light.

"What is it?" Philippe asked.

"It's not Squat Men!" said Kouram. "They're warriors of a clan defeated by the Blue Eagle. They knew that Warzmao was leading a party composed entirely of Sons of the Star, while the Blue Eagle went in another direction. They must be intent on taking their revenge, Master."

"I thought that half that clan had perished."

"Warzmao did take half the Sons of the Star with him, and he's bringing back even fewer."

"Is the route blocked?"

"Yes, Master, all the way to the lake."

Philippe climbed up on to the mound in his turn. The Moon had just set in the west. He could only see the confused forms of the ground and the vegetations. The Goura-Zannkas were also hiding in the long grass or hollows in the ground.

"Damn it!" groaned Nightingale. "This land is terribly uncomfortable. I need to get some sleep!"

"You probably can," said Kouram gravely. "Warzmao will wait for daylight before resuming the march."

"What if those sons of bitches attack?"

"We'll wake you up."

Here and there, a black body was crawling through the grass. Warzmao distributed his sentinels. A sovereign silence weighed upon the wilderness; the large predators had stopped hunting.

Muriel and Philippe sat down on the ground. The breeze seemed to be descending from the stars, and that carnivorous night, when beasts and men had been slaughtered—that night full of menace and horror—settled into a peace so gentle that the young people almost forgot the barbaric law of the world.

"Oh, Muriel!" he sighed. "See how good life is…"

"It *is* good! We must accept the proofs to which the Lord subjects his creatures. I sense that we shall be saved!"

She bowed her head and raised a humble human supplication to the heavens—and Philippe's heart, turned upside-down by love, softened, astonished by that fabulous reality…

"Are they attacking?" stammered Dick Nightingale, who had just woken up with a start.

Dawn had broken. The fleeting tropical twilight had scarcely enchanted the lake, and the red furnace of the Sun had already appeared between two hills.

"No," said Kouram. "They're a little closer. They're blocking the route completely. We shall have to disperse them or beat a retreat."

"How many are there?"

"I don't know, Master. Warzmao has shown twice ten times the fingers of both hands."

"There are 200, then?"

"How was he able to count them?" Dick put in, in a surly tone.

"I don't suppose he has counted them," Philippe said. "He's probably calculated their number by deducting the dead, the wounded and the captives."

"Also dead," muttered Nightingale, "since they've been eaten."

"Warzmao still has between 70 and 75 sound men. You, Master, Mr. Nightingale and the riflemen are worth at least 100 men."

"Oh, much more!" Dick exclaimed, forcefully.

"But how can we engage in battle?" the man went on. "They'll draw back, invisibly, to the river, while harassing us. There, we'll need to cross over, and they'll be able to remain in the reeds, and inflict a great deal of damage on us."

The threat was enigmatic and annoying. The Sun rose, still partly veiled, and climbed swiftly over the lake, spreading its salutary and redoubtable energy over the waves.

Philippe, Warzmao, Dick and Kouram tried to spot the enemy forces. For the moment, they were all invisible. At length, two fuzzy heads emerged furtively, on the crest of a small hill. Reassured by the distance—more than 300 meters—the two warriors stood up. They were both tall men. The taller brandished an assegai and proffered words that the accompanying gestures almost rendered intelligible to the white men.

"He's challenging the Goura-Zannkas!" said Dick.

"That's the chief," said Kouram, after exchanging signs with Warzmao. "If you can hit him, Master, the warriors will be frightened."

Philip had raised his gun. He hesitated. He did not have the same motives for hatred against the unknown native that he had against the Squat Men. He resolved merely to wound him, but, understanding that it was necessary to maintain his prestige, he said to Kouram: "I'm going to hit him in the shoulder. Try to make Warzmao understand that it's a warning to the enemy."

Disappointed, Kouram gestured abundantly. Warzmao was astonished—but he howled in a voice as loud as a lion's roar. "The lives of the Sons of the Red Rhinoceros are in the hands of our allies. The chief will be wounded."

These words, the meaning of which the white men and Kouram understood, caused the enemy chief to burst out

270

laughing. He did not complete the fit of laughter. Philippe had fired, and the tall man, hit in the shoulder, dropped his assegai.

"The allies of the Goura-Zannkas are infallible and their weapons have the power of thunderbolts!" Warzmao shouted. "If the Gou-Anndas withdraw, their lives will be spared."

The enemy chief and his companion had disappeared. There was a long silence. Here and there, dark bodies could be seen crawling through the long grass. Then whistles sounded, which drew replies from the lake to the first baobab precursors of the forest.

Finally, three couriers presented themselves before Warzmao, who started to laugh, and signaled to Kouram that the enemies were beating a retreat. The Goura-Zannkas' advance guard was already under way again.

"What if it's a trap?" asked Philippe, looking at Muriel.

"We're preceded by invisible watchers," Kouram replied. "At the slightest alarm, the warriors will halt."

Philippe gave the signal to depart—but the threat had not disappeared. The Gou-Anndas' retreat might conclude with an ambush.

They advanced slowly. The column stopped several times.

"The warriors are still there!" said Dick.

After an hour's march, the alarm was given. The warriors held their assegais at the ready and there was a suggestion that the enemy had moved round to the rear. Soon, that became certain: the Goura-Zannkas were surrounded!

The situation was going bad. Because of Muriel, a violent anguish weighed upon Philippe. Nevertheless, the march continued—a slow, infinitely prudent march, protected by a circle of scouts.

Suddenly, savage cries were raised.

"The attack!" cried Dick Nightingale, preparing to fire.

The cries had died away. A stormy atmosphere enveloped the men. In the distance, the sound of a trumpet was audible.

Then an enormous clamor erupted. All around the column they saw the scouts rise to their feet.

"What is it?" cried Philippe.

Warzmao was yelling victory cries.

"It's the Goura-Zannkas' giant trumpet!" said Kouram. "We're saved!"

Philippe went pale and looked at Muriel, his gaze sparkling with the joy of deliverance.

Already, the Gou-Anndas could be seen emerging from cover and fleeing in disarray. A group of Goura-Zannkas pursued them with thrown assegais, and the Blue Eagle's advance guard came in view.

Muriel uttered a loud yell, and extended her arms toward the Occident; Ironcastle was coming, with Sir George and the colossal Guthrie.

VII. Life and Death

It was the hour when the shadows were lengthening: *Majoresque cadunt altis de montibus umbrae.*[37]

In the sacred clearing, the Goura-Zannkas were gathering for the nocturnal feast. The fires were ready. Twenty Squat Men and 20 Gou-Anndas were still soaking in the lake, in order that their flesh might be more tender and flavorsome.

It was a day of supreme victory. In less than a month, the Goura-Zannkas had triumphed over the Sons of the Red Rhinoceros, the Sons of the Black Lion and their millennial enemies the Squat Men, the masters of caves and underground tunnels.

---

[37] "The greater shadows fall from the tall mountains." The quotation is from Virgil's *Eclogues*, but it became a widely cited proverb.

The Blue Eagle marched toward the camp of the Chiefs with Colorless Faces. There too the fires had been disposed for the trap-filled night.

The Blue Eagle contemplated Guthrie's immense stature admiringly, and turned to Ironcastle with an earnest expression. Repeating his words in gestures, he proclaimed, amicably: "This night will be the Goura-Zannkas' greatest night since Zaoiuma took possession of the forest. Twenty Squat Men and 20 Gou-Anndas will give their strength and courage to the Goura-Zannkas. Ouammha would be pleased to share the flesh of the vanquished with the great Phantom chiefs, for he is their friend, and he knows that they are the masters of death. Would the chief of Wisdom, the Giant chief and the chiefs who strike at a greater distance than the voice of the Sonorous Trumpet can carry care to take part in the great feast?"

Hareton understood the speech. He replied, in words and gestures: "Our clans do not eat human flesh, and it is forbidden to watch it being eaten."

The Blue Eagle's face displayed an immense astonishment. "How is that possible?" he said. "What do you do with the vanquished? Your life must be sad!" He realized that this must be the reason for their colorless faces—but because it is necessary to respect strength, and because he was full of gratitude, he limited himself to saying, perhaps with an obscure irony: "Ouammha will send his friends antelopes and warthogs…"

In the green shade, amid the tremulous reflections of the river, Philippe contemplated Muriel's fair-haired grace. Beneath her tresses woven from sunlight and moonlight, the daughter of Angels evoked blonde goddesses, oread nymphs and undines springing from the mysterious lakes of the North. She gathered around her the beautiful desires of man and the sacred fictions that made the humble primitive female into an enchanted creature.

Their eyes met. He stammered: "Muriel…perhaps you know…that without you, darkness extends over my future…"

"I'm a poor small thing," she murmured, "and I owe you my life…"

"Then," he said anxiously, "if I hadn't come, out there…"

"Oh! No, Philippe—it wasn't necessary for you to save my life…"

A breath of creation passed through the air; the river seemed to emerge from that garden of dreams in which the first rivers ran, and the trees were newly-born on an Earth recently sprung from the waters.

Footfalls brushed the grass. Hareton Ironcastle appeared on the bank and saw their emotion. Placing his hand on Philippe's shoulder, he said: "You may entrust yourself to her, my son! Her heart is pure, her soul constant and she fears the Eternal!"

Part Three

I. The Plant Kingdom

"What a strange world!" Guthrie exclaimed.

The expedition was moving slowly through a savannah whose grasses were blue and violet. As the caravan passed by, these grasses, tall and thick, emitted a euphonic sound that was vaguely reminiscent of the music of violins. At intervals, there was a clump of palm-trees with indigo foliage, or banyans with amethyst leaves. A yellow vapor covered the ground, harmonizing with the hues of the foliage and the grasses.

"We've entered the Empire of the Plants!" said Hareton, who was observing the fantastic plain avidly.

He had given orders that the animals were to be prevented from grazing, but the orders were unnecessary. The camels and the goats, and especially the donkeys, sniffed the blue cereals and violet sainfoins mistrustfully. The gorilla manifested a grim anxiety; his round eyes were scrutinizing the locale with an ardent vigilance.

"The animals will die of hunger!" Sir George complained.

"Not yet!" Hareton replied, pointing to the forage with which the camels and donkeys were laden.

"Yes, you've made preparations," said Guthrie, "but there's one evening meal and one morning meal at the most…"

"They're desert animals…and if they're put on rations, they won't suffer much for several days."

Guthrie shrugged his shoulders carelessly. A very slow and gentle breeze had begun to blow; faint voices rose up from the entire plain—the voices of minuscule violins, the voices of naïve harps and the evanescent voices of mandolins, which formed a kind of charming and confused symphony.

"One might take it for a concert of Trilbys," remarked Muriel.[38]

"Of hobgoblins!" added Maranges.

Whenever they drew near to an island of palm-trees or banyans the voices swelled slightly, like those of muffled organs.

The yellow vapors, thick and low-lying, seemed to prolong a plain of amethysts and sapphires with a plain of topazes. Occasionally, there was a patch of bare ground—purple ground—endowed with a metallic sheen, which would not even support lichens.

Enormous flies went past, the largest of which were the size of blue tits. Their red-brown swarms followed the caravan and swirled around the animals, humming like beetles. Several of them settled on the donkeys and camels, running over their coats at a fantastic speed, but they were evidently harmless.

Minuscule birds sprang up from the grass, scarcely larger than scarabs; perched on grass-stems, a few of them were chirping in shrill tones. The flies pursued them. They were not as agile, but they occasionally captured one of the tiny creatures anyway, and disappeared with their prey into the depths of the long grass.

"That's frightful!" cried Muriel, who had just seen a fly seize a little bird.

Guthrie burst out laughing. "It's surely their turn! How long have the birds been swallowing flies? It's better for us than if they were venomous."

The plain extended indefinitely, shiny and redoubtable.

"We can withstand hunger for a long time," Sir George remarked, "but what about thirst?"

---

[38] The reference is to the eponymous heroine of George du Maurier's famous novel, who was mesmerized by Svengali into becoming a marvelous singer, although her natural voice was markedly discordant.

"A river flows from east to west," Hareton replied. "We're bound to run into it soon. We'll reach it tonight or tomorrow. Our waterskins are more than half full."

The caravan stopped in the middle of the day on one of the strips of red rock from which the plants were banished.

"Here we're sure not to transgress any mysterious laws," Hareton remarked, while the natives were preparing a meal.

Thanks to the cloud cover that hid the Sun, they were able to remain outside the tent. The anxiety was manifest. This land seemed stranger than anything they had imagined.

"Uncle Hareton," said Guthrie, when lunch had been served, "if we can't eat the plants, what are we going to do? I have a suspicion that we're facing a danger worse than the Squat Men." He swallowed a vast slice of smoked meat and started laughing, for nothing could deprive him of a part of his joy.

"Don't worry," Hareton replied. "We'll find green plants—or, rather, plants partly red and partly green…and our animals will eat. If all plants or parts of plants were taboo, how would the animals of this land live? In the meantime, our camels, donkeys and goats can't graze a single stem from this immense meadow."

"Oh!" Muriel exclaimed. Her extended hand was pointing at a strange creature that was visibly observing the diners. It was a toad as large as a cat—a *hairy* toad—whose beryl eyes were fixed on the travelers. Even more than its size and coat, the voyagers were fascinated by its third eye, with occupied the top of its skull and could swivel in any direction.

"Prodigious!" Philippe exclaimed.

"Why?" asked Hareton. "Don't we find a rudimentary eye—hidden, it's true—in the majority of reptiles? That atrophied eye was probably functional among the ancestral reptiles—and batrachians are close relatives of reptiles."

The toad had taken a stride—a stride as ample as the bound of a hare. They saw it disappear into a cleft in the rocky ground.

"There must be water underground," Sir George re-marked. "Which explains the prosperity of the violet and blue grasses."

The minuscule birds went by occasionally, with little cries. One of them settled not far from Muriel. Hypnotized by the presence of the humans, it did not hear the flight of a giant fly, which suddenly descended upon it and got ready to devour it.

"Oh! No...no!" exclaimed the young girl, horrified.

She ran forward, frightening the insect—but the little bird, wounded at the base of a wing, from which a few drops of blood sprang forth, let out to a feeble chirp. Muriel picked it up gently. In the narrow extent of its body, the tiny creature had the beauty of a sunset, the brightness of clouds of beryl, purple, amethyst and topaz. No Vanessa butterfly had more delicately-tinted wings, and its scarlet head, speckled with malachite dots, seemed to be made of some unknown, infinite-ly precious material.

"What embroiderer, water-colorist or goldsmith could have wrought such a masterpiece in such a limited space?" said Hareton.

"Which cruel nature allowed to be devoured by flies!" said Philippe.

Throughout that day the caravan moved south-westwards. The plain continued, interminably, with its violet and blue grasses, beneath gold and amber clouds, and the strange music of the vegetation brushed by the breeze.

"A frightful monotony!" Guthrie declared. "The blue and violet are making me nauseous—I have a stomach ache!"

"They're wearisome colors," agreed Sir George. "We ought to have yellow or orange spectacles."

"But I have some—and I'd forgotten them!" said Hare-ton. "Yes, I hadn't given them a thought since the beginning of the voyage. My excuse is that we all have perfect eye-sight—not a myopic or presbyopic individual among us."

"Not a single hypermetrope. Not a single astigmatic!" Sydney joked.

Dusk was approaching. They made camp on another red islet.

"This rests the eyes!" said Philippe.

"Yes...but what about the river?" asked Sir George. "I can't see any end to this plain. Tomorrow evening, our waterskins will be empty..."

"The animals won't be able to drink more than once, on half-rations!" said Guthrie, supportively.

"The Lord will provide!" Hareton replied. "There's certainly water underground." He pointed to two colossal toads that were disappearing into a fissure in the earth.

"Good!" said Philippe. "A jackal might just about get through that—but not a man."

"Especially me," mumbled the giant.

They were men with solid arteries and confident souls. In spite of the threat of the terrain, they enjoyed their evening meal. The men were pensive; a mysterious dread was weighing upon their imagination.

Philippe and Muriel isolated themselves at the edge of the camp. Among the amber vapors, a fabulous Moon rose like a copper and vermilion medallion. Philippe was intoxicated by the presence of his lithe companion. In her clear visage—a compound of young lilies, nacre and April clouds—the eyes of sapphire, with flecks of jade, had a sensitive sweetness, and her hair shone like ripe wheat.

"We shall be glad to have survived ordeals and seen this strange land!" she said. "The future is less redoubtable than back there, when you were in pursuit of monsters."

"How I should like to see you again among people of our own kind! I need you to be safe, Muriel!"

"Who knows?" she said, dreamily. "There is no safety. Perhaps this savage land has allowed us to avoid graver evils. We're poor little things, Philippe...it requires no more than one false step to kill a man who has escaped lions. God is everywhere—and everywhere, He rules our destinies."

"You're not a Muslim, though!" he said, with faint irony.

"No, I believe in effort; it's commanded of us...nevertheless, we're in the care of the Almighty." In a marvelously touching voice, she sang: "For thou has always been my rock, a fortress and defense to me!"[39]

His soul saturated by love, he forgot the obscure menaces and drank his fill of the sweetness of a magical moment.

II. Water the Creator

"The animals are thirsty!" said Guthrie. "And I'm as thirsty as they are."

There was no more water. The travelers had divided up the dregs of the waterskins. Now, in the limitless plain, they were advancing through the violet grains, the blue trees and the scarlet patches of ground. The desert gripped them like a prey, and the Sun, having vanquished the clouds, was darting forth a ferocious light that dried up the blood of humans. They had to keep going, though. The buzzing of the colossal flies accompanied the music of the grass, which was becoming sinister. It seemed more and more like the vibration of distant bells. When the breeze blew, they heard the peals of the tocsin.

"I think we're getting near to the river," Hareton affirmed.

"So you believe that there really is a river?" Sir George queried.

"I believe so, yes. It has been described to me."

Sir George scanned the horizon with the aid of his binoculars. "Nothing!" he said.

---

[39] This quotation is given in English in the original; it is taken from a prayer commonly used in the Church of England, based on the text of Psalm 31.

There were no more trees to be seen. The grasses grew thick and strong.

"There's water under the ground—and perhaps it's there that we'll need to look for it," Philippe remarked.

"We've lost a lot of time," Ironcastle replied. "I ask for a few hours more."

"So be it, Uncle Hareton," said Guthrie. "But how many days can one resist thirst?"

"That's very variable. Camels can go for three, four or five days…some say more. Men…two or three days, depending on their constitution and the state of the atmosphere."

"The atmosphere is frightfully dry!" Guthrie moaned. "My skin's beginning to harden. I fear that I might be the man who resists for the shortest time…"

A bleak horror enveloped the caravan. The Sun, as it sank, took on the color of virgin gold, and then swelled up and became orange. The day's end was near.

The animals advanced painfully, the donkeys and goats giving signs of distress. Dread and suspicion had overwhelmed the men, preliminaries of a rebellion that was still muted. The great faith that the westerners' victories had established within them was crumbling away in this strange world. The lack of water made them particularly anxious, not only because it was a redoubtable threat, but because they perceived the impotence of the masters in that respect.

Hareton saw Kouram coming toward him. "What are the men saying?" he asked.

"They're afraid, Master. This is the land of death—the grass here is the animals' enemy."

"Tell them not to be afraid, Kouram! We know where we're going."

Kouram's eyes, which bore a slight resemblance to those of a buffalo, were lowered toward the ground. "Is there far to go?" he asked, with a tremor.

"Everything will change when we reach the river."

Kouram's fatalistic soul accepted the Master's word, and he went to talk to the men.

The Sun was about to disappear when the caravan reached an islet of red soil. Several times, while they were preparing to make camp, they saw giant batrachians emerge from a fissure in the ground, which did not linger long before disappearing therein.

"Those animals need water!" Muriel remarked.

"Thus, there must be a subterranean pool of water," Sir George concluded.

"Let's find out," said Guthrie. "My thirst is becoming intolerable."

The goats were bleating plaintively, the donkeys sniffing the ground impatiently.

Philippe, Sir George and Sydney examined the fissures. They were narrow, and gave no evidence of any trace of moisture.

"We have to dig," said Philippe.

"That's what we shall do," declared Guthrie. "Let's find some movable ground."

Eventually, they found a place where the soil could be worked. Guthrie went to fetch the excavator. After an hour, they had dug a deep hole. The earth soon became moist, but that moistness did not increase and then began to diminish.

"That's strange!" exclaimed Philippe. "The dampness is obviously due to infiltration. There's probably a body of water in the vicinity."

"In the vicinity!" muttered Hareton. "Even if it's only 100 meters away, it's inaccessible to our feeble forces."

They attempted a few horizontal forays, which yielded no result.

"It will be a miserable night," Sydney concluded. "We've only succeeded in increasing our thirst."

The travelers slept badly and got up before dawn. They felt one of those threats that no valor can overcome; the peril was in their own arteries. The atmosphere, like an immeasurable leech, was drinking them drop by drop. Water, the mother of life, was abandoning their blood and vanishing into space.

"Let's not waste any time," said Guthrie. "We'll make progress more easily by night and in the morning."

"It would be a good idea for two of us to scout ahead," Sir George suggested.

"I thought of that," Hareton agreed.

"Sir George and me!" Guthrie exclaimed.

"Sir George and Philippe would be better," said Hareton.

"Why?"

"Because of their weight," said Hareton, with a pale smile. "The caravan can spare two camels for the expedition, but they're weak."

"All right," said Guthrie, churlishly.

They divided the loads of two camels selected by Kouram between the other animals; they were the fastest of the group. "They'll be good guides," the man affirmed. "They'll scent water a long way off."

Ten minutes later, the two men had left the caravan. The camels went at a good speed, as they had understood that they were being taken in search of water.

The Moon turned orange as it descended into the west; it became enormous, but its light decreased, while that of the constellations became more vivid. A slight phosphorescence rose from the ground. The atmosphere was mild, and the vegetal carillon seemed to be announcing some mystical ceremony in the depths of the savannah.

"It's as if we were on another planet!" murmured Sir George. "Here, I no longer have the impression of *our* past— nor of *our* future."

"No," Philippe replied, pensively. "We're a long way from the Promised Land."

The Moon took on the color of virgin copper; there was an almost imperceptible twilight, and the fiery Sun rose over the plain. Avidly, the travelers explored the horizon. Nothing—nothing but the interminable ocean of blue, indigo and violet grasses!

"Frightful!" Sir George said. "A vegetal tomb."

Thirst tortured the two men, augmenting as the Sun climbed higher in the sky. They followed a south-western heading scrupulously, as Hareton had recommended.

They were two strangely dissimilar souls. Sir George was one of those Englishmen who can live alone, if necessary, with a dog, in a desert region. He had a latent imagination, which burst forth in an unexpected manner, while Philippe's imagination always remained active.

Thirst! It corroded the two men's throats. Philippe, in a semi-vertigo, was subject to all sorts of fresh images: springs emerging from the ground with a lively murmur, alcarazas in the shadow of a patio, carafes of lemonade covered in condensation…

Eventually, he began to murmur in a low voice: "Fountains, streams, rivers, lakes…"

"Oh," said Sir George, with a melancholy smile, "I'm thinking, most of all, of a nice public house!"

The camels were beginning to show signs of distress.

"As long as they keep going!" said Philippe.

"They'll keep going!" affirmed Sir George. "They know we're looking for water. They understand that it would be dangerous to stop."

The Sun became ferocious; the colossal flies were buzzing around the two beasts and the two men frenziedly.

"At least we can be glad that they aren't attacking us!" Philippe remarked.

"I suspect that we're poisonous to them," his companion suggested. "The camels too."

"Why are they keeping us company, then?"

"They're following their instincts."

Silence was restored—a silence that the carillon of the grass rendered fantastic. Nothing. Still the grasses, blues and violets, with the occasional feeble clump of trees.

"What will become of them, back there?" Philippe murmured, thinking about Muriel in spite of his thirst.

Sir George shook his head. He seemed impassive, but, as a man from a damp climate, he was suffering more than Philippe. "They'll drink two or three goats, if they have to," he finally replied, "or even a camel. A camel generally has a pocket of water—more than 20 gallons of blood!"

The Englishman looked down covetously at his mount. "No, we can't!" he sighed. "We have to wait for the water!"

There was a long silence. Dry, hard and miserable ideas dragged themselves through the two men's minds—and the Sun continued to drink them…

Suddenly, one of the camels raised its head, and uttered a strange and ridiculous cry. Its companion rendered a long snort. They both accelerated their pace.

"What's the matter with them?" Philippe muttered.

"I dare not hope what I think!" replied Sir George.

The terrain became uneven; on a low hill they saw *green* grass and bushes. The two men gazed at them, dazzled; the ancient vegetal color delighted their hearts; it seemed that they were re-entering real life: the life their innumerable ancestors had led.

Now the camels were galloping recklessly. They climbed the hill. A raucous cry—a loud cry of deliverance—sprang from Philippe's breast. "Water! Water!"

She was there: the sovereign mother; the mother of everything that lives; she was there, the water of Genesis, the water of origins.

A river: it ran broad and slow, entirely enveloped by trees, reeds and grass; it spread an indomitable fecundity into the expanse.

Vertigo had gripped the camels. They galloped like thoroughbred racing camels; in five minutes, they reached the edge of the river, and were already leaning forward to drink untiringly.

The men leapt down on to the bank and, plunging their cups into the current, they slaked their homicidal thirst.

"This is imprudent!" Sir George eventually remarked.

"But delicious!" Philippe retorted.

Sir George offered him a gray pill. "Against the microbes! Wow!"

The Englishman stood up, alarmed, while his index finger pointed to a long islet 20 meters from the bank. An extraordinary animal had just emerged. It had the physical structure of the huge crocodiles of ancient Egypt—the vast elongated jaws, the monstrous teeth, the short legs and the muscular tail—but instead of scales, long hair grew all over its body and skull, and its eyes, shining like those of a panther, were not at all reminiscent of the vitreous eyes of reptiles.

A third eye gleamed at the summit of the cranium.

"What is that monster?" exclaimed Philippe. "Even in prehistoric times, no saurian resembled that…"

"Nothing, at least, licenses the claim! But our knowledge is fragmentary."

The beast studied the camels and the men; instinctively, they reached for their rifles.

A kind of barking caused them to turn round. Its head tilted back, a blue antelope was coming toward the river at top speed. The predator that was pursuing it—a lithe beast with beige fur dotted with small pink patches, was making bounds of 30 feet. It was as large as the great tigers of Manchuria.

"It's a leopard, though!" muttered Sir George.

Distracted by the arrival of this formidable beast, they did not see the hairy crocodile plunge into the river.

"Look out!" said Sir George.

The antelope, and therefore the leopard, was running directly toward the promontory on which the two men were standing. They retreated toward the upstream section of the river. The swift animals had already reached the bank. The leopard hastened its course, and the antelope was on the point of hurling itself into the river when it stopped, terrified.

At the tip of the promontory, the hairy crocodile had just surged forth, its yellow eyes fixed upon the fugitive animal. Paralyzed by terror, the latter turned its slender head toward the plain. In its obscure brain, the images were swarming: over there, the long grass, the sweetness of movement and life…here, eternal night…

The leopard pounced. It knocked the antelope down with a thrust of its muscular paw.

In spite of the peril, the two men experienced the savage curiosity that caused the Romans to flock to the circus.

"Two magnificent brutes!" Sir George remarked, examining his carbine.

The leopard, with one foot planted on its panting victim, looked at the reptile, which only hesitated momentarily. Opening its immense mouth, and rearing up on its short legs, it was ready to do battle. Its mass was three times as large as the leopard's. Its three eyes were gleaming. The leopard uttered a deep cry, which resembled a roar. It advanced at an angle, seeking to surprise its adversary by leaping on to its back, but the latter had none of the stiffness of its scaly ancestors. It turned round, and charged. The enormous feline rolled on the ground. Two heavy feet maintained it there. Too short, they impeded the action of the long mouth.

Then, flattening itself out and squirming through the grass, the leopard succeeded in getting away. Frightened by the superiority of its adversary, however, it fled. The other disdainfully set about devouring the antelope alive, and its victim's cries of agony mingled with the hoarse grunts of the victor.

While it was beating a retreat, the leopard perceived Philippe and Sir George. Its amber eyes fixed themselves avidly upon the two men.

"I'll aim at the head," said the Englishman, coolly.

"That's preferable," Maranges agreed. "I'll do the same."

The leopard hesitated. Fear, rage and hunger agitated its rude body. Then, seeing those singular silhouettes, the eyes of the two men fixed upon it, and the carbines that seemed a prolongation of their limbs, it went in quest of a more familiar and timid prey.

III. Life or Death

Death was hovering over the caravan. Occasionally, the hoarse and quavering breath of the donkeys or the baroque plaint of a camel was mingled with the strange carillon of the plants. The large flies continued to harass the animals—and the men, in spite of the faith they had in the chief, darted anxious glances around, which spoke of nascent rebellion and entertained gleams of folly.

"Bad!" said Kouram, who had just harangued his men. "They're losing their heads, Master."

Hareton examined the bleak silhouettes. His own throat was on fire, and the colossal Guthrie was suffering unspeakably. Muriel was holding up better than the men.

"Tell them to wait one more hour," Ironcastle replied. "If nothing turns up, we'll sacrifice a camel."

Kouram went to convey the chief's promise to the men. Because hope took on a clear form, the men rallied. The mysterious fluid of the nerves circulated less heavily.

Hareton scanned the horizon. Where were they? Had they reached the river, or were they wandering, like the caravan, in a desert that was all the more abominable for producing plants in abundance.

"It's disgusting!" Guthrie grumbled. "I really don't know whether I can hold up for another hour. I'm having hallucinations, Uncle Hareton. My head is full of springs, waterfalls and streams. It's a vile torture. An hour!" He took out his chronometer and considered it distractedly.

Hareton had turned to the young woman.

"Don't worry about me," Muriel said. "I can wait an hour, if necessary." Philippe's absence, however, filled her with apprehension and affliction. Had this mysterious and hostile land caught him in some trap? In spite of her own suffering, she thought about that which her faithful soul loved, with an ardor that would never fade.

The hour passed. The cruel light dazzled the men and animals alike. Guthrie had the impression of circulating through an immense furnace.

A man lay down on the ground, uttering plaintive cries. Another waved his knife. They all began groaning.

Then Hareton darted one last desperate glance at the horizon. Nothing! Nothing but those blue and violet grasses, those giant flies, that intolerable sound of bells.

Are we finally doomed? Turning to Muriel, his heart ripped by remorse, he added: *What madness persuaded me to risk that young life?*

To gain time, he called a halt and had the tents set up, saying: "In ten minutes, we'll be gorging ourselves on a camel."

Beneath the hastily-erected tents, they all sought a fugitive coolness. Hareton sadly designated the two men who were to carry out the sacrifice. They went forward, armed with sharp knives.

"Not yet!" cried Kouram. Lying on the ground, he stuck his ear to it, attentively. "I can hear a trot," he said. "The trot of large animals."

Everyone listened, breathless.

"Don't move until I give the signal," Hareton said to the sacrificers.

They stood beside the condemned animal. The blades threw off silvery reflections. Kouram continued listening, with his skull to the ground. Two other men imitated him.

"Well, Kouram?" Ironcastle demanded.

"The trotting's coming closer, Master—and I think they're camels."

One of the other natives agreed: "Yes, camels." But the other said, in a low voice: "Perhaps warthogs…"

"Where are the footfalls coming from, Kouram?"

Kouram pointed toward a long bulge in the ground to the south-west, whose crest could not have been elevated by more than 20 meters, but which was sufficient to shrink the horizon.

"Come on!" said Guthrie, mounting the largest of the camels. "If it's them, I'll raise my arms!"

In spite of its lassitude and its thirst, the animal did not refuse its service. It set off slowly. Several natives, being impatient, followed the colossus.

Hareton, who had raised his binoculars, let them fall back anxiously. "As long as it's not a mistake!" he muttered, looking at the men, all of whom had their eyes turned southwestwards.

Meanwhile, Guthrie had reached the foot of the hillock. The slope was gentle; the camel climbed it without any difficulty, preceded by the natives.

Hareton and Muriel waited, distress and hope oscillating with the beating of their hearts.

A few more paces—already the men were on the ridge, capering and crying out, without it being possible to figure out whether it was in joy or disappointment.

Finally, Guthrie raised his arms.

"It's them!" Hareton exclaimed, breathlessly. He had grabbed his binoculars again. Guthrie was laughing!

"Water! They've found water!"

The entire caravan leapt up, including the animals. It did not take Hareton long to reach and scale the shallow slope.

Out there in the desert of sonorous plants, two camels were running at a brisk pace. Philippe and Sir George were distinctly visible. Full waterskins were quivering on the animals' flanks. Delirious, Guthrie howled a victory song and the men were shouting frantically; all of them had carried on running.

"Is it the water, at last?" roared Sydney, when he was close enough.

"It's the water," Sir George replied, placidly, holding out a gourd to him. "Out there, as Ironcastle said, there's a large river flowing through the wilderness."

Guthrie continued drinking the fluid of life frenetically. The natives were howling and leaping about, laughing like children.

A grave joy filled Hareton's breast. "The Lord has turned his gaze to the prayers of the humble, and has not scorned their plea!"

Already, the rations having been distributed, the men were reviving, as dry grass revives in the rain. The animals were given minimal amounts, sufficient to give them the strength to reach the river.

Having drunk, Hareton listened without any great astonishment to the story told by Philippe and Sir George.

"Samuel wrote to me about these things," he concluded. "Tonight, the caravan will camp on the bank of the great river."

All distress had disappeared. The brains of the natives, in which the future only designed feeble images, forgot the ordeal in the sensuality of their revival—and because the Masters had triumphed once again over harsh Nature, their faith became unshakable.

IV. Near the River Bank

The caravan came to a halt 1000 paces from the river. Night had fallen; a starry light shone down on the vegetation and expanded subtly into the wilderness.

Six rocky masses surrounded the red camping-ground, where nothing grew but lichens, mosses and primitive plants. The fire radiated its sparkling light, and the animals that passed by in the semi-darkness paused at a distance to peer at the strange beings agitating amid the flames.

They saw batrachians emerge, as well as large crocodiles, jackals with coppery coats, dancing hyenas, bristling warthogs, pink hippopotamuses and furtive antelopes. Sometimes, a raptor with fleecy wings soared in the gloom, and a red lion appeared at the very edge of the river. Its eyes remained fixed on the encampment for some time, and then it set off on the prowl.

"It has the coat of a fox!" Sydney remarked, while Sir George was checking his rifle.

"Its gait is odd," added Philippe.

The camels, donkeys and goats sniffed the predator's scent anxiously.

"It is not as large as the river-leopard."

"No," Philippe agreed, "and certainly less fearsome."

"Look out!" Guthrie exclaimed.

The lion had disappeared; three colossal animals had just emerged from the shadows.

"Crocodiles!" said Hareton, with a mixture of curiosity and apprehension.

"Hairy crocodiles," Philippe specified. "The same as the one this morning. The largest is positively apocalyptic."

One of the reptiles was, indeed, at least a dozen meters long. Its mass could not have been inferior to that of a rhinoceros. Its three eyes, the color of emerald frosted with amber, were scanning the surroundings.

"Its strength must be terrible," said Philippe.

"Indeed!" muttered Guthrie, picking up the elephant-gun. "Nature has done her work well."

The colossal creature gave voice to a bizarre sound, analogous to the rumor of a cataract. It did not head toward the humans, but it had scented the powerful odor of the camels and goats.

"We make a very well-stocked larder," Philippe said. "Will it dare to come through the gaps?"

There were bare zones between the fires, the caravan not having been able to gather enough wood to make up a continuous circle. An audacious beast might be able to get into the camp—but in all probability, neither a lion nor a tiger would have attempted it, being fearful of the palpitating flames.

The phantasmagorical fauna increased in the vicinity of the camp: coppery jackals, hyenas, cheetahs, panthers, nightbirds, green monkeys, fluttering bats, lizards, giant toads and serpents of beryl and sapphire. Two leopards appeared on a mound; the creeping lion had reappeared, and more crocodiles climbed out of the river. The little lamps of eyes shone in the tenebrous swarm of bodies: yellow eyes, green eyes, red eyes, violet eyes, reflecting the firelight.

One of the leopards, raising its head, uttered a roar equal in strength to a lion's.

A confused anxiety grew in the souls of the voyagers. How paltry they would have felt before that inferno of wild beasts, without their redoubtable armaments! But the infallible aim of Sir George and Philippe, so many rapid-fire weapons, Guthrie's elephant gun and—above all—the machine-gun endowed the upright animals with an imposing power.

"A vision of St. John on Patmos!" said Guthrie.

The giant crocodile yawned; its open mouth was reminiscent of a cavern; its teeth seemed innumerable, and the entire creature made them think of the age of fabulous reptiles. It was now in front of the encampment's largest gap; the camels were snorting fearfully, while the donkeys and goats sought refuge closer to the humans.

Attentively, with its large eyes fixed on a dromedary, the crocodile stretched itself. Perhaps it was hesitating, but only briefly. It advanced deliberately into the gap.

Then, a mad terror took possession of the domesticated animals—a terror comparable to the stampedes that draw herds of wild horses over the savannah. A few broke their hobbles; three crazed camels galloped toward the group of humans. The men ran to intercept them.

"This could reduce us to a state of inferiority," Hareton muttered.

"Look out!" cried Guthrie.

The crocodile was in the camp.

It headed for the dromedary that it had spotted and, which, for mysterious reasons, had obtained its preference. It was a tense moment, because the other crocodiles were approaching the camp.

"Since it's my turn," said Philippe to Sir George, "I'll take the right eye."

"All right," the Briton acquiesced, phlegmatically. "The left's mine."

Two shots rang out. The crocodile uttered a howl of distress, and started to turn round. A third bullet, cleaving through the pineal eye, blinded it conclusively.

The men took control of the furtive beasts, and the furious plaints of the crocodile immobilized the predators around the circle. Over the blue expanse, the ancient splendor of the stars trembled gently.

"Man is a redoubtable beast!" Guthrie concluded.

V. The Young Woman in the Blue Night

For two days the caravan advanced without hindrance. Hareton took his bearings every morning and directed the march after consulting the compass.

The region remained fertile, populated with innumerable and unusual animals: mauve hippopotamuses, exceedingly tall giraffes, hairy crocodiles, spiders as large as birds, disquieting insects—some of the beetles attained the size of turtles— elephants armed with four tusks, climbing fish and snakes the color of fire.

The plants were particularly astonishing. They still encountered violet and blue grasses, disseminated in islets, but a leguminous flora became more abundant the further southwest they went. Its variety was inconceivable; some were shaped like sensitive plants,[40] others attained the stature of

---

[40] The sensitive plant (*Mimosa pudica*) is so-called because of its unusual reactivity, and there are numerous other species in the same genus capable of rapid movement, including the telegraph plant and the Venus fly-trap. Rosny elects to use the more general *Mimosée* [Mimosacea] as a general descriptive noun for his superior plants, but it is plants of the genus *Mimosa*—most of which are tropical and subtropical shrubs or

birches, ash-trees and beeches, and a few colossal specimens surpassed the Sequoias of California in height and mass.

Hareton had given his companions strict warnings. "It's necessary to respect them, without exception—they're all re-doubtable."

These instructions excited Guthrie's curiosity. Had he been alone, he would doubtless have given in to his instinctive bravado, but he willingly obeyed the chief. When anyone brushed a Mimosa, of a dwarf or giant variety, the leaves clenched like fists and according to their shape, emitted sound comparable to those of zithers, lyres or harps.

"What makes them redoubtable?" Sydney asked, impatiently. "Is it their thorns?"

"Their thorns are already sufficient—a prick is painful, and causes a kind of madness. Notice that the animals are avoiding any contact."

"What shall we do, then, if they multiply to the point of rendering our passage impracticable?"

"They don't seem to want that," Hareton replied. "They leave free spaces everywhere. I wonder why." He consulted Samuel Darnley's notes.

The sky grew darker. Immense clouds ascended from the depths. A magnetic atmosphere enveloped the caravan.

"We're going to have a fine storm!" Sir George remarked.

Spiraling winds got up in a light of copper and jade; the elements took on a furious excitement, and when immense flashes of lightning filled the expanse, it was as if some obscure will of the mineral world had determined to terrify the animals and astonish the humans. Up above, the clouds displayed a sudden genesis, a formidable consciousness suddenly surging from the unconscious.

---

flowering plants—that he has in mind as "advanced" plants likely to have evolved even greater capabilities, given the opportunity, so I have used the less cumbersome term.

Then the water came down, palpitating and fecund, the ancestor of everything that grows and dies.

They had set up the tents; the poorly-sheltered animals stamped their feet in the squalls and leapt up at the roars of the thunder, as if innumerable lions were wandering in the nimbus clouds.

"Ah, how I love storms!" cried Guthrie, breathing in the humid air voluptuously. "They give me ten lives!"

"They must also cause many deaths," Sir George remarked.

"Everything causes death! It's necessary to choose, my friend."

"We don't choose—we're chosen."

All around the camp, stampedes carried the wild animals away. A herd of giraffes passed like lightning; elephants showed their rocky backs momentarily; giant lizards sought crevices; a rhinoceros lumbered like a rolling stone and warthogs galloped ponderously, while slender antelopes fled, without knowing it, into the vicinity of a bewildered lion.

"There's neither prey nor hunter now," said Philippe, who was standing next to Muriel.

Already, however, the weather was abating; a gap pierced the nimbus clouds; the rain began to fall less torrentially.

Then the ancient furnace reappeared in the depths of the sky.

"There's the Monster!" Guthrie growled.

"The authentic father!" Sir George riposted.

The end of the drama was abrupt. The earth drank the water and dried out visibly.

"We can get under way again," said Hareton. He spoke in a weary voice and, having risen to his feet, walked heavily.

"The weather's still disturbing!" said Guthrie. "It makes one feel weary."

"Very weary," Sir George agreed.

Philippe said nothing; it seemed that the weight of his body had doubled.

Even so, Hareton gave the order to depart. It proved exceedingly difficult. The humans were dragging themselves along, the animals panting hard, and they were all moving with excessive slowness.

"What's the matter with us?" Guthrie demanded. His speech was slurred, his voice leaden, and he was moving like a man in a trance.

No one replied; for half an hour the caravan continued on its way, ponderously. It had not covered a kilometer. All around it, the islets of Mimosas multiplied to the point of rendering passage difficult. Whenever anyone inadvertently touched one of the plants, the leaves stirred strangely, and an icy fluid seemed to spread through his flesh. The phenomenon was more obvious when it was associated with a tree; the branches undulated like a nest of serpents.

"I can't go on any more," said Guthrie, finally, with a dull anger. "It's as if I were dragging leaden cannonballs. Haven't your notes anything to tell us about this, Uncle Hareton? Is it some kind of narcosis? And is it these damned plants again?"

"It doesn't feel like narcosis to me," Hareton replied, in a voice as constrained as Sydney's. "No, it's not a numbness—my thoughts are clear, my sensations normal. It's just this intolerable weight. One would think that gravity had increased."

"Yes," Sir George agreed. "That's it, exactly. Everything is still normal—except for this heaviness."

"I must weigh 500 pounds!" Guthrie complained. "You haven't answered my question, Uncle Hareton. Is it the plants? If so, how?"

"I think it must be the plants," Hareton said, feeling a frisson. "Besides—as you know—here, everything depends on them. I only wish I could understand *what they want*…or why they're hindering us."

"There's no longer a single animal visible," Philippe remarked.

That was true. They could not see a single mammal, bird or reptile; even the insects had disappeared. With every step, the weight increased...

It was the camels that stopped first. They started uttering discordant cries, which gradually died away; then they lay down and refused to budge. The donkeys did not take long to imitate them, while the goats continued to move around, painfully.

"What will become of us?" Hareton murmured. His speech was slowed down as were his gestures, but his nerves retained their sensitivity and his thoughts were unaffected.

The giant collapsed. Although less affected, Philippe and Sir George were still paralyzed. It was Muriel who was most resistant; even so, she could not take a step without an extraordinary effort.

"Yes," said Philippe, painfully. "What do they want? What have we done that frightens them?"

A mysterious terror floated in the air. In front of the caravan, a forest of giant Mimosas began; they must already have been alive in the time of the kings of Assyria and the Chaldean shepherds. Ten civilizations had risen and fallen since the time when their shoots had sprung from the nourishing planet.

Is it them that are stopping us? Hareton wondered. *Perhaps, then, by turning back...*

But they could not turn back. Their legs were almost inert; when they tried to speak, the words emerged so slowly that they became incomprehensible. All the caravan's animals were lying on the ground; only their eyes were active—and those eyes expressed an indescribable terror...

Evening approached: a red and funeral dusk. With unprecedented efforts, Muriel had dragged herself as far as the food stores and brought back smoked meat and biscuits. They all watched the Sun disappear. Night fell. A pink crescent illuminated the surroundings faintly. Far away—very far away—jackals were yapping.

It occurred to them then that they were defenseless; predators could eat them alive—but the solitude remained complete; no animal form appeared in the grass, on the bank or on the edge of the forest. Gradually, fatigue overwhelmed all sensation and all thought—and when the crescent moon disappeared beneath the horizon, humans and animals slept beneath the tremulous grace of the constellations.

In the middle of the night, Muriel woke up. The Moon had disappeared; the whiteness of the stars formed a palpitating snow. The young woman stood up, painfully agitated by fever and a phantasmagorical overexcitement. She looked at her companions stretched out in the ashen light, and suddenly experienced a sharp feeling, simultaneously sad and urgent, *that it was necessary to save them.*

That sentiment excluded all logic; it was self-contained, like the impulses of creatures that live entirely by instinct. She did not even try to reason…

Prey to a sort of hallucination, and although her fatigue was still overwhelming, she set off in the direction of the Southern Cross, moved by an intuition that owed its origin to something Ironcastle had said. Periodically, she was forced to pause; her head weighed upon her neck like a block of granite…

Often, she crawled. Tired as she was, her excitement did not abandon her; from time to time she murmured: "I *must* save them!"

Deep down, she conceived the hope that, after a while, she would emerge from the dangerous zone, forgetting that she would then find herself alone in a carnivorous world—for here, the astonishing solitude persisted; no animal was stirring in the immeasurable plain.

Muriel progressively drew away from the forest of giant Mimosas.

Several hours passed, hard and slow. The young woman had not covered more than a mile. Abruptly, she felt a delightful impression. The weight had disappeared. Muriel found the freedom of her muscles again, the sweet sensation of being mistress of her own body. Instinctively, she made haste, to get further away from the deadly zone…

Then, another anxiety began to stir within her. The animal world had returned. Jackals were passing by, as furtive as phantoms; a hyena limped through the shadows; giant toads were hopping in the moist grass; nocturnal raptors were gliding overhead on their silent wings.

Subtle, disquieting life was swarming everywhere—that agitation which, since time immemorial, has never ceased to be mingled with stubborn and ferocious destruction: sounds of breathing, obscure clamors, the rustling of grass, the jerky laughter of hyenas, the curt yapping of jackals, the plaint of an owl…

Muriel's only weapon was a revolver, but she did not think of retreating. The excitement that had drawn her forth persisted, transforming itself into a sort of confused intoxication, doubtless due to her renewed agility.

Occasionally, a frisson agitated her breast. The jackals that were following her with a prudent effrontery were the symbol of everything in the savage land that was on the lookout for life in order to destroy and devour it. They were led by the eternal hunger that makes a promise to the belly of every living creature.

Dawn was approaching when a shrill voice pierced the air—and Muriel saw a long body gliding slyly through the grass. Its eyes darted two emerald gleams.

The young woman watched the terrifying thing coming: the flesh that coveted her flesh…

The jackals had stopped, their ears pricked, simultaneously full of dread, desire and hope. Muriel felt the immense solitude, and all the cruelty of the universe, weighing upon her…

Browning in hand, she murmured; "Lord, thou art my strength and my shield!"

Meanwhile, troubled by Muriel's gaze and her upright stature, the feline did not attack. The rule of its race dictated that it must take any prey capable of defending itself by surprise.

In the blue night, the human eyes held the ferocious eyes in check. Muriel was ready to fight. The predator, stretching itself out, glided through the grass like a fluid...

VI. The Scaly Men

When Hareton opened his eyes, at dawn, he remained in a kind of torpor for some time. A mist floated before his eyes. His companions were still asleep, as was the gorilla...

Vague forms were moving in the tent, like shadows on a wall. They became more precise—and Hareton, after a start that woke him up completely, discerned extraordinary creatures. Were they animals? Were they men?

Like men, they were vertical in stature, even though their feet were like the trotters of wild pigs and their legs were like the legs of lizards. Their bodies were covered with translucent plates, mixed with green fur, and their heads were not precisely reminiscent of any human or animal head: cylindrical, with a sort of mossy cone at the summit, they were the color of malachite. The triangular mouth seemed to have three lips; the nose was reduced to three elliptical holes; and the eyes were sunk into hollows whose edges were toothed like a saw. Those eyes emitted a variable phosphorescence, with purple, orange and yellow glints. Their hands had four claws, opposable to three others, but no palms...

Hareton tried in vain to stand up. Lianas as slender as cotton thread, and very numerous, bound his limbs. Slightly elastic, they stretched when the American made an effort.

Ironcastle's astonishment did not last long. As the clarity of his memory increased, he mentally recapitulated Samuel Darnley's notes and realized that these fantastic beings were those which, in this land *replaced humans*.

Instinctively, he tried to talk to them. "What do you want?" he said.

His voice caused the cavernous eyes to turn toward him, and whistling sounds rose up: deep whistling sounds that were reminiscent both of the chirping of blackbirds and the sound of gross panpipes.

Their faces were mobile, but only in a single direction, in such a way as only to form vertical wrinkles. In consequence, their expressions were quite unlike any familiar expressions.

Philippe woke up in response to the sound, and then Sir George and Guthrie. All three were bound, like Ironcastle. The lamentations of the men went up from the neighboring tents.

"What's this?" growled Guthrie, gripped by fury. His powerful muscles distended the lianas to the point that they seemed to be on the point of breaking. Ten scaly men precipitated themselves toward the colossus—but the bonds did not give way. "Where did these monsters spring from?" he howled. "By comparison, the Squat Men were celestial creatures!"

"They're human, or nearly," said Hareton, sadly, "who hold us captive!"

The natives were making a frightful racket; at intervals, the growl of the gorilla could be heard.

"Are they prisoners too?"

Suddenly, Ironcastle uttered a howl of distress, almost immediately echoed by Philippe. Muriel was not in the tent. Horror and somber dread infected him.

"What do these monsters want?" Guthrie exclaimed, after a silence.

Philippe was weeping, and Ironcastle was sobbing. "I have tempted the Lord," the latter moaned. "Oh Lord, let my sin fall back on myself alone!"

They were soon certain that the "monsters" were pseudo-humans. One by one, the travelers, the gorilla and the majority of the natives were dexterously and methodically loaded on to camels. The claws manifested an extraordinary vigor and complexity of gestures. Guthrie howled insults. Sir George, still impassive, muttered: "Where are they taking us? Do they know how to make use of animals?"

Then they made their most surprising move. They untied five of the men, including Kouram, and pointed to the tents, and then the animals.

Kouram understood. "Should we obey, Master?" he asked Hareton.

Ironcastle scarcely hesitated. Evidently, the Scaly Men held the lives of the prisoners in their hands, and resistance might unleash an obscure anger. It was better to gain as much time as possible. "Obey!" he said.

Fatalistically, Kouram had the tents dismantled, and when everything was ready for the departure, he led the caravan away, guided by the gestures of the kidnappers.

One of them—an individual scalier and greener than all the rest—seemed to be the chief. About 50 pseudo-humans were marching alongside the caravan; 20 preceded it and they were able to count about 40 bringing up the rear.

Maddened by the anxiety that Muriel's fate was causing them, Hareton and Maranges observed events imperfectly, while Guthrie was only just beginning to recover his self-composure. Sir George alone had watched everything with profound attention. The intelligence of the monsters seemed evident, their discipline perfect and their language highly-developed. To give an order, the chief did not make any gesture; his finely-modulated whistles were sufficient to make himself understood. He only had recourse to gestures when addressing himself to Kouram, in whom he had quickly recognized an authority superior to that of the other men.

Besides, the Briton thought, *he has taken care not to untie any white man. He therefore knows, instinctively or otherwise, that they are different from natives and more dangerous...*

The expedition marched parallel to the forest for several hours. Then the Mimosas became more widely spaced; a sort of heathland appeared, where pine-trees, ferns and tall bright green mosses were growing. The Scaly Men set forth into it deliberately.

"Where the Devil are they taking us?" said Guthrie, who was now observing as minutely as Sir George.

Hareton and Philippe had also moderated their agitation.

"They're taking us home, I assume," the Englishman replied. "Note that they're treating the plants here with brutality, whereas, back there, they were careful not to make contact with the trees, or even the bushes.

"There's not a single Mimosa in this place," Hareton remarked. "And the majority of the vegetable species seem primitive—cryptogams or gymnosperms…"

"All that doesn't give us any information as to our fate," Sydney complained.

"They haven't killed us," Sir George retorted, calmly. "They're taking the trouble to take us with them, and our animals…"

"And our provisions!"

"One can infer, without overmuch temerity, that they intend to keep us alive."

"At what price?" A furious quiver shook Guthrie's giant body.

"I assume that we'll be captives…and that they intend to make use of us…"

"Damn it!" the colossus cursed. What proof is there that we won't be the fresh meat at a feast? Why shouldn't these fellows be cannibals, like our friends the Goura-Zannkas? In that case, we'll have nothing to look forward to."

The heath broadened out; the mosses became enormous, a breeze stirring them like vast heads of hair; the pines were no more than stinted bushes, while the ferns formed arborescent bouquets where strange sarigues[41] and flightless birds the

---

[41] The sarigue, or quica, is a small American opossum; it is presumably included here because it is a marsupial, to supplement the observation that the flora seems primitive.

size of bustards took refuge, along with worms like threads of wrought iron.

The expedition went around the fern-thickets without the order of the march being disturbed. Hareton was now observing the Scaly Men as attentively as Sir George. Their armaments were bizarre. Each of them carried a sort of helical harpoon made of red stone, a plate carved into a half-moon, and—in a leather bag—round and spiny projectiles, also red, the form of which resembled sea-urchins. The efficacy of these projectiles became evident when a group of warthogs passed by. Three warthogs, struck by the "sea-urchins," rolled on the ground and died in convulsive agony. The weapons were evidently steeped in poison.

"You can see that they're human—and ingenious humans too," Sir George said to Sydney.

"What prevents there being animals as ingenious as humans?" the giant complained. "They can be anything you want, but not men."

At about midday, the leader of the expedition gave the signal to halt. They did so in the shade of ferns as tall as plane-trees, whose thick foliage provided shade that was almost cool.

Kouram was then permitted to communicate with his masters and the black prisoners.

"Can you understand them, Kouram?" Ironcastle asked.

"Sometimes, Master. I know, therefore, that they want me to give you something to drink and eat." The man spoke in a weary and miserable tone. He sensed a threat hanging over him direr than death—and the white man's prestige had disappeared. Another, unnamable, prestige had arisen to oppress the guide's superstitious soul…

Aided by his free companions, Kouram helped his masters to eat and drink, and then took care of the immobilized natives.

The halt was not long. The expedition got under way again, and the landscape underwent a further metamorphosis.

Chains of rocks emerged from the ground; they advanced in shadow through a bleak gorge, as red as fresh blood.

When sunset approached, another halt was commanded. The melancholy prisoners considered an immense scarlet ring sealed by high cliffs, with no other exit than the gorge from which they had emerged.

"Is this where these monsters live?" Guthrie exclaimed. "I don't see any sign of shelter."

"I assume they live *in* the rock," Sir George replied.

The chief's whistling interrupted them. They saw the Scaly Men of the escort form a circle around the caravan and other individuals appeared at the base of the red cliffs, as if they were actually emerging from the rocks.

An intense whistling replied to the chief's whistles. The camels having been relieved of their animate and inanimate burdens, Hareton, Sir George, Philippe, Sydney, Dick Nightingale and Patrick Jefferson were set down in a group with the bound natives. Then, half a dozen Scaly Men brought dry wood, with which they lit a fire, which they sprinkled with a yellowish liquid.

"This bodes ill," said Hareton, sadly, on seeing the flames spring up. "Just in case, my friends, let's say farewell!"

The monsters drew away, driving the beasts of burden to the far end of the enclosure.

"I'm guilty of having brought you all to this," Ironcastle went on. "I ask your forgiveness."

"Come on, Uncle Hareton," said Guthrie. "We're men, and we intend to take responsibility for our own actions."

The fire was blazing more powerfully; an aromatic odor spread through the atmosphere. Philippe thought desperately about Muriel and his sister Monique.

"It's a wise precaution to prepare oneself for death," said Sir George, "but all is not lost."

"Let's pray," said Hareton.

The increasing flames threw an orange light into the shadow of the rocks; the odor became more penetrating; a strange languor took hold of the men.

306

In the distance, the Scaly Men abandoned themselves to fantastic rhythmic movements, punctuated by long whistles.

One by one, the prisoners collapsed on the ground and became still.

VII. Muriel in the Unknown

The beast had only one bound to make to reach Muriel, and the packs of jackals, moving closer, awaited the denouement with a voracious impatience. The prey was too large for there not to be flesh, entrails and blood left over once the large predator was sated; they would have their turn then.

In this tragic situation it was not so much fear that motivated Muriel but an incommensurable sadness and a curious bitter humility. The daughter of dominant races that had enslaved animals and plants, she was no more than a feeble victim, vanquished flesh that was coveted by a cat, a hyena and jackals. Her entire sense of existence was inverted, as if the ancient ages had returned, when the fate of humans was confounded with that of other animals.

The unknown beast growled, and Muriel, resigned and combative at the same time, did not miss a single one of its movements. Still attempting to take the prey by surprise, the feline moved around her, and then drew closer in such a way that the young woman thought it was attacking and decided to fire.

Two shots rang out. Wounded and furious, the beast leapt at Muriel and knocked her over. A mouth with sharp canines opened above the white throat…

At that moment, a raucous cry—a fantastic clamor simultaneously reminiscent of the sound of a torrent and the howl of a wolf—rose up on the plain. Two singular animals appeared on a mound. Their scaly bodies bore some analogy to the body of a Newfoundland dog; their cubic heads were almost as large as a lion's.

The feline recoiled; the jackals and the hyena beat a retreat and the monstrous beasts ran forward. When they were no more than a few meters away, the feline fled desperately, and Muriel got to her feet.

A more mysterious danger was menacing her. Dazedly, she contemplated the creatures, as chimerical as winged bulls, unicorns, fauns and sirens. All resistance seemed vain. Muriel folded her arms and waited for the attack.

There was no attack.

Two paces away from the young woman, the animals stopped. Almost immediately, more individuals appeared—but this time, they belonged to the familiar universe. They were three natives, tall in stature, and *armed with rifles*, so similar to the men of the caravan that for a moment, Muriel thought they had come to look for her. Merely by their accoutrements, she realized that she was mistaken; one might have thought that they were clad in polished glass, but a glass as flexible as linen or hemp. Their costume consisted of a kind of close-fitting jacket, and a short skirt, hanging down to mid-thigh, a hat with a flat rim, and a kind of belt in which a knife and a hatchet were visible.

They waved their arms, and one of them exclaimed: "Don't be afraid! Friends!"

Stunned with amazement, she waited for them to come down from the mound.

When they were closer, the one who had spoken—who bore a vague resemblance to Kouram—asked: "American?"

"Yes," she said, nervously.

The man had soft, tranquil eyes. "Me too," he said.

There was a pause. The scaly animals prowled around the young woman; the men examined Muriel attentively.

Suddenly, she had an inspiration, and murmured: "Do you know Mr. Samuel Darnley?"

"He's my master."

"We're looking for him."

"I thought so," said the man, laughing and clapping his hands. "In that case, Miss...or Mrs...?"

"Miss Ironcastle."

"Come on—it's this way."

"Is it far?"

"Two hours' march."

It was one of those times when it was necessary to risk everything. She did not hesitate; she went with the men.

They led her over a savannah, and then traversed—with minute precautions—a forest in which baobabs and banyans alternated with Mimosas. Otherwise, the march was easy, the trees being spaced out or forming islets that they went around.

They came to a stream, whose bank the men followed to a place where enormous stones, not very far apart, permitted them to cross over.

"We're nearly there," said the one who had accosted Muriel.

The plants had become sparse; red ground stretched away, bounded by a rocky wall.

At that moment, the scaly beasts made their fantastic voices heard.

A tall man appeared in the shadow of the rocks. His sunburned complexion, which almost seemed black, made a striking contrast with his hair and beard, which were as blond as Muriel's hair. His ultramarine eyes fixed themselves on the young woman, and he exclaimed, in amazement: "Miss Ironcastle!"

"Mr. Darnley!" she exclaimed. She was gripped by such emotion that she nearly fainted.

Having advanced toward her, Samuel Darnley took her hands and squeezed them tenderly. Then an anxiety creased his tanned face. "Where's Hareton?" he asked.

"He's back there…with the expedition," she stammered, "plunged in a lethargic sleep…we've been unable to move any further forward since yesterday…"

Darnley shook his head, and frowned. "It's *them*!" he muttered. "You've strayed into a region that's temporarily forbidden…*they*'ve defended themselves…"

"Who?"

"The Mimosas. It's necessary to know them and obey them…"

Muriel listened fearfully, but not astonished. Suddenly, her eyes grew wide. Other natives had just emerged, along with indefinable creatures. Because of their upright stature, they were broadly reminiscent of humans, but their pachy-derm-like feet, their lizard-like legs, the scales with which they were covered, mixed with coarse hair, their heads like cylinders of bark surmounted by a mossy cone, their triangular mouths and their sunken eyes, which emitted a multicolored phosphorescence, was not precisely reminiscent of an animal or human form. In spite of having experienced so many ex-traordinary events and spectacles, Muriel was momentarily stupefied.

"They're human!" said Darnley, in response to the young woman's glance. "Or rather, they play the role of humans in this region. Strictly speaking, their organisms are as different from ours as those of a baboon and, for instance, a dog. Don't be afraid, Miss Ironcastle—they're my allies, absolutely relia-ble, incapable of the slightest treason. It's only necessary to fear those with whom I haven't yet been able to forge an al-liance." He interrupted himself, his brows furrowed. "Let's think about Ironcastle and his friends! Since you were able, in spite of everything, to get out of the afflicted territory, the acceleratory energy must already have diminished. I think, therefore, that our friends are now awake and on the move. Let's go look for them."

Rapidly, he gave orders to the four men, and then ad-dressed himself to the Scaly Men, partly by signs and partly by means of strange whistling sounds, to which they replied.

In a quarter of an hour, the expedition was ready, the men armed with rifles and each of the Scaly Men with a sort of red harpoon and a semi-circular plate. Leather bags were suspended from their waists.

"Let's go!" said Darnley.

As the troop left the red ground, he said to the young woman: "There's no reason to be anxious. The fact is that they

310

aren't murderous. Even when the acceleration and the sleep are prolonged, there's no great harm done. I've seen animals weighed down or put to sleep for three or four days without suffering any lasting damage."

"But what if carnivorous animals invade the camp while they're asleep?" Muriel objected. "Your crocodiles and giant leopards are terrible."

"Nothing to fear! Our friends will wake up automatically before any animal has reached their camp. The sleep wears off about an hour after the termination of the 'acceleration'—and during that hour, any region subjected to the phenomenon is respected...except by those who fill the roles of humans and are less obedient to instinct...but almost all the tribes in the vicinity are among my allies."

The humans and pseudo-humans followed the trail, powerfully aided by the scaly animals.

"What would they do?" Muriel asked, tremulously. "I mean, the ones who aren't your allies..."

"I don't know, exactly. The various tribes don't have the same mores. Besides, there are two races. The less numerous is the more dangerous." He shook his head, and a shadow passed over his eyes, but he smiled and added: "It's almost certain that we'll find the caravan safe and sound. Come on!"

Muriel scarcely recognized the locations through which she had passed. She talked to Darnley about the forest of giant Mimosas. "Is it dangerous to go into it?" she asked.

"The region contains several such forests. If one doesn't commit any depredation or any imprudence, and if one refrains from entering any forbidden zone, one can move freely there."

"How does one recognize the forbidden zones?"

"One perceives them, my child. The acceleration is one sign. Whenever it occurs, it's necessary to stop and wait, or go around the obstacle. A mysterious anguish is another sign: one chokes, and is gripped by dread. Sometimes, it's a fever. It gets worse the further one advances into the forbidden region. It sometimes happens that one is simply *repelled*..."

"Are there boundaries that must never be crossed?"

"No—there are only actions from which it's necessary always to abstain. You find out what they are very quickly."

They had passed the mound where the blue predator had attacked Muriel. It was now necessary to follow an unknown trail, for the young woman could only give her companions vague directions. The Scaly Men and the pseudo-dogs applied themselves to the task with surprising flair.

Finally, they all stopped. Then they explored a strip of land in every direction.

"The caravan stopped here!" said Darnley. "Here's the proof." He pointed to traces left by the tent-pegs, a box of conserves that had fallen on to the ground and a frayed rope.

One of the men uttered an exclamation, soon echoed by the others. The Scaly Men were digging in the ground.

"Master," said the man who spoke English, "*they*'ve been here—see their footprints."

Anxiety stiffened Samuel Darnley's features. "No traces of a struggle?" he asked.

"None, Master." The native looked alternately at Darnley and Muriel.

"Speak, I beg you!" said the young woman.

Samuel made a fatalistic gesture; it would do no good to beat around the bush—the young woman would always assume the worst. "Yes, speak," he said in his turn.

"*They* have taken the caravan prisoner."

"Which *they*?"

"Those who are like men."

An obscure fear chilled Muriel, and visions of death haunted her.

Samuel saw her grow pale. "I don't think they'll kill them," he said. "At least, *not for a long time*…" He seemed to regret having pronounced the last words. He went on: "Let's not waste any time! Let's go!"

The men, the animals and the Scaly Men now followed the trail as easily as if the abductors and their prisoners were visible. They passed through the heath of pines, ferns and hairy mosses. The latter became gigantic, and the tall arborescent ferns rustled in the breeze, sheltering a population of marsupials.

Darnley hardly said a word.

They reached the red gorge in this fashion. The pursuers had advanced prudently; occasionally, one of the natives would put his ear to the ground. The Scaly Men stopped periodically. Darnley knew that they were interrogating the surroundings, being endowed with a sense comparable to that of bats.

"Do you think we're getting close?" asked Muriel, timidly.

"Not yet," said Samuel. "They had several hours start. We can't count on catching them up before dusk, if they stop."

"What if they don't stop?"

Darnley raised his eyebrows dubiously.

"Do you have any hope of saving our friends?" asked Muriel, tremulously.

"I have every hope." Seeing the young woman's tearful face, he thought it as well to give her a few details. "In all probability, it's the Red Circus tribe. It has about a 150 combatants. We only have 40, but I've sent for reinforcements—so there's no need to worry. Ah!"

One of the men had just signaled the abductors' first halt. The terrain was explored in every direction, and having revealed nothing out of the ordinary, the pursuit continued. They went into the red gorge, where they halted. The natives and Darnley had a short meal; Muriel had difficulty swallowing a few mouthfuls of some sort of biscuit. The Scaly Men nourished themselves on fern-roots and a sort of mucilaginous paste made from lichens.

Afterwards, a Scaly Man appeared to spring from a rocky outcrop, and whistled softly.

"The reinforcements are arriving," said Darnley.

"My God!" murmured the young woman. "Will there be a battle, then?"

"Perhaps not. The people of the Red Circus know us; they know we're better armed than they are."

"They'll have the prisoners' weapons."

"They're incapable of making use of them."

The expedition advanced, with increasing precautions, preceded by a guard of natives, hounds and a few Scaly Men. Two hours before dusk, the scouts returned. Darnley conferred with them briefly and came back to Muriel. His expression was very grave.

"It's definitely the people of the Red Circus," he said. Our scouts don't think they've been seen. Anyway, whatever happens, it's in the Circus that the outcome will be decided. They can't abandon it, because of their women and children, and it's there that they feel strongest. Let's take our precautions."

He took a bottle from his pocket, poured a few drops into a minuscule cup, and said to Miss Ironcastle: "This is an antidote. Take it!"

Muriel drank the liquor without hesitation, immediately imitated by Darnley. She could see that the natives and the Scaly Men were doing the same. The Africans were using cups, like Darnley; the others were making use of a sort of pipe that contained the liquid.

"Now we're armored!" said Darnley. "Let's go!"

They moved forward more rapidly, but without omitting the necessary precautions.

"The tribes all possess the art of provoking sleep, by the incineration or evaporation of certain substances," Darnley said, "but they also know the remedy, which is what we've just employed. It has to be taken at least half an hour in advance in order that it has time to take effect."

"When shall we arrive?" Muriel asked.

"We're no more than three kilometers from the Red Circus. Permit me to give the final orders."

He summoned two men and two of his allies. For a few minutes, words and whistles alternated.

"We're ready!" said the explorer, having returned to Muriel. "Now we need a little luck."

Muriel was surprised to see some 15 Scaly Men climbing the rocks. As they reached the summits they disappeared.

"They're veritable experts in matters of stone," Samuel explained. "They know the exits from the Red Circus."

The march slowed down again. Humans and animals maintained a profound silence. Darnley had moved closer to the advance guard, having instructed Muriel to follow at a distance.

About half an hour passed, and then whistles burst forth. Darnley and his men accelerated to a trot. Muriel could not help doing likewise.

The Red Circus was there. Smoke was billowing, which spread an aromatic odor—and they saw several hundred frenzied creatures whirling around, while a group of white and black men lay on the ground.

"My father!" Muriel exclaimed—and added, in a lower voice: "Philippe!"

Darnley, his followers and his allies blocked the entrance to the Circus. Scaly Men seemed to surge from the rocks; they launched flaming projectiles, which burned brightly, producing green smoke. Among the troops massed at the entrance to the gorge, 20 Scaly Men were doing identical work.

Gradually, the turbulent mass relented in its movements. Two sorts of adults became discernible; some, identical to those accompanying Darnley, were presumably the males; the others, shorter and stouter, with strange pockets of skin on their abdomens, had to be the females. Finally, thinner individuals, some of whom were very small, could only be children.

Within a moment, the men gathered together, and Darnley considered them with a certain anxiety.

"They're beaten!" he said to Muriel, who had just caught up with him. "In a few minutes, they'll be powerless—but a moment of desperation is possible, and might cost lives needlessly."

315

No attack occurred. The children were beginning to collapse; then a few women fell and the men began to vacillate.

"Praise the Lord!" murmured Darnley. "We have them, and we've arrived in time."

"My father and his friends?"

"Nothing to fear. Even if I didn't have what's needed to revive them, we'd only have to wait for the narcotic to wear off—but I've been armed for some time."

Meanwhile, the people of the Red Circus were falling down one after another, so rapidly that after ten minutes, not one was still standing.

"They'll be out for several hours," said Darnley.

Muriel was already running to her father, whom she embraced convulsively. Darnley took a translucent bottle from one of his pockets, uncorked it and plunged a fine syringe into it. He gave successive injections to Ironcastle, Maranges, Farnham, Guthrie, Dick and Patrick, and then to the men, while his companions loosened their bonds.

Muriel waited, her heart beating rapidly.

Ironcastle awoke first, then Maranges and Sir George. For a few minutes, their thoughts remained blurred and slow. Finally, Hareton's eyes shone; he saw his daughter, and uttered a great cry of joy; then he saw Darnley, and memories of yesteryear came flooding back.

"What happened?" he murmured. "We were prisoners."

"You're free!" said Darnley, kissing him on both cheeks.

In their turn, Philippe and Sir George recovered consciousness.

The sight of Muriel dazzled Philippe. "Safe! You're safe!"

Guthrie was the last to wake up. When his consciousness emerged from the fog, he uttered a cry of fury. The sight of a group of Scaly Men lying on the ground fascinated him. He ran toward them, and lifted two of them into the air with a loud grunt.

"Stop!" Hareton shouted. "They're vanquished!"

Guthrie, confused, replaced the two inert bodies on the ground.

"This is my friend Darnley," said Ironcastle. "It's thanks to him that we've escaped…" He stopped.

Sir George asked: "From the jaws of what peril have we been snatched?"

Darnley smiled. "I don't know. Not immediate death, at any rate. At the moment when we intervened, you were about to serve as their prey—in a very particular fashion. They don't eat flesh, but they drink blood. When it's a matter of their own kind, or the animals of the region, it's rare that it causes death, but you might have been weakened excessively…and thus incapable of reconstituting yourselves. In this land, creatures have adapted to long fasts and considerable losses of blood."

"So these brutes are vampires!" growled Sydney, disgustedly.

"Not in the legendary sense," said Darnley, laughing.

Epilogue
The Vegetal Legend

"This fish is astonishingly reminiscent of a salmon-trout!" Guthrie remarked, eating with enthusiasm.

"Yes," Darnley replied. "As flesh, that's incontestable—but as to genre and species, that's another matter entirely. It's more closely related to goldfish…although, in fact, it has no place in the known classification."

"I'll give it a nice place in my stomach, at any rate!" Guthrie joked.

The diners were lunching in a granite room, whose furniture was due to the genius of natives and Scaly Men and the industry of Darnley. Comfort was not lacking; the seats were upholstered. As for knives, forks, spoons, plates and dishes, the caravan, having been brought back safe and sound, had furnished the necessary complement.

Through open windows, they could see an area of red stone surrounded by a locale of pines, ferns, giant mosses and monstrous lichens.

The travelers, who had returned three or four hours before dawn, frightfully tired, had slept like bears.

"No Mimosas hereabouts?" said Hareton.

"No," Darnley replied, "we're *at home*—for these pines, ferns, mosses and lichens are as harmless as those in our old fatherlands. The pre-eminence of the vegetation begins with the angiosperms and, as you already know, attains its full amplitude in the Mimosas."

Servants brought in two haunches of roast antelope, which obtained Sydney's eager and disrespectful attention.

"Is that because the animals and the sort of humans that took us prisoner don't have any means of defense against the plants?" asked Sir George.

"Against the superior plants—those, at least, that are superior *here*—they have no resource but avoidance or strict

318

obedience to their 'laws and decrees'. Free license, as I've already said, with gymnosperms and, *a fortiori*, cryptogams, but as soon as one arrives at monocotyledons, the danger commences and is subsequently aggravated, according to an irregular norm. I don't know why the all-powerful vegetables are the Mimosas, or, rather, certain gamopetalous plants.[42] One would be tempted to think, *a priori*, that the inferior plants would perish, but they remain prosperous, occupying almost as much territory as the others. I think I've discovered the cause of that. The superior plants exhaust the soil; they need to alternate with the inferior plants. The latter remake a propitious soil, sometimes by gradually replacing the dominant plants, sometimes by growing in the same terrain. In their turn, the dominant plants take possession of terrain amended by the others. It's especially where large, long-lived trees are concerned that the primitive plants grow among the others; in that case, their presence serves to maintain an efficacious soil permanently."

"That would have filled the writers who used to celebrate the harmonies of nature with admiration," Philippe remarked.

"Yes," Darnley replied. "And in this instance, they would not have been mistaken."

"What interests me more," said Guthrie, helping himself to a vast slice of antelope, "are the relationships between the plants and animals—particularly with the monsters that nearly drank our blood. After all, animals have to be able to live…"

"The relationships are complicated, but there are two major factors. Firstly, on the territories of cryptogams and gymnosperms, men and animals live as they do among us—they

---

[42] Gamopetalous means that the petals of a flower are fused together to form a solid corolla. In fact, plants of the genus *Mimosa* are not gamopetalous, the small petals of their complex flower-heads only appearing to form a single flower. Darnley would know that, but Rosny can be forgiven an understandable mistake in his attempt to imitate scientific discourse.

use plants according to their whim. Those which fill the role of humans can even devote themselves to cultivation, with the restriction that their fields are always threatened by invasion by the invincible plants that cannot be domesticated.

"The second factor is that, *if they obey the laws*, they are not forbidden to circulate among the superior plants, nor even to obtain some nourishment from them. There are times when herbivores are allowed to graze the grains with as much impunity as the mosses, lichens, ferns and young pines. They're warned as to when they cannot do so by the taste of the plants themselves, which causes them an invincible repugnance, and, complementarily, by the poison that they secrete at the appropriate time. Finally, there are sacrificed fruits—I don't know why; one recognizes them on contact and by odor. The forbidden grains and fruits immediately cause a feeling of nausea and give off an exceedingly bitter odor. No animal can make a mistake! All things considered, animal life is less precarious here than under the human regime; it is merely submissive to other restrictions, compensated by real advantages."

"We've already seen," said Sir George, "that the laws have all the more chance of being obeyed because some are unbreakable, under pain of death."

"In certain environments, they're all unbreakable," Darnley said. "Everywhere the Mimosas flourish, the rules do not tolerate any breach; even elsewhere, transgression results in a sufficiently harsh and rapid punishment for the animals and Scaly Men to obey them. To touch any Mimosa whatsoever will cause malaise or suffering; if it's a large one, it can keep you at a distance by means of a repulsive force whose nature I don't know. You've seen that with the aid of an 'acceleratory' force—I call it that because it resembles gravity, and weight is certainly caused by a gravitational acceleration—they can render all movement impossible. They also have—as you've also observed—soporific powers. They can co-ordinate their forces perfectly; no single plant, even a giant Mimosa, would have been able to paralyze your caravan at a distance. Finally, when the Mimosas are in the vicinity of endangered angiosperm plants, they can assist them by subterranean means, by charging them with defensive fluids or radiations."

"In the letter that you sent me," Ironcastle remarked, "you said that you didn't know whether your plants' actions emerged from intelligence. It seems to me, however, that all this requires it."

"Perhaps—and perhaps not. There's a certain logic to the plants' actions, but that logic corresponds so closely with circumstances that it's almost identical, in quality and quantity, when it has to ward off identical perils—in sum, it's so lacking in caprice that I can't compare it, *in itself*, to human intelligence."

"It must be a sort of instinct, then?"

"Nor that. Instinct is crystallized; its foresight produces repetitive actions, while the actions of the dominant plants often manifest a diversity of effects. They respond to stimuli, whatever the stimulus might be, provided that it is a threat. In a sense, the vegetal reaction resembles a chemical phenomenon, but with a spontaneity and a diversity that resembles intelligence. It is, therefore, an unclassifiable phenomenon."

"You believe, without qualification, that the role of plants infallibly dominates that of animals and humans?"

"I'm certain of it. Here, everything is subservient to the needs of the sovereign plants. Animal resistance would be futile. For myself, I haven't discovered any means of escaping that norm."

"But what if a race as energetic and creative as the Anglo-Saxon were to establish itself here?"

"My conviction is that it would be obliged to submit. Besides, as you've been able to deduce, even from partial observation, the reign of the superior plants does not have the destructive character of human rule. Animals are not brutally threatened; they may live in accordance with the laws, and are not constrained to any kind of labor."

"What about its evolution?"

"You have seen that it differs a great deal from evolution elsewhere. For instance, the reptiles aren't inferior to the mammals. They're almost viviparous, often intelligent and often furry. As for the pseudo-humans, they present some analogy with the marsupials. The women possess a pouch in which the children conclude their development—but that pouch is different in origin from the marsupial pouch. As you've observed, the body of these creatures is both scaly and hairy. They have a sense that we don't have—I call it the spatial sense—which *completes* the eye. Their anatomy doesn't permit articulate speech, but they express themselves perfectly with the aid of the modulations of their whistling, which involve the pitch of the sound, the harmonics, certain alternations and repetitions, and also long and short notes. The number of combinations they have at their disposal is, to tell the truth, indefinite, and would surpass the combinations of our syllables if that were necessary. They don't seem to have any sense of plastic beauty; the men and women, if I may use those terms, are only seduced by one another's sonorous qualities."

"So it's music that presides over selection?"

"A strange music that has no significance to our ears...and would have none to those of birds. However, it must have beauties that we cannot suspect—rhythms without analogy with ours. I've tried to form an idea of it—some notion, however vague—but I had to give it up. It was impossible for me to discover anything resembling a melody, a harmony or a measure. As for their degree of social development, it doesn't exceed the level of the tribe—tribes composed of several district clans. I haven't been able to discover any trace of religiosity. They can fabricate weapons and tools, subtle poisons and powerful soporifics, and mineral textiles more analogous to flexible felt than cloth; they live in the rocks, where they hollow out extremely elaborate cave cities.

"You can converse with them?"

"By means of gestures. Our senses are too obtuse to be able to adapt to their language. I've perfected a vocabulary of signs, with the aid of which we can exchange all practical ideas, but it has been impossible for me to surpass pre-abstraction—I mean, abstraction that relates to everyday events. As for 'ideal' abstraction, nothing."

"Are you safe among them?"

"Completely. They have no concept of crime—which is to say, the infraction of the rules of the race or accepted conventions—which gives rise to a singular honesty, as sure and infallible as the action of gravity. Any alliance with them is irrevocable."

"They're better men than we are, then!" Guthrie declared.

"Morally, without a doubt. Moreover, the general morality of the environment is superior to the morality of our world, for there's a sort of automatic morality in the Mimosan hegemony, thanks to which all destruction is limited to what is strictly necessary. Even among the carnivorous beasts, you won't encounter any wastage of flesh anywhere. In any case, many carnivores are merely sanguinivores; they take blood from their victims without killing them or draining them completely."

There was a pause, while servants brought unknown fruits, which were reminiscent of strawberries—but strawberries as big as oranges.

"All in all," Philippe said, "you haven't been unhappy here?"

"I haven't thought about happiness or unhappiness. A permanent curiosity keeps my thoughts, sentiments and impressions alert. I don't think I'll ever have the courage to quit this land."

Hareton sighed. An avid curiosity was awakening in him too, but his eyes turned toward Muriel and Philippe; the destiny of those young creatures lay elsewhere.

"You will be obliged to keep me company for four months," said Darnley. "The rainy season begins in a few weeks; it will render travel impracticable.

Partially consoled, Hareton thought that he could make precious observations and carry out incomparable experiments in four months.

"Besides," Samuel went on, addressing himself to Sydney, Sir George and Philippe rather than Hareton, of whose disinterest he was aware, "you won't go back ruined. There's enough gold and precious stones in this red earth to make a thousand fortunes…"

Guthrie liked the perishable things of this world too much to be insensible to riches. Sir George had dreamed for a long time of restoring his country houses at Hornfield and Hawktower, which were threatened by imminent ruin. Philippe was thinking of both Muriel and Monique, created for a luminous life.

"I'll show you the vain treasures that geological convulsions have formed in the ground," said their host. He summoned one of the men and said: "Bring the blue boxes, Darnis."

"Isn't that exposing the brave lad to temptation?" asked Guthrie.

"If you knew him, you wouldn't ask that. Darnis has the soul of a good dog and that of a good servant united in the same creature. He knows, too, that if I ever return to America—he's from Florida—he'll be as rich as he desires. That doesn't cast a shadow of doubt in his mind. In the meantime, he's perfectly content with his lot. Here are the specimens!"

Darnis had reappeared, with three rather spacious caskets, which he placed on the cleared table. Samuel opened them nonchalantly, and Guthrie, Farnham and Maranges shivered. The boxes contained immense fortunes in diamonds, sapphires, emeralds and virgin gold. These treasures were not shiny: the raw gems looked like any minerals, but Sydney and Sir George recognized them, and Philippe did not doubt Darnley's competence.

After a brief pause, while all his dreams were dazzling his imagination, Guthrie burst out laughing.

"We have a magic wand!" he said.

Hareton and Samuel Darnley considered the stones with a sincere indifference.

Afterword

"Le Cataclysme" must have seemed distinctly odd to its initial readers, who had not yet had a chance to read "La Légende sceptique," in which the seed of the idea is contained in the chapter translated as "Planetary Physiology" in volume one of this series. In that essay, Rosny had not yet developed the notion of the "fourth universe," in which the universe we observe is merely one of a vast number, each composed of its own system of mass/energy, but he was already prepared to suggest that the heavens might be full of bodies composed on an essentially alien matter, capable of interacting with ours by way of exotic forces. The idea is further extrapolated in *La Force mystérieuse*, in which there is no meteor shower to advertise the possible presence of the alien matter as it moves through our solar system, and in which the effects of the interaction are much more varied and extensive.

The notion of a shared life that features in "The Mysterious Force" was to be echoed again in "Dans le monde des Variants" (tr. in vol. 2 as "In the World of the Variants"), but in the latter story it is represented as something enduring rather than transient, albeit so tangential to the human world that only one exceptional individual participates in the duality. That participation enhances the fleeting Utopian—or, strictly speaking, eupsychian—element of the story told in "The Mysterious Force." The notion that human physiology is ill-adapted to the quest for happiness, especially in a sexual context, was to become increasingly exaggerated in Rosny's speculative works once it had been broached in "The Mysterious Force." The eupsychian modifications he subsequently attached to alternative relationships and ways of being were not counterbalanced by such terrible costs as the "carnivorism" inflicted on the gestalts featured in "The Mysterious Force."

In one of the footnotes to "The Mysterious Force," I called attention to the slight peculiarity of the list of mushrooms said to be cultivated in the farm featured in the plot, and, particularly to the fact that the species singled out to play a crucial role in the physicists' subsequent experiments is the highly toxic fly-agaric—a fact subject to some slight concealment in the text by virtue of the choice of an alternative name (*fausse oronge*). Although fly-agarics would not be cultivated as food in the same way as porcinis and other edible varieties, however, there is one motive that might inspire their cultivation: their hallucinogenic quality, due to their production of an alkaloid called (in consequence of its source) muscarine. Given that the phenomena associated with the temporary interaction of the two forms of energy include various psychotropic phenomena, Rosny's choice of agaric mushrooms as a potential explanatory link might be significant. If so, it might also be relevant to note that the genus *Mimosa*, which features so significantly in "Hareton Ironcastle's Amazing Adventure," and whose hypothetical members are there imagined to be capable of inducing exotic psychotropic effects akin to those featured in "The Cataclysm," includes *Mimosa tenuiflora*, the source of a powerful hallucinogen long used in shamanic rituals, initially named ayahuasca after the ritual but nowadays known as DMT.

As none of this is explicit in the texts, it might be a coincidence—but if so, it is surely a remarkable one. It is worth noting that many of Rosny's other scientific romances contain passages that would be more plausible if they were hallucinatory, and that it would not have been very surprising had the imaginative content of such stories as "Nymphaeum," "The Voyage" or "The Treasure in the Snow" (all in vol. 2) been revealed, in the conclusion of the relevant narrative, to have been a stress-induced vision. In fact, Rosny never did that, evidently feeling that apologetic endings in which characters wake up to find that they have been dreaming were beneath contempt—and characters in such stories as "The Young Vampire" and "The Supernatural Assassin" (both in vol. 6) are extremely adamant in declaring that their suspect experiences were completely real, and not hallucinatory at all. If nothing else, however, the insistent evocation of agaric mushrooms in "The Mysterious Force" suggests that Rosny was not unaware of the kinship between his work and the tradition of visionary fantasy.

Although it is quite usual for Rosny's longer narratives to seem fragmentary and to undergo sharp changes in narrative direction, "Hareton Ironcastle's Amazing Adventure" gives rise more than most to the suspicion that it might have been cobbled together from fragments of different stories. In the introduction I suggested that part three might have been intended as a third item of hackwork for Flammarion's *Une heure d'oubli* series, but had to be reprocessed, although it is odd, if that is the case, that there is not a single mention in parts one and two of the objective of the characters' journey. It is not implausible that the preface might have been tacked on belatedly, in order to connect the story told in parts one and two with the one told in part three, and that those two stories were initially independent, although that hypothesis does not fit well with the keen attention given in the preface to the mysterious Monique, who plays no further part in the narrative.

Whatever the process of the story's composition might have been, however, the fact remains that both of the stories making up the patchwork narrative of "Hareton Ironcastle's Amazing Adventure" duplicate the basic plot-formula of "Nymphaeum" (in vol. 2), the first one in a version much closer to the one subsequently redeployed in "The Boar Men" (in vol. 2) and "Adventure in the Wild" (in vol. 5), with a stubbornness suggestive of near-obsession. The explanation for the recurrence of the plot-structure might not be significant of anything more than Rosny's general lack of interest in plotting, his story formulae being regarded merely as convenient wrapping for his speculative ideas, but its essential incongruity—one aspect of which is brutally exposed in "The Boar Men"—is surely suggestive of a peculiar *idée fixe*, which becomes even more peculiar when it crops up yet again in a very different narrative context in "Companions of the Universe" (in vol. 6).

The two versions of the abduction story reproduced in "Hareton Ironcastle's Amazing Adventure" are reflective of a trend by which the relatively handsome and gentle alternative humans of his earliest stories gave way by unsteady degrees to extremely ugly and brutal ones, although the apologetic case made on behalf of the Scaly Men reflects a parallel trend attributing unorthodox beauty and moral rectitude to beings further removed from the human norm. In that respect, part three of the novel picks up a notion introduced in "The Wonderful Cave Country" (in vol. 2), that vampirism is at least potentially morally superior to more brutal "carnivorism," because it is not necessarily fatal to its victims. That notion is also broached, albeit tentatively, in "The Young Vampire," which originated as one of the *Une heure d'oubli* booklets; the latter story entangles consumption and intimacy in a fashion markedly different from, but nevertheless akin to, "The Mysterious Force."

From the viewpoint of the connoisseur of speculative fiction, "Hareton Ironcastle's Amazing Adventure" is bound to seem unsatisfactory, by virtue of the cursory treatment it gives to its key speculative motif—the notion of an ecosystem dominated and regulated by capable plants. If that section of the narrative really was the first to be written, the disappointment would be increased by the fact that it was supplemented by such a stubbornly unimaginative melodrama, which merely recapitulates a formula that the author had used before and would use again. If, however, part three of the narrative did start out as an independent exercise in "scientific marvel fiction," that strategy of adaptation might well be reflective of exactly the same despair that overwhelmed Maurice Renard at the same period: a conviction that the literary marketplace, at least in France, was utterly and implacably hostile to speculative material, and would only tolerate its produce in a conspicuously underextrapolated form in the context of the crudest pulp fiction.

The trajectory of Renard's and Rosny's careers provides a stark illustration of the fact that the window of opportunity in which such complex and challenging works as *The Blue Peril* and "The Mysterious Force" could actually achieve publication was always a narrow one, and that it became narrower as the two writers grew older. When one considers the difficulties that must have afflicted Rosny in securing publication for such early works as "Tornadres" and the even greater ones facing such later ventures as the story told in part three of *L'Etonnant voyage de Hareton Ironcastle*, the wonder is not so much that such material was forced into story-formulas in which they seem rather incongruous, but that any form could be found to render them acceptable to contemporary publishers and readers. The fact that "Hareton Ironcastle's Amazing Adventure" is, in essence, pure pulp fiction of a bizarre sort, should not entirely distract attention from the fact that the speculative notions that its third part attempts to embody and convey are far from uninteresting. Indeed, of all of Rosny's attempts to reconstruct the fundamental principle of Nature in such a way as to render them less cruel, the idea of dominion by wise plants is the most intriguing.

Rosny was doubtless aware that the family to which the genus *Mimosa* belongs also includes the carnivorous Venus fly-trap, but he did not want to represent the reign of plants as a mere reversal of the existing relationship between plants and animals. It would have been interesting to see, had he felt free to grant himself more space for that sort of extrapolation, how he might have developed the briefly-broached notion of the dominant plants' periodic willingness to surrender themselves for partial consumption. As the narrative stands, he obviously felt it necessary to stop short of Utopian fantasy, leaving such endeavor as the merest twinkle in Ironcastle's eye, but there is still a sense in which the real goal of the story's amazing journey was the glimpse of an unfortunately-unpromised land, in which the flow of milk and honey equivalents would be sanely regulated rather than subject to the ravages of insatiable gluttony, and all the myriad corollaries of that primal sin.

SF & FANTASY

Guy d'Armen. *Doc Ardan: The City of Gold and Lepers*
G.-J. Arnaud. *The Ice Company*
Aloysius Bertrand. *Gaspard de la Nuit*
Félix Bodin. *The Novel of the Future*
André Caroff. *The Terror of Madame Atomos*
Didier de Chousy. *Ignis*
C. I. Defontenay. *Star (Psi Cassiopeia)*
Charles Derennes. *The People of the Pole*
Harry Dickson. *The Heir of Dracula*
Sâr Dubnotal *vs. Jack the Ripper*
Alexandre Dumas. *The Return of Lord Ruthven*
J.-C. Dunyach. *The Night Orchid. The Thieves of Silence*
Paul Féval. *Anne of the Isles. Knightshade. Revenants. Vampire City. The Vampire Countess. The Wandering Jew's Daughter*
Paul Féval, *fils. Felifax, the Tiger-Man*
Arnould Galopin. *Doctor Omega*
V. Hugo, Foucher & Meurice. *The Hunchback of Notre-Dame*
O. Joncquel & Theo Varlet. *The Martian Epic*
Jean de La Hire. *Enter the Nyctalope. The Nyctalope on Mars. The Nyctalope vs. Lucifer*
G. Le Faure & H. de Graffigny. *The Extraordinary Adventures of a Russian Scientist Across the Solar System* (2 vols.)
Gustave Le Rouge. *The Vampires of Mars*
Jules Lermina. *Mysteryville. Panic in Paris. To-Ho and the Gold Destroyers*
Jean-Marc & Randy Lofficier. *Edgar Allan Poe on Mars. The Katrina Protocol. Pacifica. Robonocchio.* (anthologies) *Tales of the Shadowmen* (6 vols.) (non-fiction) *Shadowmen* (2 vols.)
Xavier Mauméjean. *The League of Heroes*
Marie Nizet. *Captain Vampire*
C. Nodier, Beraud & Toussaint-Merle. *Frankenstein*
Henri de Parville. *An Inhabitant of the Planet Mars*
Polidori, C. Nodier, E. Scribe. *Lord Ruthven the Vampire*
P.-A. Ponson du Terrail. *The Vampire and the Devil's Son*

Maurice Renard. *Doctor Lerne. A Man Among the Microbes. The Blue Peril. The Doctored Man*
Albert Robida. *The Adventures of Saturnin Farandoul. The Clock of the Centuries*
J.-H. Rosny Aîné. *The Navigators of Space. The World of the Variants. The Mysterious Force*
Brian Stableford. *The Shadow of Frankenstein. Frankenstein and the Vampire Countess. The New Faust at the Tragicomique. Sherlock Holmes & The Vampires of Eternity. The Stones of Camelot. The Wayward Muse.* (anthologies) *The Germans on Venus. News from the Moon*
Kurt Steiner. *Ortog*
Villiers de l'Isle-Adam. *The Scaffold. The Vampire Soul*
Philippe Ward. *Artahe*

MYSTERIES & THRILLERS

M. Allain & P. Souvestre. *The Daughter of Fantômas*
Anicet-Bourgeois, Lucien Dabril. *Rocambole*
A. Bisson & G. Livet. *Nick Carter vs. Fantômas*
V. Darlay & H. de Gorsse. *Lupin vs. Holmes: The Stage Play*
Paul Féval. *The Black Coats: The Companions of the Treasure. Heart of Steel. The Invisible Weapon. The Parisian Jungle. 'Salem Street. Gentlemen of the Night. John Devil*
Emile Gaboriau. *Monsieur Lecoq*
Steve Leadley. *Sherlock Holmes: The Circle of Blood*
Maurice Leblanc. *Arsène Lupin: The Hollow Needle. The Blonde Phantom*
Gaston Leroux. *Chéri-Bibi. The Phantom of the Opera. Rouletabille & the Mystery of the Yellow Room*
William Patrick Maynard. *The Terror of Fu Manchu*
Frank J. Morlock. *Sherlock Holmes: The Grand Horizontals*
P. de Wattyne & Y. Walter. *Sherlock Holmes vs. Fantômas*
David White. *Fantômas in America*